frek
and the
elixir

Books by Rudy Rucker

frek
and the
elixir

rudy
rucker

A Tom Doherty Associates Book
New York

FREK AND THE ELIXIR

Copyright © 2004 by Rudy Rucker

This book is printed on acid-free paper.

Edited by David G. Hartwell

Book design by Milenda Nan Ok Lee

A Tor Book
Published by Tom Doherty Associates, LLC
175 Fifth Avenue
New York, NY 10010

www.tor.com

Tor® is a registered trademark of Tom Doherty Associates, LLC.

Library of Congress Cataloging-in-Publication Data

Rucker, Rudy v. B. (Rudy von Bitter), 1946–
    Frek and the elixir / Rudy Rucker.—1st US ed.
        p. cm
    "A Tom Doherty Associates book."
    ISBN 0-765-31058-9
    EAN 978-0765-31058-3
    1. Young men—Fiction. 2. Fathers and sons—Fiction. 3. Quests (Expeditions)—Fiction. I. Title.

    PS3568.U298F74 2004
    813'.54—dc22

                                                                    2003020868

First Edition: April 2004

Printed in the United States of America

0 9 8 7 6 5 4 3 2 1

For my son Rudy—
remember the day we sailed
from Linekin Bay to Boothbay Harbor?

author's note

Carb's description of a portal between worlds in Chapter 10 was adapted from the "Apotheosis" section of Joseph Campbell's classic *The Hero with a Thousand Faces*. Campbell himself got the quote from J. Takakusu, translator, *The Amitayur-Dhyana Sutra,* Sacred Books of the East, Vol. 49 (Oxford University Press, 1894).

Writing notes and further background information about *Frek and the Elixir* can be found at www.rudyrucker.com/frek, the book's Web site.

contents

contents

part 1

the
departure

1

middleville, 3003

"Your room is a mess," said Lora Huggins, standing in her son's doorway. "A dog den. You're not going anywhere until it's straightened up. Poor Snaffle doesn't know where to begin." Indeed, Snaffle had stopped short at her side.

Snaffle was a suckapillar, a bioengineered cleaner creature like an oversize green caterpillar, not that there were any normal-size caterpillars anymore. Snaffle had powerful lungs and a conical lemon-yellow mouth. The suckapillar's little stalk-eyes twitched as the dim-witted beast tried to form a plan for vacuuming Frek's room without swallowing anything valuable.

Frek Huggins sighed and finished pulling on his soft leather shoe. "My room's not a mess," he said. "I know exactly where everything is. Snaffle's too stupid to understand. I have more important stuff to do, Mom." Like dreaming about being a toonsmith.

Frek had a vivid imagination; his friends listened spellbound to the stories he liked to invent. Well, that wasn't quite true. It was more that he could get his acquaintances to listen to him for quite a while before they'd eventually cut him off with a remark like, "That's kac, Frek." Maybe if he still had a father at home it would be easier to talk to people. Nothing had felt quite right since Dad left, just about a year ago now.

"Get to work," said Frek's mother. "I mean it." She started back down the corridor that curved toward big sister Geneva's room, over on the other side of their house tree. Geneva's room would be easy to clean. Her things were always lined up and orderly. "Come on, Snaffle," called Mom. "You don't have to clean Frek's room yet." The low-slung suckapillar let out a sigh, and undulated off, her legs rising and falling. Thanks to the gene-tweaks, each of her twenty-six stubby feet bore a different letter. Years ago, Snaffle had helped Frek learn the alphabet.

Frek stood up and looked out his roundish window at the sunny Saturday morning. It was a fine day in May. His room was halfway up their house tree. He had a good view of their yard, and of the neighbors' house trees and yards.

Right below Frek's window, his dog, Wow, was sleeping on the uniformly green grass in a patch of sun. Next to Wow were Mom's identically lush roseplusplus bushes, dense with blooms of every shape and color, and thornless of course. Beyond the roseplusplusses was the family vegetable garden with its super-high-yielding scions of the six canonical vegetables: yam, tomato, carrot, chard, rice, and red beans.

Between the Hugginses' garden and their garage was the elaborately filigreed mud mound where their turmite colony lived. The turmites ate organic trash and wove things. Cloth, paper, wallboard—whatever you needed, the turmites could make it from, say, a pile of dead leaves.

The garage was a dome of something like waxy brown cardboard. The turmites had put it up over the course of one frenzied afternoon. The Huggins family's angelwings lived in the garage. If Frek leaned far out of his window and listened, he could hear the angelwings softly buzzing. He'd gotten his own pair just last week—for his twelfth birthday. It made his heart beat faster to think about it. With his angelwings on his back, he could fly like a mosquito.

Frek was tempted to forget about cleaning his room, to hop out his window, clamber down the tree, and buzz on over to Stoo Steiner's house. Stoo would be playing with goggy killtoons, drinking soda, and eating greasy yam chips as usual. Stoo's mother, Sao Steiner, never made him do housework. But of course Sao didn't have a hard job like Lora Huggins did. Mom was a knowledge facilitator; that is, she gave music lessons. Some people still liked to play real instruments, others preferred pretend instruments like air guitar, gesture trumpet, invisible drums, and so on. Music urls could turn people's gestures into sounds, but they still had to know the right moves, and Lora was good at teaching them. She worked all week giving music lessons in person—and Saturdays the kids helped her clean house. No ifs, ands, or buts.

Frek sighed and looked around his messy, curvy room. Where to begin? A bunch of his clothes lay near the foot of his bed. It was hard to think what he should do with the clothes. Rather than bothering to distinguish one piece of clothing from the next, Frek kicked at the garments until they were in a mound, and then he picked up the mound and stuffed it into his closet. The floor of his room was still covered.

Frek looked at all the scattered glypher slugs he'd brought home from school this week. School. Some kids stayed home and learned from knowledge facilitator toons instead of going to school. Mostly what you did at school was watch the same facilitator toons anyway. Frek felt like he would have liked home schooling. Frek had remarkably intense powers of concentration, and he could learn just about anything faster than the other kids. So why sit around waiting until even the gurps got the picture?

But Lora Huggins insisted that her children go to a real, everyone-in-the-same-room kind of school. "Think school of fish," she'd tell Frek when he asked why he couldn't stay home. "*School,*" Mom would repeat, waggling her two hands like a pair of trout swimming near each other. "Don't grow up antisocial like your father. Society is a herd, Frek, a flock."

Carb Huggins had tried fighting the way things were on Earth, and in return the government had done some nasty things to him, like using a peeker uvvy to search for rebel secrets in his brain. Gov might have eventually killed Carb, but he'd managed to ride a space bug out to a Crufter asteroid called Sick Hindu. He hadn't asked his family if they wanted to come along—he'd just gone. They hadn't heard anything at all from him since he left, which seemed pretty crummy.

And there'd been some kind of mishap on Sick Hindu last week. Carb was a source of worry.

On the plus side, Dad was tough. He had a muscular body and a hard, angular face. He dressed like a gaussy old-time punk, complete with a Mohawk hairdo and moving tattoos on the sides of his head. Whenever anybody gave any trouble to Lora or the kids, Dad used to get right in their face about it—before Gov peeked him. After that he'd been a little vague sometimes. And then he'd deserted his family. No, Frek didn't want to grow up like his father. It was better to grin and bear it, to be a good Nubbie and go to school.

The thing was, although school was about learning to get along with people face to face, Frek wasn't very good at it. He was never on the same wavelength as the other kids, and the knowledge facilitators didn't like him because he didn't pay enough attention to their silly rules.

The glypher slugs were the perfect symbol of the goody-goody, make-work kac that facilitators liked for you to do. Every time Frek came home and unfastened his school satchel, more of the nagging glyphers slithered out, their skins aflicker with symbols. The glyphers contained permission forms and graded tests for Mom to view, requests for her to volunteer, and announcements of school events she should attend in person or at least watch on their house tree's wall skins.

Frek got busy picking up the slugs. To make his work more bearable, Frek groaned as if he were a very old man with a bad back, letting out a sharp little yelp each time he bent over all the way.

When he had all the glyphers in one hand, he recklessly stuffed them into the soft toilet that bulged out of his wall. The facilitators might yell at him on Monday, but today was Saturday. Forget school! The toilet swallowed the slugs right down, just as if they were stinky kac. The toilet bowl was part of the tree. Not only did the house tree absorb waste, it provided sparkling pure water that it got from the rain, the ground, and its own photosynthetic reactions. A fine example of Nature's alchemy as improved upon by a NuBioCom kritter.

Down the hall, Mom had herded the suckapillar out of Geneva's room and into Ida's. Geneva was Frek's big sister and Ida was his little sister. Ida's room was even messier than Frek's. All of a sudden, Snaffle's wheezy inhales changed to sharp coughs. The suckapillar had inhaled one of Ida's umpty-zillion wooden building blocks. "Ida!" called Mom. "Ida, come up here."

The only answer was the chatter of the toons on the walls of the family room. Geneva and Ida were playing with some toons that Frek didn't like. Normally he'd look at any kind of toon at all, especially on Saturday morning, but he drew the line at the Goob Dolls. The Goob Dolls were most definitely evolved to please people like Frek's sisters and not people like Frek.

Some Saturdays Frek would fight with Geneva and Ida to try and keep them from watching the Goob Dolls, who always debuted their latest skits and situations at the same time as that funny Vietnamese toon about Da Nha Duc and his nephews Huy, Lui, and Duy. Of course Frek could have watched any show he liked on the walls of his own room. But that would be giving in. Controlling which toons were shown in the big, comfy den downstairs was an important power game among the three Huggins kids.

Today, however, Frek wasn't going to bother arguing with his sisters. As soon as he could get out of here, he was going over to Stoo Steiner's to play with Stoo's new Skull Farmers killtoons, the latest creation of the Stun City Toonsmithy. Frek was itching to mix it up with the Skull Farmers. Maybe Stoo would even lend Frek the Skull Farmers urlbud, not that Mom liked for him to play with killtoons.

He heard his mother come back along the curved passageway and stop at the head of the narrow steps down to the big round family room in the base of the house tree. "Ida!"

"What!" hollered little Ida, making her voice sound deep and rough. "Whadda ya want!" She and big sister Geneva let out shrieks of laughter.

"Ida's the Goob Doll's Secret Agent!" yelled Geneva. "And I'm her contact in the Mean Queen Mansion! We're lying low for the Final Fracas!"

"Goob Dolls rule!" burst out Ida.

"Goob Dolls!" whooped Geneva, egging Ida on.

"Thank you, girls!" burbled one of the Goob Dolls. The Goob Dolls sounded full of joy. "Hooray for Ida and Geneva!"

Toons were smart. Thanks to the eyes in the walls, they always knew who was watching them. Every instance of their show was real-time tailored for the specific viewers.

"Ida, you come up here and clean your room or I'm going to tell Snaffle to eat every single one of your blocks!" called Frek's mom.

"I wanna finish my show, Mom," called Ida. "*Pleeeease.* The Goob Dolls need me for the Final Fracas!"

"You children," said Mom and sighed. "You tell those toons they're just going to have to wait a few minutes for you to clean your room." Before she hopped downstairs to get Ida, Mom looked over and saw Frek watching her from his door. "Is your room picked up yet, Frek?"

"Almost," said Frek. "And then I'm going over to Stoo's, okay?"

"I hope you don't waste the whole day in a dark room pretending to shoot things," snapped Mom. Sometimes it seemed like she could see right into Frek's head.

"You children should be outside doing something healthy on a day like this," continued Mom. "Climbing a tree or building a dam. Flying with your new angelwings. The angelwings need exercise, you know. The more you fly, the stronger they get. I didn't buy them so they could rot away in the garage." Suddenly she got an odd look on her face and stopped herself. "Listen to me," she said ruefully. "Nag, nag, nag. I'm turning into Grandma Huggins. Enough. I'm glad that you're cleaning your room, Frek. I appreciate that." She gave him a kind smile. She looked a little tired from the housecleaning.

The weary look on his mother's face made Frek feel bad about stuffing his clothes in the closet instead of sorting them. Well, maybe he'd sort them later. Meanwhile he still needed to finish clearing his floor.

Frek had a set of fifty shiny monster-shaped seeds that he'd bought from a shape-farmer at the Middleville market last November. They came from a please plant that the cheerful farmer had tutored with clay figurines he himself had made. Please plants had eyes in their flowers and you could show them models of how you wanted their seeds to be.

Last week the please plant seeds had begun to sprout, which meant

Frek would have to get rid of them soon. He'd positioned them in nooks and crannies for one last attack on the King's Quarters—which is what he imagined the little monsters calling his big, comfortable bed. Frek liked to see them poised in readiness, their taut shiny buds like purple eyes. What made it really gollywog was that the spring-wakened seeds were slowly, slowly creeping toward the Quarters, which they perhaps perceived as a moist, loamy spot good for roots.

Frek found the turmite-cloth sack that the monster-seeds had come in, and walked around the room collecting them, still giving an agonized yelp each time he leaned over. To make it more interesting, he kept count of the seeds, and made the numbers part of his cries.

"Is something wrong, Frek?" called Mom from the bottom of the steps.

"Thirty-seven," groaned Frek.

"Is something ailing you?" There was humor in his mother's voice.

"Thirty-eight. I'm picking up my monster-seeds."

"Get rid of them!" called Mom. "I don't want please plants growing in my house or yard. They're unny."

It might be easiest to dump the seeds in the toilet. They hadn't cost all that much in the first place. Frek picked up the rest of the seeds without any more yelping. When he was almost done, he noticed one last please plant seed on the floor right next to his bed. This one wasn't shaped like the others. Rather than looking like a little humanoid monster, it looked like a—spider? A tapered blob with big round eyes and a bunch of legs. He'd never noticed that particular seed before, but it was a good one. He put it in the sack with the others.

And then Frek found himself tossing the sack out his window. It would be a shame to waste these glatt seeds. The thought popped into his head that he should plant them someplace private. Yes. He'd use the place called Giant's Marbles on the slope of Lookout Mountain above Middleville. It was full of huge boulders, with no big trees, and you could see really far. Lots of please plant bushes grew along one edge of the clearing where a little stream came trickling down. Not many people went there, but it wasn't dangerous like the Grulloo Woods east of town. Frek could fly his seeds to Giant's Marbles later today. It would be fun with his new angelwings.

But first he had to finish his room, and second he had to go to Stoo's.

The next thing to pick up were the fungoid urlbuds scattered across the floor. But right away Frek came across one of his favorites, the Merry Mollusks. He went ahead and pressed the rubbery little disk to the wall. The wallpaper pattern cleared to reveal a mosaic of octopi, squid, cuttlefish, nautili, and yet odder forms. They were toons of extinct animals, dancing around, clowning, singing songs. Frek had been tweaking one of them to resemble a believable character for a story. Practicing for the day he tried to get a job at the Toonsmithy.

The arms on his virtual cuttlefish looked a bit too short today, and Frek would have started working on him, but just then Goob Doll Judy came barging in, sliding across the wall leaving a wake of yellow sparkles.

"You shouldn't be on my wall when I didn't ask to see you," said Frek.

"You should know that Gov's curious about you," said Judy, widening her pale brown eyes. "Something happened last night in the sky. It's the start of a new adventure!"

Toons had all sorts of tricks for roping more and more people into watching them. Frek quickly made his pet cuttlefish get big enough to cover up Judy. When Judy's ponytails came poking out among the tentacles, Frek pasted another urlbud to the wall, the Gaiatopia. This site was complex enough to cover both Goob Doll Judy and the Merry Mollusks.

Frek stared at the orchid-bedecked trees, at the dragonflies, the scuttling rodents, the languid snakes, the crazy monkeys, and the lurking big cats. The Gaiatopia was populated by toons of all the lost species of Earth—at least all the species that the designers could remember. NuBioCom had collapsed the Earth's biome in 2666, and the species they'd winnowed out weren't ever coming back. NuBio-Com didn't exactly advertise the fact, but if you poked around on the Net, you'd find that the old DNA codes were gone as well. Erased from all the memory archives. These days evolution was limited to NuBioCom's designs for commercial kritters, and to the toons.

Not for the first time, Frek let himself dream of finding a way to bring back Earth's real plants and animals—of going on a quest for a magic elixir to heal his home world. But he had no idea of where to begin. Visiting the Gaiatopia always made him a little sad.

When Frek peeled the two urlbuds off the wall, it reverted to looking like silvery paisley. Goob Doll Judy was gone, too. Once all the urlbuds were stored away, Frek set to work on the mess of wooden blocks left in his room by Ida, who'd been building a maze for Wow the other day. Despite Ida's injunctions, Wow had of course just stepped over the blocks to get to the scrap of anymeat that Ida had placed at the maze's end. The kids could never quite decide how smart or dumb their dog was.

Frek decided to stash Ida's blocks under his bed, which was a bouncy platform grown right out of the house tree wall, with a pair of legs at the outer corners to hold it up. A bunch of stuff was already under there, but the blocks fit easily enough, as did the curved ebony shapes of Frek's Space Monkeys puzzle, his real metal spring, and the wooden top that he could never get to work. And then Frek crammed his throwing disk under the bed, also his ball-paddles, his model rocket made of a tweaked snail's shell, and the box holding a tank-grown microscope eye you could uvvy-link to.

With all of this gear out of the way, the only thing left to get rid of was Frek's battered old Solar Trader game. He'd been playing a big tournament with Stoo over several days this week. The colorful money leaves and deed petals and hotel seeds were all over the place. The edges of the game's turmite-paper box were broken, which meant that after Frek got all of the Solar Trader stuff sandwiched in between the flattened top and the bottom he couldn't carry it very far, or everything would slide out.

He tried to push the box under his bed, but it wouldn't fit. A giant shove might have done it, but Frek was worried all the game pieces might spew out. He leaned over and peered under his bed at the clothes, blocks, and toys. In toward the middle was a pillow, a fancy pillow of Geneva's that Frek had forgotten about. He'd hidden it there last month when he and his sisters were in the middle of a great pillow fight.

The pillow had a picture of a rabbit embroidered on it. Grandma Huggins had made it by hand when Geneva was born. Frek had hidden the rabbit pillow so that Geneva couldn't hit him with it, and so that he himself would have extra artillery for the next pillow war. Geneva had asked him about her rabbit pillow a few times since then, but so far she hadn't gotten around to pitching a big enough fit to make Frek find it and give it back. Geneva had other things on her mind these days.

Frek lay down flat on his stomach and worked the pillow out from under the middle of the bed, trying not pull along the junk squeezed in around it. Just as the pillow came loose he glimpsed something odd in the farthest, darkest corner of the space under his bed. Something rounded and shiny. A dark, glossy purple, almost black. The size of a squashed bowling ball, with a dimple on the side facing him. He couldn't think what it might be. A toy he'd forgotten about?

Downstairs Mom had just told the house tree to take the toons off the walls. Ida was yelling about it, but there was no stopping Lora Huggins. "Good-bye, Ida, good-bye Geneva," sang the sweet, chuckling voices of the Goob Dolls. "I wish Frek would listen to me," called Goob Doll Judy just before Mom closed her down. "I have more to tell him." Right.

Ida's footsteps came pounding up the steps. Instead of starting to clean her room, Ida dashed into Frek's room. She was a cheerful little girl with golden skin and sparkling black eyes. She was wearing yellow turmite-silk pajamas that had black fuzzy stripes to make her look like a bumblebee.

"You found Geneva's rabbit pillow," said Ida in her deep little voice.

"I had it under my bed," said Frek. "My stockpile for the next pillow fight."

"Pillow fight!" exclaimed Ida. She snatched Frek's pillow from his unmade bed and smacked him with it.

"Ida!" called Mom from the foot of the stairs. "If you don't clean your room, you're not getting any allowance!"

"All *right*," shouted Ida. She always got rebellious when she had to clean her room. Ida was rebellious a lot. Being the youngest of three kids, she had to be. She gave Frek another good whack with his pillow and took off down the hall.

Frek decided to leave the mysterious shiny purplish thing under his bed for later. It was time to get going. Stoo would already be deep into the land of Skull Farmers. Frek pushed everything a little farther under the bed, finally making enough room for the Solar Trader set. To finish things off, he made his bed.

On his way down the hall, he tossed the rabbit pillow onto the floor of Geneva's room, making an exploding sound with his mouth as he did it. Geneva was in there, sitting on her bed, her eyes blank as she focused on the signal from the pulsing uvvy kritter on the back of her neck.

"Brat," said Geneva to Frek, snatching up the pillow and setting it beside her on the bed. She made her mouth a thin straight line and shook her fist. And then she went back to talking to her friend. Even though you didn't really have to, most people talked out loud when they were on the uvvy, and usually they even gestured with their hands. As if the other person were right there in front of them. "Oh that was just my brother," said Geneva. "Yon upstart barbarian. So what should we wear to the store, Amparo?"

Outside, Wow greeted Frek with enthusiasm, bowing and wagging his tail and squeaking, "Frek," from the back of his throat. In principle Wow wasn't allowed in the house as he still chewed things and he went to the bathroom on the floor sometimes. But Ida loved to smuggle Wow in. He was only outside today because he truly couldn't stand to be around when Snaffle was active. Snaffle and Wow were archenemies: Ms. Tidy and Mr. Mess.

Wow was the one and only kind of dog left after the Great Collapse. NuBioCom changed the design very little from year to year. Wow was a little like a collie and a little like a beagle, medium-sized with white hair, a dark tail, and an orange saddle-shaped patch on his back. Every dog in town looked pretty much like Wow—every dog on Earth for that matter—but even so, the Huggins kids felt like their dog was the best. Wow's eyes were perhaps a lighter shade of brown than those of some other dogs, flecked with gold in certain lights, and surely Wow was unusually intelligent-looking.

The garage's thin turmite-paper door opened at a touch of Frek's finger. Wow tried to push into the garage with Frek, but Frek didn't let him. The angelwings were scared of dogs.

The angelwings were godzoon goggy kritters, one of the newbio miracles that made the collapse of the biome seem almost okay. Each was about one and a half meters long and resembled a scaled-up mosquito wing, a transparent wing veined with branching struts. They had a rainbow sheen to them. Despite their name, they didn't look much like the wings on angels in old-time pictures; if anything, they looked devilish. An angelwing's body was a flexible stick along the base end of the single wing. There were left and right angelwings; they came in pairs like shoes. The sticklike body had an insect head at one end, a few padded legs in the middle, and a bunch of soft, sticky tendrils mixed in with the legs.

The six angelwing kritters dragged themselves slowly across the floor toward Frek. *Kvaar,* buzzed six sets of mandibles. *Kvirr, kvurr, kvak.* The long gossamer-thin wings were layered on top of each other like a pile of stained glass.

Frek got a bag of water-soaked beans and rice down from the shelf, sprinkled it with mapine sugar, and spilled the mush into the angelwings' trough. While they were eating—never a pleasant sight to watch—Frek used a broom-branch to sweep away the sticky pellets of waste they left on the hard dirt floor, lifting up the wings to reach under them.

You wouldn't have thought the frail angelwings could possibly have enough power to raise a person off the ground. But NuBioCom had found a way around that; their organisms incorporated a secret process that metabolized energy from the invisible dark matter known to pervade all of space. Normally you didn't notice dark matter because it was somehow perpendicular to ordinary matter. The patented NuBioCom process depended upon a certain oddly knotted molecule's ability to rotate particles of dark matter into normal space. Or something like that.

When the angelwings had finished eating, Frek brought them a bucket of water from the side of the house tree. They uncurled their long hollow tongues to slurp up the water. Meanwhile Frek took the waste pellets out to the turmite mound.

A few turmites came poking up out of their lacy mud galleries. They resembled pale, oversize ants, each with six legs and a complicated mouth. They gave Frek the creeps. Last year he'd gooshed a couple of them sort of by accident, but not really, and a swarm of turmites had instantly crawled out of the mound to begin biting him. You had to mind your manners with these little kac-eaters.

Wow kept poking his nose through the open garage door. He was always curious about the angelwings. Frek shooed him away and herded his two angelwings out onto the flat lawn. It didn't take much urging. The angelwings loved the chance to fly.

Frek lay down on his back and the angelwings scooted over next to him, clamping their padded legs around his upper arms and fastening their tendrils all along his ribs. The tips of the tendrils were fine enough to reach right through the cloth of Frek's shirt. He rocked up one shoulder, then the other, letting the wings reach behind him.

By the time he got to his feet, the angelwings had comfortably bonded to his back, chest, and arms. Frek held out his arms and flapped. The wiry muscles of the angelwings amplified Frek's shoulder motions strongly enough to lift him a few centimeters off the ground. Wow began barking.

The wingtips quickly sped up into their own rhythm, beating in figure-eights at many times the frequency of Frek's motions. From now on, the main thing he had to do was steer. With a twitch of his shoulders, Frek buzzed high into the air. He began looping around the trees, hoping someone would look out of his house and see him.

The Hugginses' yard had one each of the three standard NuBio-Com trees: a house tree, an anyfruit tree, and an all-season mapine—which was about it for trees anymore. The house tree resembled a thick, sturdy oak with oval window holes and an arched door. House trees were perhaps the finest miracle of genomics. They grew their own plumbing, saved up solar energy, showed video on their inner walls, and networked via the antenna veins in their branches. Frek glimpsed Mom through her bedroom window, folding clothes on her bed. She looked up and spotted him, then smiled and waved. He waved back.

On the other side of the house tree was their anyfruit tree. Depending on the season, it might have cherries, plums, pears, or apples. Right now it was making blackberries. Rolling his shoulders in a hover-pattern he'd just learned, Frek got the angelwings to suspend him over the highest branch of the anyfruit. He ate a handful of ripe berries.

Right about then a special feeling came over Frek, a feeling that he'd been having off and on all week. The feeling had to do with the world taking on a larger-than-life quality, and with Frek's own sensations seeming exceptionally fresh and interesting. A golden glow would spread across things, and Frek would imagine that someone was watching him and asking him to explain everything that he thought. It felt like he was a star being interviewed. He didn't know why he felt this way, but it was kind of fun.

Grinning like a newscaster, Frek threw his shoulders far back. The angelwings scooped mightily at the air, giving him the altitude to sail over their all-season mapine. The mapine bore red-yellow autumn foliage, tender new green shoots and dusty summer leaves. Some of its branches were wintry and bare, while others were dripping the sticky sap of spring. From above the mapine, Frek could see across his whole neighborhood. The three kinds of trees were scattered in an organic, natural way across the hills and dales. You could hardly tell you were looking at a Nubbie village. No roads or wires or pipes—just the house trees and anyfruits and mapines and some winding grassy footpaths, with bindmoss covering the spots where the grass had worn away. Every part of the Nubbies' lives depended on the NuBioCom kritters.

Frek and his angelwings flew toward the Steiners' house tree, which was near the highest point in Middleville, at the base of Lookout Mountain. Frek made a long and winding trip of it, with Wow running along below the trees like a bouncy brown and white toon animated onto the uniformly green lawns. The angelwings were young and playful; they enjoyed a barrel-roll or a loop-the-loop as much as Frek. Occasionally Frek would get so dizzy from his gyrations that he'd have to orient himself by peering down at Wow, always doggedly on course for the Steiners'. Wow knew where they were going and he wanted to get there. Stoo's mother usually fed him something.

When Frek touched down in the Steiners' yard, he found Stoo's father, Kolder Steiner, trying to get his shiny green lifter beetle to fly him to work. The beetle's passenger pod was of transparent chitin, with a seat made up of swirly spiral curls the same golden-green as the beetle's wing covers. At one point in the beetle's life-cycle, the pod had been his pupa-casing. The beetle himself was perched on the top of the pod with his legs hooked into it. The great insect seemed to be in a contrary mood; he was snapping his mandibles and making liquid high-pitched noises.

Even though Kolder was a high-ranking exec at NuBioCom, he wasn't good at handling his living helpers. Kolder pressed a spot between the beetle's antennae, and the kritter went *sgli-gli-hi-hi*.

"Hi," said Frek.

"Hello, Frek," said Kolder Steiner, not really looking up. He was a hairy man with strong arms. He poked impatiently at the beetle and again the kritter made the noise. *Sgli-gli-gli-hi-hi*. So far he hadn't lifted his wing covers.

"It sounds like a giggle, doesn't it?" said Frek, trying to be friendly. Frek's father had been gone for so long that Frek wasn't sure anymore how to act with grown-up men. Kolder Steiner didn't answer him. Jerk.

Frek walked past Kolder's uncommunicative back and stashed his angelwings in the Steiners' garage. When Frek came out, Kolder was glaring at the lifter beetle and muttering under his breath. Now he gave the beetle's domed back a savage slap. *Gli-squeeeek-gli-hi-hi*, said the beetle.

Inside the house tree, Sao Steiner was sitting at a table dictating a shopping list to a glypher slug. Like everyone else, she had golden skin and dark, almond-shaped eyes. But Sao was thinner than most people, and she had extra teeth in her smile. Toothbuds. She was wearing a white turmite-lace tube-top and tight, shiny, shin-length gray pants. A pile of new clothes sat on the table next to her; apparently she was planning to exchange some of them.

Sao made shopping complicated. She liked to go to the local turmite tailors who'd trained certain turmite mounds to create uniquely styled fabrics. She made forays into Stun City as well, seeking out the cured wall skin garments popular there. Sao would bring her selections home and try them on for days and then take most of them back.

She was always talking about it. Shopping was like her main job.

"Yubba, Frek," said Sao, flashing her amplified teeth. "Are you ready to rock and roll?"

"How do you mean?" said Frek. Sao Steiner had a way of saying offbeat things. It was like she was always acting flirty—or maybe like she thought it didn't much matter what she said to him. Frek found it interesting to talk with her, even though he could tell she didn't really approve of him. He was different from the other kids; his father was a Crufter and his mother had a low-status job.

"That's what Stoo's new game says when it starts up," said Sao Steiner. "*Are you ready to rock and roll?* I think it's hysterical. You'll find the crown prince in his room. Here." She stood up and got some cookies out of a drawer to put on a plate. "You can take these up with you. Nothing like some fat and sugar. Oh, look who else is here. Wowie! Want a cookie, Wow-Wow?"

"Cook-ie," said Wow, opening his jaws wide to squeeze out the sound. "Wow want cook-ie." His lips were drawn back from his teeth with the strain of using his voice, which sounded like the squeak at the end of a yawn. It was rare for Wow to talk, but Sao could always get him to do it. Lora Huggins didn't encourage Wow's talking—she said she heard enough from her three kids.

Sao Steiner held a cookie up in the air and Wow jumped for it, making a wet inhaling noise. He'd gobbled down the cookie by the time he was back on all four feet. He quickly nosed a stray crumb off the floor, then looked up at Sao Steiner, licking his chops, his gold-flecked eyes watching her every move.

"I'm thinking we should get a dog, too," said Sao. "But Kolder wants to wait for next year's model. Wow's cute, but there's already so many of him in town. Kolder says the 3004 model dogs won't mind fleas. That's why it's good that dogs don't have puppies. The new models replace the old ones."

At the sound of the word "flea," Wow abruptly lay down and started chewing at the hair on the base of his tail. Any talk about fertility was over his head. He remained prone to wandering off in search of female dogs in heat, even though nothing could ever come of it.

"When NuBioCom collapsed the biome, why didn't they get rid of fleas?" Frek asked Sao Steiner. Since Kolder was such a big deal at NuBioCom, Frek figured Sao might have some inside information. "All the ants and beetles are gone, and the grasshoppers and butterflies and lightning bugs—why keep fleas?"

"They kept mosquitoes, too," said Sao, shaking her head. "Counting everything, we're down to only two hundred and fifty-six kinds of legacy species—including mosquitoes and fleas. I've asked Kolder about it, and he says NuBioCom has a use for blood-suckers. They're vectors for spreading the knockout virus to spots where the puffball spores might not reach. We need the knockouts to keep dogs from conceiving puppies, for instance. And to keep people from having unlicensed children. Don't frown like that, Frek! You don't want to end up like your father, off in some crazy Crufter asteroid and maybe even disappeared from there. Life's gog gripper just the way she is." It grated to hear someone's mother try to use kids' slang.

"Don't talk about my father that way," snapped Frek, a little surprised at his temerity. Even though he wasn't happy about Carb running off, he didn't like other people to criticize him. "He's not crazy."

"I'm sorry, Frek," said Sao, backing off. "That was insensitive of me. You must be worried sick about him." The love of gossip glinted in her eyes. "Have you gotten any news about what happened up on Sick Hindu? I heard this googly rumor that three Crufters were abducted by aliens."

"We haven't heard a geevin' thing," said Frek with a sudden rush of fear. "Carb hasn't managed to call us since he left. Mind your own business."

Sao pursed her lips and wrinkled her nose. "How about giving me some fashion advice, then." She pulled a blouse from the bags of clothes on the table. "With your fresh eyes." She slipped the blouse on over her tight lace top and cocked her head. "How does it look, kid?"

It looked like a blouse. And Sao looked like Sao. Lively, thin, smug, theatrical, slightly unfriendly. What else was there to say?

Just then Sao's uvvy made a wet razzing noise. It was under her pile of clothes, and it took her a few seconds to unearth it. "I'll be glad when NuBioCom finally figures out how to put these things inside our heads," she remarked to Frek as she pressed the uvvy's patch of tendrils to her neck. And then she was into her call. Wordlessly she handed Frek the cookies, and gestured toward the stairs.

Frek thought he had a good hold on the cookie plate, but he didn't. The next second, the plate and the cookies were on the floor and Wow was snarfing them down as fast as he could. Furious at Wow, and at himself, Frek poked Wow hard with his foot. It wasn't exactly a kick.

Wow yelped a really nasty curse word and swung his body away, keeping his head down on the floor, eating.

Frek crouched to scoop the rest of the cookies onto the plate. He managed to save about half of them. Sao had set aside her uvvy call. She was looking at Frek with a mixture of pity and contempt.

"You drop things a lot, don't you?" she said. "You need meds. Clumsiness is a type of attention deficit disorder, you know. Lora should take you to a tweaker." She flashed her too-wide grin. "Nothing personal, of course."

"Don't need tweaking," muttered Frek. His face felt hot. "I'm good the way I am." Turning away, he hurried up the steps to Stoo's room before Sao could pick on him any more.

Stoo had his window curtains closed and his lights turned off. He was perched on a big round cushion in the middle of the floor. He was a dark-haired, bright-eyed boy a bit taller and older than Frek, and with a crooked angularity to his jaw. He was handsome and very much his own person, a kid that the others looked up to. Frek wasn't quite sure why someone as gaud as Stoo even hung out with him.

Right now Stoo was holding an imitation gun grown by a please plant. A prop gun. It didn't need an uvvy-link. Because of all the eyes in a house tree's wall, the toons could track Stoo's hand motions closely enough to tell when and in which direction he meant to shoot.

"Yubba, Frek," said Stoo. It was the standard greeting for kids their age, though it had sounded odd coming from Sao in the kitchen.

"Yubba you," said Frek. "Here's some cookies from your mother." He dragged over a cushion and sat down next to Stoo. Wow lunged for the cookies again but Frek sharply blocked him. "No, Wow! You want to stay at home next time?" He felt around on Stoo's floor and found a prop gun of his own.

The Skull Farmers were on all the curving walls of Stoo's room.

Their world was designed around an old-time Y2K theme. Frek could see at first glance that it was another Toonsmithy masterpiece. An oil refinery was burning in the distance, killer giraffes and elephants were silhouetted nearby, and six business-suited figures were flying across the sky on winged motorcycles. Loosely ranged across the foreground were three lively, individualistic skeletons in Y2K garb. Skull Farmers.

The three Skull Farmers noticed right away that someone new had come into Stoo's room. Frek happened to focus on one of them, and that one got big; his bony face filled the whole wall.

Toons had a way of enlarging whatever aspect of their world you focused on. The toonsmiths called the technique "phenomenological autozoom," but gamers just called it "pzoom." The toons were letting Frek, and not Stoo, control the pzoom. They wanted to draw him into the game.

The face Frek had focused on was a goggy shecked-out skull with glowing red eyes, a gold front tooth, and a crumpled black top hat upon the deathly white pate. A rusty nail had been hammered into one side of the skull, with a pair of dice dangling from it like an earring.

"Welcome, Frek," said the skull-faced toon. His voice was shrill and grainy, as if he'd been yelling all day long. "They call me Gypsy Joker. We need yore smarts and firepower. Seems we've got our butts into a bit of a situation hyar." He hooked one thumb toward the sky, and Frek pzoomed out to view the background. "The six Financiers of the Apocalypse is a-comin', just for openers. I cain't promise you an easy run, but it could be hella fun. You wanna sign on with the Skull Farmers?"

Meanwhile Stoo fired off a couple of shots at the business-suited Financiers of the Apocalypse, who took the damage hits in a shower of green dollar signs and circled back into the distance.

"Right on, Stoo," said the second Skull Farmer, and Frek brought him into view. He was wearing a red velvet cape and held an archaic electric guitar. He pushed himself into prominence and struck a chord of rich metallic-sounding music, sending images of roses spiraling out. "I'm Strummer," he told Frek. Some of his teeth were black and he had an old-time British accent. He struck a pose and raised his voice to a warbling shriek. *"Are you ready to rock and roll?"*

"Hold it," said the third Skull Farmer in a sharp tone. Frek was back to a medium view, now, showing all three of the Skull Farmers. The third one had a heavy ballistic-style machine-gun hanging from one bone shoulder, and his skull was burned black, as from a fire, with tendrils of singed hair and crusts of burnt skin. "Soul Soldier here. I'm just pickin' up a message for new recruit Frek Huggins. Goob Doll Judy passed it to me. Groove on it, Skulls." Soul Soldier flicked the joints of his spectral skeleton hand and blood-red urlbuds flew across the walls to the two other Skull Farmers.

"Whoo-eee!" said Gypsy Joker, catching a bud. "Frek Huggins got company comin'. Anvil fallin' down at him."

"Tell me more," said Frek, pleased to have the toons drawing him into their game.

"Anvil's what they call it," said Soul Soldier in his dark, gravelly voice. "The Govs have had Skywatch Mil trackin' it for a couple days. Came down through the asteroids. *A*Nonymous *V*ector, *I*nterste*L*lar. Last night they found out it's headed for Frek Huggins."

"An anvil from the forge of God," said Strummer in a cracked whisper. He plucked the strings of his guitar and crooned the phrase again, rounding it into a verse of song.

> An anvil from the forge of God
> Is falling toward a young man's bod,
> It's coming closer night and day
> He doesn't think to run away.

Strummer's papery voice gave Frek a chill. "What are you talking about?" he asked uneasily. Toons always mind-gamed you to get you into the play, but this routine seemed unusually gollywog.

"Lot of alien activity last night," said Soul Soldier. "Your world's gettin' real funky. After the Anvil hit the atmosphere, the sucker darted around so swoopy that the Skywatch jelly-eyes lost it in the foo-fightin' fog. And then a big fat flying saucer cruises over Stun City, with some kind of human voice on its radio sayin' as how the Anvil's addressed to

Mr. Frek Huggins. What it is, Frek. Had any company this morning?"

"Kac, Huggins," interjected Stoo. "The Skulls never ran a level like this for me yet. What makes you so gaud?"

"I don't know," said Frek, forcing a laugh. He had a sudden memory flash of that dark shiny shape he'd glimpsed in the farthest recess of the space under his bed. But it couldn't be. The toons were just playing with him was all. "I'll handle that Anvil," he said, making his voice firm. He aimed his prop gun and squeezed his trigger finger, expecting to see simulated bullets shoot across into the toons' sky, expecting to see some Y2K saucer UFO icons darting away in response. But the toons were ignoring his prop gun.

"This is realtime," said Gypsy Joker, watching Frek with his hot red eyes. "We ain't jivin' you. There's something come down to Earth lookin' for you, Frek, and don't nobody know what it is or where it's hiding."

Suddenly Sao Steiner walked into the room. Her voice was cold and all business. "Frek, I just got a message from Lora. There's two counselors over at your house to see you. Go talk to them before they have to come over here to get you. Kolder's furious. What on Earth have you been up to, you odd little boy? Stoo—he didn't ask you to do anything geevey, did he?"

2

the thing under frek's bed

A watchbird appeared as soon as Frek got back in the air, and it followed him all the way home. It was a gray, beady-eyed little thing, a tweaked hummingbird kritter with the slick bump of a tiny uvvy on the back of its neck. The watchbird's one color accent was its narrow, scarlet beak.

A man and a woman were standing by Frek's garage waiting for him. They wore uvvies and powder-blue overalls. Counselors. Mom was standing next to them. Geneva and Ida watched round-eyed from one of the house tree windows. The counselors' shimmering teal blue lifter beetle was nibbling on the grass of the lawn.

"Hi there, Frek," said the counselor woman. "I'm PhiPhi and my partner here Zhak. Gov sent us to help you." Zhak and PhiPhi had round, calm faces and pleasantly full lips. They looked like dull-witted siblings. It was said that Gov did something to the brains of those who signed on to be his counselors—Gov being the person, or the simulated person, who ran things around Middleville. The watchbird fluttered down and perched itself on PhiPhi's shoulder.

"When's the last time you talked Carb Huggins?" asked Zhak, helping Frek out of his angelwings.

"Don't bother him about his father," snapped Mom. "Carb left us last year, and that was that."

Frek was glad to have his mother stick up for him. These days it upset him to think about Carb. Sometimes he worried that it hadn't just been Gov's persecution that drove away his tough, wise-cracking father—maybe Dad had left because of something Frek himself had done. Like asking too many questions about how toons were made. Carb hadn't liked toons at all. Or maybe Frek had brought too many glypher slugs home from school.

Toward the end, Carb had always had a headache. Gov had put the peeker on him because of the Crufters, and he'd never fully recovered. He'd get confused sometimes. Gov had started talking about giving Carb this kind of brain therapy called the Three R's. And then Carb had quietly gotten hold of a space bug and flown away. Maybe it wasn't fair of Frek, but was still mad about it. Shouldn't a father stick with his family, no matter what?

"We must know," said PhiPhi, smiling blandly and fixing Frek with her eyes. "Necessary for you to answer. Otherwise we peek, most unfortunate. When was the last time you talked Carb, Frek?" She said all this as flatly as if she were reading it off a message board in her head. Counselors let Gov do a lot of their thinking, and they used Gov's ugly, gobbledygook style of speech.

"Don't you dare talk about peeking him, you Gov-skulled stooge," said Mom evenly. Somehow she'd managed to wedge herself in between Frek and the counselors.

"It's Frek's decision," said PhiPhi, holding her eye contact with him.

"What my mother said," muttered Frek. "One night I saw him at supper and the next morning he was gone."

"Do you know why we're here?" asked PhiPhi, taking a different tack.

"About the Anvil from space," blurted Frek.

"Yaya," said Zhak. "Now we get somewhere." Zhak had an extra uvvy in a mesh sack on his belt. A twitching, bright-yellow peeker uvvy. Getting peeked could mess you up for good. A regular uvvy took the words you deliberately thought at it, and sent them off to other uvvies, but peekers dug their tendrils in deep and took whatever they could find.

"The Skull Farmers told me," said Frek, the words tumbling out of his mouth. "Some toons I saw on Stoo Steiner's wall skin. They heard it from the Goob Dolls. They said something from space landed last night. They called it the Anvil. They said that someone on a flying saucer told them the Anvil was looking for me? At first I thought the Skull Farmers were making it up. And then Sao Steiner told me I should come see you. That's everything I know, honest."

"I can search the house?" Zhak asked Mom.

"Search for what?" she demanded. "Maybe Frek knows what this is about, but I sure don't. We cleaned up today, by the way, and I can tell you right now there's nothing unusual to see. Maybe you should stop busy-bodying. You should leave honest people alone." Her voice grew a little louder. "You think it's easy being a full-time facilitator and raising three children? With my husband gone? And now you Gov zombies have to come here and threaten my poor son? Because of something that a stupid game toon said?"

"The search doesn't take long," said PhiPhi, in a soothing tone. "Calm calm." She patted Mom's shoulder and displayed a big, warm smile. "What it is, Lora, the Anvil is real. It might be some kind of alien? Or it's from the Crufters? We're uncertain. It came down last night, simultaneous with a warning message regarding Frek Huggins. The message came from an anomalous unidentified vehicle, now vanished. This makes possibles. Maybe just a prank same time as a meteorite, we hope. But, Lora, for your good, and Frek's good, Gov has to be sure. Zhak and I assigned to stay and watch your home for one or two days. If you kindly permit, we plant a little shelter for ourselves—over here? It remains afterward for your guest room or perhaps shed." PhiPhi was pointing to a spot between their house tree and their garage.

"Not so close to my garden," said Mom, not entirely displeased. Recently she'd been talking about needing money for an extra room, with the three kids getting so loud and big. But house tree seeds were expensive.

"Those *are* all standard plants?" asked PhiPhi, peering at Mom's vegetables. "Carb not sending down crufty oldbio seeds, huh?"

"As if oldbio could live on Earth anymore," said Lora. "Don't you know anything? Second of all, Carb and I are unwebbed as of three months ago. There's no link between us anymore."

Unwebbed? Mom hadn't told Frek about this. The news hit him hard. Not only was Dad never coming back, it was as if he'd never been here at all. Frek had no father. His face felt so odd and stiff and silly that he turned away so nobody would see. He coaxed his angel-wings into the garage and petted them. They made soft *kvarr*ing noises, which made him feel better. He stepped back out just in time to see Zhak go slipping into their house. Mom was so distracted by PhiPhi's chatter that she didn't notice. For the moment, Frek felt too upset with Mom to warn her.

In any case, there was nothing for Zhak to find. Or was there? Frek was still thinking about the lumpy shiny purplish-black object he'd glimpsed under his bed. The Anvil? A UFO come to rest under his bed? Impossible. But what if? If the counselors found it, they'd punish him for not telling them. And if they didn't find it—what then? What was the Anvil really? Frek's stomach felt cold and hollow.

PhiPhi wasn't looking at him right then, which was good. Even though counselors were dumbed down, they had uvvy access to special Gov routines for reading people's thoughts from their expressions.

PhiPhi was busy trying to push a house tree seed into the ground. The seed was pointed at one end and flat at the other, about five centimeters long. She was trying to push the seed in sideways. It was like she was impaired. Mom squatted down and helped PhiPhi get the seed properly into the ground, point first. Lora Huggins knew how to do everything right. Frek was lucky to have her for his mother. Even if she had unwebbed from Dad.

"Where did Zhak go?" said Frek, so that Mom would look up from the seed and notice their house was being searched.

"What?" said Mom, standing up. "He's already started?" She brushed the dirt off her hands and rushed inside to supervise.

PhiPhi gave Frek an angry look. But all she said was, "Will you get water? The seed needs water." She tore open a pod of fertilizer-pollen and sprinkled it on the ground.

Frek attached a snakeskin hose to their house tree's spout and asked the tree to set a steady trickle of water flowing into the muddy patch where Mom had pushed PhiPhi's seed into the ground. In a matter of minutes, a pale green sprout appeared. It worked its way upward and unfurled into a tiny, lobed house tree leaf set upon a shiny gray-green twig. The leaf-bedecked twig twitched as if sniffing around for light, then angled itself out away from the Hugginses' house tree. Three, five, seven more shoots appeared from the ground near the twig. Soon a little thicket was growing upward, the sticks getting fatter as they rose.

PhiPhi stood off to one side, her face blank, listening down into her uvvy, communing with Zhak and Gov. Though she didn't talk out loud, her lips were moving and she twitched her hands a little. Meanwhile her lifter beetle was hungrily edging toward Mom's garden. Frek herded it away. Presently Zhak appeared in the window of Frek's room, holding up Frek's wooden top. The watchbird was hovering next to him, its little wings a blur.

"This thing," said Zhak, waving the top. "What is it?"

"It's a stupid toy that doesn't work," called Frek. "You wrap a string around it to try and spin it."

"It's too little, Zhak," exclaimed PhiPhi. "Don't be dim. The Anvil is two hundred kilograms and the size of a man's head. It's not there. Maybe coming later."

"I dunno," said Zhak. "There's so much kac in this kid's room. . . ."

"Don't you turn everything topsy-turvy," came Mom's voice from behind Zhak. "It took Frek all morning to get his room picked up. You have no idea how hard it is for him."

"Listen Gov on your uvvy, Zhak!" exclaimed PhiPhi. "Nothing's manifesting yet, and so we wait. Come out now. Don't ill-will our clients. Lora Huggins indeed of gog good standing." The watchbird swooped out of the window and lighted on Frek's shoulder. He could feel the faint touch of its little claws through the cloth of his shirt.

"He going to keep an eye on you," said PhiPhi. "Cute, yes?"

Frek could see the gray, bright-eyed little bird out of the corner of his eye. It seemed a bit mangy and, no, not cute at all. Its beak was the color of blood. The watchbird's eyes glared at him, glassy and inscrutable.

Meanwhile the bases of the new house tree's branches had merged into a bulging, gnarled trunk that was painfully pushing itself out of the ground. Frek kept on watering it. The new house tree rose up faster and faster. It had a big hole in one side and a smaller hole near it, just the right shapes for a door and a window. The thing grew to the size of a hollow tree-stump two meters across and three meters tall, then stopped. A crop of green-leaved branches sprouted from its lumpy top. The branches were tough and wiry, veined with antenna metal extracted from the soil. The inner walls of the new house tree were flickering and alive. An image of Gov appeared, visible through the door like an oracle in a cave. Gov was presenting himself in the toon form of a stylized First Nations eagle, all red and black and pie-eyed.

"Attention, counselors PhiPhi and Zhak," said Gov's toon. "Counselors are to withdraw to the temporary shelter and stand by for further notification. The watchbird will surveillance the Huggins family for events regarding the Anvil. Your inaction is correct in the meanwhile time." Gov always talked in broken jargon. You saw him on the wall skins every now and then, issuing exhortations and orders. Carb said Gov wasn't a person at all, and that he'd accidentally evolved from the code for a certain parasitic worm that genomicists had been using as a standard lab specimen years ago. A pinworm from a Quileute village called La Push in the Pacific Northwest.

"Tell them to tie up their lifter beetle," Mom told Gov. "I don't want him to eat my whole yard and garden."

"Let it be so," said Gov, gesturing with a red and black wing. PhiPhi and Zhak settled into their newly grown house tree hut, with the beetle tethered right outside.

Frek went straight up to his room. He just had to look under his bed to see about the lumpy, shiny, purplish thing, even though the watchbird was whirring along behind him. To appear less suspicious, he acted like he was tidying up. "Keeping things organized," he muttered. "Zhak made a mess." He forced himself to work on his shelves and his closet a bit before looking under his bed. Mom appeared in the room before he'd gotten to the bed.

"Are you looking for the Anvil?" she asked straight out.

"No," lied Frek, annoyed with her for making it all so obvious.

"I wonder if this really does have anything to do with Carb," said Mom, plopping down on Frek's desk chair. She looked keyed up and chatty. "The counselors said they got a message when the Anvil came down? Those toons you saw, did they talk about him?"

"No," said Frek. "But the Anvil came through the asteroid belt. Where Dad is. Not that you care what he does anymore. Can you leave me alone now, Mom?"

"Are you mad about me and Carb getting unwebbed?"

"Do we have to talk in front of the watchbird?" said Frek.

"That thing?" said Mom. "It doesn't matter. The house tree has eyes and ears, too, you know. And for sure Gov taps into that; you know his puffball has plenty of brain nodules to monitor what the counselors don't watch in person. So forget about the watchbird. He's mainly for following you outside."

"I don't want to talk," said Frek stubbornly. "And I'm not looking for the Anvil. I'm only cleaning up."

"Suit yourself," said Mom. "Come downstairs in a bit; we'll have lunch."

Frek worked on his closet a little more, folding a few of his mounded clothes, and then he walked over to his bed. He lay on the floor beside it, shifting the objects about, all the while peering to see the thing that was maybe the Anvil. The watchbird strutted back and forth on the floor right beside him, turning its head this way and that. Frek was almost glad the watchbird and the house tree were observing him. If there really was an alien under his bed and it came darting out at him, it wouldn't be so bad to have Gov and the counselors ready to help.

But he saw nothing but toys and games. Had he imagined the shiny thing before? No, wait—there was a funny spot by the wall, a spot where things didn't want to go. He pushed with his Solar Trader game box, bulldozing some toys toward the mystery corner. His throwing disk slid off to one side of the special spot and the model rocket slid off to the other. Yes, something was there, but you couldn't see it. The air in that spot had a warped quality—as if a lens were floating there. Scooting forward and stretching his arm out as far as he could, Frek reached into the place where nothing wanted to go. And, yes, he felt something. Bumpy, smooth, faintly vibrating. He swept his hand on past the spot, so that maybe the watchbird and the house tree wouldn't realize what he was doing, even though his heart was pounding so hard that it seemed like everyone must be able to hear. He took a deep, shuddery breath, sat back up and brightly said, "No sign of the Anvil! And now my room's nice and tidy." And then he went downstairs to the kitchen.

It was cozy in the kitchen. Their little yellow-white marble statue of the Buddha looked friendly up the wall shelf. Seeing the Buddha always made Frek feel safe and good. Mom and Frek's sisters were eating grobread and anymeat with carrot sticks and sliced tomatoes from their garden. "Help yourself," said Mom, nodding to the kitchen counter. "But don't let that dirty little watchbird kac on anything."

The grobread and anymeat loaves were there with the knife. Frek had thought he was too worried to eat, but when he saw the food he changed his mind. He sliced off a piece of the puffy white grobread, enjoying, as always, the way the new-cut surface of the remaining loaf immediately started plumping itself up, growing the loaf back to its original size. The surface puffed up like foam. But somehow the new-cut slice in his hand knew not to grow. Frek had experimented with this a few times: slicing the grobread loaf first from one side and then from the other, making a whole lot of slices in a row, or cutting the whole loaf exactly in half. But it was always just one of the grobread pieces that would renew itself, and this always seemed to be a piece that you weren't biting into.

Slicing off a piece of anymeat wasn't so dramatic; the smooth pink loaf of anymeat renewed itself at a slower pace than the grobread. He took a tomato and some carrot sticks and sat down with the others. The watchbird sat on the back of his chair.

"What does it mean for you and Daddy to be unwebbed?" Ida was asking Mom just then. The girls had heard the conversation with the counselors, too.

Mom didn't answer right away, preferring to busy herself with pouring them mugs of tree-juice from a pitcher she'd filled.

"It means they're not married anymore," put in Geneva. "And that Carb's never coming back."

"That makes me feel sad," said Ida in a low voice. "I hardly remember him at all anymore."

"Maybe we'll see him again when we get big," said Geneva.

"Don't count on it," said Mom, setting down the pitcher with a clack.

"I could go visit him," said Ida quietly. "Just to say hello."

Lora Huggins started to say something more, then stopped herself. She reached over and patted Ida's head. "Of course you can, Ida. And maybe one of these days you will. It would be nice of you. I'm sure Daddy misses you."

"If he misses us, how come he never gets in touch?" asked Frek. That was the thing that really rankled him. Carb's continued silence. If he'd been off on a secret mission of some kind, working to save the Earth, well, that would have been one thing. But it seemed like he'd just found an easy way to save his own neck. Probably he was flirting with other women, and maybe even starting a new family. Didn't he care about his kids at all?

"Dad would call us if he could," said Geneva loyally. She was the one who remembered Carb the best. She'd been his favorite. "But Crufters don't have uvvies," she added, as if Frek and Ida were complete gurps. "They don't use any newbio at all."

"Except for the rockworms that hollow out their asteroids for them," said Mom a little harshly. "And the oxymold that makes their air. And the space bugs they use to get around. It's all pretty bogus, if you want my opinion. The Crufters think they can pick and choose, but in the end their world's as compromised as ours. I'm afraid Frek's right, Geneva. If Carb tried hard enough, he could find a way to send a message. But probably his new girlfriend doesn't want him to."

"How do you know he has a new girlfriend?" asked Geneva.

"He was talking to her on the web before he left," said Mom. "I didn't want to tell you before. A woman called Yessica Sunshine. What a stupid name."

"What is the Anvil anyway?" interrupted Ida, maybe to change the subject. "Is it going to hurt us?"

"I doubt if there's anything to it at all," said Mom. "Gov is pretty paranoid. He put a watchbird on Linz Martinez last year just because

Linz was hiking around counting trees for a teaching project." Linz was a fellow facilitator who'd been spending a lot of time with Lora.

"Liiiinz," sang Ida, sweetening her voice. She liked to tease Mom about having a boyfriend. "Linz and Mommy under the tree. K - I - S - S - I - N - G." Geneva joined in and they sang it again.

Lora Huggins smiled and shook her finger at her daughters. Then she changed the subject. "Frek," she said, "I noticed your bag of please plant seeds in the yard. Could you either feed them to the tree or fly them out to the woods? I told you I don't want them growing in our yard. Why not get away from all this foolishness about the Anvil and have some fun with your new wings."

"Yes," said Frek, remembering his plan to plant the seeds up near the Giant's Marbles. "I'd like that." But right then of course he had to knock over his half full mug of tree-juice.

"Every meal, Frek?" said Mom a little impatiently.

"I'm sorry," said Frek, and got the cleaner tongue from its pouch in the wall. The tongue was glad to wipe the table off, for the tree-juice was sweet and sticky. When Frek had finished with the tabletop, he noticed that the juice had dripped down to the floor. He knelt down there with the cleaner tongue, and when he was finished his eyes felt hot and achey.

"Frek's crying," said Geneva.

"Am not!" he shouted. "Nosy brat!" He stamped across his kitchen and shoved the cleaner tongue in its pouch.

"Poor Frek," said Mom. She got up and put her arm around the shoulders. "I'm sorry I snapped at you. It's upsetting having the counselors snooping around, isn't it? And all this talk about Carb."

"It's not just that," said Frek, turning away from his sisters so they wouldn't see him dry his eyes. "Sao Steiner said I'm so clumsy that I should get special meds. She said you should take me to a tweaker."

"That dumb grinskin!" exclaimed Mom. "Meds are all she thinks about. Meds and clothes. Maybe I'd be that way too if I had to live with Kolder. Have you ever seen that man smile, Frek? Even once?"

"No," said Frek, feeling a little better. "You don't think there's anything wrong with me? You don't think I need a tweaker?"

"What?" said Mom. "Dumb you down with a med leech? Of

course not. You're fine, Frek. You spill things and knock things over, and sometimes it's annoying. But so what? It'll be a cold day in hell when I let one of Gov's tweakers put a med leech on my smart son. Don't even think about it." Mom held Frek out at arm's length and smiled at him. "Go sow your please plant seeds. Have some fun. Just remember not to fly near the Grulloo Woods."

So Frek got his angelwings back out and flew to Lookout Mountain, with the watchbird whirring along in his wake. On the way, he uvvied Stoo to ask if he wanted to come, but Stoo said his mother wouldn't let him. They talked for a few minutes. Stoo was eager to hear what the counselors had said to Frek about the Anvil, not that, come to think of it, they'd really said much. Stoo was impressed that the counselors had grown their own field quarters, and that Gov had put his eagle toon on its wall skin. He started to ask Frek to stop over on his way back home, but Sao in the background shouted no. Evidently she'd starting thinking of Frek as a bad influence.

Grinskin, thought Frek.

It was a lovely day, the sky clear blue with creampuffs of cloud. The rocky little Lookout Mountain rose about three hundred meters above Middleville, with the Giant's Marbles halfway up. To make his flight more exciting, Frek spiraled straight up until he was even with the patch of boulders before heading across to it. It was incredible to be so high in the air, and just a little scary.

Frek glanced at the heads of his angelwings, sticking out from beneath his armpits. At first it seemed like you couldn't read much of an expression off an angelwing, as they had compound eyes: smoothly curved reddish-gray mosaics of lenses. But once you got to know an angelwing, you could read its mood from the motions of its mouthparts in particular. Frek's angelwings had their jaws wide open to the air, and they were rocking their heads from side to side. They were loving it up here.

The beady-eyed little watchbird was laboring along just off Frek's starboard wingtip. It made Frek feel sort of important to have Gov watching him. But also a little worried. Probably he should have told the counselors about the thing under his bed. It might well be the Anvil. If it was really from another world, then maybe it had a way of making itself hard to see. The counselors would do something awful to him if they found out he'd lied. They'd call him a sociopath, or worse. But who wanted to be on the side of those bossy gurps? And maybe, just maybe, the Anvil held a message from his father.

The sunny air washed away Frek's worries for a time. He landed atop the biggest boulder in the Giant's Marbles, spotted a likely spot on the bank of the stream at the edge of the clearing, buzzed over there, and temporarily took off his angelwings. The wings crawled down to the edge of the stream to drink water, and Frek pulled up a few wild carrots for them to gnaw on. The watchbird perched on the branch of a low anyfruit tree, overseeing the goings-on.

The plants out here weren't any more diverse than the plants in town. Besides the generic grass and the ground-covering bindmoss, Frek could see roseplusplus bushes, scrubby anyfruit trees, please plant bushes, yams, tomato vines, carrots, bean bushes, stalks of rice, and clumps of chard. House trees tended not to grow outside of the towns; they needed special watering and fertilizer-pollen to get off to a good start.

Frek used an anyfruit stick to poke a bunch of holes into the mossy mud along the edge of the stream, and one by one he planted all the seeds in his bag. It took awhile. Again he noticed that one funny-looking seed he'd found near the bed, the one with all the legs. Might it have something to do with the Anvil? Not wanting to excite the watchbird by staring at the special seed for too long, he planted it in the ground like the others.

The seed came to life; it wriggled out of sight. A munching sound filtered up through the shaking earth. A little circle of soil collapsed. The watchbird chirped; it was taking all of this in. The ground vibrated beneath Frek's feet. Accompanied by a high-pitched burrowing sound, a line of disturbance etched its way across the hill. Bushes trembled, boulders gently shifted, the ground was dented with the ghost of a trench. What had Frek unleashed?

It was getting on toward evening when he got home. After supper, Frek's family watched some toons. Suzy Q the statewide newstoon presented a brief item about the counselors standing guard over the Huggins house in case the mysterious "Anvil" from space were to turn up. It was quite unusual for Suzy Q to mention Middleville at all. Some friends uvvied Mom right away to talk about it. At least the news didn't say anything about Frek's weird seed. He listened to Mom talking for a while, and then he went up to his room and played with his Merry Mollusk toons.

His customized cuttlefish was like a squid, but with a fatter body. Just like a squid, a cuttlefish had a bullet-shaped "mantle" covering the rear of its body, with its head and arms and tentacles sticking out of the mantle's open end. And, like a squid, a cuttlefish had eight short arms and two long tentacles, all of them with suckers. When they were just floating around, the Merry Mollusk cuttlefish had a demure way of bunching their arms together to make a pointed cone beneath their large, yellowish eyes. Frek found the cuttlefish cute, even though their pupils were shaped like the letter W. He was teaching his cuttlefish toon to stretch out one arm to shake hands.

But it was a little hard to focus on his Merry Mollusk tonight. All he could really think about was the Anvil. And the faintly etched line across the hillside at Giant's Marbles. Of course with the house tree and the watchbird spying on him, he couldn't go poking around under his bed again. He did allow himself one quick glance, and spotted the same warped-looking blank region near the wall. When he went to bed, he lay about half an hour in the dark waiting for something to happen. And then he fell asleep.

Frek's dreams were so strange that when the noise woke him he wasn't sure he was really awake. He'd been dreaming about his father, Dad talking to him and intensely nodding his Mohawk-crested head, and then he'd dreamed about a spiky glowing shape floating in the air with a smiling girl his age inside it, and then about his Merry Mollusk cuttlefish jabbering really fast, and then about a yellow peeker uvvy worming its feelers into his head.

Here came the noise again, a twitter as of some animal. Frek listened with all his might. The house was dead silent. Another chirp came, followed by a hiss. Yellow light spread across Frek's floor. Light from underneath his bed. Frek leaned over and, yes, the purple thing he'd seen that morning was visible again. He knew now that it was the Anvil.

The Anvil was disk-shaped, like a big red blood cell, except it was purple. It was tipped up so that the flattish top faced Frek's way. A bright triangle of yellow-orange light glowed in the top's dimpled center. The triangle was a door with a thing coming out: a tiny form dark against the light, growing bigger, moving forward, its shape coming clear as it approached. It was a flattish lump with a cluster of arms or legs sticking out the front end. It had two shining eyes. Frek wasn't scared. Surely the Anvil's passenger was his friend. It had come all this way just to see him.

The watchbird started squawking. The house tree turned the room lights on. Already the counselors in the yard were hollering. There wasn't much time.

The shape beneath Frek's bed had grown into the form of—a cuttlefish, just as if it had read Frek's mind. The cuttlefish gazed up at Frek with large, kind, wise eyes. The eyes were a pleasant shade of gold, with dark, wiggly pupils. The cuttlefish's flesh was shaded in tints of green. "You're the one," said the cuttlefish in a low voice. "You'll save the world." The voice sounded human, manly, comforting. The cuttlefish stretched out one of his short sucker-arms and twined it around Frek's hand, just like Frek had been teaching his toon to do. The creature's touch was smooth and warm and—tingly.

An instant later, Zhak and PhiPhi came charging into Frek's room. The cuttlefish scooted awkwardly backward toward the Anvil, but Zhak caught hold of him. Zhak had a transparent glove on his hand, and as soon as he'd grabbed the space cuttlefish, the glove turned itself inside out and sealed the cosmic emissary in a clear bag. The alien was squealing and flailing about. He no longer sounded at all human. He bit his way out of the bag almost right away, using a large beak that had been hidden down in his tentacles. PhiPhi drew a light sword and carved the cuttlefish into five pieces. The pieces flopped around wildly and continued to scream, each piece screaming in a slightly different voice.

News reports of the ongoing struggle were on the house tree walls; it was an emergency wake-up bulletin about the invasion, narrated by Suzy Q. Frek could hardly believe Suzy Q was talking about his room and broadcasting a realtime picture of him in his pajamas.

PhiPhi and Zhak took the five bagged pieces of the cuttlefish outside, with Frek and his family tagging along. Down in the yard, two of the writhing chunks of mollusk flesh burst their bags and tried to crawl away. More counselors arrived and caught them.

A crowd of curious Middleville locals was gathering, Stoo Steiner and his parents among them. Alerted by their house trees and borne on angelwings, people were dropping from the sky like ripe fruit. They seemed anxious, even vengeful. With their biome so pruned-down, Nubbies had a deep-seated fear of new species. What if the alien cuttlefish were to breed explosively and run amok?

"Burn the invader!" shouted Kolder Steiner. "I brought alcohol," he added, rushing up to PhiPhi. He was carrying two seedpods filled with liquid. "You have to burn that thing fast. Every bit of its tissues. I know all about biohazard. I'm a genomicist. There's no substitute for immediate incineration."

"Burn the sport!" chimed in the other onlookers. "Burn it now!"

"Yes," said PhiPhi, after listening down into her Gov-linked uvvy. She and Zhak quickly started a fire with a pile of alcohol-soaked mapine sticks and leaves. The mapine wood was rich with a sticky pitch that burned exceedingly well. The neighbors stoked the blaze, tearing off branches from all the nearby trees they could reach, and once the fire was roaring, the counselors hurled in the pieces of the space cuttlefish. The tentacled globs continued to writhe and scream even as the flames ate them away.

Sao was leaning tight against Kolder, with her head thrown back against his neck. "Burn," she crooned, arching her body and glancing around to make sure people were looking at her. "Buuuuuuurn." The firelight flickered across Kolder's hard face, all angles and crags. Seeing Frek, he glared.

Kolder wasn't the only one looking mean. Most of the neighbors were blaming Frek for the creature from the Anvil. Mom stuck close to Frek, ready to defend him. His sisters were right next to him, too.

Two of the counselors got the Anvil from under Frek's bed and lugged it outside. It looked almost like a meteorite: a shiny, bumpy purplish rock, a disk with dimples on the top and bottom. The triangular door was gone. The Anvil sat there by the fire, glinting in the light. The cuttlefish's screaming had stopped; the flames were guttering down.

"Did the octopus try to bite you?" asked Geneva.

"He was starting to talk to me," said Frek. "He was friendly. He was a cuttlefish, not an octopus. I wish they hadn't killed him so fast."

"Did he tell you his name?" asked Ida.

"He only said one thing," said Frek. "He said I'm going to save our world."

"You?" said Geneva.

"From what?" asked Ida.

Just then Zhak came over and took hold of Frek's arm. "We must take you to our service center," he said. "It requires a full debriefing."

"Frek hasn't done anything," cried Mom. "It's your fault you didn't find that monster this afternoon. My poor son could have been killed."

"This is not negotiable," said Zhak. More counselors were at his side. "Come, Frek."

Lora Huggins threw her arms around Frek; it took three big counselors to pry her away. Zhak dragged Frek to the pod of his lifter beetle. Geneva and Ida wailed for help, but none of the Nubbies raised a hand to save Frek.

As the counselors pushed Frek into the pod, he noticed that the yellow peeker uvvy was gone from Zhak's belt. And then he felt something settle onto his neck. The peeker had crawled up from behind his seat.

Frek tried to reach back and claw the thing off him, but Zhak held down his hands. As the lifter beetle carried them into the sky, the tendrils dug deep into Frek's brain.

The next few hours were odd, like watching a toon show. Frek kept hearing a boy's voice, slow and shy and hesitant. Sometimes he'd feel his throat vibrating in synch with the voice and he'd remember that it was him talking.

He and Zhak were in a room at the counselors' service center, which was a large house tree in a deserted area outside of town. Nobody much was there; the service center was mainly for housing specialized, seldom-used kritters. Also it was a spot to interrogate someone out of the public view.

A being was in Frek's head asking him questions. Gov. Now Gov looked like a First Nations raven mask instead of like an eagle. He was red and black and white with a clacking beak a meter long. Gov didn't actually say his questions out loud. Instead he bobbed his head forward and pecked the answers right out of Frek's brain. Frek had a dim, sick feeling that the pecks were damaging him.

He told Gov everything. About seeing the Anvil in the morning and about how it had hidden itself behind some kind of space lens in the afternoon. About the please plant seed that had looked a little like a squid, and where he'd planted it. About what the space cuttlefish had said. You're the one. You'll save the world.

The raven kept pecking and a sad boy's voice talked on and on.

The pecking might have killed Frek then and there, but his mind possessed some hard kernel that the beak wasn't able to break. It seemed Frek's consciousness held a deep-buried core that could heal itself from the peeker's wounds, an inner seed to regrow his personality. But by the end, the seed was very dented and small.

Then Frek was up in the air with Zhak again. It was morning. Zhak had the window of the lifter pod open; the wind was blowing in at them. Gov wasn't in Frek's head anymore.

"Okay now?" said Zhak.

Frek didn't answer. He felt the wind and listened to the buzz of the lifter beetle. He saw trees below. His house tree. The beetle landed. Frek's legs weren't working right. He fell down on the ground, onto his own yard's grass. It was so wonderful to be back home that he was crying. PhiPhi and Zhak dragged him to his door, then flew off in the lifter beetle right away. They were done here.

Frek spent the next few days in bed, hobbling over to the toilet in the wall when he needed to. Mom, Geneva, and especially Ida came in to visit him, solemnly sitting on a chair by his bed. Sometimes Mom would bring up the yellowish little family statue of the Buddha and hold hands with Frek and pray.

Mom kept telling Frek he'd get better soon. Even though he still hadn't started talking. At first he didn't remember how to talk, and then he didn't want to, and then he was scared to try. If he tried to talk and he couldn't, he'd get a med leech or even the Three R's. Nobody was allowed to be handicapped anymore. They fixed you, no matter what. On the highest shelf of his room perched the watchbird, observing him.

Another health issue was that Frek was having trouble remembering what he was doing, much more so than ever before. It was tricky, for instance, to fetch a mug of water from the tap in his wall. After he filled the mug, he'd maybe notice something else in his room, and when he got back to his bed, he wouldn't be holding the mug anymore. And then he'd have to search all over the room to find it, repeatedly forgetting what he was looking for, but all the while anxiously aware that he *was* looking for something. Finally he'd spot the mug of water—on a shelf or a chair or sitting on the floor—the mug kind of sneering at him, it was a reddish-brown thing from a please plant, with a face on it like a monkey. Can't catch me, the mug would seem to say. Imagining the voice of the mug would make Frek think of the pecking of the raven and the slow halting droning of that tormented boy's voice. Things were bad.

Late one afternoon, Ida got bored while she was visiting with him and put the Goob Dolls on his walls.

"There he is," said Goob Doll Judy, staring down at Frek from the wall skin. As always, she had long, skinny arms and legs, lively ponytails, and hazel eyes like saucers. Two of Judy's Goob Doll friends were with her: Tawni and LingLing. When they moved, pixie dust showered off them, red yellow blue. They were in the Goob Doll House, a place of cheerful colored trapezoid walls and sketchy cartoon furniture.

"Frek Huggins," echoed LingLing. She was the brainy one of the Goob Dolls; she wore those old seeing-things on her face. Glasses. "Are you being nice to him, Ida?"

"Yes," said Ida. "We think maybe the peeker uvvy broke him."

"What's broken gets fixed," said Tawni, nodding her head. She wore her hair in a high, round bun that bounced as she moved.

Frek shook his head no.

"He doesn't want to be fixed," said Ida. "He wants to be well. How can he get better?"

"I'll look it up for you, Ida," said Goob Doll Judy. She gestured at a stylized shelf of books behind her and one of the books hopped to the floor and became a cheerful little facilitator toon with a white mustache and a bald head.

"Peeker exposure of more zan five minutes iss known to cause trauma to the hippocampus, parietal lobe, and structures of the corpus callosum," said the facilitator toon in a thick European accent, pacing back and forth as he talked. "Treatment? Vhy not ze Three R's! Ja, ja!" He did a quick, elbow-waggling dance-step with Tawni, then raised his finger for attention.

"Three R's iss the physical rrremoval, rrrecycling, and rrreplacement of damaged cortical structures," continued the toon. "Vatch!" He drew an imaginary line around the hairless cap of his head. The top of his skull swung open like it was on a hinge. His brain popped out, dropped into a jar of liquid, dissolved, regrew itself, and hopped back into his head. The toon's skull flipped closed with a little clanking sound. The facilitator rolled his eyes and wriggled with delight.

And then he shoved his face forward, filling up half the wall. "Time iss of the essence!" he warned. "Ja, some healing of peeker damage may occur spontaneously after the cerebral insult. But, should lesions remain at six days, the Three R's is strongly, strongly rrrecommended, lest morbidity set in. Never fear, Three R's is a vell-tested procedure vith an exceedingly high zuccess rate!" He flipped his skull top open and closed one more time. The hinge on the lid squeaked, and when it flopped shut it made that little clank. The toon did a final pirouette and turned back into a book. The tome thudded to the Goob Doll House floor, sent out a puff of dust, rebounded into the air, and slid back into the flat wall-pattern that represented a bookshelf.

Frek gathered his courage and finally tried to speak. For a full minute he couldn't get his tongue to respond. But then finally it did. "How many days?" he asked Ida. His voice slid up on the last word.

"You can talk!" exclaimed Ida.

"How many days since I got sick?"

"I don't know," said Ida. "Are you well now?"

"I have to be," said Frek. "I have to." He got out of bed and walked to his closet to get some clothes, but when he got to the closet he'd forgotten what he was looking for. "Kac," he muttered. He knew he had to be well or they'd kill his brain—he wasn't going to forget that—but what did he need from his closet? He looked up and down until he saw rumpled pants and shirts on the floor and remembered.

"What's wrong?" asked Ida.

Frek started to tell her about his short-term memory problem, then stopped himself. The house tree and the watchbird would overhear and tell the counselors, and they'd use it as an excuse for the Three R's. Gov was probably looking for a reason to do something else to him. Frek had the feeling that Gov and the counselors hated him. And he hated them back. It felt bad. He'd never hated anyone before. He'd been mad at Carb for leaving, but he'd never hated him. And the way things were going, Frek was beginning to see why Dad had gone. Gov had peeked Dad too, and Dad had never let on how really horrible it had been. No wonder he'd been a little out of it after that. Maybe he'd been right to leave Earth. But surely, if Carb had tried harder, he could have brought Mom and the kids along. At the tail end of this long train of thought was Ida, standing there looking at him, waiting for the answer to her question.

"Nothing's wrong," said Frek, forcing a smile. "I'm fine. I'm all better, Ida. Thanks for coming to sit with me so much." Grimly he clutched some sturdy blue turmite-silk pants in one hand, a yellow T-shirt in the other. Get these on and then some leather shoes. Shoes, shoes, shoes. But first the—pants. "Stop watching me, Ida. You're making me nervous. Get out of here and let me dress."

"Mom," yelled Ida, running downstairs. "Frek can talk!"

A bit later Frek and his mother were sitting alone in the kitchen, the Buddha looking warm and friendly on his shelf on the wall. They'd had an early supper—though now Frek wasn't sure what they'd eaten—and then Mom had sent Wow and the girls over to Amparo's to play. "Call the counselors and tell them not to come," said Frek. "I'm all better now. I don't need help. I don't want the Three R's." He kept thinking about the squeak and clank of the lid on the top of that little facilitator toon's head.

"The counselors," said Mom with a heavy sigh. "They'll want to test you anyway. They've been coming around every day. They carried that Anvil thing off. They can't get it open. They don't trust you at all. Oh, Frek, if only you'd told them about the Anvil as soon as you saw it."

"I didn't know it would turn out this way," said Frek wretchedly. "I'm sorry. I wish—I wish we could go back to the way things were before." He wanted to form a plan, but thinking was so hard. "What else have the counselors been up to?"

"They decontaminated your room while they had you at the service center," said Mom. "And the last few days they've been up at Giant's Marbles where you planted those seeds. Killing everything with poison and flame-puffers. They keep coming here to ask about you. It's Thursday now. You were sick five days. They said they'd decide about healing you on the sixth day. Tomorrow. Thank Buddha you're better." Her hands were shaking. "You're really better?" Perched on the knob of a kitchen cabinet was the tiny gray watchbird, one of its eyes fixed upon them.

"Oh yes," said Frek, looking at his mother's familiar face. Would he still recognize her if he got a new brain? "Completely well."

Mom stared back at him. Of course she knew. Lora Huggins always knew. "That's wonderful," she said slowly. "I'm so glad. Let me show you the garden. Those nosy neighbors trampled most of it last week, but I used fertilizer-pollen, and the plants are just about like new. We can play a game. I bet you need exercise. Oh, and, Frek, there's apples on the anyfruit tree. You can use your angelwings to get the ones off the top. Your wings have missed you."

It was the first time Frek had been outside since they'd brought him back from the peeker. Spring had moved a notch further along; it was practically summer. Everything was green and rustling, except for some yellow leaves on the mapine. The air was soft and sweet. A crow was cawing. Everything about their house and yard looked so cozy and familiar. Frek's heart overflowed with the simple joy of being alive.

For the moment he and Mom didn't talk about anything real. The watchbird was hovering right next to them. Mom showed him the garden and he said it was nice. They picked some apples from the low-hanging branches, and he said they tasted good. Mom went and got his angelwings out of the garage. Frek wasn't quite sure why she wanted him to fly. To run away? But the watchbird would track him and bring the counselors.

He stared hopelessly at Mom laying out the wings. It was going to be a mess trying to put them on. No way was he going to be able to do all the right steps in the right order. His mind was like a sieve. He stood there worrying, soon forgetting all about the angelwings.

He felt sure he'd get well on his own if Gov would just give him more time. He could feel the healing at work within him; it was a combing sensation, like fingers running through his hair—as if he were combing his brain, fluffing up his familiar old modes of thought, getting his personality back together, bringing his memories on line. But tomorrow the time was going to run out. Some people said you had an immortal soul. Would he get a new soul when they changed his brain? If the Three R's even worked, that is. The facilitator toon had talked about a high success rate. That was a roundabout way of saying that some patients died. Maybe Gov would deliberately make sure Frek ended up being that kind of patient. Yes, tomorrow Frek was probably going to die. He probed the thought, weighing it against the feel of the late afternoon breeze, the smell of the garden, the light slanting through the gathering clouds.

"Don't look so gloomy, Frek," said Mom, actually laughing at him. "Oh, I'm sorry, but you should see your face. I'm going crazy. Let's not give up yet. You don't feel like flying?"

"Uh—"

"Well, then, let's play badminton first!" she exclaimed, as if she'd been waiting to say this. "It's a new set, I got it this week to distract the girls from worrying about you. Look." She darted into the garage and brought out a pair of long-handled racquets, beautifully gnarled wood with springy meshes of fibers.

"They're from a please plant," said Mom. "The strings are good, aren't they? And, look, Frek, here's the *birdie*." She produced a rubbery little pellet with a fringe of feathery fronds.

They went over to the lawn beside the garage so as not to step on the angelwings. They played without a net, not keeping score, just batting the little birdie back and forth. It was easy. The watchbird was intrigued by the shuttlecock's motions; it kept buzzing back and forth, chasing it.

Mom began lobbing the shuttlecock higher and higher. It would settle slowly down toward Frek with the watchbird buzzing after it, and then he'd whack the badminton birdie back to his mother.

"Oops," said Mom. She'd just kicked a hole in the lacy turmite mound, and you could already see some of them swarming out. A pungent, vinegary smell came from the angry turmites. Mom casually moved a few steps away from the mound and hit the birdie to Frek again. He was down past the far end of the garage.

As they continued to volley, Frek noticed something odd about Mom's motions. She kept looking from him to the watchbird to the turmite mound behind her, which meant she had to keep awkwardly turning her head. Doing this over and over. At first he thought it was that she was worried about the turmites stinging her, but then, all at once, he got the picture.

"Ow," said Mom, suddenly stepping to one side and bending to brush a turmite from her ankle. The shuttlecock and the watchbird were flying straight toward Frek. This was it.

Focusing all of his attention, Frek swung his racquet through a full sweep, stretching the length of his body from the tips of his fingers to the tips of his toes. He caught the watchbird full-on with the center of the racquet and sent it hurtling toward the turmite mound.

If the watchbird wasn't dead when it hit the ground, it was a few seconds later. A mass of the angry, tweaked insects crawled over its body, biting.

"Yes, Frek!" called Mom in a low, intense tone. She radiated urgency. "Quick! Let's get your wings on. Come over here and lie down on them. I'll help. And listen, I'm going to give you the mate to Carb's ring. He left it for you. It's exactly like his." She drew a heavy shiny ring out of her pocket and slipped it onto his finger. She'd wrapped some sticky bark tape around the band to make the ring small enough to stay on.

"I'm supposed to run away?" whispered Frek, not quite believing it. He looked down at the ring. It was indeed exactly like Dad's, a solid gold band, thicker on one side, with a glowing dot of red set into a depression in the thick part. The red spot wasn't a gemstone; it was, rather, a shimmering ball, like a tiny, immaterial fire suspended at the base of a little golden cup in the ring. Frek had studied Dad's ring many times.

He ran his finger over the smooth metal, oddly warm to the touch. The origin of Dad's ring was a bit mysterious; Dad had once told Frek that he'd gotten it in a dream he had the night before Frek was born, a dream about some kind of magic pig. But Carb had never filled in the details, nor told him about this copy. Wearing it was almost like holding hands with his father. Frek smiled down at it, then looked up at Lora.

"I'm supposed to run away?" he repeated.

"Not so loud," hissed Mom. "The house will hear you. Yes, run away before Gov takes you again. Your brain will get better by itself. You still have something wrong, don't you?"

"I can't remember what I'm doing," breathed Frek. He was lying on the wings now. "Things slip away from me."

"Oh, Carb had that too after they peeked him," said Mom with another anxious glance at the house tree. "He was getting better, but Gov didn't want to give him time. You'll be fine." She leaned over and helped with the angelwings, her voice even lower than before. "Hurry. There's a Crufter hideout five kilometers west of town. Follow the river upstream. The hideout's in the ruins of that old hydro plant. You've seen the ruins, we've been there for picnics. There's a door down near the base on the other side. Pound on it and show them the ring and someone will help you for sure. Your father, he always thought you were destined to do something special. Maybe he was right." The angelwings were tightly attached now. Mom stood back. "Hurry, Frek!"

Frek got to his feet and flexed his wings. He was still holding the racquet. What all had Mom just said? *Where* was the hideout?

"Here," said Mom, showing him a folded piece of paper and then shoving it into the pocket of his pants. "I wrote everything down for you. Take it one step at a time. First you fly to the river." She pointed away from Lookout Mountain. "You know where the river is, Frek."

She took hold of him and turned him so he was facing downhill. "You take off, and you fly fast and low. Stay under the trees whenever you can. The counselors will be looking for you. Got that much?"

"Fast and low," said Frek. "Where's the hideout again?"

"Upstream," said Mom. "When you get to the river, fly toward the sun. To the left. It's all on this paper." She gave him a fierce kiss on his cheek. "Go now, Frek. And be careful."

"I love you," said Frek, hugging her.

"Buddha bless you, dear son. You're my heart's delight."

Wow suddenly came trotting into the yard, his ears pricked and alert. He poised himself, ready to run along on the ground after Frek. "No, Wowie, you stay here with me," said Mom, grabbing his collar. She was crying.

Frek lifted into the air.

"Good-bye Frek," squeaked Wow, straining at his collar and staring up at him. Even the dog could tell this was a big deal. "Good-bye."

3

in the grulloo woods

Frek's angelwings were well fed and well rested; he buzzed down the shady pathways of Middleville at a tremendous speed. Pretty soon he'd left the house trees behind. He was in a zone of all-season mapines, thick and uniform. The ground was a carpet of sticky red and yellow leaves, pocked by turmite mounds intricate as little cathedrals.

Frek noticed he held something in his hand: the badminton racquet. He savored the sudden memory of how he'd swatted the watchbird. That had been so godzoon goggy. He'd slammed the watchbird and the turmites had finished it off.

Speaking of turmites, they were crawling all over the fallen mapine leaves, feeding. Bolts and swatches of turmite-woven fabrics and garments rested beside their mounds: denims and silks and wools. Middleville was known for its tailors. They cultivated these turmites and harvested the cloth. Off to the right, Frek saw Shurley Yang, the tailor who'd sold Mom her one fancy dress. Shurley glanced over at Frek and waved. She didn't know he was running away.

Running away from what? Frek looked over his shoulder. Nothing was following him. But then his mind played the squeak-clank sound of the brain-lid on the facilitator toon's head. He was running away from the counselors and the Three R's.

The mapine forest stopped abruptly, and Frek was flying across patchwork fields of vegetables, the fields rolling downhill to where the bank dropped off to the clear, rushing waters of the River Jaya. This was the first time he'd used his angelwings to fly down here.

The fields were for yams, tomatoes, carrots, chard, rice, and red beans, the same vegetables as always, the plots butted together upon the rich land of the river bottom as far as Frek could see. Farmers were at work, supervising their crews of pickerhand kritters. Some of the scampering little hands were planting, but others were harvesting as well. The tweaked crops yielded all year round. The harvester pickerhands were loading the produce into elephruks who would carry the produce off to the Nubbies of Middleville and Stun City. So much to see!

Frek's attention fixed upon a rice paddy in a slough just below him, teeming with pickerhands. A massive bull elephruk rested on his knees beside the paddy, taking on a load of the winter-ripened rice. A gangly, thin farmer stood twitching his elbows as he talked with the elephruk's mahout. It was nearly quitting time. Frek slowed and circled to take in the scene. He loved elephruks.

The pickerhands were like living gloves, propelling themselves across the muddy water of the paddy by fluttering their fingers. They were picking each ripe stalk they came across. Once a pickerhand had collected as big a sheaf as it could clasp between thumb and palm, it would clamber up onto the banks of the slough and trot to the elephruk. The hands had a cute, twinkling way of running on their fingertips.

The long, gray elephruk had let his back sag all the way down so that the pickerhands could more easily get into his hopper. The hands beat the stalks against the hopper's inner walls, incrementally mounding the elephruk's freight-bed with grains of rice.

Just then things got even more interesting. The elephruk decided that the load upon his back had grown heavy enough. He rose slowly onto his six legs, unkinking himself from front to back. When a last few pickerhands leaped into his hopper with more sheaves, the elephruk reached his trunk back and plucked up the pickerhands one by one, hurling them into the waters of the rice paddy.

The elephruk's mahout began screaming at his beast. He was a wiry old man in orange tights and a turban. His shrill, cracking voice was so instantly and disproportionately furious that it made Frek laugh to hear it. The elephruk paid the mahout no mind at all. The dusty behemoth rocked from side to side, settling his load, then began making his way around the slough toward the mossy lane that followed the River Jaya to Stun City. The mahout stopped yelling, bid the farmer good-bye, and hopped onto the elephruk's back.

"Frek! Frek Huggins!" The voice came from above, mixed with a clattering in the air. It was PhiPhi, leaning out of the same shimmering green-blue lifter beetle that had carried Frek off to the peeker session last week. No! Frek had forgotten he was running away!

He spurred his wings to a supreme effort, darting toward the river. The high clay riverbanks were green with bindmoss. Frek's mind was empty of any idea about whether to turn left or right, so he took the direction the elephruk was walking in. He had a bit of a lead on the lifter beetle; perhaps he could outfly it.

Frek sped downstream just above the river water, putting every bit of his nerve energy into making his angelwings beat faster.

The River Jaya was crystal clear to the bottom, inhabited only by mosquito larvae and the amplified trout who fed upon them. Frek envied the calm of the great trout, hanging there in the clear water like birds in the sky, gently beating their fins against the current.

He made it past two bends of the river before PhiPhi's lifter beetle drew even with him. PhiPhi was alone, sitting sideways to face him. She was holding a large, hairy, crooked webgun: a heavily tweaked spider. Its spinnerets pointed Frek's way.

"It is easier on you if you land over there and let me take you in," PhiPhi called to Frek. She gestured toward the high bank of the river. "Otherwise I have to net you."

Squeak-clank, thought Frek. They want to eat my brain.

He went a little gollywog then. With a sudden lurch, he dug his angelwings into the air, managing to get behind and above the lifter beetle. And then, faster than thought, he swooped down at the lifter and slashed the edge of his badminton racket against the base of beetle's tiny head. The shock sent the racquet twisting out of Frek's grasp.

Though the lifter's chitinous head was too tough to break, the blow was enough to stun it. The teal-blue beetle dropped its passenger pod and fell to the river itself. The pod and the beetle skipped across the surface like a stones. A wad of web stuff came shooting up from PhiPhi, treading water in the stream. Frek dodged the web and flew on. Yes!

He made it past another bend of the meandering River Jaya. And then he realized he had no idea where he was going. PhiPhi would be uvvying in for reinforcements. What had Mom told him to do? Frek couldn't remember.

He'd pushed his wings so hard that they were drawing strength from the muscles of his chest and arms, not only from his normal energy molecules, but from his body's hidden reserves of dark matter. The alchemical transformation of dark matter was essential to balancing the angelwings' prodigal energy budget. At first his arms had ached, but now they were starting to go numb. He glanced back and saw the glint of a lifter beetle two bends behind him. It was time to go to ground.

Here came another river bend. The carved-out left bank was bluff-high with a fringe of roseplusplusses and please plant fronds against the cloudy sky. Frek went part way round the bend, then quickly angled up to the top of the bank, his arm muscles a mass of pain. Above the bank he found an overgrown slope with no sign of human habitation. In a momentary flash of insight, he realized he'd ended up in the Grulloo Woods. He'd never been here before. Well, it was better than letting the counselors get him. A deep gully gouged the slope above the bluff. Frek dove for the spot where the vegetation looked the thickest.

As soon as he hit the ground, his angelwings peeled themselves off him. They were trembling with fatigue. They wanted to start foraging, but Frek stopped them. He gathered them in his arms, collapsing them like umbrellas. And then Frek scooted under the thickest, lowest-hanging bush he saw—a please plant bush with a bundle of thin branches that rose up from a central clump to droop back to the ground, leaving plenty of room underneath. The branches were set with little oval leaves of a lovely spring-fresh green.

Frek lay there for a while crooning softly to his angelwings and rubbing their domed eyes and their complicated mouths against his cheeks. Up through the bush he could see the clouds turning pink with the setting sun. As he shifted around, trying to be invisible, he felt some hard lumps under his hips. Last year's please plant seeds.

The seeds were shaped like smooth little rods with round disks on the top—like spoons, but not cupped like spoons. Each of the rods had a tiny hole in it. Something about these shapes seemed familiar, but in his present condition, Frek had no hope of remembering what they were. He held some of them up to the mouths of the angelwings. The famished kritters gnawed avidly.

For the next hour or so, Frek lay beneath the bush feeding please plant seeds to his angelwings and looking at his new ring. Frek had always hoped he might get a special ring like Dad's some day, but he'd never thought it would be so soon. Dad had left it for him, and Mom had been saving it for when he got older. Dad cared.

The ring was nicely made, with its cup fashioned into a perfectly parabolic dish. The mysterious red light at the base of the cup glowed equably. Frek prodded at the light with a bit of twig; the stick moved right through the red dot.

Mom had wrapped enough bark tape onto the band to make it a tight fit. With a little effort, he slid the ring off and had a look at the underside. He'd never actually seen Dad take his ring off, and he wondered if you could see the red dot from underneath. But he found smooth gold metal all across the back of the hemisphere—lightly flecked with subtle crystalline structures, the crystals making a delicate pattern that teasingly seemed to change when you stared at it. Frek turned the ring right side up and stared into its glowing red dot. For a second the light seemed to be painting a pattern in the air, like a laser limning a hologram. A face? Could Dad be using his matching ring right at this moment to try to talk to him? But then the thing was once again just a ring. Frek slid it back on, pleased at its weight upon his finger. Having the ring made him feel better about Dad than he'd felt for a long time.

Too bad Dad wasn't here, though. He'd know what to tell the counselors, all right. Dad was the one to have on your side when there was trouble.

While Frek was thinking about Dad and the ring, the rest of his memory kept blanking out on him, but not so much that he ever forgot that he was hiding from the counselors. At first he kept hearing their lifter beetles flying along the river, but after a while the buzzing went away. The clouds grew orange, then shaded down to purple and gray. Maybe he could fly farther down the river tonight. He wished he could remember where Mom had told him to go. He'd forgotten about the paper in his pocket and he'd forgotten he was in the Grulloo Woods.

In the distance, farther up the slope, an occasional thud sounded, as if someone were chopping wood. Just before it got completely dark, the chopping stopped. A moment later a glistening teal lifter beetle set down on the ground some thirty meters off. It was PhiPhi and Zhak with some kind of animal—oh Buddha, it was Wow.

"You smell him near here, Wowie?" said PhiPhi in a sweet voice. Frek could hear her perfectly. With the coming of dusk, the air had grown very calm. "Good, smart dog. Poor Frek needs help. Find him! Find Frek!"

"This the fourth place that dog think he smell Frek," said Zhak impatiently. "We should get real counselor watchdog, a dog with an uvvy so you know what it thinking. Get real counselor dog come back tomorrow morning. If Gov gave Middleville better funding we have dog like that in the first place."

"Tomorrow morning the boy could be in Stun City," said PhiPhi. "Where Gov lives. Gov doesn't want that."

"Little geever," said Zhak angrily. "He supposed to head upstream to that old Crufter hideout. Like Lora Huggins tell him to. I waiting there all afternoon and he never come. His brain's fubbed, yes? Let's just K-I-L-L him, hey PhiPhi?" He spelled the word to keep Wow from understanding.

"Gov doesn't want that," said PhiPhi again. "Gov wants the boy for bait to reopen the Anvil. We bring him in alive. We do like Gov says, Zhak."

"Yaya," said Zhak wearily. "Go on, you stupid dog! Find Frek!"

Wow gave a low growl. But PhiPhi started up the sweet-talk, and soon Wow was nosing around in the brush. It took all of three minutes till his head appeared under Frek's bush, his soft golden eyes glowing with pleasure at having found his friend.

"No, Wowie," whispered Frek before Wow could bark. "Go away. PhiPhi bad. Zhak bad. Frek hide. Go away."

The angelwings twisted in Frek's grasp, trying to escape the smell of dog. If they started chirping he was doomed.

"Go away, Wow," hissed Frek.

Wow bared his teeth in his version of a smile, and went crackling off through the bushes, moving on past Frek, pretending still to be searching, and having himself a good look around. He kept it up for quite a long time.

When it was fully dark, Zhak and PhiPhi started hollering for Wow. And then, finally, Wow went to them.

"Frek not here," squeaked Wow from deep in his throat. The sound carried clearly in the calm evening air.

"Curse you," said Zhak. "We go now, PhiPhi. These woods not safe at night. The Grulloos thinking about suppertime. Grulloos eat people. If Frek here, he won't get to Stun City. We posted watchbirds all along River Jaya anyhow. Enough now, PhiPhi. We go."

"I wish we have one more watchbird," said PhiPhi. "I got a feeling Frek's under one of these bushes. Listening to us. I bet Wow lying to us. I wonder if Frek come out if we start T-O-R-T-U-R-E his dog?"

"Yaya," said Zhak with a snicker. "I like your think. Hang on. I'll—" He broke off in a yelp. "He bit me! There he goes! Don't let him get—"

Frek heard frantic crashing in the bushes and then a distant splash in the river.

"I'm bleeding, PhiPhi," said Zhak mournfully. "I need med leech. We go. Forget curse you dog. Maybe he drowns or a Grulloo eats him or we catch him tomorrow, who cares. We go."

The lifter beetle buzzed away, invisible against the black sky. It was a cloudy, moonless night.

Frek was trying to process all the different things he'd heard. It was like juggling—and he couldn't juggle. One by one the memories dropped from his grasp and rolled off. Eventually he gave up and began putting on his angelwings. He knew for sure that he should keep running from the counselors—he just didn't know which way.

A noise was coming from uphill. A quiet sobbing. It had started soon after the counselors left, but only now had Frek identified it. Someone up there was hurt and crying. Frek headed up the dark slope, using his angelwings to move in long, low leaps. When he got closer to the sound, it turned into words.

"I've pinched my tail," said a man's rough, high-pitched voice. "Please help me, Frek."

Startled, Frek flew straight up into the air and found a perch on the high bare limb of a rotted-out mapine tree, pale in the darkness. He'd just remembered he was in the Grulloo Woods. The clearing beyond the dead tree was a pool of night.

"How do you know my name?" called Frek into the gloom.

"Your dog told me," said the little voice, growing conversational. "He said you might come. Please help me. I'm trapped."

"How do you mean?" asked Frek.

"My long, clever tail," came the raspy tenor from the blackness. "It's pinched. I was splitting logs this afternoon to get at the veins of nutfungus. It's got a spicy taste my folk are fond of. I was holding the wedge with my tail, and when those counselors came buzzing in I was so frightened that I let the wedge pop out. The log snapped shut on me." The unseen little man dropped his tone nearly to a whisper. "If Okky finds me like this I'll meet a sorry end. Hop down here and free me, Frek. Drive in the wedge and pry the log open."

Frek was on the point of flapping down when something stopped him. "You have a tail?"

"A fine woodsy one," confided the voice, growing stronger again. "It looks like a stick, but it's terribly strong and leathery. I can lie in a bush and stick my tail up into the air and when a little bird lands on it—*zickzack,* Jeroon's got his lunch! Come on, boy, don't keep me waiting."

"You're a Grulloo," exclaimed Frek. "You eat people."

"Your Gov promotes that toony tale to make you hate us. Grulloos all cannibals? Poppycock! I live on fruit, vegetables, and the odd fowl. I'm a simple woodsman; I gather what I can—rugmoss, nutfungus, please plant seeds—and I barter my takings for what I can get from my fellow Grulloos. Groceries, in the main, with the rest going toward furnishing and decorating my burrow. I've a hand-made chair, a bed, and a fine Grulloo carpet of cultured rugmoss. Once my home's to the liking of my Ennie, the two of us can hatch out an egg, Gaia willing. Yes, yes, Grulloos are family people, as peaceable as you Nubbies. Precious few of us are man-eaters." The Grulloo lowered his voice again. "But if I'm trapped here much longer, it's the dreadful Okky who'll make a meal of me. She eats her victims' heads, you know, starting with the nose and ending with the brain. I've chanced upon her grisly leavings more than once. It's said that Okky sells our refined cerebral essences to NuBioCom, as she's got no eggs to offer them. Free me, Frek, free me before Okky finds us. She'll eat you, too!"

"You won't hurt me?" asked Frek.

"Aid me this once and I'm your friend forever. Such larks we'll have, Frek. I've always wanted to know a Nubby. Jeroon's my name. I'm the fellow to have at your side."

"I do need help," said Frek. "The counselors broke my memory."

"Peeked you, they did, eh? I've got some stim cells in my burrow that'll heal that. Come on down here, boy. My axe is next to me, but the wedge flew off to the other side of the clearing."

Still Frek hesitated. "Can I look at you first? Can you make a light?"

The Grulloo grumbled a bit and began rustling in the dark. A spark shone as he fired up a matchbud and lit his—pipe? Except in toons, Frek had never seen anyone smoke before.

In the darkness of the woods, the glow of the pipe was enough to light the clearing. The Grulloo was little more than a man's head with a pair of arms—or were they legs? Little legs with hands that he walked upon. He had a big nose and browned, leathery skin. His eyes were hidden by the brim of a dark blue felt cap worn tight and low on his head. He carried a knife tucked beneath a strap of the cap, the blade lying along one side of the crown. A tight little red jacket rose up to his chin, with many pockets, and a pouch of nutfungus at the waist. He flexed his cheeks, pulling smoke out of the pipe. Rather than breathing the smoke in, he let it trickle up around his weathered face.

The Grulloo—he'd said his name was Jeroon—had a bit of a body that tapered out from the back of his head like a fish's, thinning down to a branching, sticklike tail. Much of his tail was buried deep in the heart of a thick old log with a red strip of nutfungus along one side. He cocked back his head and peered up imploringly with his pipe clenched between his square yellow teeth. His face was tight with pain.

"Poor Jeroon," said Frek, his heart opening. He fluttered to the ground. It was a matter of minutes to fetch Jeroon's wedge and to pound it into the log with the little axe. Jeroon's wedge, axe, and knife were elegantly formed; they were the products of please plants cunningly tweaked to draw metal from the soil.

"Oh, that's good," said Jeroon when his tail came free. Although his tail was camouflaged to resemble a branching stick, it was completely flexible. He set his pipe down on the ground and brought the tail around to his face, sniffing and licking at the injured spots. And then the pipe was back in his mouth and he was scrambling about on the split log, prying at the thick veins of shiny red nutfungus and stashing the pieces in his pouch.

Frek caught a whiff of the pipe smoke. He'd always wondered what tobacco smelled like. Sort of good. You couldn't get it in Middleville.

"Hist," said Jeroon, suddenly looking upward. He ballooned his cheeks to draw the smoke from the pipe, turning his head from side to side, the smoke leaking out of his mouth and up around his nose. He slowly stalked all around the clearing, listening. He moved with a bow-legged rocking motion, tossing his tail from side to side to keep his balance. He was like a two-limbed toon tyrannosaur—but less than half a meter tall.

Now Frek, too, could hear what Jeroon was listening to. The whir of wings. A lifter beetle? No, this sounded different. More of a flapping sound.

"It's Okky," whispered Jeroon. "We're for it, lad. Let's bolt!"

"Which way?" asked Frek, crouching down to face the Grulloo.

"Can you carry me?" asked Jeroon, hand-walking forward. He'd pocketed his wedge and his axe hung from a loop in the side of the coat.

"All right."

"Friends for life," said Jeroon, leaning far to one side and extending the hand at the end of his right leg. "I'll give you something wonderful when we get to my house. A boon."

"Friends," answered Frek, shaking Jeroon's hand. The Grulloo's grip was firm and strong, his skin hard and calloused.

Jeroon got his arms, or legs, around Frek's midsection and they lifted up into the air. The overburdened angelwings weren't liking this, they were chittering in dismay.

"That way," said Jeroon, speaking around the pipe stem still clenched in his teeth. He was pointing with his tail, curved around to gesture in the direction they flew. The pipe smoke floated up into Frek's face, making him cough. Breathing tobacco was a different story from smelling it.

"Put out the pipe, Jeroon."

"Not yet," said the Grulloo, puffing out his cheeks so hard that the pipe bowl glowed bright orange. "We may need it against Okky." The color made Frek think of the door in the UFO under his bed—which seemed like a lifetime ago. Frek worked his wings, staying ahead of the smoke.

They were above the tangled dark shapes of the Grulloo Woods, heading away from the river. This was wild, unknown country. Nobody ever came here. It was all Frek could do to avoid hitting the trees, but Jeroon seemed to know exactly where they were going. His arms aching with a wholly new level of fatigue, Frek followed the pointing of Jeroon's limber tail, dimly visible in the light from his pipe.

"Look out," said the Grulloo suddenly. "Here she comes." Nimble as a nightmare demon, Jeroon scrabbled up Frek's chest and hauled himself onto Frek's shoulders, his coarse hands digging into the nape of Frek's neck. The pouchy base of Jeroon's tail swept past Frek's face and wedged itself against the side of his head. From the corner of his eye, Frek could see that Jeroon had stuck one hand up high into the air, the hand clutching both his knife and his glowing pipe. Hard as it was to believe, Jeroon was also singing at the top of his lungs— bitter, joking verses about Grulloos, each chorus ending with the line, "So don't you call us freaks!"

There was a hooting sound followed by a whoosh of air laden with the smell of corruption. Jeroon's singing rose to a fierce shriek.

Something thumped against Frek's back, crumpling one of his angel-wings. The poor wing gave a dying insect chirp of alarm, then peeled off and fell away. Frantically Frek feathered the air with his remaining wing, sweeping it from side to side to break their fall as best he could. Jeroon seemed to be everywhere at once, on Frek's shoulders, at his waist, on the side of his leg, all the time singing his defiance of Okky, who swooped about them, pressing her attack.

They crashed into the top of an anyfruit tree, and as luck would have it, the impact snapped Frek's other wing, sending the ichor of its torn, dying body oozing down his side. Frek initially took it for his own blood. But then he realized that by some miracle he himself was unscathed. Thank you, Buddha.

Jeroon leaped off him and clambered onto a thick branch just overhead. His pipe and its coal were long gone, but he was still roaring out his song and stabbing his knife at the dark form that hooted and beat the air with stinking black wings. For a terrible, confused, instant Frek thought the shape was Gov in his raven form, somehow risen out of the wall skins to physically hunt him down. But it was Okky, and then the deathly beast had flown away.

"Your poor wings," rasped Jeroon, nimbly dropping to a branch at his side. "Gaia bless 'em, they saved our lives. We'd never have gotten this far on foot. You're a good friend, Frek. I hope you're hale enough to push on? We're not safe yet. My burrow's just a bit farther."

They climbed down the tree. Frek followed the sound of Jeroon's steps through some brush into the bed of a gurgling stream. They walked up the stream for a while, the banks getting higher on either side. Frek's feet grew wet and muddy. He felt thoroughly miserable. And by now he couldn't remember what he was doing here. There was nothing for it but to press on.

Finally Jeroon came to a stop and began fumbling at a spot on the bank. Frek heard the creak of a little door.

"Welcome to my home," said Jeroon.

Frek reached out to feel the shape of entrance. It was a round hole, nicely framed in stone, less than a meter across. "I don't want to go in there," he said. "I'll suffocate."

"Oh it's roomier than you think," said Jeroon. "Plush and airy, with a well-stocked larder. There's windows and a fireplace with a clean-drawing chimney. Don't be frightened, Frek."

Jeroon disappeared into the burrow, but Frek stayed outside. A few minutes passed. Frek heard clatters, bumps, and crackling. A warm, flickering light appeared within. Peering through the open door, Frek could make out a low, arched hallway with its floor tiled in contrasting square and octagonal stones, nicely polished. The warm light came from a doorway in the right side of the hall. Jeroon peeked out of the lit door, and beckoned with his curled-around tail.

Frek heard a hooting not very far off. The memory of Okky's attack flashed back. He took a deep breath and crawled into Jeroon's burrow, slamming the round door behind him.

The hallway was gog tight, but once he'd wormed his way down the hall and through that lit-up door at the end, he found himself in a room nearly tall enough to stand in. He rose to a crouch and looked around.

The room had a smooth, redbrick floor and, wonder of wonders, a thick Turkish-style carpet, glowing with patterns of red, blue, and yellow. A cozy fire burned in a hearth on his left and, true to Jeroon's promise, the smoke was drawing nicely up into the flue. The arched ceiling curved down to merge with walls of hard-packed earth that were brightened by a coat of whitewash. Two barred, round windows were in the right wall, and one was propped open to let in the fresh, cool night air. A door on the far side of the room led to a kitchen, with a door beyond that leading to a bedchamber.

Jeroon had perched himself on a tall chair with two low arms and no back. His tail dangled behind him, so that his head seemed to sit alone upon the high chair's cushion like the dot of a letter "i." He was sipping at a mug of something that smelled sweet and spicy. "My home is your home, Frek," said Jeroon, clearly savoring the moment. "Have a seat over there, you'll be more comfortable. Take off your wet shoes. I'll be bringing you some food."

Frek sat down on a square flat bolster in the corner between the hall door and the open window. For a moment Jeroon stared at him, grinning. And then the little Grulloo clambered down from his chair and ambled hand over hand into the kitchen, slowly beating his tail.

While Jeroon was gone, Frek looked around the room some more. There wasn't much furniture besides Jeroon's chair. Most of the floor was covered by the rich-colored carpet. A bowl beside the fireplace held a dozen little lumps of half-dried—were they meat? They looked too soft and greasy to be please plant seeds. Frek wondered if they were to be part of supper. He was quite hungry. He reached out to pick one up but, unsettlingly, it twitched at his touch. He left it in the bowl.

His attention kept being drawn back to the rug. The pattern was slowly changing, smoothly cycling from one symmetry to the next. It was gog gripper. He leaned forward to examine the carpet. It wasn't turmite-fiber. It was a mat of soft bristles tinted in colors that slowly changed. In a way, the rug was like a house tree's wall skin, but it was a living colony on its own. Frek had never seen anything like it before. For some reason he thought of Sao Steiner. He wondered if she'd ever seen a Grulloo rug. And then his memories drifted off, and he was just staring at the rug's colors.

Jeroon reappeared with a cold plate of boiled carrots and roast yams, a thick slice of anymeat on grobread and a cup of tree-juice spiced with nutfungus. He held the plate and the mug balanced over his head with branches of his curled-up tail. Though the tail's surface resembled bark, the tail was like a set of four tentacles.

Frek ate and drank, thinking of nothing but the food. The nutfungus had a pleasant scent that tickled the back of his nose. Slowly the ache went out of his arms.

Jeroon watched him closely, bringing seconds, and then thirds. "I can't get over it," he said when Frek was finally done. "I have a Nubby as a guest in my own home. Wait till I tell Ennie and her family."

"Ennie?" said Frek. "Is someone else here?" He wondered if he'd forgotten meeting more Grulloos. Had they been in the room while he was watching the rug?

"Your memory!" exclaimed Jeroon. "We have to set it right. I'll mix you up a stim cell potion. It's not to be had amidst your

Middleville Nubbies." Jeroon reached over to the small bowl by the fireplace and picked out a couple of the drier gobbets of meat. "These are from the Kritterworks artigrows. They're like belly buttons, you might say, scraps of umbilical cord. NuBioCom harvests them special for us Grulloos, useful kritters that we are. And in return we give them our eggs, which just so happen to be ideal for making embryo blanks. A nice little circle there. We give 'em eggs to seed their kritters into, and they give us stim cell nuggets left over from where the kritters grow." Jeroon brandished the two winkled nodules. "Loaded with bioactive repair cells," he said. "Just the thing to fix your brain! Not that the counselors would have told you about them. Gov much prefers the Three R's for troublesome lads like you. The removal, recycling, and replacement of a bad boy's brain." The Grulloo let out a snort of laughter.

Frek hadn't really been following Jeroon's meandering discourse. But at the last words, he instantly imagined the terrible squeak-clank sound again. He lurched up onto his knees. "The Three R's?" he choked, looking for a way out. It would be hard to make his escape with the ceiling so low.

"Don't startle up," said Jeroon soothingly. "*No* Three R's. It's but a foamy health-drink I'm after making you, my boy. You'll drink, you'll sleep, and you'll be able to remember again. We Grulloos know firsthand about the beastly things your counselors do. Did you see the Raven when they peeked you?"

"Yes," said Frek, slowly lowering back onto his cushion.

"Gov is kac," said Jeroon shortly. "A bully and a coward. A parasitic worm. Don't budge!" He scuttled into the kitchen.

Gov is kac. Frek had never heard anyone say that before, not even Dad. It was music to his ears. The fact that Jeroon was free to say it made him feel safe. And then Jeroon was back with a mug of something lukewarm. It was cloudy, and smelled of rancid meat, and it made Frek's lips numb, but at Jeroon's urging he drank every bit of it down. All at once Frek could feel how tired he was from the long day. Jeroon pulled over another cushion. Frek lay down and slept right through the night.

He was roused by something lightly jumping on his stomach, then hopping off. He heard high little voices all around him, and the burbling of a stream. Light slanted in through a round window nearby, stained green by overhanging bushes of a type Frek had never seen. The voices belonged to five Grulloos, their bodies variations on Jeroon's, each of them with a head, a pair of legs ending in hands, and some kind of tail. They all wore colorful jackets around their middles. Two of them were quite small. Children.

"He's awake!" shouted the littlest Grulloo, the one who'd just woken him by bouncing on his stomach. "The Nubby's awake!" She had a sweet round face and two pink leg-arms sticking out of the side of her head. Her jacket was little more than a pink sash. The bulge at the back of her head tapered out into a little ponytail that waved about on its own. "Hi, Nubby," she cried, hopping onto Frek's chest again. "I'm LuHu!" Her ponytail rose into the air like an exclamation point.

"Roar!" said the other young Grulloo. "Are you scared?" He had short orange hair and sharp yellow teeth. His tail resembled a tiger's, and his jacket was striped to match. He'd been feeling Frek's belly with one of his black-nailed hands, but when Frek moved, the little Grulloo twitched away.

Next to him was a mermaidlike Grulloo with a scaly, silver tail and a fair, thoughtful face supported by two well-formed arms. Her jacket was of flowing, sea-green cloth. Beside her was an orchid Grulloo, a heavy-set woman with white petals upon her legs and tail. Her jacket was of white turmite-silk. She was pressed tight against the male Grulloo at her side, a tough-looking fellow with a green lizard's tail and a dirty red suede jacket with four pockets. The Grulloos were shifting back and forth on their legs, torn between curiosity and fear, the little ones alternately darting away beneath the adults and creeping forward for a better view. Though the Grulloos' tails were like parts of plants or animals, they all had human faces.

"Hello," said Frek a little warily. "I'm Jeroon's friend." Sounds of cooking came from the kitchen.

"Good morning," said the Grulloos.

Remarkable as the Grulloos were, Frek's attention turned inward. His memories were back, including everything he'd heard and seen the day before.

The first bit to grab him was something Zhak had said: "He supposed to head upstream to that old Crufter hideout. Like Lora Huggins tell him to." How had Zhak known what Mom told Frek? Had the house tree overheard them? No, Mom had been too careful for that. One of those supposedly helpful Crufters must have spilled the beans. Given what a thoughtless opportunist Carb was, it figured the Crufters would foul things up. Frek felt a burst of anger at his father—and that reminded him of his new ring. There it was, still on his finger. The Grulloos were interested in it, the little ones had already come over to touch it, fingering the depression on its top.

The next thing Frek remembered was faithful Wow. Wow had jumped into the river. Had he found his way back home?

And then came the memory of Mom putting a paper in his pocket. Hard to believe he'd totally forgotten to look at it yesterday. He'd been gog fubbed. It was wonderful to have his mind back. He felt like his old self for the first time since he'd been peeked.

Frek rocked to one side, toppling the Grulloo with the long lizard's tail and the powerful, green legs. He apologized, then pulled the folded paper from his pants.

"Don't smother him," said Jeroon, hand-walking out from the kitchen with a big plate of pancakes balanced on his tail. "He needs his breakfast. What do you have there, Frek?"

"It's a note my mother put in my pocket," he said. "My memory's all better again, Jeroon. Thanks."

"My pleasure," said Jeroon, setting the plate of pancakes beside him. "You saved my life." He smiled tenderly at the mermaid Grulloo. "Keep your niece and nephew off him, Ennie, while I make enough pancakes for everyone." The Grulloos cheered and continued chattering. Soon Frek had sorted them out. The green one in the grubby red suede jacket was Gibby, his plump petal-covered wife was Salla, their children were LuHu and Bili, and Ennie was Salla's younger sister.

Frek wasn't good at reading, so it took him a while to get through his mother's note. He ate most of his pancakes while he was at it. They were made of grobread dough, fried and drenched in blackberry syrup. One by one the Grulloos got pancakes too, Ennie first.

The note went as follows.

Dear Frek,

(1) Go to the river.
(2) Fly upstream toward the setting sun.
(3) Stay AWAY from the Grulloo Woods on the other side of the river.
(4) Upstream you'll find the old hydro plant.
(5) There's a door in the base on the other side.
(6) Pound on it and a Crufter will help you. They know you're coming.
(7) They'll hide you and take you to live with Carb.

Love,

Mom

Well, Frek could forget about (2) through (7). He'd flown the wrong way down the river, he'd gone into the Grulloo Woods, the Crufters had turned out to be double-crossers, and he didn't want to live with selfish Carb one bit. What a mess.

"He's done reading," shouted LuHu, who was grasping a last sticky bit of her pancake with her prehensile ponytail. "Let's get him, Bili!" She and the tiger-tailed Grulloo boy scampered across the pulsing rug and leaped onto his lap.

"Not just yet," said Frek, smiling and pushing them off. "I'm still thinking. I haven't been able to think for a week, you know. Jeroon only just now fixed my brain."

Fixed it with stim cells. Tiny one-celled kritters that had made their way from his stomach into his bloodstream and up to his brain. Might the stim cells take over his personality? His heart began pounding. Was that the stim cells in action?

"Jeroon," he croaked, clutching his throat. "Are the stim cells—"

"Don't kac your britches," said Jeroon, proudly perched on his lofty chair. He'd just started eating his own plate of pancakes. "They'll leave your system soon enough. It'd be better for us Grulloos if stim cells lasted longer. Then we wouldn't need to dose ourselves so often." His head was at the back of the cushion with the plate in front of him and his arms around it. He bit off a piece of pancake, chewed it, and then paused as if waiting for the mouthful to go down. Frek noticed that Jeroon had a stim cell nodule on his plate beside the pancakes.

"You eat stim cells all the time?" asked Frek.

"Look us over," said Jeroon, gesturing at himself and the other Grulloos. "You think we could live without some help? That big body you're the master of, it's full of life-support. Stomach, lungs, heart, liver, kidneys—you've got the whole shebang." He tapped the thick base of his tail. "I've got a few rudiments in here, such as lungs, yes, but nothing like what's needed for a proper long life. It's the stim cells that keep me going, you know. I don't have a stomach or a liver, no digestive tract. Take a gander!" He chewed up another big bite of pancake and opened his mouth. Him doing this reminded Frek of Geneva, who sometimes showed him a mouthful of food when Mom wasn't looking, just to be gross.

Jeroon's mouth simply ended at the back. A little hole on the roof of his mouth connected with his nose and lungs, but he lacked any gullet-type throat-hole. The back of the mouth was a dead-end sack with the wad of chewed pancake just sitting there. But the flesh at the base of Jeroon's tongue was busy; a thousand pink projections were tugging at the dough, picking it to pieces, pulling the pasty mush into the tongue's fissures.

"Quit it, Jeroon," said Salla, shaking her petals. She had a mother's firm voice. "You'll teach bad manners to Bili and LuHu."

"My breakfast," said Jeroon, partly closing his mouth. "Once the food particles are in my tongue, the stim cells turn them into nourishment."

Little Bili was imitating him now, skipping about the room with his mouth wide open. The backs of Bili's and Jeroon's tongues were both engorged with pancake. So googly, so shecked-out.

Frek asked another question so Jeroon would close his mouth. "You said the stim cells are from the Kritterworks?"

"To be sure," said Jeroon. "From the artigrows. The NuBioCommers found a use for the stim cells when they made Grulloos. Around three hundred years back. A little after the Great Collapse."

Hearing about the collapse always made Frek feel wistful. First Earth's genetic heritage had been driven extinct by the NuBioCom knockout virus, which broke the reproductive cycle of non-NuBioCom organisms. And then, on June 6, 2666, the NuBioCom labs had purged all the archived DNA information. Erased Eden's blueprints. "I wish we had butterflies," said Frek softly. "And octopi—I'd love to see an octopus or a squid. The alien I saw looked like a cuttlefish, you know. He was green."

"What alien?" asked Jeroon, surprised.

"I didn't tell you?" said Frek. "You didn't hear? Don't you watch the news on your wall skins?" But then, looking around the burrow, he remembered that Jeroon's walls were packed dirt, very far from the live inner surfaces of a house tree.

So now Frek told his new Grulloo friends about the Anvil and the cuttlefish, about the peeker and his brain damage, about the smashed watchbird and the escape.

"Where's the Anvil at?" asked Gibby when Frek was done. He was like a two-legged lizard with a man's taut, sallow face. "Maybe there's goodies inside it." Gibby rocked back onto his tail and rubbed his rough hands together, blinking his flat round blue eyes. "I'd surely like to have a look-see. We could make a nice buck off a thing like that."

"Gov's got it," said Frek. "One of the counselors said Gov wants to use me for bait to make the Anvil open up again."

"Gov," said Jeroon thoughtfully. "The mighty toon who rules the local Nubbies. He's based in the big NuBioCom puffball in Stun City. I'd wager three eggs that's where the counselors carried the Anvil. It would be a treat to see what happens if the Anvil opens *without* Gov's stooges around, eh? I daresay your cuttlefish alien had a boon to share. I've a half a mind that you and Gibby and I should steal what's in the Anvil, Frek."

The word "boon" reminded Frek that Jeroon had promised to give him something for saving his life. Was it just going to be that healing dose of stim cells? Usually a boon was something a little more gripper than medicine. But Jeroon seemed too wrapped up in his own plans to remember his promise. Frek felt a bit annoyed. Here these Grulloos were scheming to ransack the Anvil and they hadn't even asked Frek what he thought of the idea.

"You'll reap a whirlwind!" put in Ennie, and thumped her mermaid tail on the ground for emphasis. "Don't do it, Jeroon."

"Our world's a paradise just the way it is?" asked Jeroon, his voice rising to a shrill buzz. "With NuBioCom pinching off the very dance of life? Things grow more wonderful all the time?"

"But Jeroon," said Ennie, her voice breaking. "Maybe you're forgetting some of the important things you've already got."

"How would we get inside the puffball to find the Anvil?" interrupted Frek, curious about the proposal in spite of himself.

"Our man Gibby goes there once a month to trade our tribe's eggs for stim cells," said Jeroon weakly. Ennie's plaint had knocked the wind from his sails. "I often travel along to help. Gibby was planning to go today, as it happens. I'd thought we might bring you with us and try our odds." He glanced over at Ennie. "But perhaps not."

"What about hatching out our egg?" wailed Ennie. "Instead of trading them all away for Gov to use in the Kritterworks. You'll die in his horrible puffball and we'll never have hatched even one!"

"You're ready right now?" asked Jeroon, lowering his voice.

"I've been waiting and waiting for you to ask," said Ennie. "But you want to run off to play the hero and—and—" She lowered her eyes and turned away.

"Oh, my dear Ennie," said Jeroon. "More fool I. Of course we should hatch out an egg together. It's been my fondest dream, my sweet. Yes, yes, let's do it now. The Earth's blessings upon us!" He trotted over to Ennie. They leaned forward on their short little legs, pressing their faces together, kissing. LuHu and Bili cheered and capered around them. Salla's plump features were wreathed in smiles.

"Wal, I'm going down to Stun City anyhows," Gibby told Frek. "Gotta get them fresh lumps of stim cells. The folk got better'n a hundred eggs for me to cart along. If you're game, you're welcome for the ride, boy."

"Do you think it's safe to take him?" wondered Salla. "He's wanted by the counselors."

"He can wear a disguise," said Gibby, calmly fishing out a pipe from one of his jacket pockets. "That Anvil could be worth a king's ransom. Is it heavy, Frek?"

"I think so," said Frek. "Too heavy for me to carry, if that's what you're thinking."

"I bet you can get it to open up again. Or if that don't work, maybe we could roll it onto the back of my elephruk."

"You have an elephruk?" said Frek, enchanted by the notion. Gibby wanted him to ride to Stun City on an elephruk? Life in Middleville had never been this interesting.

"An elephruk, but she's a sorry one," said Gibby, grimacing against the smoke from his pipe. "Grulloos don't get nothing unless nobody wants it. I say let's do it. You ready to go?"

Across the room, Ennie and Jeroon were staring raptly into each other's eyes, all but lost to the outside world.

"How long will it take those two to hatch out their egg?" asked Frek. He felt a little shy of the gruff Gibby. He'd rather wait for Jeroon.

"Some men might say three days," said the petal-covered Salla with a comfortable laugh. "But really it takes the rest of your life. Jeroon won't be wanting to step out with you today, Frek, nor tomorrow, nor the day after that. And on the third day, we'll have the wedding party, right, Gibby? My big sister Pfaffa will help. With Ma and Pa in heaven, the wedding's our responsibility. Stop racing around like that, Bili and LuHu. Leave Aunt Ennie alone."

"I've a fine nest ready in my bedroom," Jeroon was telling Ennie. "It's lined with the softest of turmite-silks, and I'll dust them down with stim cells. How I've longed for this day, my love."

"Oh, Jeroon," said Ennie, blushing all the way down to the flukes of her tail. She took a little step toward the door that led to the kitchen and Jeroon's bedroom.

Jeroon's rough, plain face was shining with joy. As he turned to follow his bride, his gaze fell upon Frek. "Gibby will take care of you," he said casually. "Depend upon my good brother-in-law-to-be!"

Certainly his vows of lifelong friendship weren't weighing very heavy on his mind.

Frek had never been particularly good at speaking up for his rights. But the little woodsman had promised him a boon for saving his life, and he'd be a fool not to ask for it. Maybe asking for the boon was part of the test. So he looked Jeroon in the eye and said it straight out. "Weren't you going to give me something?"

"Ah yes," said Jeroon, looking just a bit shifty. "It nearly slipped my mind. Thanks for reminding me."

"Good on you, boy," said Gibby. "Jeroon's a tight-fisted little runt. Don't short him, Jeroon!"

"Fine, fine," grumbled Jeroon. He swung across the floor and pulled a loose brick from the wall by the fireplace. "I'll give you—"

"Give him *two* things," put in Gibby. "He got your tail out of the log, and he flew you home. He saved you twice."

"I'm to have this troublemaker as my brother-in-law?" said Jeroon, barely managing to keep a pleasant tone. You could see that he didn't like to give up any treasure.

"Get it over with," said Ennie. "We've got more important things to do." She skipped over to give Jeroon another kiss.

"All right then," said Jeroon in a brighter tone. He handed Frek a translucent seed pod filled with a sparkling gel. "This is chameleon mod, Frek. There's three doses in here. To use it, you take off your clothes, dab it onto any part of your skin, and for the next half hour you might as well be invisible." Frek had heard of chameleon gel, in fact he'd seen Da Nha Duc use it in a toon. But he hadn't quite understood it was real. He studied the pod. The shiny gel contained colors upon colors.

Jeroon continued rooting in his hidey-hole, looking for something else he was willing to give. Frek heard the clink of some gold coins, but those stayed hidden. Finally Jeroon produced an unimpressive-looking brown twig shorter than Frek's little finger. Its bark was slightly scaly.

"Forgot I had this," muttered Jeroon and then, after a moment's hesitation, he handed it over. "It was one of Gov's experiments," said Jeroon. "A crowd-control device, you might say. We tested it out in a corner of the Grulloo Woods. It's called an Aaron's Rod. A plant that grows and branches and grows and branches till it fills up—oh, I don't know, how big would you say the Aaron's Rod thicket is, Gibby? You were there when we tested it."

"Filled up a hundred meters of woods easy," said Gibby. "Was a whole gully eaten up in less than a minute, all stuffed with that damned wad o' twigs. And then it dies the next day. What good is a present like that, Jeroon? Don't you got nothing better in that hidey-hole?"

"Mind your own business," snapped Jeroon. "The Aaron's Rod could come in handy for Frek sometime. Whatever you do, don't start it up anyplace you're fond of, Frek. All it takes is a splash of water to wake it. Think of it more as a weapon, like. Here, you can keep your treasures in this. It'll keep the Aaron's Rod dry." Jeroon produced a sticky little purse-fungus for holding the mod-pod and the twig. The fungus was a little pouch, pink with a flap covering a smooth green interior, and small enough to fit in the palm of Frek's hand.

"Well, thank you," said Frek, taking his gifts. "And good luck to you, Jeroon." He examined the mod-pod and the mighty twig. Three doses of invisibility salve and a plant that would grow to fill a large building in less than a minute. Calling them treasures seemed like something of an exaggeration. Oh well. He tucked them into the purse-fungus.

"So let's clear out and give these love-birds some peace," put in Salla, registering a coaxing glance from Ennie. "I'll start the fixings for the wedding feast. Only three days from now, and so much to do! Gaia bless you, Ennie. Congratulations, Jeroon!"

"I want to watch them push their eggs together!" cried LuHu. "That's what they're gonna do, isn't it, Pa?"

"Get along with you, sugar-pup," said Gibby as little Bili guffawed. "Don't be poking your nose into grown-up ways."

The children skipped down the hall to the door of Jeroon's burrow, with Salla and Frek following them and Gibby taking up the rear, having said a quick last good-bye to Jeroon. And then they were outside on the banks of the gurgling stream.

It was an overcast May morning, with the clouds low in the sky.

For a few minutes Gibby busied himself snapping stalks off the overhanging plants that all but hid Jeroon's round windows in the steep mud bank.

"Fresh baccy for the wedding party," he explained to Frek. "If I hang it by our chimney it'll be fit to smoke in three days. You about ready to hit the road?"

"Let me come, too, Paw," put in Bili.

"Absolutely, positively not," said Salla. "Paw's going to have his hands full taking the Nubby to Stun City. Do you really think you might get the Anvil, Gibby? It could be worth a lot. But it sounds so dangerous."

"Easy as pie," said Gibby. "I'll hit the Brindle Cowloon by dark, wash off the road dust with a mug of moolk, and get a good night's sleep. In the morning we'll trade the eggs for the stim nuggets over to the NuBioCom puffball. With his chameleon mod, Frek can slip in and likely find that old Anvil laying around lonely. He'll empty that thing out, or roll it out a window into the elephruk sure enough, light and lively, don't blink or you'll miss it. We'll be home tomorrow night. By the way, Frek, Jeroon said to be sure and bring you back for the shindig. Grulloo wedding's a real treat."

"Does the chameleon mod really work?" wondered Frek, patting the little lump in his pocket. It hardly seemed possible. And if it did work, would he want to come straight back to the Grulloo Woods? Well, no need to decide everything right away. First of all he'd have a look at Stun City.

"If the mod works?" said Salla. "Oh yeah. We'll show you about mods over at our place."

Gibby and Salla's burrow was only a few score meters farther up the stream. Gibby went inside to hang the tobacco and pack up his store of Grulloo eggs. Salla gave Frek a bunch of carrots and told him to fetch the family elephruk.

"Bili and LuHu can help you," said Salla. "Be careful not to run out of carrots."

"Our elephruk's name is Dibble," LuHu told Frek. "She's old."

"Old and mean," added Bili with a grin. "Like Paw."

As they walked through the woods, Frek made friends with Bili. Though the Grulloo was small, it turned out he was ten, just two years younger than Frek.

After about half an hour of searching and calling, they found the gray elephruk, nearly a kilometer from the burrow. Dibble was tearing low-hanging branches off an anyfruit tree with her trunk and stripping them with her drooling, pendulous mouth. She was smaller than the elephruks Frek had seen carrying the Middleville crops to market—though she was still plenty big enough to carry a load of goods and a few people.

"Yoo-hoo, Dibble," called LuHu. "This is our new friend, Frek. He's a Nubby. He's going to help you and Paw take the eggs to town. He has carrots."

The elephruk made a snuffling noise in her trunk and tore another branch off the tree.

"Roar," said Bili, as if to give himself courage. He twitched his striped tail. And then he hopped into the low, flattened bed of the elephruk's rear and scampered up near the beast's head. The elephruk gave an angry squeal and flipped back her trunk, trying to grab the boy Grulloo, but Bili kept out of his reach. LuHu joined her brother, her ponytail lashing so fast that it was practically invisible.

"Give Dibble a carrot, Frek!" squealed the excited LuHu from her perch at the base of the elephruk's head.

The elephruk was half again as tall as Frek, with six wrinkled gray legs like tree trunks. Frek gathered his courage and stepped out in front of the elephruk, holding a carrot at arm's length. The elephruk glared at him for a minute, then stretched out her long flexible trunk to pluck the carrot from Frek's hand. She swept the carrot into her loose-lipped mouth and pulverized the offering with big, yellow teeth.

"Another?" said Frek, holding a carrot up in the air and starting off toward Gibby and Salla's burrow. Dibble followed along, moving faster with each carrot, frighteningly heedless of whether she might accidentally trample Frek underfoot. It felt like running down a hill ahead of an avalanche. Bili and LuHu rode cheering upon Dibble's back. Frek made the carrots last all the way back to the stream.

Gibby was waiting for them in a clearing atop the bank with four woven hampers of pink, baseball-sized eggs packed in bindmoss. The tough old Grulloo went over to Dibble and said something into the creature's great, dusty ear. Gibby must have had some kind of hold over the elephruk, for now the beast became much easier to control. For one thing, she stopped trying to grab LuHu and Bili. For another, she no longer acted like she wanted to step on Frek. Placidly she knelt, lowering her back. To further calm Dibble, Salla dragged over a block of salt. Dibble nuzzled the block contentedly.

Frek helped Gibby drag the baskets of eggs onto Dibble's flat back, jostling the baskets a bit on the washboard of the elephruk's ribs. The eggs didn't have shells; they were more like balls of gelatin, translucent and pink with dark clots and threads near their centers.

Gibby produced a wad of mapine pitch and used it to stick the egg-baskets into place.

"Are we going now?" asked Frek. He was excited about the trip to Stun City. He'd never been there before. And to arrive upon an elephruk beside a Grulloo! This was really living. If Frek remembered right, today was a Friday. The kids back in Middleville were sitting in school listening to a facilitator.

"Not so fast," said Salla, hand-walking up the bank from the burrow. Though quite round in her body, she was very nimble. She held a rolled-up cloth between her flowery tail and the back of her head. "You need your disguise, Frek. From what you said, Gov's counselors are looking for you."

"Maybe I should use Jeroon's chameleon mod?"

"Weren't you listening? The chameleon mod only lasts about half an hour a dose and you only got but three doses. The chameleon mod's too precious to fritter away. We need to use some cheap, all-day type mods to get you in and out of town."

"I say get rid of his legs and make him a Grulloo," said Gibby. His thin-lipped mouth showed no humor at all. He knuckle-walked across the gray elephruk bed and felt Frek's calf with his callused hand. "Just for a time, son. I'm not talking knife, so don't have no heart attack. It'll be easy as pie to dwindle down your legs with some of that khora-khora mod. I believe I got a pod of it on me." Gibby lowered himself to the ground, and began fumbling with both hands in the many little pockets of his yellow leather jerkin.

"Khora-khora!" hissed Bili, baring his jagged yellow teeth.

Though Frek couldn't quite be sure, it seemed like they were serious. What had he gotten himself into, hanging out with Grulloos? Suddenly it seemed like time for some major changes to his plans. Get to Stun City and find the Anvil on his own. Faster than he could think all this, he'd jumped off the elephruk and run across the clearing, heading for the trees.

"Wait!" Salla yelled after him. "Don't listen to Gibby. He's not going to shrink your legs." She took a few steps after Frek. "Don't run off, Frek! You need us. If you go off on your own, you'll never get out of our woods. Not all the Grulloos are as friendly as us. And did you forget about Okky? She likes to hunt the road to Stun City—daytimes, too. Gibby can get you to Stun City safe and sound."

Frek hesitated at the edge of the forest. Okky. Maybe he could use the chameleon mod to get past her? But he'd need the mod when he got to Stun City. "Why did Gibby say that about my legs?" asked Frek finally.

"He's trying to scare you so he can feel big," said Salla, shaking her head so that her petals shook. "He says crazy things to scare people. He thinks he has a sense of humor, but he's just mean. Don't even think about khora-khora."

"LuHu ate khora-khora right after she hatched," put in Bili, teasing his sister. "And that's why she's so small. She ate it in a shrinking pill."

"Did not!" yelled LuHu, rocking over to one side so she could hit her brother with her free hand.

"No more nonsense about khora-khora," said Salla, unrolling her cloth on the ground. Frek saw lots of bright little pods in there. "Come closer, Frek. I'll fix you up a nice disguise. It's for your own good. I've got all sorts of mods. NuBioCom's always letting us try them out."

"Gibby has to take back what he said," said Frek, feeling stubborn.

"I'm sorry," rasped Gibby. "I didn't mean to upset you, boy. I was just funnin'. 'Course you need your legs. How else you gonna steal that Anvil for us?"

Frek thought things over for a minute, and then he walked back across the clearing. His chances of making it out of the Grulloo Woods were definitely better on Gibby's elephruk. He only hoped there wasn't any such thing as khora-khora.

LuHu and Bili were very much underfoot as Frek looked at Salla's mods. The cloth's pockets were filled with pointed please plant–grown pods, translucent enough to reveal the colored spots of mod-gel nestled in their bottoms. Salla was resting on her stomach, her flowery head next to her unrolled cloth. She was fiddling with her mod-pods, now and then cocking back her head to look up at Frek.

"Here," said Salla, holding up a pod with curly lines drawn on the top. "Every disguise should start with a beard."

"Is it safe?" wondered Frek. Lora Huggins had always said terrible things about mods. Nobody in Middleville used mods—or at least nobody admitted that they did. Frek knew from the toons that if you rubbed on a little mod-gel, the stuff got into your cells' nuclei and mitochondria and made them start doing gollywog things. Supposedly the effects wore off. But, according to Mom, "It's like making ugly faces. You might stay that way."

Salla had a set of thin wooden sticks in her kit, like chopsticks with dents in one end. She used one of the chopstick things to scoop up a little of the beard mod-gel. The gel was pale green. "Okay now?" said Salla, her moon face smiling reassuringly up at Frek. "Lean down so I can reach you."

"Do it, Frek!" said Bili. "We want to watch."

Frek hunkered down and Salla used her chopstick to smear the gel along the sides of his face and jaw, carefully going over his face several times to get the stuff smoothly spread out. Right away Frek's skin began to itch, but he was scared to scratch it, not wanting to get the mod-gel on his hands.

"Lips," said Gibby. "Give him the blub lips too."

"Mmm, okay," said Salla.

"How do you mean, blub lips?" said Frek.

"You know," said Salla. "Puffy kisser. I use this mod myself sometimes. If you put it on even, it looks fabu."

"Your beard's already startin' to come in," said Gibby. "Your own maw wouldn't know you. You look ten, twenty years older. All grown up."

Indeed Frek could feel a steady prickling along the sides of his face. Meanwhile Salla used a fresh chopstick to scoop out a bit of red gel from a pod. Frek pursed his lips and she dabbed it on, a spot here and a spot there.

This mod hit harder than the beard-gel had. Frek's lips began to twitch around like glypher slugs; they tingled and swelled up to what felt like three times their size. In a sudden panic, he scrambled down the bank to the stream and began washing his face. He had hair all over his cheeks and chin, a full beard. Very gollywog. When he felt his lips with his fingers, they weren't as big as he'd imagined. He wondered if it would be hard to talk.

"Hello," he said tentatively. "My name is Frek Huggins." The lips worked fine.

LuHu, who was still at his side, echoed him. "Hello. My name is Frek Huggins."

Frek gave her a smile.

"Look at yourself," said LuHu, splashing across the stream to a calm pool.

Frek peered into the pool, taking in his new appearance. Quite a change. The beard was gray. And his lips—they'd swollen unevenly, setting themselves into a deformed snarl. What if he did stay this way for good? Again he felt the urge to run away from these Grulloos.

When he climbed back up the bank, Gibby and Salla abruptly broke off their conversation and walked over to him.

"His left arm," said Gibby finally.

"What about my arm?" asked Frek sharply. It still wasn't too late to run away.

"Gotta change your body too, you wanna fool Gov," said Gibby. "Like I was gettin' at before. We don't disguise you good, Gov's gonna give you the Three R's and we're never gonna see what's in that Anvil."

Even as Frek tensed himself to flee, Salla said, "Now," and abruptly dabbed the back of Frek's left hand with a chopstick that seemed to come out of nowhere. A deep, fluttery sensation went up Frek's arm. It happened before he had time to react.

"Khora-khora!" said Bili in an awestruck tone.

Frek's fingers withered like a balloon leaking air. His ring dropped to the ground. In seconds his hand shrank to half its size. They'd ruined him! His fingers had become limp little worms. His forearm was shrinking as well. It was a nightmare, but he couldn't wake up. His fingers disappeared into five little nubbins at the tip of his arm. The deflating arm shrank up past where his elbow used to be—and stopped.

"Noooooooooo," moaned Frek, hopping from foot to foot. Yet, as he felt around within himself, he realized that the shrinking of his arm hadn't actually hurt. It was terrible to see, and to think about, but he felt no pain. In fact, in his mind, the arm felt just the same. But in the real world it was a crooked flipper. He stooped to pick up his ring with his good hand, and managed to use his thumb to push it onto one of his good fingers.

Dibble the elephruk had turned her head to see about the yelling. Bili and LuHu were dancing around in excitement, trying to look at Frek's flipper-arm from every side. Salla looked sympathetic, but Gibby—Gibby was up on the elephruk's back laughing.

Frek saw red. He jumped onto the elephruk and aimed a kick at Gibby. But the lizard-tailed Grulloo was too fast. He skipped to one side and yanked Frek's foot as it went by. With his arm the way it was, Frek's balance was off. He fell heavily against a basket of eggs, tipping it over.

"Careful there," said Gibby, worried about his cargo.

Frek snatched up a Grulloo egg and smashed it into Gibby's face. The egg liquefied when it hit the Grulloo, drenching him in goo. That stopped his laughing. Frek picked up another egg, and got Gibby again. And then Gibby was at his throat, up close and smelling of tobacco and sweat. Frek grabbed onto one of the Grulloo's arms, pulling hard to keep Gibby from choking him. Frek outweighed the Grulloo four to one, but with his left arm missing, it was all he could do to hold his own. Straining and snarling, the two of them rolled off the elephruk bed and onto the ground. Frek hung onto one of Gibby's hands; he held the Grulloo out at arm's length, shaking him back and forth to keep him off balance. Gibby was shrieking curses.

Meanwhile Dibble had lifted her trunk and started trumpeting. Salla was screaming at them to stop. LuHu was crying, and Bili had run off yelling.

And now, before things got any worse, help arrived in the form of Jeroon, dragging a big skin of water that he squirted into their faces. It was a good excuse to stop fighting. Gibby and Frek released each other and lay there panting.

Frek could hardly believe he'd had the courage to attack the tough old Grulloo. And he'd done pretty well in the tussle, too. Gibby showed no desire to resume the fight.

"Gaia save us all," exclaimed Jeroon, pausing to adjust the buttons of his jacket. "Is this how you treat our Nubby guest, Gibby? The boy who saved my life? You've made him look like a brainfubbed tramp. Like a gump."

"He needed a disguise," said Salla.

"And never mind that NuBioCom pays you every time you test out one of their new mods," said Jeroon. "What did you put on the boy's arm?"

"It's called khora-khora," said Gibby, who was smoothing back his hair. "It don't last but a little more than a day, feller said. Same as the beard and lip mods we put on him." He rose up on his hands and walked over to Frek. "You a fighter, son. I'm proud to be your partner. No hard feelings?" He leaned to one side and stuck out a hand.

"Okay," said Frek after a moment's thought. He needed all the allies he could get. "Maybe I shouldn't have gotten so upset. You're sure about my arm coming back?"

"If it don't come back, we'll make NuBioCom fix it," said Gibby. "Before we steal the Anvil. You and me, Frek, we in this together."

"That's more like it," said Jeroon. "Gaia speed your way, Frek. I'll be getting back to—" His dark brown skin reddened. "You know." And then he was down the bank and back in his burrow with Ennie.

After loading up a few more supplies for the trip, Frek and Gibby were ready to start on their way.

"Now Gibby, you take it easy with the cowloon moolk," cautioned Salla as they left. "Remember what happened last time."

"I remember," said Gibby. "You done talked about it enough times. Don't worry a bit. Just one mug and I'm in beddy-bye."

"Bye, Paw!" called Bili and LuHu.

And then they were off. The elephruk crossed the creek and found her way to a winding, sandy track that angled through the Grulloo Woods. Once they were on the road, Gibby produced a little fiddle from his travel sack and began to play it with some skill.

The sweet sound of live music held a nostalgic tinge for Frek, as Mom had a real guitar that she strummed sometimes. Carb was musical, too; he had a harmonica, and at the family's very happiest times, he and Mom would play together, joining their voices in song.

Where was Carb now? Had he really made it to the asteroids? Frek glanced down at his ring, wondering. Why didn't it talk to him? And what about Mom? Had the counselors done something to her? For now there were no answers, only the steady rhythm of the plodding elephruk and the plaintive notes of Gibby's music.

"Did you make the fiddle yourself?" Frek asked Gibby when the Grulloo paused to tune his instrument.

"We grow the pieces on please plants," said Gibby, drawing his bow to make a long, sweet tone. "Fiddles are a Grulloo specialty." He paused to adjust one of the instrument's tuning pegs, a little rod with a round disk on the end. And now Frek realized what those please plant seeds had been last night—he'd been hiding beneath a tuning peg bush!

They were coming into an unwholesome part of the woods. Many of the trees were blighted and bare, and the ground was thick with a rubbery yellow fungus. The air smelled of decay.

"Okky and her sisters live over there," said Gibby, using his bow to point—though without interrupting his playing. Frek glimpsed the edge of a ragged shape peeking down from the blasted top of a dead tree. He and Gibby were quite exposed in the elephruk's bed. Gibby goaded Dibble to go faster and redoubled his sawing at the fiddle. "Listen up and sing along," he urged Frek. "Music's the one thing Okky can't stand. We have one song in particular. We call it 'Grulloo's Apology.' "

Grulloo's Apology

Hey there bio science, my arm just bit my hand,
I took a mod for dentures; it jiggered up a gland—
Got teeth inside my armpit since your latest tweak.
And we're the ones,
Who done got spun,

We know the score,
From way before,
So don't you call us freaks.

Papa was a rooster, you changed him to a duck,
We sat down at the table, and he was out of cluck,
His legs and wings flew off—and left a googly beak.
And we're the gang,
Not scared to sang,
We test your mods,
On our own bods,
So don't you call us freaks.

You whittled down my body to tail and arms and head,
My wife and me lay eggs instead of making love in bed—
You use us for your research to get the inside peek.
Yay for Grulloos,
The ones you choose,
For finding out,
What life's about,
So don't you call us freaks!

It was the same song Jeroon had bellowed at Okky last night. As Frek learned the words, his gaze darted between Gibby and the rotten tree. He saw one, two, three dark, toothy winged heads up there.

"Here she comes," cried Gibby as they started the song over from the beginning. "Okky. You can tell her by the scar on the side of her head. Grab that long knife out of my sack and sing out, boy, sing out! It helps fend her off."

Frek bawled the verses with the full force of his lungs as Okky swooped down to within five meters of them, close enough for Frek to pick up a smell of rotten flesh. Gibby played as if possessed, the two of them fairly screaming the choruses, with Frek holding up the knife, clutching it in his fiercest grip. And then Okky and her sisters flew away.

"Yee haw!" whooped Gibby. "Awright!"

What with his tweaked-away arm, Frek felt like a Grulloo himself. People were so quick to think the worst of these little people, just because they looked strange.

"I was wrong not to trust you," he told Gibby. "Wrong to judge you by the way you look."

"You like a younger brother to me now, boy," answered Gibby, his hard face splitting in a grin.

The path rose to the crest of a ridge looking down on the River Jaya. Slowly the gray sky cleared. They rode along the wiggly ridge for a couple of hours, and then the path began working its way down to meet the river, golden in the late afternoon sun.

A watchbird buzzed them near the river bank; as a matter of course Gibby rocked over onto one arm and threw a stone. The watchbird easily dodged the missile and buzzed closer, getting a good look at them. For the next half hour Frek was worried about counselors, but his disguise must have been working. No lifter beetles appeared.

Gibby pointed out a prickly spot on the horizon: Stun City. They began passing isolated country homes; they were red, yellow, and purple with irregular towers and arches. Frek wanted to run over and get a good look at one, but Gibby warned him not to.

"It's rich people living out at this end of Stun City," he told Frek. "Rich people always think they's about to get robbed. You hop off a Grulloo elephruk lookin' the way you do right now and go running up to them aircoral mansions, why, they'll shoot you with a webgun and feed you to the turmites. No gumps allowed!"

"The houses are aircoral?" said Frek. "I've never seen aircoral except on the toons."

"You gonna see a whole bunch of it pretty soon," said Gibby.

More and more houses appeared as they approached Stun City, mostly made of variously colored and textured aircoral—which was hard, lifeless stuff like stone. Where did it come from? Frek got his answer when they passed a house under construction. Around the growing walls were heaps of sand. The air was alive with a fog of glinting, darting animalcules. Some of these gnat-sized kritters drifted across the road as they passed; Frek caught one of them. It was like a flying worm; Gibby called it an airpolyp. The polyps carried specks of sand in their tiny tentacles; they were assembling the building like a reef.

Across the rolling river landscape, Stun City kept popping in and out of view. Just as the sun went down, they topped one last rise and the town finally lay spread out before them, a lush parkland of house trees and aircorals, with its famous central cluster of enormous, odd-shaped buildings.

The huge NuBioCom puffball had just turned on its lights, sending bright beams out across Stun City, as if reaching for its citizens. Frek studied the portholelike windows for a minute, imagining the inner structures and the hidden Anvil. The windows were aligned one above the other, forming ribbons that ran from top to bottom like the stripes on a gourd.

Gov lived in there. Who or what was Gov? He showed himself as First Nations–type bird designs like the Eagle and the Raven, but those were just toons. Behind the toons was—depending who you asked—a man, a worm, or nothing but a computation distributed across the tissues of his home puffball.

Frek tried to visualize himself running naked up and down the halls of the puffball, his skin indistinguishable from the walls and floor, looking for the Anvil. He no longer doubted that the chameleon mod would work—but what would he find inside the Anvil?

A bit closer than the puffball glowed the Kritterworks cube, set close to the banks of the River Jaya. As Frek knew from watching documentaries and news shows, four sides of the cube were solid, and the two end-walls were cored out with great and small tunnels. Frek could see a big central gallery and at least eight smaller galleries running the length of the cube. The side-walls of the Kritterworks were alive with billboard toons. Frek recognized ads for the latest kritter models: massage starfish, passenger crickets, mattresses made of big flat downy ducks, uvvy-controlled personal pickerhands, and the 3004 model dog. The 3004 dog wasn't going to be nearly as cute as Wow, who'd been artigrown in 2999. Frek wondered again what had become of Wow after he'd jumped into the river. Had he gone back home? Had he gotten a chance to tell Mom about seeing Frek? And was Mom okay?

The Stun City structure that interested Frek the most of all was the legendary Toonsmithy—this was where the very best toons were crafted. The Toonsmithy was a giant beanstalk, trained into the shape of a corkscrew that spiraled up into the sky. Jittering like visible music, colored pulses of light wound along the helical tube, up and up to where its gyres tightened to a point. At the apex hung a firefly hologram, a dancing fog of scenes from the Toonsmithy's latest shows and games. Frek saw the Skull Farmers: Gypsy Joker, Strummer, and Soul Soldier. He wished he had gotten to spend more time gaming with them. But then again, he was living a real-life adventure wilder than he ever could have imagined. Fingering his twisted lips and his gray beard—his beard!—he glanced down at his flipper arm, imagining what Ida and Geneva would say if they could see him now.

The Brindle Cowloon Inn was beside the river on the near edge of Stun City, a two-story aircoral building with a grassy pasture. No two of the windows were the same shape. Fantastically formed turrets and antlers stuck up higgledy-piggledy from the cornices and roof. The inn's smooth, undulating walls were creamy white with a few large patches of orange—like a giant cow.

"Advertising," said Gibby, nodding at the walls. "The cowloon itself is out back. It's the only one in town; draws a good crowd this time of day. I'm sure enough ready for my moolk. But first we gotta stash our cargo and pasture Dibble."

Dibble came to a halt before the asymmetrically arched entrance. While Gibby went inside to arrange for a room, Frek helped drag the four moss-packed hampers of eggs off the elephruk. With his arm missing, it was hard work. Suddenly he heard a woman's clear voice.

"Who's the gump?"

"Just a drifter helping me out," said Gibby. "Don't need to ask no more, Phamelu, we call him—Huckle."

"Hi, Huckle," said Phamelu. She was a middle-aged woman with a pleasant, open face. She reminded Frek a little of his mother; she wore that same air of humor and intelligent self-possession. But her black hair was tweaked to a honey-colored shade of blond. "Welcome to my inn," said Phamelu. She gave Frek a friendly smile that crinkled the corners of her eyes. "That's a nice ring you have. I've never seen anything like it."

"Leave him alone, I say," rasped Gibby, and then he and Frek were wrestling the egg baskets up the stairs, with Gibby putting his powerful tail to good use.

"Phamelu seems nice," said Frek when they were ensconced in their small slant-ceilinged room. Phamelu. He liked the sound of the kind innkeeper's name.

The Grulloo gave a short laugh. "Didn't you tell me you was through judging people by their looks, boy? Me lookin' like a lizard don't make me bad, and Phamelu's apple-pie smile don't make her good. There's razors in that pie. The woman's robbed me more than once. That's why I brought a guard-toad for the eggs. Anyone comes in our room without my say-so, they gonna get bit."

Gibby dug down into the egg basket nearest the door and came up with an ordinary-looking toad. The toad had been sleeping, but now he perked up and yawned. Frek glimpsed stubby fangs, sticky with green venom.

"Good toady," said Gibby. He fished a pod of grub-worms out of his travel sack and fed the toad three of them. It gave a low croak of thanks. And now Gibby emptied out his pockets and put everything of value in his travel bag, which he set, in turn, behind the baskets of eggs. Just to be safe, Frek tucked his purse-fungus back there too, with the chameleon mod and Aaron's Rod inside it. They left the room with the watch-toad perched on the egg-basket closest to the door.

They found Dibble impatiently waving her trunk, sniffing the breeze from the river. They led her down through the inn's riverside pasture, lush with shoulder-high grass. Some other elephruks stood at the edge of the stream. After an introductory round of snuffling and trumpeting, Dibble sprayed some gallons of river water into her mouth. And then she lumbered over and set to work tearing up huge sheaves of grass. The grass's biorhythm must have been tweaked to an insane speed, for it grew back nearly as fast as Dibble could eat it.

"Don't bust your gut, Dibble," chuckled Gibby. He grinned up at Frek. "Now let's get ole Gibby his moolk."

The lighter-than-air cowloon bobbled above the center of the courtyard, surrounded by a Friday evening crowd of drinkers. Two bright-looking young women were talking and gesturing, one of them was showing the other one designs on the back of a turkle. Their jokey, stylized clothes looked almost like something the Goob Dolls would wear. It struck Frek that these two were probably toonsmiths. Maybe they worked for the Goob Dolls show! Maybe they'd even helped design the Skull Farmers! It would be gog gripper to talk to them.

"Follow me, Gibby," said Frek. He screwed up his courage and walked over to the women.

"Hi," he said. "Are you toonsmiths?"

"Are you and your friend looking for a modeling gig?" said one of them with a laugh. She was tall and willowy, with her hair in black curls. Her shirt was a live wall skin playing, just now, a loop of a smug Da Nha Duc, throwing back his shoulders and curving his beak in triumph. "Deanna always needs new trolls," added the curly-haired woman. Frek suddenly remembered that he looked like a gump, like an unhealthy bum.

"Oh, don't be mean to him, Sooly," said the other toonsmith, the one with the turkle. "He's just an ugly fan." Her blond-dyed hair was cut into a spiral pattern circling her head up to a tiny topknot. She smiled kindly at Frek, her eyes warm in her smooth brown face. "Do you play a lot with the toons?"

"As much as I can," said Frek. He gestured self-consciously at his face and his stub arm. "This isn't how I really look." Gibby gave him a sharp poke.

"If that's a costume, someone's done a glatt job," said the spiral-haired Deanna. She glanced down at her turkle and made a few quick lines with a little stylus. A tellingly accurate caricature of Frek and Gibby appeared in the iridescent skin of the turkle's leathery back. "Save," said Deanna, and the image melted into the recesses of the turkle kritter's brain.

"Now leave us alone," said Sooly, her Da Nha Duc's expression switching to a fuming scowl.

"Sorry," added Deanna. "Sooly and I have some things we have to work out. It's hard to find time to talk when we're at the Toonsmithy."

"That's okay," said Frek humbly, and took a few steps back.

"Time for my moolk, Huckle," said Gibby.

Beside the toonsmith women were a group of five Kritterworkers. Their overalls had stiff spots from the colorless ichor that fed the Kritterworks artigrows.

Just arriving were a trim lady exec and a lower-ranking junior exec. She wore a NuBioCom pin of rank upon her lapel. They seemed a bit out of place here. Perhaps they didn't want to be seen by their usual friends. They gave Frek and Gibby a wide berth.

Closer to the cowloon were elephruk-handlers, farmers, fishermen, turmite-cloth tailors, off-duty counselors, and young couples out partying. Gibby sprang up onto the curved wooden bar that circled the stalk of the cowloon. Frek leaned his single elbow on the bar and watched to see what would happen next.

The floating cowloon was a taut bag resembling the headless, legless body of a cow. Buoyant with methane, brindle orange on white, it floated three meters up in the air, attached to the ground by a thick stalk, all of it covered with hairy hide. The cowloon's great, hanging udder was in service, squirting moolk into the mugs the bartender held up to it.

"Back for another bout, eh Gibby?" chortled the bartender, a slender, weasel-faced man with a pencil-line mustache. He raised a half-pint pottery mug into the air.

"This time's gonna be different, Pede," said Gibby, sounding a little defensive. "I'm only havin' just the one. Got some important business tomorrow. Me and my partner Huckle."

"Good to meet you, Huckle," said Pede, setting Gibby's moolk down next to him. "Should I give him a mug on your tab, Gibby?"

"No moolk for Huckle," said Gibby sharply. "He's too young to be getting messed up."

"Young?" said Pede, cocking his head and giving Frek a careful once-over. "If you say so." He turned his attention to some other customers.

The moolk had a powerful effect on Gibby, who immediately began cursing and slurring his words. It was unpleasant to see, and the other moolk-drinkers weren't nice to be around either. A plate of free anymeat and grobread sandwiches sat upon the bar; Frek snagged two of them, wormed his way out through the crowd and headed across the pasture. Deanna the toonsmith was the only one to notice him leaving. She didn't exactly wave or smile, but she didn't frown either. Maybe he could get her to give him a tour of the Toonsmithy one of these days.

Down on the riverbank Frek sat a little upstream from the elephruks, eating his sandwiches and drinking from the clear River Jaya. It was getting dark. A crescent moon hung low over Stun City, exquisite against the skyline's fantastic shapes.

Idly Frek watched the images atop the Toonsmithy. Before long they cycled back to the Skull Farmers: Gypsy Joker, Strummer, and Soul Soldier. Seeing them set Frek to thinking about all the stuff that had happened to him.

The adventure had started last Saturday when he'd been gaming with the Skull Farmers at Stoo's. The counselors had come to ask about the Anvil and he hadn't told them it was under his bed. Then in the middle of the night, the Anvil had opened up, the alien cuttlefish had talked to him, and early Sunday morning the counselors had peeked him. After that he'd been fubbed in the fog till Thursday afternoon, when Ida and the Goob Dolls woke him up. Then right away Mom helped him run away and he'd ended up with the Grulloos. Jeroon had fixed his brain with stim cells, and today, Friday, he'd ridden to Stun City with Gibby, disguised as a gump. Tomorrow he was supposed to sneak a peek at the Anvil.

Gibby was up by the torch-lit cowloon drinking moolk; even from here Frek could hear him yelling and playing his fiddle. Frek's new pal. It was hard to believe he was friends with a Grulloo. Downstream the elephruks were making a peaceful, rumbling noise. And out across Stun City, dogs were barking, especially near the Kritterworks.

Frek rubbed the stump of his arm, feeling a slight tingle. Was it starting to grow back? Hopefully not before tomorrow afternoon; till then he'd need his disguise. He wondered if he had any chance of finding the Anvil within the fortresslike puffball. And, assuming he could get the Anvil open, what would he find inside it? It was a shame the counselors had killed the cuttlefish. For the first time since he'd gotten his memory back, Frek remembered that one funny-looking seed he'd planted. And the way it had immediately grown into something that burrowed off beneath the soil. Surely it had been from the alien. Mom had said the counselors burnt and poisoned the ground all around Giant's Marbles. But by the time they got there, the mysterious digging thing would have been long gone.

Frek looked out across Stun City. The sliver of moon was higher now, cupped upward like a bowl. And, hard as it was to believe, two of the buildings on the skyline had changed shape. One of them definitely had a new spire that hadn't been there before. Those aircoral polyps were fast.

There was so much he didn't know about Stun City. Frankly, it seemed hopeless to try to loot the Anvil with Gibby, especially after seeing the Grulloo hitting the moolk. Being like a chameleon for half an hour wouldn't make that big a difference. Would the NuBioCom guards just stand there and watch while a funny-looking patch of floor coaxed open the Anvil—or shoved it out a window to land on Gibby's elephruk? The idea was kac.

What to do? Fred couldn't go home yet or the counselors would get him. Go live with the Grulloos? Not an appetizing thought. Maybe he could get a job in Stun City, or if things were too hot for him here, go farther down the river to some other town. Grand-sounding words, but the thought of having to travel even farther from Mom, Ida, Geneva, and Wow made Frek feel sick and hollow. And how far would he have to go to escape Gov's influence anyway? Carb had gone all the way to the asteroids. Must Frek find a space bug and ship out, too?

School and the toons didn't teach all that much about the government. The basic setup was that the planet was divided into little regions, with each region run by its own Gov, all of them more or less the same. They had one top-level Gov called Prexy. They weren't told more than that; the main message was don't worry about it. Thinking of Gov set Frek to remembering the Raven toon pecking him. To get his mind off that, he lay down flat on his back and stared up at the stars.

Right before he fell asleep something funny happened. He'd turned his heavy new ring around so he could rub the little dent with his thumb. It was soothing to feel the nice curve. It was something he'd been doing off and on all day. But now it was as if he'd finally triggered something in the ring, for one of the stars high up in the sky suddenly seemed to get brighter. In his drowsy state, this didn't seem all that remarkable. The bright star flew down; it found its way to him and hovered over his ring. A spiky yellow halo surrounded the glowing ball. In the center Frek saw a girl with pigtails and a friendly, open face. "Come to me, Frek," she said. "Come soon and help me." She smiled, and the smile shone like the sun.

When Frek woke he was cold and damp. It was the middle of the night. Having a stub for a left arm surprised him at first, but then he remembered what was going on. By tomorrow afternoon he'd be back to normal. Briefly he recalled the image of the girl in the ball— but surely that had been a dream. He checked his ring; it wasn't doing anything.

Frek could hear a few drinkers still at the cowloon; their voices were fubbed and mean. But he didn't hear Gibby, which was good. He headed up through the pasture toward the inn. The six-legged ele-phruks were standing in the high grass now, sleeping with their heads and trunks hanging down.

Frek bent his path so as not to get too close to the guttering torches and noisy people by the cowloon. The toonsmiths Sooly and Deanna were long gone of course; they weren't the type to stand around get-ting messed up. At first Frek saw no sign of Gibby. He was hoping his friend had made it safely to bed. But then he noticed a small still form lying in the dirt by the inn's back door, with someone leaning over him. Phamelu was going through the unconscious Gibby's pockets.

"What are you doing?" asked Frek, walking up to her, his pulse beating fast.

"Oh, hi there, Huckle," said Phamelu, flashing an easy smile and pushing back a hank of her thick blond hair. "I'm just loosening his jacket so he can breathe better. I would have liked to have carried him upstairs, but I think there's some kind of watch thingie in your room?" She gave Frek a concerned look and shook her head. "When

I checked your room, I heard this fierce croaking sound and I figured, careful, Phamelu, don't go in there. Anyway, I think he's too heavy for me to carry. Good thing you're here."

"Yep," said Frek shortly. He wasn't sure if she'd been trying to rob Gibby or to help him. Maybe just help. Phamelu did seem so nice. "I can carry him," he said, and hoisted Gibby onto his shoulders. Gibby's fiddle lay smashed on the ground where he'd collapsed. Poor little thing.

"You're strong," said Phamelu. "Come back down when you've got him settled. I'll give you a snack."

Frek didn't know what to answer, so he didn't say anything. Upstairs, the toad gave a warning croak when Frek pushed open the door. Frek held Gibby out in front of himself and pinched the Grulloo's tail until he made a noise. This seemed to mollify the toad. To seal the deal, Frek found Gibby's pod of grub worms and fed some more of them to the toad. The warty little creature gazed up at him with a kindly look in the pupil-slits of his yellow eyes.

"If I go downstairs for another minute, will you let me back in?" Frek asked the toad as he tucked Gibby into his bed. The toad didn't say anything one way or the other. Frek fed it another grub and took the pod with him when he went downstairs.

Phamelu was perched on a stool behind her inn counter. "I don't know if you ever got any supper," she said. An anyfruit apple sat on the counter between two mugs of moolk. "Pede said you'd wandered off, and then nobody could find you when Gibby got sick."

"Sick?" said Frek. "He drank too much."

"He always does," said Phamelu, smiling and shrugging her shoulder. "You'd think he'd learn. Not that there's anything wrong with moolk, if you know how to handle it. Here's a nice apple with some moolk for you. On the house."

"Well—" said Frek. "I'll be glad to eat the apple, but I think maybe—"

"Pede heard Gibby say you're too young for moolk," said Phamelu, nudging one of the mugs forward and giving Frek an encouraging smile. "Funny you don't look young."

"Uh-huh," said Frek, once again at a loss for words. He took a bite of the apple and then, just to show Phamelu he wasn't scared, he took a tiny sip of the moolk. It tickled the back of his throat.

"If you're interested, I might be able to offer you a job," said Phamelu, taking a sip from her own mug. "I need an extra hand around the inn. Just to help the suckapillar clean out the rooms, you know. And tend to the elephruks. I don't have any extra money these days, but I could give you a place to sleep and plenty of food."

This sounded very glatt. It was right along the lines of what Frek had been thinking of doing, in fact. Lie low in Stun City. Phamelu smiled at him and he took another sip of moolk. It tingled all the way down to his stomach. He quickly took a big bite of apple. The apple was delicious. Frek felt wonderful. He smiled happily at Phamelu.

"You're not really old, are you, Huckle?" said Phamelu, looking deep into his eyes. "Tell me. Once I know the truth, you can have the job. Tell me. We can work things out."

She was certainly insistent. "Well—I might look younger tomorrow afternoon," allowed Frek. "But you say I can still have the job even if I'm young?"

"Of course," said Phamelu in a caressing tone. "You can keep the room you have right now. It's just a Grulloo room. I'll let you have it for free and you can work here as long as you like."

"That's really nice of you, Phamelu," said Frek. Things were happening faster than he could think them through.

"A toast," said Phamelu, raising her mug.

They clinked mugs, and Frek took a much bigger swallow of moolk than before. When he set the mug down it made a loud sound on the counter. His ears were ringing.

"I imagine that's quite a valuable ring," said Phamelu, nodding toward the shiny cup with its dot of red light, then tossing her head a bit to get her blond hair away from her eyes. "You're lucky to have it."

"I got it from my dad," said Frek carefully.

"I wonder what you look like without the mods Gibby put on you," said Phamelu in a dreamy tone, as if she were just thinking out loud. "I bet you're a nice-looking boy. I wonder what your real name is."

"Frek," said Frek, before he knew what he was saying. And then he put his hand over his mouth and giggled. The moolk was seriously getting to him. He reached for the apple and, as usual, knocked over the mug. The moolk rushed across the counter and dripped onto Phamelu's lap.

"Oh oh," she said mildly, not acting a bit mad. She drew out a rag to wipe up the moolk. But as she glanced up from the rag, Frek saw something hard and mean in her face. He remembered what Gibby had told him: there's razors in that apple pie. He was in way over his head.

"I better go to bed," said Frek. "We can talk about this tomorrow. I'm sorry about the spill."

"Good night, Frek."

The counselors came just before dawn.

Frek woke to a great croak from the watch-toad, followed by the sound of a man screaming. The wall lights came on. The counselor who'd been bitten by the watch-toad was on his knees clutching his hand. It was Zhak. And the other counselor was PhiPhi. She needled the toad with a pulse from a fat laserbug mounted on one of her fingers. Phamelu stood blocking the door. PhiPhi drew out her webgun and aimed it at Frek, once again ready to tangle him up.

But she hadn't reckoned with Gibby. With a snap of his tail, the little Grulloo sent himself flying out of his bed and into the wall. He caromed off the wall into PhiPhi's head, knocking her flat on her back.

"You gleeps ain't stealin' my eggs this time!" hollered Gibby. "Stun City's a free trade zone!"

Phamelu had the door covered, but the window was wide open. In seconds Frek had his feet out the smooth aircoral window hole. He paused to glance back, bracing himself with his flipper arm. Desperate though things were, it was wonderful to see his friend back to his old self again, not like the pitiful unconscious figure of last night.

"Come on, Gibby. We gotta run!"

"I ain't done nothin' wrong," protested Gibby. "I'm stayin' to protect what's mine." Zhak and PhiPhi were still on the ground. "Take this," said Gibby, passing Frek the sticky purse-fungus with his chameleon gel and his Aaron's Rod. "Now git."

Right then PhiPhi sat up and splatted one of Gibby's legs with a glob of goo from her webgun. Gibby whirled and grabbed her wrist with his free hand, shaking the webgun loose, all the while arguing with her about his rights.

Frek slid down the slightly slanted wall, his ring clattering on the coral. He took off running toward the river. The sky off to the left was the faintest shade of pinky gray. Some birds were starting to chatter.

When Frek got to the high, dew-soaked grass, he encountered two wet, prancing shapes. Dogs. He started to dodge around them, then stopped.

"Wow!"

"I smell you," squeaked Wow from the back of his throat. "I wait." He sniffed the stub where Frek's arm ended and whined in sympathy.

"Run away," said the other dog. "Follow me home." She looked much like Wow, though her hair was perhaps a bit curlier. She might have been a 3000 or a 3001 model.

PhiPhi was yelling from the inn window, but she wasn't coming after him yet. Gibby was probably still hanging onto her. And there was no sign of Zhak. Frek had been thinking he might need to use the chameleon mod, but now it was looking like he could just run away.

He followed Wow and the other dog down to the river's edge, the tall grass rippling around them. They turned left and cut under the abutments of a bridge that crossed the River Jaya less than a hundred meters downstream. Beyond the bridge, the waterfront got complicated.

In the growing light of dawn, the dogs led Frek through a maze of wharves, boatyards, warehouses, and ruined old dwellings, finally coming to a stop in a big ironwood culvert just behind the Kritterworks. If anyone had been following, Frek and the dogs had lost them on the way.

"This Woo," said Wow, introducing his friend. "Woo have heat."

"Home," said Woo. "Woo den." The culvert held piles of rags and bedding, some bones and chewed-up old shoes, and a pervasive doggy aroma. Wow and Woo had long since shaken themselves dry. They lay down side by side, tongues lolling, looking calm and friendly.

"Thanks, Woo," said Frek. "You came by at just the right time, Wow. How did you get here?"

"Run in water," said Wow, meaning that he swam. "I smell Woo." He gave Woo's muzzle a lick.

"I smell Wow," said Woo. "Wow strong. Make good puppies."

"Puppies!" exclaimed Frek. He didn't have the heart to try to tell the dogs that they couldn't have puppies unless someone gave them doses of the latest update of the NuBioCom antidote for the ever-changing knockout virus. Not that the dogs would understand. All over the planet, plants and animals were fruitlessly trying to repro-duce themselves the same way they always had, enjoying sex as much as ever. But these days—unless the would-be parent or parents owned a paid-up NuBioCom reproduction license and installed the latest twenty-four-hour wetware upgrades into themselves—making babies didn't work. The knockout virus threw a monkey-wrench into repro-duction's intricate genetic dance, fouling up the proteins used in meiosis.

Frek patted Wow on the head. "Tell me, Wow, did the counselors do anything bad to Mom when they came to get you?" Wow didn't understand, so Frek made the question simpler. "Lora okay?"

"Lora lie down," said Wow simply. "Lora crying."

Frek felt an anger stronger than any he'd ever felt before. He had to do something to stop the counselors, something to show Gov he couldn't ride roughshod over everyone forever. Frek wasn't going to run off down the river. He was going to fight Gov here and now. Yes. What had the alien cuttlefish told him? "You're the one. You'll save the world." Somehow, some way, the cuttlefish had come to help Frek smash Gov's power. Even though the counselors had incinerated the alien being, there just had to be some remaining trace of what he'd come to do. Maybe that funny seed had already made a difference. And the answer would lie in the Anvil.

"Can you take me to the puffball?" Frek asked Woo. The curly-haired dog didn't answer. Frek gestured with his arms. "Big, big round building. I want to go there."

Woo didn't understand, or wasn't interested. She could talk, but she was still a dog. She got up, walked a little farther back into the culvert and came back dragging a rather large bone. You rarely saw bones like this, since all the meat these days was from anymeat loaves. Frek guessed the bone was from the Kritterworks trash. Maybe from a recycled elephruk. Wow began chewing one end of the bone, and Woo the other.

"I'm going to the puffball," repeated Frek after resting for a while. He would have liked to have Gibby along for this—but he had a feeling that the counselors might not release the Grulloo anytime soon. And if Gibby was in fact free, he'd probably think of going to the puffball too. One thing for sure, Frek wasn't going back to the Brindle Cowloon.

He took Jeroon's special mod-pod out of his pocket and looked at it. When Dha Na Duc had used it in the toon, each of his feathers had begun automatically tinting itself to be the color of the nearest background object. It hadn't always worked right, particularly when enemies were looking for Dha Na from two different sides. And a dose of chameleon mod only lasted half an hour. Well, he'd just have to see how it turned out. He was going to the puffball no matter what.

Meanwhile the dogs were still chewing. Frek went over to say good-bye. His foot bumped against the big bone, and Woo unthinkingly growled. Frek hunkered down next to his dog. "I'm going, Wow. You don't have to come if you don't want to."

Wow paused in his chewing and looked up at him. "Wow have bone. Woo have heat." He was in heaven just now, and clearly in no mood to go anywhere. Frek sighed. Well, it wasn't like he should expect Wow to follow him into the jaws of death or down the river or wherever the heck he was headed—though, really, that might have been kind of nice.

"You go home soon," Frek told Wow. "Tell Lora Frek fine." He gave Wow a few more lingering pats, and then he left the culvert. He was going to miss that dog. The sky was yellow in the east, and clear lavender-gray above, with a few high, pink cirrus clouds. It wasn't hard to locate the puffball. It was a few blocks up the hill that led away from the river. Its great bulge blotted out a good bite of the sky.

Despite the early hour, others were out and about on the tough bindmoss walkways of Stun City. Workers were coming and going from the Kritterworks. A turbaned man on a coffee-camel was selling mugs of java warmed by the flames of the beast's combustible breath. *Whooosh!* It was a gripper thing to see. The coffee came from a leaf-covered pouch slung across the camel's back; a kind of plant that produced coffee as its sap. The pouch was symbiotic with the camel; its roots grew right into the hot-breathed beast's hump. "Coffee here!" called the man in the turban, setting out a row of fresh-filled mugs. "Piping hot."

A heavily modified couple came bouncing up for some coffee; maybe they'd been out all night. A young man and woman, they had long floppy ears and elastic balloons of skin growing from the soles of their bare feet. *Boing,* they went up into the air, bouncing on their foot-puffs, and came down, *boing, boing, boing,* in smaller and smaller increments, finally coming to a rest. The really weird thing was that their knees bent backward. *Whooosh* went the coffee camel, lighting its breath with a spark from its flinty back teeth. Sipping their drinks, the ball-foot couple stared absentmindedly at Frek—as if *he* were the odd one—all the while talking a funny city slang that he couldn't understand.

"Goggy Glen, it's goo to googoo you," said the woman, laughing and leaning against her boyfriend. The letter 'G' was very much the gripper thing to use these days. "Glim me a guzzle, gurgle my genes." She licked the side of his cheek. Her tongue was green.

"It's godzoon gauss to glawk with you, Gillian," said the man, spicing her coffee with a bit of mod gel he drew out of a pouchlike pocket in his skin. "Glug the grog, my guddly gollywog!"

"Gump dump grew you?" the woman asked Frek, swishing the modified coffee around her mouth. "Going Gov grotto for stim?"

"I'm going to the puffball," said Frek.

"What I said," answered the woman in clear. Her dangling ears were covered with animated tattoos. But despite her wild, uncanny looks, she meant to be helpful. "Up two blocks that way, one right, one left to the NuBioCom sample door." Frek's twisted lips and shrunken arm must have given her the impression he was testing mods for NuBioCom. Like a Grulloo.

"Geevey khora-khora goo on you," observed the man. His green-gummed smile and his backward-bending legs made Frek very ill at ease.

With the briefest of nods, Frek hurried up the hill toward the puffball in the direction the woman had pointed. He passed some men unloading an elephruk full of metallic dust and uncorking casks of aircoral polyps. They were adding a story to a shiny restaurant. A fish market stood next to the eatery; here in the big city people wanted something more than simple anymeat loaf every day. The fish were amplified trout from the River Jaya, identically plump and healthy. A little man with webbed fingers was busy laying them out.

At the end of two blocks, Frek was right up against the NuBio-Com puffball, its shadow spreading across the green moss of the street. The building wasn't an aircoral, it was a single living thing, a giant fungus with brain nodules amid the computational richness of its mycelia and hyphae. Gov's home. The air in the shade of the puffball was cool and moldy-smelling, though now and then the breeze seemed to bring out a scent of corruption, as of rotten vegetables and decaying meat.

Remembering what the bouncy woman had told him, Frek turned right, then left, skirting around the edge of the puffball. The puffball presented a blank, greenish-gray surface to the outer world. Its walls had glassy black eyes set into in them; Frek wasn't sure if they noticed him or not. Thanks to Phamelu, Gov would know his disguise by now. Frek took out Jeroon's purse-fungus and stuck it to the palm of his hand. It clung tight there. Soon it would be time to put on the chameleon mod.

At the far side of the puffball, Frek found a square with a queue of gumpy mod-testers, waiting for admittance to the puffball's low, arched rear door. There was so much traffic here that, rather than being covered with bindmoss, the square was paved with live cobblestones, which were gray, rocky tubers grown right into place. The nearest gumps in line included a man with long antennae protruding from his head, a woman with an extra pair of arms, an old Grulloo woman with a squirrel tail, and a couple whose heads were partly melted into each other. A pair of beefy counselors were admitting the testers a few at a time. The puffball door opened onto a little chamber that flickered with colors; the walls inside the puffball were alive with images. Inside the door Frek could glimpse NuBioCom counselors taking blood samples from the mod-testers, and shadowy tunnels leading deeper into the puffball. That's where Frek wanted to go.

He squeezed up against the wall of the puffball and took the chameleon mod-pod out of his purse-fungus—and not a moment too soon, for now he heard the buzz of a lifter beetle drawing near. It pulled into view and angled down for a landing. PhiPhi. She hadn't noticed him yet. Frek squashed himself into the pinched crack where the puffball met the ground, taking off his shoes and slipping out of his blue turmite silk pants and his yellow T-shirt.

Just then Dibble came marching into the square. The Grulloo egg-baskets were back in her bed, plus an unhappy Gibby, propped up against a basket with his hands bound together by a wad of gunk from the webgun. Dibble's driver was none other than blond, kind-faced Phamelu. Frek guessed she'd come to sell Gibby's eggs for herself—and probably to sell Gibby, too. Gov wasn't likely to show the cantankerous Grulloo much mercy. Frek realized that it was up to him to save his friend.

Phamelu's bright gaze fell upon Frek; instantly, she pointed at him and raised her voice.

"There he is! The boy who ran away!"

5

professor bumby

Already naked, Frek dabbed a third of the chameleon goo onto his bare stomach, and willed his body to start looking like the gray-green puffball and the reddish dirt beneath his feet.

It happened fast as thought. The effect began with a stippled pattern of dull red and green dots that spread from his stomach to his chest and arms and legs, the dots racing across his skin. They covered every bit of him, even sliding out along his hairs. The color spots split into smaller and smaller dots with ever finer shadings. Frek's body looked like a house tree's wall skin bringing a scene into focus. And then his feet were indistinguishable from the dirt, and his upper body was a perfect match for the slanting puffball's skin.

But of course the counselors were still running straight toward the spot where Frek stood. There was PhiPhi, and one of the guards from the puffball entrance, and two more counselors who'd appeared from inside. Phamelu remained perched upon Dibble, guarding her plunder.

Frek darted in a direction his pursuers might not expect: toward Phamelu. As he moved, his body matched itself to the appearance of the square's cobblestone tubers and the appearance of the buildings and streets beyond. It was like having a perspective-warped toon show playing on his skin. Magical. The chameleon mod worked without his having to control the details consciously.

But when he was out in the open like this, the illusion couldn't fit together for every direction at once. Though Phamelu was still pointing at the spot by the wall where he'd started, the guard from the door was easily following Frek across the square. Reaching Dibble, Frek pressed himself against the elephruk's gray flank, figuring the chameleon effect would work better against something flat.

Meanwhile—accidentally on purpose—the gump with antennae had gotten in the guard's way, and the Grulloo woman with the squirrel tail had tripped up PhiPhi.

Frek's skin was an elephruk shade of gray now, complete with darker lines to mimic the beast's wrinkles. By the time the guard had reached the front of the elephruk, Frek had scooted along its body to the rear. For the moment, nobody knew exactly where Frek was.

Except for Gibby. The Grulloo was less than a meter away and he could hear Frek breathing.

"Didn't I say git?" hissed Gibby.

"I'm going to save you," murmured Frek, though he didn't know how. With the four counselors after him, and only his naked body, there was no hope of cutting Gibby's bonds. And he wouldn't get very far if he tried to carry him.

Phamelu must have heard them talking, for now she was turning around. "Thar he is!" shouted Gibby to distract her. "Headin' off downhill! Look! Look! Look!" It was the oldest trick in the book, but Gibby was yelling so loud that Frek's pursuers couldn't help but look down the street toward the river. The gump mod-testers took up Gibby's cries and kept getting in the way of the counselors. The counselors now wasted a few precious moments in clearing the riffraff from the square.

Meanwhile Frek dropped to the ground, crawled under Dibble, finding his way among her legs, and came out on the elephruk's other side. He realized that his ring was still visible. He used his thumb and fingers to work it loose, and tucked it into the purse-fungus pasted to the palm of his hand. And then he flattened himself on his stomach against the cobblestones and began worming his way across the square, moving quite fast. His stub-arm was fine for this kind of crawling.

With Frek flat on the ground, the chameleon effect was perfect. Looking down as he slid his hand across the ground, he could see every detail of the street's surface echoed upon his skin. If he moved his arm across a pebble, the image of a pebble moved across his skin; if a leaf was beneath his fingers, the image of a leaf was displayed upon his knuckles. Frek recalled hearing that the chameleon mod made your skin photosensitive, effectively giving it the ability to see. One side of his arm could tell the other side what color to use. The effect was as if Frek were made of glass, except that the purse-fungus glued to his palm didn't show through.

Frek worked his way over to the far side of the square, and then crawled around the square's edge to get back to the puffball's wall. Meanwhile, the counselors were ineffectually milling around. Gov was trying to think for all of them at once, and not doing too well at it. Only if one of them happened to blindly step on Frek would they find him. And that wasn't likely, now that Frek was back under the bulge of the puffball. A bad smell, as of a dead animal, drifted past again. Frek crept along the wall toward the waiting door.

Getting through the door was going to be tricky, as counselors kept rushing in and out, for all the world like turmites in a hill. The only thing to do would be to wait for a lull and make a dash for it. Somebody might glimpse him going in, but once he was inside the puffball there'd be hundreds of meters of smoothly curved walls against which he could hide himself. Even if the walls were covered with toons, Frek felt sure his chameleon skin could keep pace with them. His mod still had maybe twenty minutes to go. He crouched beside the door, waiting for the counselors to clear out of his way. He felt just a bit hypnotized by the slowly changing colors he could see inside the entrance.

Sitting still like this, Frek entered a strange, yet familiar, state of mind. The world took on a kind of golden glow, as if Earth were an exotic place and he were seeing it for the very first time, being sure to clearly characterize everything that he saw. It wasn't just the puffball that looked goggy—it was everything around him that looked new: the forms and faces of the people, the colors of the plants, the clouds in the sky, the live cobblestones. The gentle whisper of his breath was deeply significant; the counselors' footsteps were like an orchestra. Most of all, the play of Frek's consciousness felt like a performance, unique and miraculous, like some exquisite piece of craftsmanship with all of its components on display. This was the same golden glow sensation he'd been having off and on for the last couple of weeks. Ever since, come to think of it, the mysterious trouble on Sick Hindu. What did it mean?

"If you can't find him, better take my goods and close the door," called Phamelu right about then, breaking the spell. "Frek and this little Grulloo were planning to get inside the puffball and find the Anvil. The Grulloo was bragging about it last night when he was drunk. Might as well give him what he asked for!"

"You poisoned me!" shouted Gibby. "I'm bein' kidnapped and robbed! The boy ain't here, he's run off, I tell you, he's goin' down the river!"

Ignoring his cries, five puffball counselors converged on the elephruk, one for each basket of eggs, and one for Gibby. Meanwhile the color-lit puffball door was drawing itself together like an anxious mouth. It was time to act. While the door was still waiting for the counselors to carry in Gibby and the baskets of eggs, Frek ran for it as fast as he could.

"There he goes," cried the alert Phamelu, who'd been watching for him. The guard by the door glimpsed him too, and almost caught him, but Frek managed to dodge past his grasp. And then he was inside the puffball.

The room had four, no five, tunnels leading off it. The walls were flowing with pastel hues like watercolors melding on wet paper. Frek's skin took on the same shades. The center of the room was full of equipment growing out of the floor: chairs, desks, lamps, hoses. Gov's disembodied voice called out a warning. Three counselors jumped up.

The wall skins went creamy white, as if to make Frek easier to see. But of course he turned the same shade of white all over. Nevertheless, at least one of the counselors had gotten a good visual fix on him when he came in, and they were closing in.

Small and quick as he was, Frek was able to dodge past them. He took off into the handiest of the tunnel mouths. It proved to be a spiral ramp winding up to the next level, and then to levels above that. Frek kept going up, hoping the counselors would tire before he did. But they remained close behind. As if to make it harder for Frek to stay in synch with his background, the walls now began to flicker rapidly through an irregular sequence of solid colors. It was dizzying.

By the fourth level, Frek didn't have the breath to climb anymore. He branched off into a level hallway, and ran fifty yards along that. The hall seemed to circle along the outer edge of the puffball. Every few yards an oval door gave upon a chamber with a window. People were in many of these little rooms, NuBioCom techs and genomicists. All the while, Gov was broadcasting warnings from the puffball wall skins, and some of the workers joined in trying to capture Frek.

By dint of some tricky turns and reversals, Frek managed to lose his pursuers for a bit; they thundered off down the hall ahead of him, leaving him camouflaged against a wall. He dropped to the floor and crept into a room off the hall. It was a kind of meeting room, with two men and two women standing by a table. NuBioCom execs. Frek didn't take time to really look at them. A window faced out on Stun City; it occurred to Frek that if all else failed, he might use a chair to smash open the window and then slide down the curving puffball wall.

The execs had jumped up in response to Gov's alarm, but now that the chase had moved off to another part of the puffball, they were settling back down.

"Terrible business, that runaway boy getting inside our headquarters," said one of the women. Her face was so flat that the bridge of her nose was level with her eyes. It almost looked as if her eyes could see each other.

"I know him," grunted one of the men. "He's a misfit, practically a mutant. Four sigmas off the genomic norm. Frek Huggins. His father went over to the Crufters last year. Young Frek was always wanting to come over to play with our son, Stoo. I did what I could to make him feel unwelcome."

Wedged down against the curved corner where the wall met the floor, Frek recognized the voice. It was Kolder Steiner talking. Frek had never realized the Steiners thought quite so poorly of him. It made him ashamed to think back on all the times he'd tried to be nice to them, and them just thinking he was a gleep.

"Well, let's get back to the business at hand," the second woman exec said. She was dark-skinned, with slowly writhing copper hair. "The internal uvvy, to be known as the *ooey*. We need to get the ooey genome finalized so we can give the product a full-court press. We're targeting a ten percent early-adopter rate in the first quarter and a front-porch bulge of sixty percent by the end of the second year. After that, Gov makes them mandatory."

"Mandatory?" said the second man at the table, who sounded a little surprised. He was younger and more thoughtful looking than the other three. A genomicist.

"Makes things easier to just have one kind of uvvy," said Kolder dismissively.

"But—what if somebody doesn't want a voice in their head?" asked the young genomicist. "That's what's bothering some of us. We want the internal uvvy to have an 'off' mode. A user-activated pause control."

"Excellent that you mention this," said the copper-haired woman. "It's exactly the main topic we planned for this meeting. The point is that an off mode would defeat our goal. Gov wants everyone online, all the time, everywhere. A hundred percent connectivity. This is absolute and nonnegotiable. The internal uvvies are to be universally adopted and always active. Why? Think of the marketing possibilities. The educational benefits. Gov feels this will be the most important thing he's ever done."

"I think it's fabulous," enthused the flat-faced woman, who seemed to be a corporate cheerleader type. "An age-old dream come true."

Whose dream? thought Frek with silent sarcasm. Hucksters and salesmen, tyrants and dictators, bullies and snoops—that's who wanted an always-on communication channel to the inside of every citizen's head. He had to find a way to stop Gov. NuBioCom had already collapsed the biome and now, with that ooey internal uvvy, they were planning to make people's minds all the same.

But then Kolder said something that totally caught Frek by surprise.

"We already have other beings in our heads," said Kolder. "Ever since the Sick Hindu incident. Gov told me I could share this with you. But perhaps you've noticed?"

The young genomicist glanced around at the others, a little embarrassed, maybe even wondering if Kolder had gone gollywog.

"A special feeling," said Kolder in a coaxing tone. "Things take on a warm, rich appearance. Your sensations and thoughts seem unusually interesting. You view yourself from a certain remove."

The young genomicist's face remained politely blank. He hadn't risen this far in the ranks without knowing when to hold his tongue.

Kolder gave a sudden short bark of laugh. "You thought it was just you, didn't you? Well, guess what, boy, these days lots of people are feeling like they're the stars of their own shows. It's a pattern Gov's picked up from people's conversations. Analyzed it. He thinks it's because of those aliens who abducted the three people from Sick Hindu. We believe they've instigated a mind surveillance operation whose scope is the entire human race. So the sooner Gov gets out ahead of them, the better."

"That's—incredible," said the genomicist quietly. He didn't seem to believe Kolder at all. But Frek did. Kolder was talking about the golden glow sensation that Frek had noticed outside the puffball.

"Let me make it simple for you," Kolder told the doubtful genomicist scornfully. "Implement the always-on ooey genome. Do it now."

"Thanks for clearing this up," said the genomicist in a neutral tone. "I'll get my team right on it."

Just then the wall-colors flipped from beige to dark gray. It took a split second before Frek's skin could catch up. Maybe nobody in the room would have spotted him, but the rooms had eyes all along the tops of their walls, and one of the eyes saw him.

"Intruder alert," said Gov's voice from the wall. "He's right there next to the door. Grab him."

But by then Frek was off and running down the corridor again. Alerted by Gov, the counselors were coming back down the hallway toward him. Frek did a U-turn and ran the other way, back past the conference room. For the moment nobody was ahead of him, but that wasn't going to last long. He needed a plan, or he was headed for the Three R's—if not outright execution.

Rounding the next corner, Frek noticed a shape sliding along on the wall next to him. It was a dark green toon of a cuttlefish with light spots, a tentacled creature wearing one of those funny old skull-caps with a square on the top of his head. A mortarboard. Facilitator toons sometimes wore them. Except for the mortarboard, the toon looked exactly like the Merry Mollusk Frek had been working on. Or, more to the point, it looked like the alien Frek had seen under his bed.

The toon began talking to him, vibrating its voice from a moving patch of wall.

"Follow me," it said in that same familiar male voice the alien had used. Like a mixture of the voices of Frek's friends, of Dad's voice, of toon voices, and even the voice of Frek himself. A voice that evoked instant liking and trust. "I know what to do," said the cuttlefish on the wall.

By this point, Frek was ready to try anything. For the moment his pursuers were out of sight. The tentacled toon darted around the lip of a doorway that led to a little side corridor. Frek followed the cut-tlefish, hoping he wasn't being led into a trap.

The short corridor quickly hit a dead end—but the final chamber had a sizable hole in the floor and a similar hole in the ceiling. The room seemed to function as a kind of air vent. Glancing up, Frek could see a series of holes in the chambers above him leading all the way up to a faintly glimpsed patch of sky. Though he would have preferred to head upward, the green cuttlefish toon thought different.

"Crawl down through here," the toon's voice told him. The im-ages of his tentacles writhed and beckoned at the edge of the hole in the floor. For a minute Frek just looked at him. Unlike a real mollusk, the toon creature had had a slight corkscrew twist to his tentacles, like the tendrils of vines. It gave him a lively, springy look.

Just about then the counselors went thudding down the main cor-ridor, right past Frek's cul-de-sac. They hadn't noticed yet that Frek had branched off. Even the eyes in Gov's main hallway seemed to have missed his move, and by some stroke of good luck, Gov didn't seem to have any eyes or ears in this side corridor's walls to notice Frek talking to—who?

"What's your name?" Frek asked the toon on the floor.

"Call me Bumby," said the toon, and then made a sound like a laugh. "Professor Bumby. 'Professor' being the old-time Earth word for a super-duper facilitator, you understand. I boned up on your planet's mighty culture whilst I've been waiting for your next move. When I call myself 'professor,' I mean that I have an advanced level of practical knowledge about the manipulation of physical reality. Get down, Frek, down through the hole. I'll waltz us out of this corner fine and dandy."

So Frek squeezed through the rubbery hole. It was a little awkward with his half-missing arm. The next chamber down had a hole in its floor too, and Frek followed the toon through that hole, and down through a hole in the floor of the room below that, which brought him back to the bottom floor of the puffball.

"We've lost those creeps for now," said the Professor Bumby toon in that cozy voice he used.

"You *are* the same one who was under my bed, right?" asked Frek, just to be sure.

"That was a wetware me indeed," said Professor Bumby. "I'm a software instance. We'll unearth the new scion before you know it."

"And you told me I can be a hero and save the world?" persisted Frek.

"I did, and you will, my boy. You're off to a bang-up start. You sowed the backup scion into the soil of Giant's Marbles, the new Bumby inflated, and he headed here. Flying underground—for us Orpolese your earth is soft as fog, you understand. Soon, very soon, you'll meet the kick-ass Bumby scion, the amazing cuttle who'll fly you to the elixir. And in return you'll say a few words to the branecasters."

"You're saying we'll find the Anvil?" asked Frek, a little bewildered.

"My ship," said the toon. "The solid Bumby's ship, that is. Don't call her 'Anvil.' An anvil is heavy and it falls. I've been overhearing the brutish Gov-worm saying 'Anvil' all week. I've been out and about your infospace, Frek, all eyes and ears, demurely waiting for my hero. You. I was just listening in on the same conversation as you, in fact. About Gov's plans to put a controller uvvy in each Earthling's brain. And about the branecasters opening up a channel to your minds."

"Gov wants to make us into—components," said Frek. That much he understood. The rest of it was still vague, the part about aliens watching their minds. "I have to do something."

"You have to be the hero," said the Bumby toon quietly. "I'm here to potentiate, to open the gate, to aid your quest, to be your race's producer. Just in the nick of time. We're ready to fly, to grow beyond all measure like a soul striving toward the All. My Orpolese ship is no anvil; she's my *slobber-tweet*. I call her Ulla."

Not that "slobber-tweet" was exactly what the toon said, but the sound was something like that, with the *tweet* coming right on top of the *slobber*. The toon's odd, rapid talk was a little hard to follow, and the fact that he was using such a familiar-sounding voice made it extra goggy.

"Yes, Frek," continued the Bumby toon, "My superfine *slobber-tweet* Ulla will carry you to the galactic core, you'll meet the scary branecasters and contract the Orpolese as your producers. You'll win the elixir, hooray! But before all this sundry adventure, we'll dig the new me in Gov's graveyard."

"Look out," interrupted Frek, pointing upward.

Somebody was poking around in the fourth-floor corridor they'd started from, peering down through the air hole. Professor Bumby slid along the wall, leading Frek into an empty hallway with softly throbbing yellow walls. With a little squirt of visual ink, the toon sped off toward the center of the puffball. A bad smell was coming from there, the stink of death. Frek hesitated and stood in the middle of the corridor for a minute, thinking.

Go to a graveyard? Cross the galaxy? Branecasters? Fine concepts for a fantasy game or a killtoon, but this was Frek's real life. He was a little frightened of following Professor Bumby toward that unsettling smell. The toon barely made sense. What if Frek just got the heck out of here before his chameleon mod wore off? He wished he could be a regular kid again and go back home to Mom. But that was over now. He had to get even with Gov. The cuttlefish toon would help him.

Right about then the wall flickered from yellow to green, but Frek's skin didn't. He'd reverted to his usual golden tan. The chameleon mod had expired. He fumbled at his fungus-purse, hurrying to smear on more.

"Come on!" urged Professor Bumby, his image darting back down the corridor to Frek's side. "Hurry up. We have to meet me in Gov's graveyard. Be a hero, Frek, not a cluck. The graveyard's just a decomposing compost heap." The cuttlefish toon jiggled back and forth, the image excitedly curling and uncurling his helical tentacles and sucker-arms.

"Stop rushing me," said Frek. "I need to put on more goo. So they can't see me."

"Save it for a rainier day," said the toon, undulating the skirtlike fin that ran along his body. "You won't need camouflage once we reach the compost heap. The solid Bumby's coming back. They'll all be screaming and running away."

So Frek took the toon's advice and refrained from rubbing on the chameleon mod. By now the Gov eyes in the corridor's walls had seen him, anyway, and even if he put the mod on, the eyes would track him like before. He took off running after the toon.

The puffball was a bedlam. Counselors were shouting as they came down through the air vent, counselors were yelling to each other in nearby halls, somewhere Gibby was hollering, and dogs were barking, too. Wow and Woo?

Professor Bumby twisted and turned through the maze of passages, managing to keep Frek always out of sight of the counselors. And soon they'd reached Gov's graveyard. What a stench. The puffball was like a hollow ring, with a big hole in its middle, and a patch of ground like a courtyard garden. But instead of grass and trees, the ground was mounded up with piles of rotting vegetables, with chunks of unused factory meat, and with the foully decaying corpses of people, of animals, of Grulloos. The shapes were slumped and soft. Frek gagged. Hair-fine white fungus tendrils shrouded the stinking refuse. The ground underfoot was puddled with vile, dark juice. Food for the puffball.

Breathing shallowly through his mouth, Frek looked around for the cuttlefish toon. He saw no sign of it. The puffball walls surrounding the courtyard of death were a leathery monochrome.

The walls had windows, though, and at every level of the puffball, NuBioCom workers were leaning out into the courtyard, pointing and yelling at Frek—Frek standing there in plain sight, completely naked save for the fungus-purse holding his mod, the Aaron's Rod, and his new ring. And here came blank-faced PhiPhi yet again, buzzing down into the puffball's hole upon her teal blue lifter beetle.

Just then the ground under Frek's feet bucked up. Something was digging out. A rubbery shape, a fluked arrowhead of flesh worming its way out of the ground, dark green spotted with light green dots. Yes. A pair of extremely large and intelligent eyes appeared at the wide lower end of the body. The eyes were golden, and the dark pupils were shaped like the letter W. The space mollusk finished digging its way out of the sodden, reeking soil. It shook out its eight boneless arms and two long tentacles, each of them dotted with suckers, each of them with a slight clockwise twist. Squeezed in with the arms was a protruding flexible tube—which Frek recognized as the "siphon" used for rapid cephalopod propulsion.

"*Eadem mutata resurgo,*" said the alien cuttlefish, flinging a comradely tentacle across Frek's shoulders. "That's Latin. The same yet changed I rise again. I'm a Professor Bumby, too." He raised an arm and delicately aimed one of its tips at PhiPhi's noisy beetle. The tip glowed and lengthened itself into a curving ray of energy that lashed out to touch the tweaked insect. The lifter beetle plummeted from the air, landing on a soft mound of rotten fruit. PhiPhi spilled into the stinky mush, and when she tried to stand up and fire her webgun, a second burst from Bumby knocked her onto her back, kicking and yelling.

Professor Bumby's other arms were spread out and squirming, each of them with tips that dissolved into living lines of—light? No, it wasn't light, but rather some cosmic form of energy new to Earth.

The beams were moving in arcs and loops, they were branching like vines. The ropes of energy writhed across the faces of the counselors and NuBioCom workers.

"I can't see!" shouted a counselor, and the cry was taken up by the others. Bumby had temporarily blinded them, one and all.

"Let's go liberate Ulla," said the green cuttlefish, gazing at Frek with his W-pupil eyes. The eyes were in humps that stuck up above his bunch of arms. "My *slobber-tweet*. Gov has her stashed in one of the puffball's tiptop rooms. Wrapped inside a space bug." The cuttlefish inflated his body like a balloon. He was hovering half a meter above the ground, and he'd grown to the size of a couch or a bed.

"We have to save Gibby before we do anything else," said Frek. "And Wow. I heard him barking. Are you going to help me fight Gov?"

"Yes, in spades," said Professor Bumby. His voice came from inside the cluster of arms and tentacles he had in place of a face. Frek recalled that a cuttlefish had a razor-sharp beak, with the top half fitting into the bottom. Maybe it was just as well not to see Bumby's mouth. *"Gubernator delenda est,"* continued Bumby. "Gov must be destroyed. I came in peace. Gov's counselors lynched me. It's payback time."

"Why didn't you protect yourself, anyway?"

"I was weak from my long journey, enfeebled, on the ropes. A yunch trip takes the juice out of a traveler. And, you know, I hadn't been expecting Gov to know I was coming in. Someone tipped him off, I think it might have been a Unipusker saucer, it flew over Stun City right after we landed. Anyway, I'd formed my yunched little body into a nice-looking cuttlefish shape to meet you, and right away those Gov-zombies hacked me up and burned the pieces to ashes. But, thanks be to the Many, you planted my scion, and I quickly instantiated a new Earth-type body in the rich soil of Gaia. I'm most peppy indeed, most thoroughly revivified, with all relevant memories downloaded from my Bumby crypton. *Gubernator delenda est!*" His talk was a mixture of facilitatorlike formality and freewheeling poetic elaboration.

By way of punctuation, Professor Bumby extended his siphon and shot a gundo goggy blast of energy, charring a hole the size of an elephruk in the nearest puffball wall. An angry scream split the air, coming from the whole fungus at once.

"Gov doesn't like it now," said Professor Bumby. "We'll deconstruct him, eh, Frek?"

"Get away from me," boomed Gov's voice, coming from every side of the courtyard. "Tell this monster to leave, Frek, or I tear your friend and your dog in two."

"A challenge for the hero and his noble steed," Bumby said to Frek in a calm tone. "*Whinny*. Where do you think Gov has laired your companions?"

"I heard them near the entrance," said Frek, pointing. He was a little in awe of the strength of his new ally. The siphon blast had surprised him even more than those goggy curving energy rays that the cuttlefish controlled like extensions of his arms. And on top of it all, Bumby could fly! The space cuttle was remarkable, to say the least.

"I can magic-carpet us there in a flash," proposed Bumby. "I'm full of helium." He used his two long tentacles to lift Frek onto his broad, gently domed back, leaving a spring-coiled tentacle stretched back like a bridle for Frek to hang onto with his one good hand. Beating his skirt fin in smooth waves, Bumby shot forward through Gov's corridors. Every bit of the wall skins was wallpapered with Bumby toons. They were jeering at Gov and warning all the counselors and workers to get out of the puffball right away. People were leaving in droves, many of them still blinded. None of them were in a mood to confront Bumby.

Frek had plenty of experience with finding Wow, who was known for wandering in search of female dogs. It was only minutes till he and Bumby had tracked Wow down. On the way, Frek worked his ring out of the purse fungus and put it back on his finger. It comforted him to wear it, and with the chameleon mod worn off, there was no reason not to. He wished Carb could see him riding the alien cuttlefish.

They found Wow, Woo, and Gibby imprisoned within a chamber near the puffball's entrance, a kind of holding cell. A blast from Bumby's siphon tore the cell door apart like turmite paper. The Grulloo and the two dogs were bound at the ankles by tough stalks growing from the puffball wall, one stalk for each ankle.

"Halt," intoned Gov's voice again. His menacing raven toon appeared upon the wall skin to drive his message home. "Stop now, Frek, or I'll rip them to pieces. Surrender. Only a matter of time till the counselors catch you. If you keep this up, you make things worse for self—and for your mother."

Seeing the raven frightened Frek; it brought back the nightmarish memories of his hours with the peeker uvvy. But the threat to Lora redoubled his determination.

"We're going to kill you," he told Gov evenly, then turned to his new alien friend. "Help us, Bumby!"

Gov's wall-stalks crawled apart, spread-eagling his captives. Gibby grimaced, and the dogs yelped in pain.

"Quite unacceptable," said Professor Bumby. Again he grew light-tendrils from the tips of his arms. A few well-aimed twitches burned the shackles in two. At the same time his multiple Professor Bumby toons squeezed Gov's image right off the wall skin.

"Thankee kindly!" exclaimed Gibby, producing a longish knife from within his jacket to cut the remaining circlets of puffball from his ankles—or wrists. He glanced up from his work, squinting at Professor Bumby. "This would be that space alien you tole me about, hey Frek? Proud to meet you, Mr. Cuttlefish. I'm Gibby the Grulloo, and this here is Frek's dog, Wow, and the dog's lady friend, Woo. We been making ourselves acquainted here, passin' the time till they started dissectin' us."

"Call me Professor Bumby," said the floating cuttlefish. "Glad to meet you."

It was cozy to hear Gibby again. And a pure joy to see Wow. Frek hopped off Professor Bumby's back and ran to hug his dog. Wow and Woo's story was simple enough. Once the bone was chewed down, Wow had decided to follow Frek after all. Woo had come along, and some NuBioCom workers had caught them while Wow was sniffing at Frek's discarded clothes.

As it happened, the counselors had thrown the clothes into the cell along with Gibby and the dogs. So now Frek was able to get dressed again, which he found a great relief. His soft leather shoes felt good on his feet, and it was nice to cover his nakedness with his blue pants and yellow T-shirt.

"Let's go, Frek, yes," said Professor Bumby, bobbing in the middle of the room like a friendly balloon. He beat his fin to bring himself down to the ground. "On the road. From what I'm overhearing on the uvvy links, we'll be in for a dash to catch my *slobber-tweet*. But once we save my lady fair, we'll take you to meet the branecasters and fetch the elixir that will restore the biome of your Earth."

So that was the plan. Frek hadn't realized all that before. It sounded glatt. Restoring the biome was exactly what he wanted to do. It was like Bumby had read his mind. "Elixir" was just the word Frek had always thought of. But he did wonder why it had to be specifically Frek Huggins who fetched the elixir. Why hadn't Professor Bumby just brought the elixir along in the first place? Maybe it wasn't so easy to get hold of the elixir, maybe somebody had to snatch it away from those branecasters, whoever they were, and maybe Bumby was choosing Frek to do this because Frek was so clever. Or so pure of heart. Frek guessed he was fairly pure of heart. He loved his family, he didn't sneak if he didn't have to, and he never stole things or picked on other kids.

Once again the golden glow suffused Frek's surroundings; again his sensations seemed like artifacts in a store window. It was that same feeling that had come over him just before he'd darted inside the puffball. Savoring the sensation more distinctly than ever before, Frek realized it was as if there were a stranger inside his mind, tasting his sensations and sharing his thoughts, getting him to make everything unambiguous and clear. The glow was a nonspecific pleasure tingle, as if designed to make you enjoy having the stranger watch you. The glow felt good, but being watched was distracting. And it caused you to think simpler thoughts, as if you were explaining things to someone, having to name every sensation and emotion.

This was what Kolder had been talking about. Aliens were peeking into people's minds. Frek wished he could turn off the glow. This was supposed to be his own real life, not a toon show for some invisible beings' entertainment. Perhaps freeing humanity of the galactic eavesdroppers should be part of Frek's quest as well as fetching the elixir. A tall order. Gazing at good old Wow and tough little Gibby, he realized he needed them as helpers.

"Will you guys come with me?" he asked. "I know I'll do better with you along."

"Wow come," said Wow immediately.

"Woo come," added Woo. She and Wow had really bonded. So much the better. An extra dog could be a good thing.

"Where all did he say he's takin' you?" asked Gibby, still not quite decided. "To catch what? What was that noise he made?"

"He calls the Anvil *slobber-tweet*," explained Frek. "Or Ulla. The Anvil is his starship, you know. I think he's going to take us to a different part of the galaxy. I'm sure Bumby could make stim cells for you."

"Anything you need," chimed in Bumby. "Food, air, spacesuits—I make it all from kenner."

"I always wanted to travel," said Gibby slowly. "Bein' a Grulloo and not all too welcome in most spots, I ain't been able to get no further than Stun City. I'd surely love to come, Frek. But—" A shadow crossed his face.

"What?"

"Long way to go without tellin' Salla," said Gibby. "She'll think I got moolked up like never before. Wouldn't put it past her to declare me dead and find a new husband. I'd hate to see Bili and LuHu raised by some other guy."

"Uvvy her," urged Frek. "Tell her to wait."

"We don't got no uvvies," said Gibby. "We're off the grid."

"Could we fly by Gibby's house on our way out?" Frek asked Professor Bumby. "And visit my mom, too? Lora Huggins?"

"Your planet has sky-jellies, I'm sure you're hip to that," said Bumby a little edgily. "The Skywatch Mil satellites, tools of the Govworms that tyrannize your poor green world. Even now a jelly is getting ready to try to blast me. It's goggling down, charging up its laser-cells, crooning and scheming till Frek and Bumby pull clear of Gov's puffball. And then you'll see some zick and some zack. We're going to be whisking out of here faster than you've ever seen, my merry friends, and not all that likely to be stopping door to door."

"You won't escape," said Gov's voice from the walls. A true voice of doom, carefully modulated in the deepest, scariest, most psychologically effective way.

"It's *your* clock that's running out," snapped Bumby. "It's over for you, stink worm. We're the ones to finish the job. Saddle up, Frek, and it's fine if you bring the hounds. There's scads of room inside Ulla. She can shrink us on our way in, you understand. And you come too, if you like, Gibby, but get with it, runt!"

"Don't call me runt, you space squid," said Gibby, never one to stand still for any kind of insult. "Do you know what it's like to travel off and leave your wife?"

"My wife travels with me," said Bumby imperturbably. "I mean, I might as well call her a wife. But you've no need to stew about your absence being unbearably long. A yunch trip is over almost before it starts. And for a hero like our Frek, it won't take much time to get hold of the fabled elixir."

Frek wondered why Bumby was so convinced Frek was a hero. The cuttlefish knew next to nothing about him, right? Or maybe he'd done some kind of deep scan data search on the whole planet before landing? Even if he had, it was a little hard to see why Frek's name in particular would pop up on the top of anyone's list. But if Bumby thought Frek could be a hero, who was Frek to say no? He was certainly ready to try. Destroy Gov and restore the biome—these were tasks worth risking your life for.

"We supposed to ride your back?" whined Gibby. "Looks mighty slick."

"We'll grab onto his tentacles," said Frek. "Stop stalling. We've got important things to do."

"Easy for you to say," said Gibby, still dithering. "You got feet and hands both, which is more than me and the dogs can say."

"I'll lash you down," said Bumby shortly. He laid his long tentacles along his back. "Come or don't come, it's no tearful worry thing for me. Only Frek matters."

"Oh, what the hey, I'm in for this tune," said Gibby, clambering up. "Nothin' gambled, nothin' gained."

Frek, Gibby, and the two dogs settled onto the hump of Bumby's back. Frek was lying on his stomach with one of the dogs under each arm. Gibby was wedged beneath his ankles, and Bumby's tentacles were criss-crossed over them all.

"Going up," said Bumby, puffing up his girth with more helium. "And we'll take out Gov on the way." He pointed his siphon toward the ceiling and blasted open a shaft five meters across. Gov screamed again. Beating his fin like a hula skirt, Professor Bumby drifted gently upward.

They passed a diverse assortment of puffball chambers. Everything lay quite open to the newly blasted shaft. As well as officelike cells, they saw large laboratory rooms, with dozens of experimental kritter prototypes growing in tanks. Other rooms were completely filled with fungus filaments suspending convoluted fleshy knobs. These were the puffball brain nodules that watched the Nubbies through the eyes of the house tree walls. Bumby used scathing blasts of energy to clean out every chamber he saw. But still no Gov. What if they couldn't find him?

As they passed the second-to-last floor, Frek noticed a flutter in one of the shaft's walls. With sudden conviction, he knew that Gov lay behind it.

"Gov's there!" he cried. "Behind that wall."

Bumby flipped out one of his long arms and ripped the sheet of mushroom flesh away. And, yes, they'd found Gov's hidey-hole, a foul-smelling chamber filled by an immense coiled-up worm, partly grown into the flesh of the puffball.

The worm's cold gray eyes glinted with hatred; the beast opened its little disk mouth to show its weak, spiteful fangs. Gov himself.

"Kill him!" said Frek to Bumby.

"Don't you dare!" hissed the worm as Bumby prepared to blast him. His voice came both from his body and from the puffball walls. "Don't you think I stored my memories across the puffball's brain nodules? Don't you think I have a hidden clone? Killing me accomplishes nothing. You have no time, Bumby! I launch the space bug to take your Anvil to the Sun!"

"Kill him, Bumby!" repeated Frek.

And Bumby did. A single blast from the cuttlefish's siphon scoured out the chamber, crisping the cruel worm into a greasy cloud of smoke. Bumby kept his siphon blast going, burning out more and more of the puffball, and riding the blast up into the sky. They emerged from the top of the puffball's great curve. The sun was high; it was early afternoon. A space bug had just crawled out of the puffball's flesh at a spot nearby.

Frek had seen space bugs before. They were like big maggots or grub-worms, pointed at one end, with strong skin and combustible flesh. Basically space bugs were live tubes of rocket fuel who happened to be stupid enough to light themselves if you asked them to. They had a trio of tough little wings to steer themselves. The one leaving the puffball was furiously beating its wings to get a bit out of range before actually lighting its torch. It was narrow with a faint bulge in its middle—that would be the Anvil. The space bug was only a few score meters distant, its tiny wings laboring. It looked as if the space bug would be easy to catch, but just then its rear end kindled into a blinding bright flame and it shot into the sky.

"I'm coming, baby!" shouted Bumby. Tightening his tentacles around Frek, Wow, Woo, and Gibby, the airborne cuttlefish swung his pointed rear end up into the air and unleashed the strongest blast yet from his front-pointing siphon, coincidentally charring another huge hole into the puffball. The blast sent Bumby rocketing up into the air after the space bug. The dogs howled and clawed at Frek's sides, Gibby moaned, and Frek gritted his teeth. Still they rose higher.

It was only when they were nearly a thousand meters up in the clear blue sky that Bumby drew even with the space bug. And then he wasted no time. He seized the ridged body of the space bug with his sucker-arms. Though Frek couldn't see the details from where he lay, Bumby's mollusk beak must have been a goggy one, for in an instant the space bug had been torn to shreds. Its still-burning tail went spiraling crazily down toward an open field outside of Stun City. And Bumby was clasping the thick, purplish disk of the Anvil with his sucker arms, crooning over it like a long-lost lover. It was less than a meter across.

Frek barely had time to wonder how they were all supposed to fit in something so small when Bumby called out a new warning.

"Now's when the air show *really* begins," he said. "The sky-jelly is about to shoot. Now you see me, now you won't."

The space cuttlefish belched out a shape the size of his body; it was the classic mollusk stratagem of squirting out a decoy cloud of ink. Rather than being a simple mist, Bumby's "ink cloud" was a network of interlinked tendrils, with holographic colors shining out of the tendrils to produce an overall appearance identical to that of a large flying cuttlefish bearing a boy, two dogs, and a Grulloo upon his back.

At the same time, the true Bumby's skin took on the colors of the earth and sky, rendering him all but impossible for the Skywatch Mil satellites to see. He didn't need a chameleon mod to do this, for a cuttlefish was a chameleon all the time. Perhaps out of a concern that Frek and the others might stand out against his back, Bumby rolled his belly up so as to have a nice smooth expanse of skin facing the eyes of the distant sky-jelly.

And then he blatted out his helium, cut the jet-power of his siphon, and dropped tail-first like a stone, using his bunched-up arms like a rudder to steer them away from the vertical.

Nothing but Bumby's two long tentacles and some folded-over bits of his fin prevented Frek, Gibby, and the dogs from dropping a thousand meters to the ground. The landscape below was shifting about at crazy angles. Wow vomited onto Frek's neck. Frek pressed his face forward along the sky-blue-camouflaged cuttlefish skin and gasped for fresh air. Gibby's hands were clamped so hard onto Frek's ankles that his feet were going numb. And for some reason his arm stub was tingling like mad.

A cruel, twitching beam of pale red light appeared behind them. A Skywatch Mil laser ray from the nearest orbiting jelly. The beam passed through the decoy Bumby and down into, as it happened, the vicinity of the Brindle Cowloon on the edge of Stun City, possibly endangering Phamelu's establishment, though it was hard to be sure from up here. Though smoke was rising from the spot where the beam hit the ground, the decoy Bumby hung in place, imperturbable as a cloud.

Bumby's subterfuge was working perfectly. Everyone's attention was fixed upon the ink cloud and the hot, red beam of the laser. Meanwhile, Bumby and his passengers were gliding toward an overgrown stretch of the River Jaya, downstream from Stun City. Rolling his eyes back in his head and squinting against the whistling wind, Frek watched the ground rush up at him. They were going to crash quite soon.

At the last possible minute, Bumby swelled himself with helium and sent down a series of rapid blasts from his arm-tips and his siphon. Their fall slowed to a bearable rate, and their motion became more horizontal than vertical. Bumby rolled himself right side up, and they skipped a few hundred meters along the river's surface like a well-thrown stone. They drifted to a stop beneath some overhanging anyfruit trees at the river's low, marshy edge.

Bumby unwound his tentacles and rowed to the shore, where he set the Anvil down upon the low, soggy riverbank. Anyfruit trees hung low overhead. The cuttlefish reached up and took a peach, found it good, then took another.

Not minding about getting his clothes wet, Frek slid into the water to wash off the mess from Wow. For a moment he wondered if he could properly swim—but then his left arm pushed against the current, and he realized that it had grown back. He'd been too terrified during the long fall to notice consciously.

Treading water and running his hands over his face, Frek found that his beard was gone and his lips were back to normal as well. He switched his ring from his right hand back to his left, leaving the watertight fungus-purse with the Aaron's Rod twig and the chameleon mod pasted to his right palm.

"Come on, Wow!" called Frek. Still atop Bumby's bobbing body, the dog took a step forward, a step back, a step forward—and then finally jumped into the river as well. Woo followed suit.

Bumby gobbled one more peach, then uncoiled his tentacles out into the river water. Moments later he'd snagged an amplified trout, which he fed into the busy beak at the center of his arms.

Gibby was on shore investigating Bumby's slobber-tweet. The thing was dark, smooth, and bumpy—well-worn as an ancient meteorite, glossy as a new toy. In the light, Frek could see that its surface had a twisting grain to it, like dough or taffy—a spiral twist that led into the dimple on its flattened top.

"How the heck we goin' in thar?" asked Gibby. "Does it unfold or some such?"

Bumby was still too busy eating and drinking to talk. Frek was hungry, too, but just now he was too shaken up to eat a peach. The dogs scrambled ashore and shook themselves dry. Wow sniffed at the slobber-tweet, which wasn't any bigger than him. He seemed on the point of lifting his leg against the purple pumpkin, but just then it made a sudden noise that sent him scampering a few meters off. A chirp, followed by a smooth hiss.

"But soft," said Bumby, raising his head from the river. "What light through yonder window breaks? Ulla's wavy sunny soul. Meet and greet her, fleshapoids." Still in the water, Frek could see a glow from the Anvil.

Frek paddled to the bank and climbed onto the shore. A bright triangle had opened up in the dimpled flat top of the slobber-tweet, a hole not all that much bigger than a rabbit-hole. Odd little colored shapes seemed to be crowding around the inside: green spheres, blue cones, and red cubes, briefly appearing and disappearing.

With the door open, the slobber-tweet looked just like it had looked under his bed, except then it had been propped up so that the door on the flat side pointed toward him. The Anvil was alive.

Woo, braver than Wow, walked over to nose at the door. As she extended her snout, something visually strange happened. Her head and forelegs shrank. It was as if her body had suddenly tapered to a point. Wow yelped in worry, but Woo seemed not to be feeling any discomfort. She hopped onto the top of the Anvil, with her rear legs shrinking to the size the front legs had been, and her front legs shrinking yet further. Now she looked like a small-headed rat. Finally noticing Wow's desperate barking, Woo turned around to look back at them, gave a yelp of surprise, hopped off the Anvil and came trotting right out of the slobber-tweet door's zone of influence, growing back to her normal dimensions as she came. Frek thought back on how the original Professor Bumby had seemed to grow as he came out of the starship.

"I see you big," she told Wow, and sniffed him. "Wow same now," she concluded.

"Ulla unwinds your strings," said Professor Bumby. "So the space inside her seems big. Like an air bubble in a flat pancake, a tasty bonus beyond what old Euclid would allow. Not that Euclid knew about string theory, hey? He wasn't a Y3K professor." Bumby took a bite out of a last twitching fish that he held with the suckers of the clublike tip of his left tentacle. Frek could see Bumby's bloodstained beak down in the midst of his sucker-arms. It wasn't exactly a sight that made Frek want to get into a sealed cabin with the space cuttle-fish. But the trip had to be done; Frek had to get the elixir to restore Earth's flora and fauna.

And there was also the task of bringing down the Govs. It was crazy to think that people had let these monstrous things become their rulers. Yes, Frek and Bumby had killed the Gov worm. They'd won a battle, but the war wasn't done. There were govvy tyrants all over the planet, not to mention the orbiting jellies of Skywatch Mil.

Frek took a step toward the alluring orange-yellow light of the slobber-tweet's door and stretched out his arm. It seemed to shrink—not again! But as soon as Frek yanked back his arm, it was the same as ever. He stuck out his leg next, watched it get small, pulled it back. It was as if the slobber-tweet were a magic suitcase that made things shrink small enough to fit inside. Above and beyond any chances of saving Earth, an adventure in this craft would be gog gripper. Frek just had to see this journey through.

He looked at Bumby again, disregarding the beak and focusing on the big golden eyes with their dark, wavy pupils, the eyes set into bumps on the top of the cuttle's head. Taken all together, his head was shaped a little like a valentine heart: the two eyes on top, the pointy bunch of arms below. For the first time, Frek noticed that when Bumby put away his two long tentacles, he coiled them into springs and *boing* they snapped into pouches at the side of his face.

As if sensing Frek's doubts, Bumby scrunched his eyes in a friendly way, and demurely bunched his arms to cover his beak. "Take the magic trip," he urged. "To my sweet home Orpoly, comfortably near the galactic core. I'll show you a tunnel to the Planck brane there.

You'll meet the branecasters, they'll help you score your elixir, and then it's back in a flash with the stash and a crash. Inward and downward, Frek, upward and out! Let me hoist you and your pals into Ulla. You'll fit. She shrinks her passengers to ants on the front stoop."

"Just a dang minute," said Gibby from the riverbank. "You haven't told us what's in this for you, Bumby."

"I'm a branecast producer," said Bumby. "Throughout our universe certain, *harrumph,* highly evolved species enjoy themselves by snooping on others. Universal peeping tomfoolery—we call it esping. Ulla and I scour the galaxy for talent races suitable for esping by our fellow Orpolese. And, finding same, we produce exclusive Orpolese branecast arrangements. Now, thanks to the Unipuskers visiting Sick Hindu, the branecasters have already opened a channel on your race. You're in play. Viewable by free read-only public access—until a producer is registered for you. So I want you to register Ulla and me as your producers."

"We Grulloos don't cotton to bein' snooped on," said Gibby. "I can tell you that."

"I really doubt if the average Jezebel or Jamul will notice the branecast action at all," said Bumby, giving Frek an odd look. "At most you'd feel a pleasant buzz."

Frek remembered the golden glow he'd been getting lately, that feeling of experiencing his perceptions and thoughts as something completely fresh. The alien watchers that Kolder had been talking about.

"I'm already being esped by branecast viewers!" exclaimed Frek. "I keep noticing."

"You're waving with it," said Bumby admiringly. "Yes. Think of it like your old-time religion of God in His heaven watching the world," he continued soothingly. "God as an invisible eye, so laid-back that people argue about whether He even exists. Though the more sensitive talent race members can wig to it. People like you, Frek. Once the branecasters locate a talent race, there's no stopping them. Until you register for a producer, you'll stay on open access like you are now. Aliens all over the galaxy peeking in on you for free, looking at your rock-star underwear. So you might as well hook up with a decent producer and get paid! I'm asking that you come along and take one tiny meeting with the branecasters. I'm sure they'll give you your elixir. It'll be no trouble for them at all. A sweetheart deal all around. Not only do you have the elixir, when the Orpolese esp you, you get those feelings of exaltation and importance. Yes, there may be the occasional Good Word or two of 'guidance' passed into the hearts of the talent race from the producer's race. But it's all happy pie in the sky. I'll tell you more later, lad, but let's depart this vale before that filthy sky-jelly finds us again. Get on me, and I'll fly you through Ulla's door."

With a side-to-side wallowing motion, Bumby freed himself from the river water and floated into the air. Gently beating his fin, he drifted over to the bank and lowered his rear end like a boarding ramp. Fecklessly as children following the Pied Piper, the four travelers clambered aboard.

Bumby positioned himself above the slobber-tweet and descended. It took him nearly a minute to traverse what had seemed to be the last half meter. All the while they shrank. The anyfruit trees towered overhead like the now-extinct redwoods might once have done. Relative to the dwindling size of Bumby and his riders, the slobber-tweet became vast as Gov's puffball, its triangular door a mighty arch.

As soon as they pulled inside, the door hissed and closed up behind them. Frek repressed a brief twinge of fear, a sense of being trapped. The inside of the ship was, after all, quite lovely.

The air was filled with flying colored shapes like living, toony toys. A flock of yellow pyramids darted toward Bumby and his passengers, then veered aside to orbit them. Acid green hearts flew among the pyramids. The swoop of shapes felt like a greeting, and perhaps it was, for Bumby made the by-now-familiar *slobber-tweet* noise and then added in English, "Hello, Ulla! Meet my friends."

New clouds of bright forms came to swirl about them—cones and helices and saddle surfaces and cubes—four separate flocks, one to investigate each of Ulla's passengers. A few of the lavender saddle-shapes brushed against Frek, but their touch was insubstantial, little more than a feeling of changed temperature in the air.

Bumby steadily rippled his fin, propelling them toward the center.

Although from the outside, the starship appeared no larger than a dog, its inside was like the nave of one of those great stone churches Frek had visited on the history urls. A cathedral, with free-moving shards of stained-glass light.

Glancing past the lively forms to the curved walls, Frek observed a number of knobby little masts or antennae pointing inward. These spikes acted as fountains: They were bubbling over with bright blocks of color that flew into the air to join the others. Set in among the fountains were drains—whirlpools where the three-dimensional confetti spiraled back into the substance of the Ulla's walls.

The shapes began as simple compounds of angled faces, little more than square balloons. As they aged and moved about, they gained smoothness and complexity. Some of them looked biological, like pieces of plants and animals; others were harder-edged and with a curious dimensionality that made them seem constantly to be turning inside out.

"What are they?" Frek asked Bumby.

"They're what we call tweets," said Bumby, making half of the noise that he used for Ulla. "They're made of kenner, the stuff that your race calls dark matter. An Orpolese can do all sorts of things with kenner. And one thing is making tweets."

"What about the slobber?" asked Gibby, not missing a beat.

"You're not hearing me right," said Bumby in a curt tone. "I'm saying 'Ulla,' not 'slobber.' If her name were Susanna, I'd call her—" Bumby made a noise that sounded very much like the same old *slobber-tweet*.

Frek let it pass. Right now he was more interested in staring at the oddly patterned pale purple saddle-shape hovering near him. The design on it was like a sea of suns. Right about then the saddle flapped its lobes and flew right though Frek's head.

Though it didn't hurt, Frek shouted, and when he saw that his noise was driving the shapes away from him, he shouted some more. It wasn't nice, having all those googly tweets come at him, right after the thousand-meter daredevil-dive from the sky to the riverbank. Gibby began yelling along with Frek, and then they went ahead and sang a little bit of another Grulloo song that Gibby had taught him on the ride to Stun City.

> I'm a head with two arms,
> But my arms are my legs,
> And my head's where my butt should be.
> Folks treat me like dregs,
> But they don't know jack,
> 'Cause Grulloos live a life that's free.

> The hole where I live
> By the bank of a stream
> Is all mine with no ads bothering me.
> I'm out in the woods
> And off of the grid
> 'Cause Grulloos live a life that's free.

Frek had only learned these two verses, so they sang those through three or four times. When they were out of breath and couldn't bawl out the words anymore, Frek glanced down at Wow and Woo for comfort. The colors were reflecting off the dogs' eyes, but they didn't seem disturbed by the phantasmal shapes. The tweets had no smells attached, and the dogs didn't take them seriously. Wow and Woo looked up at him, each with a half-open mouth and a lolling tongue, quite at ease—even though a glowing orange shape like a skinny pointy pyramid stuck straight through Wow's head, and a pale blue cube protruded from the back of Woo's skull.

"Fella could just about lose his marbles in here, I reckon," said Gibby. His lizard tail was trembling. He was even more frightened than Frek. "I wish I hadn't of drunk so much moolk last night. Tell me you're seein' all this too, Frek. That orange arrowhead pokin' through your dog's head, I ain't dreamin' it, am I?"

"I see it," said Frek. "And that spring coming toward us, too." A shape like the wound-up tip of a vine tendril was bouncing across Bumby's back, with its free tip disappearing and reappearing as it moved. Taking a final off-kilter *boing*, it passed right through Gibby, then flew up toward one of the little tornadoes feeding into the walls.

"I feel like I'm goin' gollywog kac crazy," said Gibby staring after the green helix. "Didn't your overgrown squid friend say this trip wasn't gonna take no time a-tall?" He raised his voice querulously. "You hear me, Bumby?"

"If you lose your marbles, Ulla can round them up," said Bumby, not sounding very concerned. He made a little gesture with a twisting tentacle. "She's got photorealistic mental images of you four by now. Commemorative coins in the old memory bank. These tweets are how Ulla talks and finds things out, you understand. She puts out kenner that's lean and hungry for info exchange. Her tweets are words that listen."

"I'd say she talks too geevin' much," said Gibby. "Tell her to pipe down, would ya? She's makin' me sick."

"Ulla is divine," said Bumby. "She knows—ah, compared to Earthlings, you can flat-out say she knows everything. She's my wife, did I mention that before? Ulla and me." He'd stopped undulating his fin; they'd reached the center of his ship's interior.

"How can Ulla be your wife?" blurted Frek. "You two don't match at all."

This remark seemed to annoy Bumby very much. "You pipsqueaks got no inkling of my own true face," said the green cuttlefish in a snappish tone. "Nor any clue of Ulla's secret form, nor of how deeptwined a pair of soul-mates we are. You're a clod from a boondocks dirt world. You came aboard of your own free will, and we're going to wheel and deal you fair and square, but don't ever dream you're on some high horse to sling stones at the marriage of Ulla and Professor Bumby. And don't you be hinting that a pure rassen like her is all muddy and low for linking with a znag like me; I bet that's exactly what's in your monkey mind."

It was hard to grasp exactly what had set off Bumby like this. Evidently he wasn't going to act so nice anymore, now that he'd gotten them inside of Ulla. What kind of idea was it to let this eccentric cuttlefish's race have branecast access to the minds of humanity? A terrible idea, that's what.

Frek spoke up. "If you want to just put us back down on Earth and tell the branecasters to leave humanity alone, that would be—"

The alien gave his back an impatient twitch that sent them tumbling into the space near his body. But they didn't drift away. Some kind of gentle force field kept them near the center of Ulla. The bizarre shapes began congregating around them again, arcing inward along writhing paths. Gibby let out a despairing moan.

"Oh, maybe you better lay off trying to confab with them, Ulla," said Bumby, relenting a bit. "We don't want the passengers flipping their wigs. Better just mime the view. That's something their little minds can digest."

And instantly the walls of the slobber-tweet began to show the outer world. It wasn't like the walls had turned transparent, nor were the images like a wall skin's video. The pictures were coarse; they were made of tweets irregularly tiled upon the domed inner surfaces of the star craft. The tiles weren't in any kind of orderly grid; they arranged themselves so as best to fit the various parts of the image.

The sunlit overhanging branch of the anyfruit tree was represented, for instance, by a mounded ridge of granular tweets; the leaves of the tree were mimed by green tweets that twisted and turned in their own private dances, yet managed, as if by a serious of miraculous coincidences, to continually outline exactly the shapes of foliage upon a tree. For Ulla, imitating Earth's shapes was a trivial task, as easy as holding your hand in front of a light to make a duck-shaped shadow, and she was amusing herself by doing it in complicated ways.

The branches of the tree waved languidly in the breeze, seamlessly imaged by Ulla's hyperintelligent color shards.

Seeing the lush fruit on the trees, Frek wished he'd eaten some when he had the chance. He was very hungry. A little bird came flying right up to the outer surface of the walls, the bird's image as vast as a toon upon the electronic billboards of old Tokyo.

It was a watchbird.

"Look out, Bumby!" shouted Frek.

The anyfruit tree burst into flame. A blinding red beam swept toward the slobber-tweet. The sky-jelly had found them.

6

yunch!

Ulla made her outer surface like a mirror. She continued putting images of the world on her walls, but the colors grew fainter than before. Frek could make out the silhouette of the blasted anyfruit tree and the red glow of the laser beam rebounding into the sky. The Skywatch Mil sky-jelly could do the cunning Ulla no harm.

"Fall up now, Ulla," said Bumby in an unhurried tone. "Fall sky high into the Govs' jellyfish, yes. Follow that aggro red line."

Ulla answered with a flock of tweets; Bumby concluded the conversation with a gargle in his native tongue.

Then came a brief shuddery feeling, as if from an earthquake, with a blank instant at the center of the shake. The starship fell upward.

They were accelerating into the sky, repelled by the entire mass of planet Earth. Ulla had reversed the effects of gravity upon them.

Looking downward, Frek watched his homeland drop away. Stun City shrank to a spot beside the River Jaya. A few bends upstream lay Middleville. Frek strained to make out his home tree. As if reading his mind, Ulla briefly made that particular spot of green bigger, tweeting extra kenner to bulge Frek's part of Middleville into bold relief.

"Bye, Mom," said Frek softly. "I hope you're okay. Bye, Ida and Geneva. I'll be back soon." Wow nudged him with his nose, recognizing the familiar names. Frek ran his hands over the dog's smooth head, hoping everything would be okay. He wondered if, somewhere out in space, he might find his father.

"Wait for me, Salla," added Gibby, staring down at his patch of the Grulloo Woods. Ulla didn't bother to magnify the spot that Gibby was looking at. Frek was starting to notice that nobody ever liked Grulloos. That was all the more reason for him to be loyal to Gibby. He gave his little friend a pat on the shoulder, that is, he laid his hand upon the thick spot where the Grulloo's arm or leg came out of the side of his head.

Their upward motion continued apace. The countryside around Middleville and Stun City unfurled like a map, revealing the hamlets beyond the Grulloo Woods, the town behind Lookout Mountain, and the winding course of the River Jaya toward the sea.

Soon they'd risen high enough to see the wrinkled sea itself and, in the other direction, the inland mountains. They fell higher, faster. The sky above turned dark purple, then black. Finally Frek could see the actual curve of Mother Earth. Seeing it in person was different from hearing about it, different from seeing a picture on a wall skin.

An uneasy thought struck Frek. He wasn't truly seeing Earth from space, he was looking at shifting patterns of Ulla's tweets. Suppose Ulla was tricking him, kidding him along so he wouldn't realize, say, that this cavity was her stomach and that she was about to digest him!

Frek pushed the fear away. Far better to believe that he was the size of beetle, at the center of an antigravity pumpkin falling into the sky. Godzoon googly indeed.

"There's the killer jellyfish," said Bumby. "Twelve o'clock high. Try to splatter it, Ulla." A fresh shoal of tweets came spiraling down from Ulla's fountains, the bright shapes passing through Bumby and back out to the wall.

Peering up at Ulla's shiny dome, Frek could make out the sketchy form of a sky-jelly overhead. The creature had long since abandoned its fruitless attempts to blast Ulla with its laser ray; its energies were now focused upon lumbering out of the way. The jelly was pulsing and twitching, sending waves racing across its great unclean body. With so little air up here for its bell to beat against, the monster was making scant progress.

But just before Ulla would have smashed into it, the jelly spat a house-tree–sized gout of wobbly goo to its right, propelling its main body to safety on the left. They fell up past it, missing the unsavory behemoth.

Bumby wetly warbled a command to Ulla, then turned to Frek and Gibby. "She'll open the door so I can shoot the jelly, and while I'm on the job, I'll scour away the rest of your world's so-called defense systems. The jellies defend the Govs only against their enslaved citizenry, against you and your people."

"Fry the jellies!" exclaimed Gibby. "Yee haw!"

An equilateral triangle opened in Ulla's lower side, a twin to the old door on top. Ulla's subtle force fields were able to keep their air from rushing out, but the resulting turbulence buffeted Frek, Gibby, and the dogs from side to side. Woo began barking. Meanwhile Bumby had propelled himself to the doorway.

The sky-jelly was very clearly visible below them. Blandly, unthinkingly aggressive, the floundering jelly was turning over so as to shoot its laser at Ulla's underside. If Frek still had any doubts about the reality of this trip, they were gone now. Earth hung below them, crystal clear, unimaginably huge, a vision of beauty blemished only by the ragged, evil disk of the Skywatch Mil jelly.

The jelly's flesh glowed white at the center, as the monster prepared to lance a fresh laser beam their way. With the door wide open, Ulla wouldn't be able to protect them. Holding onto the doorsill with two of his arms, Bumby stretched out his two long tentacles and his other arms. Was his strength equal to this task?

Ulla sent an excited avalanche of tweets down upon Bumby. Wifely advice. Bumby's arms and tentacles began to shine and grow. The tentacles became ropes of fire, ten kilometers long. And at their touch the sky-jelly became a cloud of steam and ash.

Bumby wasn't finished. Though Ulla was racing into the heavens at an even greater rate than before, his tentacles were lengthening faster still, growing to magic beanstalk lengths and branching all the while. The filigreed tentacles grew to hundreds of kilometers long, then to thousands and tens of thousands of kilometers in reach. It was hard to fully process the sight. Earth's entire upper atmosphere was covered with the glowing mesh of Bumby's branching tentacles. The space cuttlefish held the entire planet in his grasp.

"He zapped another," exclaimed Gibby, peering out into the distance with squinted eyes. "And another. Poof! Another and another!"

Frek couldn't make out the explosions, but he took Gibby's word for it. And then Professor Bumby was done. His ramified arms and tentacles shrank back to normal, and Ulla's door slid shut.

The alien cuttlefish had killed off every one of the Gov's sky-jellies. The people of Earth were free of the constant threat of being laser-blasted from the sky. That was the good news. The bad news was that Earth now lay quite open to invaders from space. But when, in the entire history of humanity, had the sky-jellies actually stopped a single invader? They'd killed, rumor had it, any number of insurgent citizens; they were good at that. Yet when it had come time for the jellies to truly defend Earth against aliens, the "Anvil" had come and gone without a scratch.

"That felt good," said Bumby.

"I can't believe you made yourself so big," said Frek.

"Comes natural to me," said Bumby. "Back home, Ulla and I are a thousand kilometers long. When we yunched down to Earth, we overdid it enough to scrunch down to your size. Like you turning into a paramecium, you might say."

"What kind of world do you come from?" asked Frek, trying to imagine a sea large enough for thousand-kilometer cuttlefish.

"You'll see soon enough," said Bumby.

The view on Ulla's inner surfaces was bright and crisp again. Earth shrank to a very clearly defined ball: alive, vibrant, divine. The pocked Moon went flying past them; they sailed into the gulf between Earth and Mars.

Frek was bursting with more questions for Bumby, but he was a little leery of again being called an "ignorant boy from a boondocks dirt world."

Fortunately Gibby was there to speak up.

"You got some kinda hyperdrive on tap or what?" asked the Grulloo. "Sure we're truckin' along right smart, but this ain't gonna get us to no galactic center."

"*Festina lente,*" said Bumby in a calm tone. "Means hurry slowly. Ulla will yunch us soon."

"Yunch?" asked Gibby.

"She winds up our component strings to make us the size of the galaxy," said Bumby, curling his tentacles and puffing up his body. "Then we take a seven-league step to the center, Ulla unyunches us and forsooth! Behold! We're in Orpoly, back to our own right size. Yunch, unyunch, plop."

"Oh, of course," said Gibby sarcastically. "Anybody would o' thought of that."

"We have to get to a nice clear spot before we yunch," added Bumby. "If you yunch or unyunch near too much mass-energy, then you might pooperoo into the Planck brane. Entering the Planck brane through a branelink is one thing, the branecasters don't mind that, it's a business call, welcome and how do you do. But if you drop in on account of you goofballed a yunch trip, especially while they're having lunch, well, they're roaring demons then, they're cruel and vengeful, they deal you a living death, and I don't meant that as a metaphor, boys, it's precisely and literally like being dead without being destroyed. Decoherence is what it's called. Strains the brain, eh, Gibby? *Festina lente.* Do you know Latin?"

"What's Latin?" muttered Gibby in a confused, resentful tone.

"Maybe it's what they talk on Orpoly," suggested Frek, trying to get in on the conversation. Wow glanced up at him, happy to hear his voice.

"Wrong and wrong," said Bumby. "I'm starting to have the odd wee doubt about you, Frek. If the choice of an Earth's hero had been up to yours truly, I don't know as I would have picked a twelve-year-old small-town boy. But we had a strategic reason to pop your name from the hat. I'm talking about your father."

Frek felt his stomach drop. "What do you know about him?"

"He was living with some others in a hollowed-out asteroid, yes? They call themselves Crufters, and they brag on avoiding biotech. Ulla and I caught their act on our way in. We'd unyunched ourselves into the far-flung vacuum outside your planetary system. Why so? I could talk all day! Snap my suspenders around the cherry-red stove. Wal, the point is, the more highly evolved solar systems have webs of force-field tubes connecting their worlds, which means that their interplanetary spreads aren't really empty. If you unyunch near one of those tubes you can't stop when you should. You keep on shrinking, help, help, help, and then our plain brane pinches you off and drops you down into the Planck brane, and you're in Dutch or lowlander than that with the branecasters. We played it all cautious and egg-walking because we didn't realize how bush-league your civilization is."

They were sailing smoothly through space. Every one of Bumby's arms was moving about, each one illustrating some arcane subtlety of his discourse, perhaps for the benefit of Ulla's attentive tweets. Frek held his breath, waiting for the news about his father. "And the motion on the galactic table is that we've found solid branecast talent in your very home-sweet-home solar system," continued Bumby unconcernedly. "Suffering struggling humanity, yes indeed, information-processing self-reproducing symbol-using communicating beings, very tasty. But, tsk, your levels are crude. No yunching, no force fields, no kenny crafting. Aside from a few barely eking space colonies, there's nothing happening on your outer planets, nary a peep on your moons, and only the dullest of spheromak loops inside your sun. And to top it off you've collapsed your biome! Blind, lost, benighted, tragically fumbling screwballs. I see great doomed, primitive nobility here. The branecast ratings could blast the roof. And your appearance and customs are wigsville, man, absolute maximum in alien oddness. So I'm here to pound the drum and shout that we Orpolese are the best independent branecast production group that—"

The maddening thing about listening to all this rigmarole was that Frek could feel the golden glow again. Some alien was tuning in on him sitting here listening to Bumby's mumbo-jumbo, possibly relishing his anxiety about his father. Maybe the watcher was Bumby himself. "Tell me about Dad!" cried Frek, actually reaching out and giving one of Bumby's writhing arms a yank. Though the tapering, leathery shape slipped quickly from Frek's grasp, the gesture got the cuttlefish's attention. At the same time, Frek clenched his mind in an effort to force the invisible watchers out.

"Well, the Crufters weren't all open arms," said Bumby. "They'd already slogged through some caustic psychodrama with the Unipuskers. Did I mention that a couple of Unipusker producers got here before us? Old rivals of ours. Hawb and Cawmb. We tracked their progress, sly sniffers that we are. The Unipuskers came in skittish same as us, a couple of weeks previous. They unyunched outside of your system and visited the same First Chance Asteroid as us. Being Hawb and Cawmb, they used up the good will, acted like ugly spooky saucerians, left a miasma of hard feelings. Unipuskers are scaly two-leggers with big clamshells for their heads. Monoculture missionaries. Yeah, when we showed up after Hawb and Cawmb, the Crufters actually shot off some kind of catapult at us."

"What happened to Dad?" demanded Frek, his voice rising. "What did the Unipuskers do to my father?"

Bumby paused. Frek, Gibby, and the dogs were floating in front of Bumby's twisty mass of arms. The dogs weren't paying attention to the conversation, they were sniffing and licking each other, now and then batting each other about with their paws. Gibby was temporarily absorbed in loading and lighting his pipe, unconcerned about polluting their ship with smoke. Meanwhile Ulla was winging a steady stream of multicolored disks their way to keep abreast of the conversation, with some of the disks passing through their heads. Ulla's walls continued to faithfully represent the space outside, black and empty, with the Moon and Earth shrunken to little disks, and the Sun still too bright to look at. Waiting for Bumby's answer it occurred again to Frek that he was very hungry.

"Those two Unipusker producers snatched your father in their UFO," said Bumby finally. "Hawb and Cawmb. Well, either they snatched him or they got him to volunteer. Space cadet number one. They no doubt promised some kind of reward to him or to his woman friend. Yessica Sunshine. But of course it wouldn't have been a restorative Gaia-healing genomic elixir like we promised you. Hawb and Cawmb's empty bivalve heads don't know from diversity. Those Unipuskers, get this, they've whittled their biome down to three, I said three, species: a plant called rickrack, an animal called a vig, and the pullulating 'Puskers themselves. All the same. Not like

Orpolese at all. Yes, they took your father." Bumby gazed mildly at Frek, blinking his big, W-pupil eyes.

"What about us?" put in Gibby, exhaling a curling cloud of blue smoke. "Sure you're promising us an elixir, but what good's a promise from a face full o' slimy grabbin' arms? And I don't get the point of this branecast stuff you keep talkin' about, Bumby."

"Don't butt in," snapped Frek. Then he caught himself and softened his words. "I'm sorry, Gibby, but I need to hear more about my father."

"There's not much more to tell," said Bumby, making a blooming, expansive gesture with his sucker arms. A cuttlefish shrug. "As for Gibby's last question—a rich vein of info there. The branecasters have you on open access to attract a production deal, sure as death and Texas. Branecast producers like Ulla and me—or like Hawb and Cawmb—the way we wangle the branecast rights for a newly contacted race is to get a representative of the talent race to register in person with the branecasters. To keep things simple, the branecasters fixate on the first representative they meet; they give them full negotiation rights for their whole race. Can you relate? That's what Ulla and I have pegged you for, Frek, the human race representative for our branecasting deal. You're the man, Frek, with Gibby as backup, assuming you can call him human, too. With any luck, you'll yak with the branecasters before your father does, and you can register Ulla and me as humanity's branecast producers with, *harrumph*, exclusive distribution to the Orpolese consumers. Yes indeed. So shoulder the load, face your fate, and pick the best producer with the wiggiest audience. An Ulla-Bumby production exclusively for the Orpolese. It's a race for the deal. And your father, he's the representative for the Unipuskers. Him and that woman and her daughter—a girl about your age called, um—what was her name, Ulla?"

A shape like a drum drifted down from Ulla's wall. "Renata," said Bumby as soon as he'd reached out a tentacle to touch the drum.

Though Frek didn't think he'd ever heard the name before, it had a familiar feel to it. Like something he might have heard in a dream. He repeated the name to himself. An image of a girl popped into his mind: a pleasant-faced girl his age with pigtails. It was a little sad to think of Carb having a whole new family. A tweet drifted through his head.

"I savor the pang of the father-son bond," said Bumby as if reading his mind. "It's fresh. We have a different parent-child pattern on Orpoly. We're cloners. It's easy enough to divide off a new one, eh? Could your parent-child emotions run so high precisely because you're *not* identical?"

"Don't ride him, you slimy squid," said Gibby. "You kidnapped Frek because the other guys took his Dad? Tell the dang story and don't beat around no bush."

Bumby primly bunched together his arms and tentacles, collecting his thoughts. The tentacles had a cute clockwise twist like a cowlick, or like the top of a soft ice-cream cone. "When Ulla tweeted the Crufters, we found out about the Unipusker producers taking Carb Huggins. So, yes, Ulla and I integrated the inputs and hatched the plan of snatching Carb's son, Frek. If you get a father's son, you've got psychic judo. But somehow it must have been that the Unipuskers found a way to tip off the Gov worm about our plan, because, as we noticed, the counselors were after us as soon as we got to your house, Frek. And Ulla and I were still too bone-weary from the big yunch to fend them off."

"The flying saucer that came when you landed, that was the Unipuskers?" asked Frek.

"Must have been," said Bumby. "I was surprised they got it together so fast. But all's well that ends. Ulla and I are hale and hearty now. We're scheme-dreaming that maybe Frek will talk some sense to good old Dad." Bumby thinned one of his arm tips down to the size of a worm and tapped Frek's ring with it. Frek yanked his hand out of the cuttlefish's reach.

"Oh, Ulla and I know your father has a ring like this," said Bumby in a smug tone. "We know all your secrets. And we know what these rings are for. They're connected by a higher dimensional tunnel. We godlike aliens use them to communicate. At any rate, the Unipusker scout ship took your father and Renata and Renata's mother, I think I mentioned her? A person named Yessica Sunshine. Took them all to Unipusk, which is an Earthlike moon circling a gas giant called Jumm. Welcome to the *Strangers in Unipusk* show!"

"Will it be safe for Dad on Unipusk?" wondered Frek.

"Any place is safe as houses if you're with Orpolese," said Bumby, not quite answering Frek's question. "What your race grovels to as the Laws of Physics—well, for us, those so-called rules are local ordinances, and the fat cop is asleep. Don't litter, keep off the grass, no spitting—ha!"

Professor Bumby stopped talking and carried out a rapid sequence of miraculous transformations. He tripled his tentacle count, turned inside out, transmuted his flesh into something very like chrome metal, shrank to the size of a thumb, burst into flame, and then grew a fresh green cuttlefish body from the thick smoke. "We advanced beings can keep you Earthlings alive just about anywhere," said the reconstituted Bumby.

Frek didn't say anything. It sounded like Carb was okay for now. He started thinking about the golden glow again. He was being esped almost continuously. Again he struggled and failed to drive the intruders from his mind.

"Don't tense up, it ruins the empathy," said Bumby in a low tone. "And, yes, we're taping you. Ulla's got a flickerball inside her. I'll get out of your way and let you have some lunch." Bumby rippled his fin, flying out to fasten himself to a spot on Ulla's ceiling.

A flurry of bird-shaped tweets swooped down from Ulla's walls. The shapes circled tantalizingly close to the dogs, causing them to snap and bark. The tweet birds slowed down and drew closer. Wow finally caught hold of one, and then Woo had one too. At the dogs' touch, the tweets changed form. They looked and smelled like pieces of anymeat. Apparently the Orpolese had the power to transform invisible dark matter first into tweet and then into solid, familiar food.

"You really think they watchin' us?" Gibby was murmuring. "All kinds o' weird lobsters and slugs lookin' at us right now from other planets?" Either the vast alien branecast audience out there wasn't interested in Gibby—or the Grulloo was too coarse-natured to sense the watchers within his mind.

Frek's sense of a golden glow was, if anything, getting stronger all the time. Bumby might not be the only one watching Frek. Creatures could be tuning in on him from all over the galaxy and, who knew, from other galaxies as well. Frek imagined the numbers spinning on a popular url's hit-counter. The Frek site.

"Gundo goggy," said Frek, distancing his faint sense of panic by acting gaud. "Way shecked-out." It would be better, really, not to think about the branecast at all.

So he caught hold of one of the edible tweet birds, a nicely browned slab of white anymeat with a pair of grobread wings. Given that there might be an endless number of branecast viewers watching him, he did the generous thing and handed the tweet off to Gibby, who hadn't yet managed to grab one. And then he snagged another for himself and bit in.

It was delicious.

Frek, Gibby, and the dogs ate in reverent silence. And then, just as Frek's throat grew dry, some big, jiggling drops of water came floating by. The round globules had force-fields around them, like nets. They tingled a bit to the touch. Frek held one of the charged balls near his face and pursed out his lips to sip at it. The water was cool and clear and fresh. Gibby followed his example, and then Frek held some water balls steady for the dogs.

To top the meal off, a few nuggets of stim cells drifted to a rest right in front of Gibby's nose. "Lookin' real good, Bumby," said Gibby, and chomped down his medicine.

For a few minutes the four travelers simply floated there, savoring the energy filling their frames, admiring the awesome orb of space on Ulla's walls, velvet black and besprent with stars.

"Can you believe we're out here?" Frek asked Gibby, finally beginning to enjoy the trip. "Look how small Earth is."

But knowing that he was on live branecast made everything he said sound a little staged and false. Rather than talking any more, Frek held his hand out at arm's length. He could easily cover Earth's disk with the tip of his little finger. He nudged Gibby, pointing this out. Gibby held out his arm as well, testing the same thing.

Wow and Woo made running motions in the air, trying to come over to sniff at Frek and Gibby's outstretched hands. One of Wow's legs caught against Woo's side, sending her spinning toward a wall. The collision sent Wow flopping into Frek. Frek cradled his dog,

savoring his old pal's furry feel. Woo bounced and came slowly drifting back toward them, yapping all the while. Dogs much preferred
barking to human speech.

"Wonder what that squid's got planned next," muttered Gibby,
rolling his eyes toward the spot overhead where Bumby had fastened
himself.

"I guess we're gonna yunch soon," said Frek, and gave a reckless
giggle. He was so excited that he was feeling giddy. "Lunch and
yunch!"

"I don't like the sound of that yunching," said Gibby uneasily.
Some little scraps of tweet were moving among them. Whether by esp
or by tweet, everything they said was overheard.

"Yunching likes *you,* Gibby," called Bumby from on high, using a
soothing tone tinged with mockery. "Don't be flummoxed, little
freak. Yunching is how we jump far. Your so-called elementary particles are wound-up strings of space, knots of nothing. No matter,
don't worry, nothing's the matter. String-wise, there's a trade-off, a
duality of winding versus scale. Let's make it butt simple. If you wrap
your strings tight, your size is huge. If you wrap your strings loose,
your size is small. When it's yunch time, which will be in, oh my, fifteen seconds or so, Ulla and I will wind all of our strings so tight that
we're a third the size of the galaxy. Then we'll fly till we're spang centered on Orpoly. At our yunched-up size scale, moving across the
galaxy will be easy. And then we unwind our strings. Yunch, scoot
over, unyunch and fall into cozy, bustling Orpoly. We'll reach maximum expansion at chime five, and we'll be back to normal at chime
ten. It'll go off slick and painless if you characters relax and ride
along. And that's all I need to say. Toodle-oo!"

"No!" screamed Gibby. "Don't!"

Bumby remained silent for a long moment. Gibby yelled again.

"Listen here, Earthlings," snapped Bumby, "Don't fight it. Once
we start yunching, we're synched together, closer than close, like
peanut butter and jelly. If one of you even *thinks* about holding back
you can throw the whole thing out of kilter. You can make us unyunch too soon. And that's a doubleplusungood no-no. Understand,
Gibby?"

A spark crackled viciously through the air, and the Grulloo let out a yelp.

"Understand?" repeated Bumby.

"Understand," muttered Gibby, rubbing a spot on the side of his tail.

"Yunch!" said Bumby.

A clear, musical tone filled the air. *Chime one.*

Ulla and Bumby began to glow. Ulla's walls grew opaque and turned a deep shade of purple. Bumby's green, writhing arms fanned out across the spherical inner surface of Ulla, branching and forking as when he'd attacked the sky-jellies before. But this time the substance of Bumby's body was melting out into his arms. In a matter of moments nothing remained of the cuttlefish but a livid tracery of green veins embossed upon Ulla's dark lavender walls.

Wow had twisted loose from Frek; he and Woo were barking frantically. Gibby was shouting for help. A golden note reverberated from the flesh of Ulla/Bumby. *Chime two.*

Some objects drifted down from the green-veined purple walls, coming at them from every direction. The shapes were glassy, curved planes, shaped a bit like troughs and bowls. Two of them converged on Frek's left leg, crystalline half-cylinders. He tried to move his leg out of the way, but then the troughs had clamped onto him, garbing his leg in a transparent, close-fitting tube. This stuff may have been made of kenner, but it had more solidity to it than the tweets. Pieces were converging on his arms, his other leg, his body and even his head. Looking over at the bellowing Gibby, Frek saw the same thing happening to the dogs and the Grulloo. Ulla and Bumby were covering them with a kind of armor that fit together to make spacesuits.

In less than a minute, the four of them were dressed in Orpolese-crafted kenner. Frek reached out to touch Gibby's lizard tail. Through the armor he could feel the shape of the tail and the scales of Gibby's skin, but even so, he had a sense of not quite touching his friend. As if thin transparent membranes lay between them.

And what about air? Somehow there seemed to be plenty of it inside Frek's spacesuit. It was very fortunate to have this armor and its air supply—because right about then two great holes opened up in

Ulla's body where the top and bottom doors had been, and this time the ship's air rushed out in a *whoosh,* leaving a brief sparkling of ice crystals.

The sharp, lancing pinpoints of the stars were visible amid the growing disks of black above and below. Larger and larger grew the holes, until finally Ulla was but a belt girdled around them, a hoop of deep purple with Bumby's green ridges twisted upon her like a vine.

So there they were, Frek, Gibby, and the dogs free floating in empty space, circled by the braided wreath of Ulla/Bumby. It was hard for Frek not to have the feeling that he was falling. And he wasn't the only one. Thanks to yet another feat of Orpolese reality-hacking, his transparent spacesuit was transmitting the voices of his companions.

"Fall," whined Wow, fruitlessly churning his legs. "Frek hold me." But he was well out of reach.

"In case we're about to die, you've been a good friend, Frek," said Gibby. "Tell Salla I love her."

"Far," said Woo. "Woo too far."

"We're safe in this armor," said Frek, sounding calmer than he felt. "I think we'll be okay."

"Are we yunching yet?" wondered Gibby.

The armor rang like a bell. *Chime three.*

The yunch trip began with a dropping sensation in the pit of Frek's stomach, a feeling like he was in a rocket rushing upward very fast. The Sun seemed to be getting closer. He was growing.

A side effect of their growth was that their bodies quickly began to overlap. They'd started out only a few meters apart from each other, and they weren't moving apart as they grew. This meant that they were soon layered upon each other; their particles were shuffled together like decks of cards. But their interpenetrating bodies could move independently from each other.

Their growth was a bit ragged and irregular, that is, the sizes of Frek's companions seemed to vary as their individual growth rates lagged behind or pulled ahead of each other. One instant Gibby was the size of a please plant seed soldier in Frek's pocket, a moment later Gibby engulfed Frek like an ogre in a toon. The Ulla/Bumby hoop shrank to a tight belt around Frek's waist, then wobbled out like a vast auditorium. One moment Wow and Woo were a matched pair of toy magnet dogs, the next moment Wow was an elephruk with Woo a watchbird hovering about their common center. Even the pieces of Frek's body were phasing in and out of scale with each other.

Frek's clothes and other possessions grew along with him, including his ring and his fungus-purse with the Aaron's Rod twig and the two remaining doses of chameleon mod.

As soon as the yunch began, the ring started tingling, buzzing at him for attention. He held it up to his eyes to study it. The red light in the cup was twinkling in a way he'd never seen before. A cloud of red flecks appeared in the air above it, and then yellow seeped into the red. The red-yellow haze spread out into a pattern of spikes and a pink form appeared in the middle—the face of a girl? But then the shape was gone. The others seemed not to notice.

Gibby's excited hooting brought Frek's attention back to his surroundings. "I ain't small no more!" crowed the Grulloo, surrounding Frek like a kind of fog.

Frek had been missing the forest for the trees. They'd reached an astronomical size. Their overlapping bodies stretched as far as the Earth. Frek was perhaps a billion times as big as he'd been when he started.

Gibby pointed excitedly to little Earth, twisting himself around to get a better look. And then, to Frek's horror, the amped-up Grulloo's tail dealt Gaia a whack. Even though Frek himself felt Gibby's motions through his body as but a faint breeze, he half expected to see his home world go sailing off like a badminton shuttlecock. But Gibby's tail passed through Earth with no visible effect. They'd yunched up to a size where their heavily-wound component strings had no discernible interactions with the loosely-wound strings of ordinary matter, and very little interaction with each other.

Curling himself into a ball, Frek brought his face right up to his home world. It was a sweet little marble, blue and patterned with white clouds. Frek had a brief, horrifying thought of some sheckedout yuncher plucking his planet like a berry, shaking off her ice caps, and sinking his teeth through her crust and into her hot, liquid core.

How small and vulnerable she looked. It made Frek proud to think that he was setting off to find an elixir for her.

Briefly he wondered if the Earthlings could see him in their night sky. Probably not. Nobody had noticed when Bumby and Ulla unyunched into the outreaches of the solar system. Given that Frek himself was seeing Earth, that meant tight-wound matter could see loose-wound matter. But probably it didn't work the other way around. Frek could have tried asking Bumby, but he had the feeling that for the duration of the yunch trip, the Orpolese were not to be disturbed.

Frek's thoughts were interrupted by the sound of a gong that seemed to fill the expanses of planetary space. *Chime four.*

Now things really took off, with the expansion proceeding at a superexponential rate. The Sun dwindled to a point as dozens, scores, hundreds of neighboring stars moved into view.

Frek, Ulla/Bumby, Gibby, and the dogs were expanding together as one, only occasionally getting out of synch enough for one of them to seem a bit too big or too small. The flesh of Ulla/Bumby was rolling over and over within itself, like the smoke in a smoke-ring. Frek felt the steady motion as a churning of his own flesh.

An avid whine filled Frek's body, as if his own particles were circling too, as if his body were the fuel for a starry dynamo of night.

What was that Bumby had said? "Yunching likes *you*."

Slowly the great wheel of the galaxy came into view around them. They were as a group of swimmers, raising their heads from the surface of a glowing pond.

"We're clouds of dust," Gibby fretted. "How we gonna make it back?"

Frek looked at his hands. Sparks of starlight were visible between his spaced-out particles. He felt overextended, fragile. Still his body grew. Bumby had said they'd expand till they were a third the size of the galaxy. They were out near the edge of the star-puddle. Orpoly was in the galactic disk's central bulge.

Frek's ring buzzed, again sending out a ball of red and yellow spikes with something in the middle. This time he could see the image quite clearly. A girl with two braided pigtails was tentatively smiling at him, leaning toward him as if she were hovering over a lens. The light around her was greenish. She was wearing a pale blue jersey. She looked sweet and friendly. She was saying something, the sound lost in the whining of the yunch. But Frek could read her lips.

"Help," she was saying. "Please help me."

The others seemed not to notice her. She was only visible to the wearer of the ring. The girl was gesturing for Frek to look at something; she was pointing off into the Milky Way pinwheel of stars. With her head turned slightly away from him, Frek could see the lovely gentle curve of her features: a high round forehead, a smooth firm cheek, a perfect arc of chin. She was the prettiest girl he'd ever seen.

She turned back to gaze at him again, her eyes wide and pleading.

"Help," she said once again, and now he could faintly hear her. "Please help me."

Could this be the Renata who'd been abducted by the Unipuskers along with Carb and that Yessica Sunshine? But why was the ring showing the girl instead of showing Frek's father?

Frek's armor sent an echoing sound into his ears. *Chime five.*

The whining in Frek's body was damping down; they were rising above the galaxy at a decelerating rate. And then the upward yunch had ended. A moment of cosmic silence spread across the galactic pool of stars. All was still, so very still.

The band of Ulla/Bumby caught hold of their particles with a gentle force field, and began slowly, slowly moving them across the galaxy as one being. In toward the galactic core.

All the while, the ring was sending pricks of pain into his finger. Certain positions of Frek's arms and body made the ring hurt less, others made it hurt more. Much as Frek was attracted to the girl, he slapped at the ring, wishing she'd go away. This was no time to make complications!

Frek was half tempted to remove the ring and hurl it into the intergalactic void. But his ring was the mate to Dad's ring. He had to hang on to it.

He found that if he kept his hand pointed toward a particular location halfway in toward the galactic core, the ring would let him alone. And then he was able to tear his attention away from the sweet, pleading girl and look at the wonders spread before him.

Gazing across the surface of the galaxy, Frek noticed a kind of shimmer along the far edge. With a bit of effort he brought it into focus. It was a huge, translucent thing with claws, creeping along the rim. Another yuncher. And there, off to its right, three purple worms came yunching up, layered onto each other like a multiheaded hydra. They seemed to be in a hurry. In a matter of seconds, they'd wriggled across the galactic disk and unyunched back down.

Now that he had the knack, Frek began to see yuncher after yuncher boiling up, crawling about, simmering back down. A few of them expanded on past him, growing toward the distant dots of lights that were the other galaxies. It was fascinating to be up at this level. Frek noticed that when yunchers got appreciably bigger than him, he couldn't see them anymore.

The troublesome ring sent a fresh pain up Frek's arm, demanding his full attention. Frek frowned at his hand. His finger was pointing toward his stomach. The girl in the spiky aura was wearing an expectant expression. Frek guessed that Ulla/Bumby's slow progress had brought them to a point where they were roughly centered upon the world the ring was making him point at. Probably the world the girl was on. He overhead the faint sound of a man talking. The girl looked away from Frek, and then the perspective in the spiky ball shifted to show—Frek's father.

Carb had his same old Mohawk hairdo, with the slowly shifting tattoo molds embedded in the bare regions of his scalp. His face was hard and craggy as ever. A rope was tied around Carb's neck. He had a bruise on one cheek and a bloody split lip. He could see Frek, Frek was sure of it, for when their eyes met, Carb formed his lips into a small, pained smile and silently shrugged his shoulders, as if to apologize for being such a screwup. An alien figure stood behind Carb, a creature with muddy-looking body, approximately humanoid, but with a stubby tail and a head like a clamshell resting flat on his shoulders. This must be one of the Unipusker producers that Bumby had talked about.

The creature tightened the rope around Dad's neck, and he winced. Frek had to do something.

He stared down into the sea of stars within his body, straining to pick out the exact dot he was pointing to. He felt certain that their current position matched that of the world that held his father captive. They had to unyunch to save Dad and the sweet-faced girl. Right now.

But how could Frek initiate the downward yunch? Even as he thought the question to himself, something within him answered that he knew. It had to do with the spinning feeling that he'd felt within the particles of his flesh on the way up. Frek could initiate the opposite motion. He could wish for them to shrink.

He put his whole soul into the wish. For a moment he could sense Bumby and Ulla's minds fighting his; he could feel the galactic wisdom of the Orpolese aliens pitted against his own small experience. Frek redoubled his effort, visualizing the familiar, unhappy face of his father.

"We're coming, Dad," he whispered. "We're coming to save you."

Frek felt within himself for the spot that held his father. He found it, locked their overlapping bodies onto it, and willed them to unyunch toward it. The faintest of whining, spinning sounds began. Bumby and Ulla sent out another push of their own willpower, trying to block the premature downward yunch. But Frek was stronger. The song of the downward yunch rose.

One more time Bumby fought him, once again Frek won. They shrank. Ulla/Bumby, Frek, Gibby, and the dogs—they were deflating. Frek had a clear sense of his particles spinning and singing. Spinning differently from before.

Bumby began calling out a phrase in the Orpolese tongue. Though filled with urgency, his voice remained level and clear. Over and over he said it.

"*Alilallah tekelili eheu uborka Orpoly.*"

Perhaps it was an SOS signal, a call for help.

Meanwhile the dogs were howling in fear. The spiky aura with its images of Dad and the girl had disappeared.

"What in tarnation did you do, Frek?" yelled Gibby. "We're gonna come down wrong and rile the branecasters!"

"I saw a girl," said Frek. "And my father. We have to help them."

The stars were rushing past them like the falling blossom petals of an anyfruit tree. Great, warped clouds of bright gas flew by on either side.

The purple and green hoop of Ulla/Bumby jostled from side to side, trying to control the collapse. They were congealing right into the plane of a planetary system that had two stars at its center, a dozen gas giant planets, and a remarkable network of bright lines connecting the planets and their moons.

The nearest moon was bluish white, and with a bright tube connecting it to the most overwhelming part of the view, an enormous pink and yellow gas giant planet. They were close enough to the giant that it seemed more like a plane than like a sphere. It ran from horizon to horizon. And they were falling toward it.

"Frek," came Bumby's quiet voice. "The big planet is Jumm. And Unipusk is the Earthlike moon up above. The one with the transport tube. There's too much mass-energy here, Frek. We've landed very badly. We're going to break through to the Planck brane. The branecasters will decohere us." He'd all but dropped the poetic elaborations from his speech.

"Living death," cried Gibby. "You said it's a living death."

"Yes," said Bumby, and paused for a long time. They were shrinking at a steady rate. The binary suns of the system were two bright disks far off to one side, and in the other direction hung the intimidating Jumm. A side-effect of their shrinking was that both the suns and the planet seemed to be moving away from them. But the transport tube from Jumm to Unipusk lay quite nearby, and, if anything, it seemed to be getting closer. Suddenly a messy flare sputtered toward them from the tube.

"They'll turn Ulla and me into things," said Bumby finally. "Zombies. But they'll probably let you four go. Especially if you give them a little chunk of matter to chew on. You're not Orpolese, not a professor of any kind, and they won't view you as the responsible yunchers. They'll yell at you and try to trick you. Keep your head." Bumby sighed and spoke again, his voice very low. "Frek, I want you to do one thing for me. Tell the branecasters your race wants Ulla and me to produce your branecast channel. Pick us even though they've decohered us. Frek, if you do that, then Ulla and I—we'll have a chance. Once the other Orpolese learn that we're humanity's producers, they'll come and bail us out."

"Damn, but he's layin' it on thick," exclaimed Gibby. "Let me break out my cryin' towel."

"Open your pinched heart, you pawky elephruker," said Bumby without raising his voice. "Listen to me, Frek. The Unipuskers lured you here. Until someone bails out Ulla and me, we'll be suffering the torments of the damned. This wouldn't have happened if it weren't for you. You owe us. Don't let us suffer in vain. Don't let the Unipuskers win. Wait for an Orpolese rescue party. Eventually they'll come."

A spiraling line of energy led to them from the nearby transport tube, branching in five to wreathe each of them with a faint glow of white light. The energy leakage was making it impossible for the Ulla/Bumby to halt their unyunching. By now they'd shrunk back to their starting size—Frek could tell because their bodies were no longer layered onto each other. They were separate. As the shrinking continued, they drew steadily farther apart. If you were the size of a dust mote, a meter's separation looked very big.

"Will our spacesuits keep protecting us?" called Frek. He felt selfish to be asking this just now, but he urgently wanted to know.

"These spacesuits can do anything you need," said Bumby distractedly, his voice seeming to come from an ever greater distance. "You only have to ask."

Frek was shrinking at a radically accelerating rate and dwindling, he imagined, to the size of a cell, a molecule, an atom, an electron, and beyond. The planets and suns of the Unipuskers' system had long since shot off into the distance. Frek's companions were out of sight as well. He could see nothing but a single writhing tendril of light from the impossibly distant transport tube.

And then Frek's world collapsed to a point.

At the ultimate moment, Bumby, Ulla, Gibby, and the dogs slapped back into him. All were merged into a single infinitesimal body the size of a dot.

Which exploded into the Planck brane.

It looked like a painting over there, with everything in bright, strange perspectives. Beneath a pearly gray sky were mountains, rolling hills, plowed fields, orchards, and on the horizon a city. Frek and the others had landed on the side of an improbably steep hill painted in rainy-day shades of green, a toony hill with star-shaped white splotches for flowers.

Frek no longer had the sensation of being watched by aliens across the galaxy. He was in the land of the branecasters themselves, off stage, behind the scenery.

The images here had a way of changing in size. That is, whenever Frek focused on something it got bigger. It was like in a dream, or perhaps more to the point, like a toon site with pzoom.

Bumby was a cuttlefish again, and Ulla a lumpy ball. They were screaming in horror, tormented by a swarm of small shapes with buzzing wings. Thanks to the rapidly reacting pzoom, Frek caught a close-up of one of attackers. It was an ugly little beast, something like an insect-winged fish with the gaping, fanged mouth of an angry cat. Its eyes were artful dots of glowing red.

The flying demons were snapping at the Orpolese, herding them down the hillside and across the plain. In an instant, the vicious creatures had chased the Orpolese all the way to the hazy blue spires of the town and into a jail cell in the basement of a turreted stone building that looked like City Hall. *Clank* went the metal door, damping the dreadful cries of the Orpolese. Frek's pzoom snapped back to normal; he was still on the hill.

Halfway up the hill was a red-and-white-checked square, a gingham tablecloth laid upon the ground with a stylized picnic basket. Six humanoid shapes had been sitting there when they appeared. Somehow Frek immediately knew them to be branecasters. They had gold auras around their heads like icons in old-time religious paintings.

And now the branecasters turned into big crude heads, still outlined by golden disks. The heads came tumbling toward Frek, Gibby, and the dogs. Frek braced himself for pain. The heads flattened themselves into squares, into six large squares like walls. One square scooted beneath Frek's feet, another came down overhead.

Frek and the others were penned in a cell with gold-edged faces painted onto the walls in shades of yellow purple green. Three cruel men, three mean women, dressed like old-time business people.

"Let's hear an explanation, or else." The words sounded within Frek's Orpolese spacesuit. He sensed the words as coming from the branecaster on the ceiling, a man's face with heavy-lidded eyes and a sarcastic, bullying mouth. "I'm Sid," added the man. "This is my wife, Cecily, and we've got two other couples here, too, Batty and Bitty and Chainey and Jayney." His eyes twitched, pointing the others out.

"I'm sorry," said Frek, peering up. "It was an accident. We didn't mean to pop through. I only wanted to help my father on Unipusk. Please put us back." For the moment all thoughts of the elixir had flown right out of his head.

"In other words, you're a moron," snapped Sid. "You unyunched almost inside Jumm. Right beside the transport tube to Unipusk. With that kind of energy-feed, you unwound your strings completely. Your space connection went away. That's why you shrank through from the plain brane to the Planck brane."

"And ruined the branecasters' picnic!" shrieked the branecaster on the wall on Frek's right. This was Batty, twitchy and scrunched-up, asymmetric, with a lunatic's glittering eyes. But like the other two men, he wore a white shirt, a black suit, and a gray necktie. The gold aura surrounding him was fainter than that around the others.

"Let's decohere them same as the Orpolese," said the branecaster face in the floor, a thin-lipped woman, strict and cold, her skin modeled as smoothly as plastic. Jayney. She wore a powder blue power suit. "Make them into puppets, guinea pigs, couch potatoes. Right, Bitty?"

"Never forget," quavered the unseen Bitty's gollywog high-pitched voice from behind Frek, and the others took it up as well.

"Never forget, never forget, never forget, never forget, never forget!" The scary thing was, each time Frek heard the phrase, it actually made him forget a bit more about what he was supposed to be doing here.

Frek's memories were all he had, all that really made him Frek. He couldn't let the branecasters drive his personality away. He fought them. He thought back to how he'd recovered from being peeked by Gov. He recreated the feelings of his convalescence; he mentally mimicked the healing action of the stim cells.

The branecasters' voices faded away. Frek focused in on his memories, hugging them to himself. Lora, Geneva, and Ida. Their house tree. Dad. The girl he'd seen in the ring. Bumby's W-pupil eye. Bumby had promised the branecasters would give him the elixir. Yes. As soon as he got a chance, Frek would ask the branecasters for the elixir to restore planet Earth. He wouldn't let the branecasters send him away without it.

"Never forget they ruined our picnic!" repeated the deranged Batty on Frek's right. At Frek's side, Gibby and the dogs were looking this way and that, their eyes rolling.

"How 'bout this," cried Gibby before Frek could say anything. The Grulloo's sun-browned face was blotched pale with fear. "We got a deal for you folks. Tell 'em about the Bumby production angle, Frek!"

Frek hesitated. Did he really want to commit humanity to being made into a show by horrible creatures like these? But Gibby had a point. Talking about a business deal could be a way to get this conversation onto a better footing. And then he could ask for the elixir.

"I might, um, want to register a branecast producer for the, um, human race," said Frek, feeling hollow in his gut. "Bumby and Ulla producing us for the Orpolese. They told me I should talk to you."

"You hear that, Sid?" sneered the branecaster on Frek's left. She had a coarse, piggish face, rich in pinks and purples. This was Sid's wife, Cecily, dressed in a frilly white blouse and a gray cashmere suit. "The little big shot's all set to pick his race's producer. Do you even know what branecasting means, junior?"

"No," said Frek in a small voice. It was hard to keep up his spirits against the branecasters. "Not really. Can you tell me?"

The sound of a vast laugh track bloomed around them: cackles, haw-haws, giggles, guffaws, tee-hees, titters, chuckles, belly-laughs, ho-ho-hos, snickers, chortles, hoots, and snorts, the noise going on for much longer than was at all comfortable or reasonable.

Suddenly Frek remembered one of the last things Bumby had said to him. Keep your head. He didn't have to let the branecasters get the better of him. "Stop it!" he yelled. He felt as strong and focused as when he'd hit the watchbird with the badminton racquet. "Forget about the branecast and put us back in normal space, you unny gleeps! We don't need a producer! We don't want to be branecast at all!"

"Tough luck," said the sixth branecaster, who was a man's face on the wall in front of Frek. He was even more unfriendly-looking than the others, bald and pudgy, with old-fashioned spectacles, a tight necktie, and a tiny straight mouth like a slot, his golden aura tight and perfectly round. It struck Frek that he resembled one of the Six Financiers of the Apocalypse in the Skull Farmer game—a cunning, humorless businessman with a bag of bills in place of a heart. His skin was all in shades of gray; he spoke in curt, clipped tones. "Except for those rare moments when you're in the Planck brane with us, every member of your race is available for live branecast, around the clock, forever. That's that. As soon as the Unipuskers happened to find your system, we opened up the human branecast channel. And we never, but never, close down a channel, son. It's a revenue stream. You start out on unrestricted read-only access, and when you're ready you pick a producer. I'll be the one to set up your deal. My name's Chainey, in case you've lost track."

"It's really up to me to select the producer?" asked Frek. "Why me, anyway?"

"You're the first member of your race to make it from the plain brane to the Planck brane," said Chainey. "Since we like to be paid in good solid matter from the plain brane, we're not interested in anyone who can't actually get here. To keep things simple, we appoint the first individual we meet to be a given talent race's sole negotiator, for however long he or she lives. You might say that you've won yourself an honor. A big day for a small boy."

"I already told you what kind of production I'd like," reiterated Frek. "No branecasting at all."

"Just kill him and wait for the Unipuskers to send over his father," snapped plastic-faced Jayney from under Frek's feet. Chainey's wife in her powder blue suit. "He's too dumb to close a deal." Her aura contained a spiral design that was continually turning inward. Like a whirlpool.

"Don't try and stampede me," said Frek, glaring down at her. "I want to know what I'm getting us into." He glanced up at the icy Chainey. "What if we don't have a producer at all?"

"Jayney's serious, you know," said Chainey, with a nod toward the floor. "If we find a talent race's current negotiator to be uncompanionable, we liquidate him or her and wait for the next one. We never have to wait long. Now that the humanity channel is open, producers will be all over the opportunity. Eventually they'll bring over one of you who's able to make the deal. It might as well be you, Frek."

"I'm listening," said Frek, a little surprised at how calm he sounded. "Tell me more."

"All right," said Chainey. "The standard procedure is that the talent race's negotiator makes an exclusive distribution agreement with a producer. Branecast access to the talent race becomes available solely to the producer's customers, who are normally limited to one particular esper race. In other words, only one kind of alien is esping you—or watching you—via the branecast access that we're able to provide. I *will* tell you that if you don't have a producer, we don't pay you anything. I'll also tell you that as long as you don't have a producer, you're going to be under extreme pressure. Producers will be importuning you to get them a deal. They might even seek to terminate you so as to bring their own hand-picked negotiators into place." As Chainey talked, the legalistic words seemed to crawl out of his mouth and into his gray skin. He looked like the fine-printed page of a law book.

"Won't the competing producers be after me even if I do pick a producer?"

"Your producer will provide you with protection. It's in their interest to preserve the status quo. Other producers may in fact come to you with attractive offers. Do note that, as sole negotiator, you're always free to return to the Planck brane and recast our agreement. We believe very strongly in the free market."

"I see," said Frek carefully. "Before I commit to a producer, let me ask you about our payment. We'd want a genomic elixir to restore the lost species of planet Earth."

"Restore your biome, eh?" said Chainey. He sounded like it was a request he'd heard before. For how many eons had he been doing this? With how many races? "I don't suppose your people happened to save the missing genetic codes?" asked Chainey.

"I think they're all gone," said Frek, remembering what he'd heard of the Great Collapse. In their zeal to make their changes permanent, NuBioCom had rooted out all the old genomics books and papers, all the digital files, all the databases. In order to make the world completely safe for their patented proprietary life forms, they'd destroyed every trace of Gaia's heritage. "But Bumby said you could fix it anyway."

"Bumby's not feeling so good right now," said the branecaster with a slight upward curve in his tiny little gray mouth. "He's waiting for somebody to bail him out."

"Will you give us the elixir or not, Chainey?" snapped Frek.

"It would mean letting you go rooting around in your past," said Chainey. "Dipping into the time pool of the appropriate Exaplex projection room. Not something we especially like to see clients do. You'd have to ask Zed, in any case."

"Just kill him!" hissed mean-faced Jayney from the floor. She was every bit as heartless as Chainey.

"I'm talking here, Jayney," said Chainey's little letter-slot mouth. "Are you going to pick a producer now, Frek?"

"I—I guess so," said Frek. Since they were already planning to branecast the human race, it couldn't do any harm for Frek to pick their producer, right? Especially since Chainey said that otherwise some other producers might kill Frek to get their own negotiator in. If you could believe what Chainey said. It wasn't like Frek knew a lot of producers to pick among, though. Bumby and Ulla, or those Unipuskers, what were their names—Hawb and Cawmb. Maybe he could ask Chainey for a list of other producers. But the branecasters' patience seemed to be wearing pretty thin. The real goal, of course, was to get the branecast turned off entirely. But it seemed like that would have to wait. For now Bumby might as well be the producer. He was in some kind of jail anyway, which meant nothing much would happen soon.

Frek took a deep breath and said, "Bumby and Ulla can produce us for the Orpolese."

"Done," said Chainey, his mouth bending into a pleased U. "Deal one, step one."

"And now can I have the elixir?" asked Frek.

"Why would I give you anything?" said Chainey impatiently. "Haven't you been listening? We never make direct transfers to the talent. That's what the producers are for. They get paid by their subscribers and their advertisers, then they pay you. And they pay us. That's the important thing: *They pay us*. And there's a penalty for you and your people having screwed up the start of the deal so badly. The Orpolese pay us the bail for Ulla and Bumby before anything else happens at all. Ten trillion tons of gold. Until then, we'll leave the humanity channel on open access. Other producers may be contacting you, of course. A completely different deal could develop."

"But the other producers might try to kill me!" protested Frek, not wanting to believe what he'd just heard. Something else occurred to him. "And Bumby and Ulla can't protect me now—they're in jail! I don't understand what you mean about bailing them out. Why would you want all that gold?"

"Food!" screeched crazy Batty on Frek's right, the white slashes of his teeth seeming to take up half of his face. "I want to eat a dog!" The wall with the frenzied face bulged up, forming a pseudopod that reached out as if to touch Wow. Wow backed away, snarling.

"Leave him alone!" shouted Frek.

"Matter's what we like, kid," came the voice of the pig-faced Cecily woman on Frek's left. "If you were smart, you'd give us a sample now. For good will, you know what I mean? You don't want us thinkin' you're, um, *uncompanionable*." She grinned over at the branecaster bulging from the other side. "Right, Batty?"

Frek felt his body through the flexible field of the spacesuit. All he had was his yellow T-shirt, his blue turmite silk pants and the little fungus purse with the chameleon mod and the twig of Aaron's Rod.

"Do you want my shirt?" offered Frek.

"Offer rejected," said Cheney, making a fishlike face. "Don't try evading, Frek. It's going to take ten trillion tons of gold to bail out your Orpolese friends. I'm talking about a solid gold asteroid ten kilometers across. That'll earn us some wham, right, guys? And, yes, like Batty and Cecily said, you have to give us something with some heft to it right now, just so we see you're ready to be a real business partner. Why *not* feed us a dog? You don't need two of them."

"Take my knife," said Gibby, suddenly rocking over to one side and feeling against his body. The bubble of his smart kenner spacesuit allowed him to get into his coat, to produce his knife, and to push it out through the spacesuit. "Here you go," said Gibby, and nimbly lunged forward to plunge the blade right into the center of Chainey's smug face.

The branecaster's image puckered up and flowed onto the knife's handle. A burst of mint green bloomed across his distorted features. The knife melted away like a piece of ice in the sun. Shades of green and blue washed across the walls, down to the floor, and onto the ceiling.

"*Tasty!*" whooped Batty. His face was bile green; his aura had brightened and grown.

"Real glatt stuff," agreed Sid on the ceiling, his sarcastic eyes glinting a brilliant aquamarine, the air around him gleaming with gold. "Good wham."

"Thanks for that," said Chainey, his skin turning as blue as Krishna's. His aura was twice as bright as before. "Iron is good. I'll put you back where you came from, with no elapsed time. And Frek, don't forget to tell your Orpolese friends to bring us that gold asteroid to bail out Bumby. Bring it through a proper branelink, of course. Tell them to hurry. You're a marked man; the other producers are going to be after you. You need Bumby and Ulla out of decoherence so they can set up your security. Oh, and once they're bailed out, they ought to be able to help you get your elixir." Chainey favored Frek with a mirthless, unkind smile. "See you again—maybe. Cheers."

The cube of faces around them became a swirl, Frek heard a *deedle-deedle-deedle* as of a sound being played backward very, very fast, and then, lo and behold, Frek, Gibby, and the dogs were floating in space again.

part. 2

the
elixir

7

renata

The vast marbled surface of the pink and yellow gas giant planet Jumm loomed before them. Behind them was the blue and white disk of the gas giant's moon, Unipusk. The cylindrical tube from Unipusk to Jumm was still quite near them, but it wasn't flaring at them anymore.

Frek's first feeling was one of joy at being back in what the branecasters called the plain brane, back in normal space and safe in his Orpolese spacesuit. Compared to the Planck brane, even the gas giant looked almost friendly. They were falling toward it, yes, and away from the Unipusk moon, but maybe that was all right. The distances out here were vast. They still had some time to work with. And Bumby had said the Orpolese armor could do anything they needed.

About then Frek noticed that the world had that golden glow again, and again he had that feeling of being watched from a viewpoint only very slightly outside himself, with an accompanying sensation of having his thoughts simplified and flattened out. An alien was esping him on the branecast, and it wasn't Ulla or Bumby. Bumby and Ulla were decoherent zombies, waiting for a ten-trillion-ton ransom. Until they got free, it was open season on Frek.

"Chainey didn't give you that elixir, did he?" asked Gibby. "To bring back the animals and the plants? I was so fired up from usin' my knife that I didn't exactly catch what happened at the end."

"Chainey didn't give me jack," said Frek dejectedly. And then all his self-doubts came tumbling out. "I'm not the right one for this quest, Gibby. I'm a gump. I'll never save the Earth. I've done everything wrong and I'll be dead before long. If it weren't for me, we wouldn't have crashed here; we would have gone on to Orpoly and done it right. I got us in deeper with the branecasters and I didn't get the elixir at all. And the other producers are going to try to kill me pretty soon."

"You did better than I could have," said Gibby. "Me, I about kacced the floor in there." He reached out and caught hold of Frek's hand. "You had a reason for landin' us here, Frek, a good one. You wanted to save your dad. We'll get him, and then we'll get that elixir, and then we'll turn the branecast off. You the one, Frek. We countin' on you."

"Thanks, Gibby." It was good to have a friend. "Thanks for giving up your knife. I know that knife meant a lot to you."

"Hey, at least I got to stick it into Chainey's face," said Gibby. "Man, that felt good. Not that he minded. Chomped it down like a carrot, he did. I would have hated to see him eatin' one of the dogs."

"We should grab hold of the dogs," said Frek. "Before they float away."

The dogs were about five meters off and, adrift in space as they were, there seemed to be no way to reach them. But then Frek thought of asking his Orpolese spacesuit to move him. Frek pointed toward Wow and, considering his words very carefully, said, "Move me slowly toward the dog and stop me when I touch him."

Frek felt a slight vibration in his heels, yes, a flicker of energy coming from his feet. He glided toward Wow, towing Gibby behind him, and when he got there, another drizzle of energy from his spacesuit brought him to a stop.

"Frek good," said Wow, nuzzling Frek through his kenner armor.

Woo began barking in excitement, then composed herself and called, "Touch me too." Frek powered himself, Gibby, and Wow over to her.

"Want eat," said Wow, when he and Woo had finished pawing each other in greeting.

"Frek feed?" asked Woo.

Even though they'd had lunch less than an hour ago, right before the yunch trip, Frek too was hungry. He recalled Bumby saying that a yunch trip took a lot out of you. He was exhausted and starving. Maybe that was why he'd felt so low a minute ago, telling Gibby he couldn't do the quest. At home, when Frek was sad or cranky, Lora usually asked him if he'd eaten.

So, all right, thought Frek, why not ask the spacesuits for food? "Feed me a mouthful now," said Frek, testing the concept out. And, yes, a nugget of grobread and anymeat popped out of the spacesuit faceplate just in front of his mouth. He chewed it down, and when he said, "Give me a little ball of water," a one-gulp blob of water appeared as well. "Feed the others the same way," he said. "And give Gibby some stim cells, too." Their suits heard him, and it was so.

"Where do them Unipuskers live?" Gibby asked when they'd finished eating. "Down to that monster planet? We gonna fall right into it?"

"That's Jumm," said Frek, who still felt quite fatigued. "We don't want to go there. Unipusk is the moon up there. We missed it."

They rolled back and gazed at the blue disk of Unipusk. It had clouds, seas, and continents. A lot more inviting than the turbid, curlicued surface of Jumm. But how to fly up there?

Frek and Gibby got their spacesuits to start pushing them away from the gas giant world, towing the dogs along, but the progress, if any, was slow. At these distances it was hard to be sure. What if they simply fell into Jumm's maelstroms of pink and yellow storms, forever to be lost? Jumm was so big; they were so small. Even if the miraculous Orpolese spacesuits could keep them alive, they'd grow old and die alone in those chaotic clouds. Frek didn't say these thoughts out loud, but a glance at Gibby's wrinkled forehead made it clear his friend was worried, too.

"Let's try something else," suggested Frek. "Let's head for the transport tube."

The Jumm-to-Unipusk tube was less than a kilometer off. Abandoning any attempt to fly upward, they simply angled over toward it. By now the dogs had grasped the notion of using their spacesuits to fly, or maybe it was that the spacesuits had come to understand that when the dogs made running motions they wanted to move. In any case, Wow and Woo flew along with Gibby and Frek.

"Is it gonna spark at us again?" worried Gibby as they approached the tube. "Or send us back to them branecasters?"

"I think it'll be all right since we're not yunching or unyunching anymore," said Frek. And he was right. No energy flares flickered out at them, no tendrils of light.

They peered into the transparent tube. It was filled with a cloudy fluid, something like methane or liquid helium, moving somewhat sluggishly in the direction of Unipusk. If they could have gotten inside the tube, they could perhaps have ridden the current up to Unipusk.

In any case, try as they might, they couldn't get inside the tube. The surface was completely impermeable. Rather than being either ordinary matter or dark matter, it seemed to be a force field. It didn't want to let them in, and there wasn't much they could do about it.

A discouraging aspect of being next to the tube was that by watching it they could better estimate how rapidly they were falling toward Jumm. Even when Frek commanded his Orpolese spacesuit to rocket up upward as forcefully as possible, the suit's power wasn't sufficient to do more than slightly slow them down. Things were looking grim. But in his weariness, it was all Frek could do to keep from dropping off to sleep.

And then Frek remembered his ring.

He slowly brought his hand up to his face and stared at the ring, at the red dot nestled in the golden cup. Though he was exhausted, the yunch trip seemed to have sharpened his mental abilities. He was able to visualize a flow of energy passing down his arm through his finger and into his ring.

"I want to call Dad," he said. "I want to talk to my father."

His finger tingled; the dot began to twinkle. A haze of light formed, grew red and yellow spikes. And there in the middle of the ball was Dad's face.

For a moment Carb seemed to be unaware that his ring was in contact with Frek again. His head was bent to one side, the fan of his Mohawk spreading out like Saturn's rings. The tattoos on his temples had sketched out clams with eye stalks—Dad's tattoos tended to show things he'd recently seen. Right now Carb was rubbing his face with a wet rag, blearily wiping black makeup from his cheek and red makeup from his lip. His injuries had been faked.

And then he glimpsed Frek watching him.

"There you are!" said Carb. Now that Frek wasn't yunching, the ring-aura voices were much easier to hear. "We lost sight of you for a second. Good thing there wasn't any trouble when you unyunched so close to that tube." Apparently Carb didn't realize that Frek had already been to the Planck brane and back. He called a name over his shoulder. "Hawb." An alien appeared next to him.

It was one of the Unipusker producers, probably the same one as before. The flat disk of his head bulged up in the middle. Two eye stalks stuck out of the head's top surface, just like in Carb's tattoos, with each stalk tipped by a piercingly bright blue eye. The top of the disk was separate from the bottom, like the two halves of a clamshell. The halves were tightly joined except in front, where they split apart to make a lipless mouth.

"Greet Frek," said the mouth in a high, sweet tone. It was dark yellow on the inside.

"Hawb will come get you," said Carb. "Now that we've got a fix on you. He'll be there before you fall too far. Hurry, Hawb!"

"Hear," said Hawb, bending his eye stalks forward toward Frek. "Inform Frek he and companions have eight more hours until they reach the atmosphere of Jumm. Mention that our saucer will take seven point nine nine hours to arrive. Alert Frek of airborne enemies in the Jumm atmosphere. Thousand kilometer bobblies. Hurry, Hawb." The Unipusker turned to one side and stumped off, his stubby tail swaying from side to side. His body was all brown, except for the tail, which was wrapped in shiny gold material. After two or three steps he was beyond the ring-aura's field of view.

It seemed like a good sign that the Unipusker producer had bothered to give Frek a safety warning. Hopefully this meant he wasn't going to kill him right away. Maybe he'd try and sweet-talk Frek instead. If Chainey was to be believed, this was all about the production deal. Carb seemed to care more about the deal than about his son.

"Why did you help them trick me?" Frek asked his father. "You're not hurt at all."

"I hurt inside," said Carb with a wry smile that sent wrinkles all across his face. He laid his hand upon his heart. "Does Lora miss me?" Just like Carb to focus on himself.

"Tell 'em we need help," said Gibby at Frek's side. Though he was unable to see or hear the images from Frek's ring, he gathered Frek was talking to Unipusk. "That geevin' gas giant's too close!"

Frek glanced down, or was it up? Out in space like this, his body's sense of direction had a way of unexpectedly switching around. Jumm was huge and eerie. The folded, wavy convolutions of its colored clouds were no place for human life. The closest point was a large whirlpool of pink and yellow, a maelstrom of whorls and eddies ten thousand kilometers across. They were rushing toward it. But everything was so big that, according to the Unipusker, they'd take another eight hours to get there.

It did make things worse to learn of predators in the garish skies of Jumm. Frek and the others should really be in a state of maximum alert, prepared to use their spacesuits' feeble rocket powers as best they could. But that was later. What had Hawb called the monsters? Bobblies, a thousand kilometers in size. Were they giant flying jellyfish? Frek was too tired to worry about it.

Though Carb was still waiting for a response, Frek sullenly denied him an answer. He wasn't going to tell Carb anything about Lora. If he was so curious about Mom, he could have stayed home with her or, having left, he could have called her once or twice in the last year. There wasn't much use talking to him at all if he was going to lie.

"I'm sorry we tricked you," said Carb, reading Frek's expression. "I wore the makeup to make sure you'd come. It was Yessica's idea. We had to be sure and get you away from those Orpolese. Humanity's looking at a very big opportunity, and the Orpolese could fub it up. Whatever you do, don't listen to them. That's great that you were able to crash their yunch trip. I hope they can't hear me talking. Well, our friends the Unipuskers ought to be able to take care of them." Carb sighed and rubbed his face. He looked tired. "It's the wee hours on Unipusk," he explained. "The Unipuskers have picked me to do some very important negotiations, you know." Carb livened up a bit as he said this. He'd always been looking for a way to make himself important. "Did the Orpolese tell you about it yet?"

"No," said Frek shortly. He was mad at his father for tricking him. And there was no point going over the details for him. The Unipuskers would esp Frek and figure out everything anyhow. In fact, given the intensity of the golden glow around Frek, they were probably doing it right now. Carb was the only one out of the loop. "We can talk it over later, Carb."

"Right you are," said Carb, always quick to read Frek's moods. He shifted to one side, revealing the cute, friendly-looking girl Frek had seen before. Neither of them was wearing a spacesuit. They seemed to be in a green room with dark windows.

"This is Renata," Carb offered. "She's eager to meet you. Her mother and I are friends."

"Hi, Frek," said Renata, bobbing her head. Her dark brown pigtails swung with the motion. Frek wondered if by now his father liked her more than him. But she looked like she could be a good friend. Frek didn't know many girls besides the ones who hung around with his sisters.

"It's great that you came," continued Renata. "We've been waiting up. It's like three in the morning." She looked sleepy, too. "Mom says you can help us get home. I hope you aren't mad that we called you." She smiled. "It's goggy here. I've been having fun drawing the Unipuskers and the vigs. The rickrack cities with Jumm in the sky. Are you close to Jumm right now?"

"Yeah," said Frek, feeling almost at a loss for words. He wanted Renata to like him, but he didn't know what to say. She looked smart, and maybe a year or two older than him. He was too tired to think. "I draw a little, too." Meanwhile Gibby was tugging at him, wanting to know what the ring-aura had told him. "I think I better say bye for now, Renata," said Frek with a yawn.

"See you soon," said Renata. "If they let me, I'm going to come along on the saucer."

As surely as he'd known how to turn his ring on, Frek now understood how to turn it off. It required a certain mental gesture akin to reaching out and pinching a candle flame. He did it.

Frek, Gibby, and the dogs spent a few minutes fruitlessly staring at Unipusk's distant disk for a sign of Hawb's launch. And then their attention returned to the fever dream of Jumm's turbulent bands of clouds, an eight-hour drop below them. To slightly slow their fall, Frek got them all to set their spacesuits to be pushing them upward as strongly as possible. And then, finally, they fell asleep.

Frek awoke amidst wisps of cloud. It was like being in the treetops of an endless gauzy forest. Quite lovely. The enormous yellow and red whorl of Jumm's great spot seemed like it should be making a noise. But all was silent. Gibby and the dogs slept at Frek's side, limply adrift, the dogs' legs occasionally twitching.

Frek hung there in the silence, savoring the moment. He felt strong, rested, optimistic. As before, his perceptions were tinged with the golden glow that resulted from having aliens esp him on the branecast. He would have liked to ignore it—like an actor learning not to stare at the camera. But in the end there was always a background awareness of his observers, for the process changed the very texture of his thoughts. Everything was simplified, black or white, with hardly any shades of gray. Oh well.

Frek turned his mental focus to recent events. How far he'd come! Today was Sunday, May 15, 3003. On Friday, Gibby had taken him to Stun City and had gotten drunk at the Brindle Cowloon. Saturday, yesterday, the counselors had come for him at dawn, and Frek had run off to attack Gov's puffball, armed only with his chameleon mod. Incredibly—with the help of the reborn Bumby—he'd succeeded. He'd killed Gov. If nothing else came of all this, that was something to be proud of.

Yesterday had been a very long day. Bumby and Ulla had yunched them halfway across the galaxy, supposedly in search of the elixir to restore Earth's biome. Thanks to Carb and Renata, Frek had crashed them into the Planck brane and met the branecasters. And now Frek,

Gibby, and the dogs were entering the outer atmosphere of a giant planet that made Earth look like a glass bead. Supposedly some creatures lived here, big hostile things called bobblies. Where was that rescue saucer?

At this last thought, Frek couldn't help but chuckle. *He was waiting for some aliens in a flying saucer.* Maybe he'd be dead in half an hour, but while it lasted, he was having a goggy adventure indeed. This was a far cry from glawking around watching wall skins in Middleville. Still smiling, he gave Gibby a poke.

Gibby woke with a startled yelp and a colorful curse that made Frek smile the more. And then the dogs started barking at Jumm. The warmly tinted cloud tops were beginning to pile up around them like mountains.

Right about then the Unipuskers' shiny flying saucer appeared. It was shaped something like the imaginary flying saucers Frek had seen in toons: a broad disklike base with a dome on top, the dome blending in very smoothly. One unusual feature was that the saucer had a number of flexible feelers. The scale of the saucer seemed excessive; it was at least two hundred meters across.

The silvery disk hovered above them, and four beams of light lanced from some of the stubbier feelers on its underside. Tractor beams. They latched onto Frek, Gibby, and the dogs, then drew them toward the saucer's underside. The saucer base had a big round window in it. When they reached the window, it shimmered like a curtain of water and let them pass through.

As they slid through the skin of the Unipuskers' saucer, their Orpolese spacesuits melted away. Frek was in the same clothes he'd started in, his tough blue turmite-silk pants and his yellow T-shirt. He still had his ring, and his waterproof fungus-purse with the Aaron's Rod twig and the two remaining doses of chameleon mod. He and the others were alone for the moment, in a large room with a transparent floor that was the window they'd just passed through. This was an entrance hall, with doors leading off it. The saucer immediately started accelerating upward, providing a weak kind of gravity.

Cautiously Frek inhaled his first breath of the saucer's air. It was humid, with a sulfur smell, as of firework-reeds on a rainy night.

This was, he'd soon learn, the smell of the Unipuskers. The odor also held a touch of rotting leaves and hints of fungus. If Frek had wanted to paint the smell, he might have made it dark purple with smeared orange dots.

Wow and Woo were sniffing like mad, holding their heads up and flexing the delicate whorls of their moist black noses, drawing their own conclusions.

"Stinks," said Gibby simply.

And now here came two Unipuskers. Though Frek had already glimpsed one of them in his ring's aura, this first face-to-face meeting was unforgettable.

They were the size of men, with arms and legs, and with heads like clamshells. They were a muddy-brown all over, with an iridescent sheen. Their skin was thick, taking the form of overlapping leathery plates. They had three fingers on each hand, and four toes on each foot, with the toes splayed out like a chicken's claws.

They wore hardly any clothes, and their exposed crotches were as featureless as those of dolls. Their short tails were the one part of their bodies they seemed to be modest about. These were covered by gold-colored sheaths held in place by straps around their thighs.

Although the heads were shaped and ridged like shells, they were the same iridescent brown as the skin, with eye stalks alertly twitching this way and that. The eyes were a very pale blue, veined with lines of a darker blue. As well as the two eye stalks, each head bore perhaps a dozen more flexible projections—feelers, radio antennae, or scent organs.

The Unipuskers bounced along, effectively feather-light in the false gravity of the saucer's gentle acceleration. They were talking in their own language, their speech a series of hisses and gurgles. It almost seemed as if they were arguing, with their yellow-lined mouths tensely clacking open and closed. Seeing Frek and his companions, the Unipuskers broke off their quarrel.

"Greet Frek," said one of them. "Introduce self as Hawb. Introduce Hawb's companion Cawmb. Comment disingenuously upon the absence of the Orpolese."

The second Unipusker bowed. They looked very similar, though

Cawmb's tail was a bit thicker, and his gold tail cover was patterned in circles, as opposed to Hawb's, which was embossed with squares.

"Greet Frek," said Cawmb. "Ask names of Frek's fellow travelers."

"I'm Gibby," volunteered the Grulloo. "And these are Frek's dog, Wow, and his dog's friend, Woo." Gibby swaggered forward, rocking exaggeratedly from side to side, leaning far over so as to hold out a hand.

"Inquire about nudity of your tail," said Hawb, peering at Gibby's hand and then shaking it. "Speculate about your tail's lack of fecundity."

"Inquire away," said Gibby with a puzzled smile. "Those are real pretty underpants you two got on your tails, by the way."

"Is my father on board?" put in Frek.

"Explain that Carb was asleep in his bed when we left," said Cawmb. "At our rickrack mansion. Assure son that Dad will be eager to greet him later and—"

"Notify Pilot Evawrt to take rapid evasive action!" shouted Hawb. "Advise guests to take a seated position to withstand extreme burst of acceleration! Point out the attack of a Jumm bobblie visible through the deck!"

The ship shuddered, lurched, and shot upward, pressing Frek hard against the floor. The window wasn't like a water curtain anymore; it was, rather, like an impermeable sheet of diamond. The acceleration was so strong that lying on his stomach was more comfortable than trying to sit up. Face pressed against the transparent deck, Frek peered down.

Sure enough, something was coming toward them from the surface of Jumm. The thing was so big that it took a mental effort to see it as a whole. It was like some old-time paintings Frek had seen on the Net, where an artist would make, say, a woman's face out of a bunch of different fruits, or paint a landscape that, if you looked at it differently, became a hunched man with a hill for his back, a lake for his beard and a tree for his nose. Far from being a simple flying jellyfish, a bobblie was—a living weather pattern.

Close as they were to Jumm, it seemed like half the visible surface was peeling up toward them. Mountainous clouds closed in on them like teeth; one whole side of the great red and yellow spot rose up like a dragon's tail.

A hum filled the Unipuskers' saucer as it strained upward. The acceleration was so intense that Frek felt his bones might snap or push through his skin. He was pasted to the transparent deck, with one eye staring through it at the rising cloud-creature, a thousand kilometers long. Gibby lay panting at his right, with the dogs beyond him softly whimpering. To Frek's left, Hawb and Cawmb sat on the deck, effortlessly holding themselves erect with their bodies' tough plates.

One of the bobblie's tendrils seemed to pass over the saucer. The craft shuddered, but its surface held firm. They climbed higher. And then they were free.

Twisting in a spasm that could only be a fit of anger, the bobblie hurled itself at the world-spanning shaft of the transport tube, then sank back down into the swirling colors of Jumm. The tube's force field walls quivered, but stood firm. It occurred to Frek that the bobblies might resent the Unipuskers for siphoning material away from their world.

"Request Pilot Evawrt to reduce acceleration to a less taxing intensity," said Cawmb, the second Unipusker.

The acceleration lightened up again. Frek sat up and began asking questions.

"Are you sure it's safe for us to breathe your air? It has all the right gasses in it? Isn't there a danger of contamination, like us infecting you or you infecting us?"

"Affirm the similarity of our atmospheres," said Cawmb. "Inform that our genomes are two-dimensional molecular tiling patterns as opposed to your one-dimensional DNA. Minimize any possibility of cross-contamination."

"Are you and Hawb a married couple?" was Frek's next question. "Is one of you he and the other one she?"

"Summarily state that all Unipuskers are one sex," said Hawb. "Remark that we use a type of genomic exchange for variation. Snigger that you will not be privy to the details. Admit that Cawmb and I are like a couple in that (a) we do exchange genomic sub-tilings, and (b) we are raising seven hundred and eighty-three children together, with thirteen more expected in the coming week. Qualify with the information that we bud off our children individually from our tails, and are capable of reproducing solo. Suggest that you refer to all Unipuskers as he."

"Point out Hawb's insensitive and careless error regarding our number of children," said Cawmb in an irritated tone. "Supply the correct numbers of seven hundred and seventy-nine children, with seventeen more expected this week."

"Impugn Cawmb's knowledge in this context," said Hawb, his voice rising. "Assert the accuracy of my original count. Report that I personally visited each of the children's rooms yesterday evening to tuck them in."

"Expose Hawb's deceit and poor partnership," screamed Cawmb, his mouth opening very wide. "Reveal that four of those children died of ickspot two days ago, leaving four beds empty. Bewail my bereavement. Complain that I alone had to fumigate, lest the ickspot spread. Reiterate that seventeen children are expected this week, as Hawb would know if he were paying proper attention to his partner's tail!"

"End this topic thread," bellowed Hawb, his clamshell head splitting nearly in two. "Present a pleasant facade to our transgalactic guests! Usher Frek, the dogs, and the deformed thing to our feeding-chamber!"

"I've got a name, you two-legged piece of kac," snapped Gibby. The Unipuskers' ill-humor was contagious.

"Express an insincere apology for my partner's slight," said Cawmb. "Reformulate his botched invitation to use the name 'Gibby.' Invite Frek, the dogs, and Gibby to share a meal of rickrack and vig."

Cawmb and Hawb smiled at each other as if their fight were all over, linked arms, and waddled through one of the entrance chamber's arched doors, conversing in their native tongue of whispery burbles. Frek and Gibby followed along, Gibby muttering in an angry undertone. The dogs pushed ahead of them, sniffing at the Unipuskers' legs and gold-wrapped tails, bouncily enjoying the acceleration's weak pseudogravity.

They found themselves in a kind of dining room with a table and several stools. A planter box of green shoots ran along one wall. Each plant was a single, thick, segmented stalk with horizontal branches sticking out. Rickrack. Sleeping on the deck by the table was a fat orange beast with floppy, triangular ears. A vig. He looked a bit like Frek imagined a pig might have looked—though of course NuBio-Com had let pigs go extinct many years before. No need for them, really, with anymeat cultures in every kitchen.

The vig had some features in common with the Unipuskers, that is, eyes on stalks and a half dozen other stubby antennae protruding from its long-lipped head. The eyes were bright green. In place of legs, it had six bumps on its belly; perhaps it used them to creep along like a caterpillar. For the moment the vig's eye stalks were flopped down flat upon its head, which was a long bulge shading seamlessly into its corpulent body.

Wow trotted right over to sniff at it. At the touch of the dog's wet nose, the vig woke and let out an angry squealing noise that Frek would later learn was called a vheenk. As well as vheenking, vigs could vark, with the vark sound being like an abrupt, echoing cough.

The vig's mouth was longer than Frek had realized, reaching nearly a third the length of its body, and lined top and bottom with ragged saws of bone. Wow barked with excitement and fear, Woo joining in. The vig rose up on its stubby cushion-legs and began angrily vheenking as hard as it could.

"Observe that this is too aggressive a vig!" exclaimed Cawmb. "Find fault with Hawb! Reprimand Hawb for bringing an attack-minded vig." He turned his attention to the vig, shaking his fist at it. "Silence!" shouted Cawmb. "Serve meat!"

Although you could tell the vig heard and understood Cawmb, it ignored him, preferring to frantically vark at the dogs. Evidently smarting from Cawmb's criticism, Hawb kicked the vig. The vig let out a surprised, pained vheenk and meekly settled down, holding its round rear high in the air.

"Extol the taste of vig," said Hawb, producing something like a very sharp knife. With surprisingly graceful gestures of his clumsy-looking arms, Hawb sliced eight steaks from the vig's orange rump.

This seemed to cause the vig no pain at all. In fact, being carved seemed fully to calm the beast down. "Describe as very fine," said Hawb, laying six of the bloody steaks along the edges of the table, and setting two of them aside.

Meanwhile Cawmb had walked over to the planter box to snap off some of the segmented shoots of rickrack plant, two shoots to go with each steak.

The Unipuskers were slightly surprised the dogs couldn't sit on their stools, but they didn't object when Frek put the dogs' vig steaks on the deck. The vig itself growled a bit at this, disliking to see its new enemies eating its flesh, but now that it had been carved, it no longer seemed to be in so combative a mood.

Frek and Gibby were hungry once again, and, after some preliminary sniffs and tastes, they went ahead and ate the red vig meat— tentatively at first, and then with gusto. It was sweet and stringy; it didn't taste as bloody as it looked. It was a bit like anymeat, but with more texture to it. And, yes, it had a faint taste of sulfur, reminiscent of the Unipuskers' smell, but oddly enough the taste grew on you. The rickrack stalks were crunchy, fresh, and succulent, a fine counterpoint to the vig meat. They smelled like violets. To complete the meal, Cawmb set out some pods of water and a few damp cloths.

"Steer conversation around to the missing Orpolese you traveled with," said Hawb when they were done eating and were busy cleaning the vig blood from their faces with the cloths.

Gibby started to say something, but Frek interrupted.

"They got eaten by the bobblie right before you came," asserted Frek, hoping against hope that the Unipuskers hadn't esped the fact that he'd already met the branecasters. "We were really scared."

"Request amplification and clarification," said Cawmb in a flat tone. "Speculate upon how deep into this deception you are willing to go."

"We were falling down toward Jumm and all of a sudden a cloud reached out and grabbed Bumby and Ulla," said Frek. "They screamed, and then they were gone. They weren't that close to us right then. They were mad at me for making us crash." He nudged Wow with his foot, hoping to get the dog to create a diversion.

"Express sarcastic doubt that a bobblie would harm an Orpolese," intoned Hawb. "Point out that the two species are allied by their opposition to Unipusk, and by their chaotic disposition. Dramatically exclaim that we know you're lying. Sorrowfully state that your deceit disappoints us."

"Well, maybe the bobblie wasn't eating them," said Frek weakly. "I couldn't tell for sure. It happened fast. Maybe it was welcoming them. Whatever happened, they were gone. And then you guys saved us." Wow was on his feet, sniffing at Cawmb's tail.

"Demand an end to your futile attempts to deceive us," yelled Cawmb. "Declaim that your lies insult us. Question whether it will in fact be possible to negotiate in good faith. Reveal that we are quite ruthless."

Right then, good old Wow bit onto Cawmb's tail cover and gave it a sharp tug. One of the tail cover's straps snapped, and Wow, bracing his legs, began trying to worry the thing loose. "Scream with embarrassment," screamed Cawmb, twirling around to hide his tail.

At the same time, Cawmb leaned forward and dealt Wow a slap that sent the dog halfway across the room. Woo joined the fray and yanked at Cawmb's tail cover from the other side. The thing came entirely loose. Shrieking and trying to turn every direction at once, Cawmb ended up giving Frek a good glimpse of his rear end.

"Finally I get to see one of your tails," came a girl's voice from the door. "How gnarly. No wonder you cover them up!" She giggled.

Frek looked over and, yes, it was the girl he'd seen in the ring. In person she was even nicer looking than the ring-aura had led him to believe. She had a broad smile, two long, braided pigtails, bright intelligent eyes, and a casual way of standing there. She had a turkle drawing pad attached to her belt.

"Hi, Frek," she said. "I got Hawb and Cawmb to bring me along, but I fell asleep right before we got here. I'm Renata, the one who's been pestering you from your ring. I hear you're twelve? I'm fourteen." Her voice was sweet and low-pitched, with a slight roughness to it. A musical yet raspy sound.

"Hi," said Frek. He stuck out his hand and stepped toward her, but in his eagerness, he overdid the step and went flying through the air. Gracefully she caught his shoulders and swung him around, damping his motion without falling over. For a second, Frek was practically in her arms, as if they were dancing. He had time to notice that Renata smelled good. Like sunshine. And then they were standing face to face. She was exactly the same height as him.

"Look at Cawmb's tail," said Renata. "It's a stack of babies. I should draw it."

Indeed, what had seemed to be a stubby cylindrical tail was in fact a pile of miniature Unipuskers. The ones closer to Cawmb's body were less developed, consisting of little more than soft clamshell heads, while the ones out near the tip were very nearly fully formed, with the very last one even moving his arms and legs. And now in fact the tipmost baby Unipusker broke free and dropped to the floor, no bigger than a gingerbread man. He looked around uncertainly, then toddled toward Gibby.

"Come here, Wow!" shouted Frek, lest the dog do something dreadful. "Woo! Come to me, too!" Sensing the possible danger, Gibby had already let the baby Unipusker hop onto his hand. The Grulloo smiled at the tiny being and held him to his grizzled cheek.

"Demand privacy," roared Cawmb, trying both to hide his tail and to bend over to retrieve his new baby from Gibby. "Direct nosy human guests to ascend to the cockpit with Pilot Evawrt and remain there! Order Hawb to lock up those vicious dogs! Request Gibby to unhand my baby!"

Renata had freed her turkle from her belt and was quickly drawing on it with her index fingernail. Her nail was shaped into a point like the nib of a pen. Her deft strokes had not only captured the image of Cawmb's tail, but the angry, embarrassed expression of his shell-shaped head.

"Save it," Renata told her turkle, and smiled up at Frek. "Maybe we should get out of here now. Cawmb is turning gollywog." Her turkle took hold of her belt again. She stepped back out into the big hall with Frek following her. "Do you get how the Unipuskers talk?" said Renata. "Every sentence is in the imperative." They started across the transparent deck. "Your dogs are cute. If I was a Unipusker, I'd say, 'Remark upon the cuteness of your dogs.' It always sounds like they're planning to do stuff instead of just doing it. Or telling someone to do it instead of doing it themselves. Actually that kind of reminds me of my mother." She paused, looking back toward the dining area, seemingly wanting to see more of Cawmb's uncovered tail.

"Are your mother and my Dad—" Before Frek could figure out how to finish the question, Hawb came bounding after them. The Unipusker scooped up one dog with each hand, flung them through yet another of the doorways off the entrance hall, and made a special gesture that sealed a dark panel across it. Frek could hear muffled barking.

"Take it easy!" cried Renata. "They're man's best friend!"

"Loudly echo Cawmb's belief the dogs are vicious," shouted Hawb. "Inform Frek the beasts must be quarantined while his party visits Unipusk."

"You mustn't hurt them," said Frek, making an effort to sound calm and in control. "They'll need food and water. And I have to be able to visit with them. If I have my own room in Unipusk, let me keep them with me. I'll make sure they're good. I can reason with them, a little bit. They don't mean any harm. They're just dogs." Meanwhile Renata was circling around to get one more peek into the dining area.

"Grant your request," said Hawb after a pause. He lowered his voice so Renata couldn't hear him. "Equate your Unipusk-side living quarters with your dogs' quarantine area. Add that we will imprison the Gibby thing there as well. Warn that all of your lives are contingent upon your good behavior. Stipulate that good behavior will mean to register Hawb and Cawmb with the branecasters as the producers of the humanity channel for exclusive esping by the Unipuskers. Amplify that this will involve canceling your existing but not yet active agreement to let Bumby and Ulla be your producers. Reveal, if still necessary, that we've been esping you and that we know all of your thoughts. State that we are not fools to be trifled with. Suggest that—" Hawb broke off to look back at his tail cover, which was beginning to shake and jiggle.

At the same time a vigorous wail sounded from the dining area.

"Frek, look at this!" called Renata, who was back peering into the door, her pigtails hanging to one side, her finger scratching at her turkle's back again. Frek ran over to join her. Cawmb's new baby was crying, opening his little clamshell head all the way. His voice was amazingly loud.

"Give him to me," Gibby was telling Cawmb. "He likes me better."

Sure enough, when Cawmb handed the baby Unipusker back to Gibby, the newborn instantly ceased his uproar. He smiled blissfully up at the Grulloo's craggy face and made cooing noises.

"Grieve that my baby prefers the deformed thing to me!" wailed Cawmb.

"My name's Gibby, damn you!"

"Suggest Gibby be our baby-sitter," said Hawb in a placating tone. "Point out that being nursed by an alien is a good formative experience for a future branecast producer. Confess that I too may be about to shed a baby, inspired by you, O Cawmb. Note that another of your babies seems about to come loose as well. Mention that we could use some help, dear."

"This one's a cute little guy," said Gibby. "Look—he's holding my finger."

"Inquire if you have children of your own," said Cawmb in a calmer tone, after taking a quick glance back at his tail.

"Sure," said Gibby. "Two of them. The oldest is—"

"I think Renata and I'll go up to the cockpit to look around," put in Frek. "Will you be okay down here, Gibby?"

The Grulloo shot Frek a knowing look. "Far be it from me to get between a boy and a girl."

"Whatever that's supposed to mean," said Frek, blushing a little. "Come on, Renata." Another of Cawmb's babies showed signs of being about to work himself loose. And Hawb was reaching back to unfasten his tail cover. Enough of all that.

Frek and Renata crossed the transparent deck together, moving in big hops. The receding surface of Jumm was like a magical rug. Frek felt as if he were walking on air.

Renata led him through a doorway to a vertical shaft that ran up past four decks of the saucer. The acceleration was low enough that it was easy to pull themselves up with the handholds on the shaft's side. The appointments on the decks they passed grew more and more sumptuous. The walls were covered with murals and filigrees, the furniture was plush and heavy. The light globes were shaped like Unipusker heads and the ends of the heavy chairs' arms were embossed with Unipusker heads as well. Images of Unipuskers were everywhere among the decorations, but none were present in the flesh.

"Is Pilot Evawrt the only other one on board?" Frek asked Renata as they paused at one of the unoccupied decks to catch their breath. The floor was covered with a rug resembling vig-skin but with brindle spots shaped like Unipuskers. The murals were patterned with vertical stripes of delicate green, overlaid by horizontal branches inset with images of windows into little rooms with Unipuskers in them. A city of giant rickrack plants. Four easy chairs were invitingly grouped around an octagonal gold table holding an object resembling a crystal ball. A glowing logo rotated at the ball's center.

Being a Nubbie, Frek found it odd to be in a room whose furnishings were a collection of disparate objects—rather than component parts of a single living thing like a house tree. Could the Unipuskers actually have made these furnishings by hand? It was hard to imagine an advanced civilization doing something so tedious.

"Hawb and Cawmb chartered this saucer from Pilot Evawrt just for themselves," answered Renata in her low voice. "The Unipuskers are pretty extravagant. A big change for me, after five years of simple living in a Crufter asteroid. I barely remember Earth. Yessica moved us to Sick Hindu when I was seven. On Sick Hindu, a new blanket is a big deal. Especially since we weave them ourselves." Renata bounced across the room and flopped down in one of the chairs. "There's no special rush to see Pilot Evawrt. He's just another bossy Unipusker. We've got about seven more hours till we get back. Tell me about Earth."

Frek took the chair next to Renata. The back had a big hole near its base to accommodate a Unipusker tail. Other than that it was quite comfortable. He looked down at the chair's intricately patterned arms, which were sort of like wood, yet somehow artificial. The material was smoother than real, and warped into impossibly perfect curves. The chair was like a toon, like the *idea* of a chair.

"Where do the Unipuskers get all this stuff?" he asked Renata. "They don't—they don't use tools and machines, do they?"

"No, no," said Renata, and laughed. She gestured at the room and at the saucer around them. "The Unipuskers' things are what they call kennies. It's a stage beyond biotechnology. Instead of using live matter, you use live kenner. Kenner is this odd kind of matter—the Unipuskers said we call it dark matter? Supposedly any piece of kenner is a little bit awake. Like a plant, maybe, or a pet. Funny that we humans never noticed that."

"The angelwings have a way of metabolizing dark matter," said Frek. "That's what makes them so strong. And the Orpolese already showed me some kenner tweets. I'd always thought dark matter was supposed to be invisible—at right angles to ordinary reality. How do the Unipuskers do it?"

"I'll take you to see a kenny crafter when we get to Unipusk. They're goggy," said Renata. "A kenny is an indoctrinated chunk of kenner, right? A kenny knows how it's supposed to look and how it's supposed to act. To make, like, a chair, the kenny crafter just tells a wad of dark matter to start acting that way. This ship we're in—it's a kenny that thinks it's a flying saucer. The three big high-status jobs on Unipusk are branecast producer, saucer pilot, and kenny crafter. Those are the ones who have the biggest rickrack plants and the most children. I talk a lot. You look confused."

"This is a long way from Middleville," said Frek, smiling at Renata. He was having so much fun watching her face and listening to the melody of her voice that he wasn't following everything she said.

"What's it like there?" asked Renata. "Tell me about Earth."

So Frek talked to Renata for a while about his life back home. He hadn't expected it would seem particularly interesting to her, but she hung on every word, asking lots of questions. She loved hearing about the Goob Dolls and his sisters. It didn't seem to matter to her that she was two years older than he was.

"You guys must miss your dad," said Renata presently. "I like him, he's nice. And funny. A little—disorganized, though."

"He's living with your mother and you?" asked Frek.

"Sort of. On Sick Hindu there aren't any real family groups. We all sleep together in a row of pods." She positioned her turkle in her lap. "I have lots of pictures of Sick Hindu. Show the pods, turkle." A drawing of pointed hammocks appeared, delicately hatched, and with tints from the turkle's skin. "Usually Carb takes the pod next to Yessica," said Renata, pointing. "She has him enchanted, only Brahman knows how. And they spend a lot of time together in the day. After me, Yessica likes Carb more than anyone. Or, no, Yessica likes *herself* the most, then me, then Carb. Or maybe Carb, then me, I guess it depends. Show my drawing of Yessica, turkle." A vain-looking woman appeared, wearing an exaggerated crown and with a forked tongue. "She's mad at me a lot, but she gets even madder at Carb when he flirts with other women. She was the one who wouldn't let him send a message to your family. He kept trying to, but she always found a way to block it. Until she got the idea of tricking you with the ring. I'm glad to be off on this outing without them, to tell the truth. That's enough Yessica, turkle."

It made Frek sad to think of Carb being tangled up with a woman who kept him from talking to his real family. And a little jealous to think of Carb taking care of Renata.

"Who's your father?" he asked her.

"I'll tell you some other time," said Renata, looking a little embarrassed.

So Frek changed the subject. "When we get back, you could come visit us in Middleville," he said. "I could take you out flying on the angelwings. And we could look at lots of toons."

"You know what I'd really like to be when I grow up?" asked Renata.

"What?"

"A toonsmith. That's one reason I like to draw."

"I want to be a toonsmith, too!" exclaimed Frek. "I thought the Crufters didn't have toons or the Net, though."

"We have this archival, static Net," said Renata. "Like for a library. If you go to the right url in our archive, there's a whole bunch of classic toon shows stored in there. The boss Crufters don't know about it. I've watched all the old shows and practiced drawing the characters. Show him my Goob Doll Judy, turkle." A little animation of Goob Doll Judy juggling the Earth, Moon, and Sun appeared on the turkle's back. "Toons are the best," said Renata. "I'd love for my drawings to think and talk. On Earth, when you watch the Goob Doll show, can Judy really see you move?"

"Oh yeah," said Frek. "*Especially* Judy. Goob Doll Judy doesn't miss a thing. On my way here I spent a night in Stun City, and Gibby and I were at this cowloon and I met two women toonsmiths. Sooly and Deanna. Deanna had a turkle just like yours. I could probably introduce you to her. Maybe you and I should work together on a show about our trip! Do the Unipuskers have toons?"

"No," said Renata. "They watch that thing instead." She pointed at the crystal ball on the table. "The flickerball. Go ahead and esp some brane." She made a face.

"So that's it, huh?" said Frek, leaning over to study the ball. It was preternaturally smooth and shiny. A kenny of some kind. The slowly rotating logo in its center was an image of cube with shiny blue rods for its edges and slow-moving happy faces on each of six sides, six kinds of aliens, each of them smiling down at a little flickerball. Satisfied branecast customers. "Esp some brane," mused Frek.

"They say that because our universe is a brane. You know, short for 'membrane,' it's that word from string theory. And using the flickerball feels like extrasensory perception would be." Renata paused and looked at him. "The Unipuskers and the Orpolese have talked to you about branecasting, right? They're competing for the right to produce the humanity channel. Branecasting is the whole reason they abducted us."

"I know all right," said Frek. "I just met the branecasters."

"You did?!?" exclaimed Renata. "Already? Hawb and Cawmb aren't going to like that. They wanted your dad to be the first one to talk to them! Oh Brahman, what'll they do when they find out?"

"They know," said Frek, and sighed. "They've been esping me all along. I bet lots of aliens are esping me—not just the Unipuskers, but the Orpolese and who knows what other alien races. Megahits on the Frek site."

"You can feel it too?" said Renata. "My mother and your dad can't tell. I started noticing it right before the Unipuskers showed up.

I'd almost been wondering if I was going gollywog. Tell me how it feels to you."

Frek looked around the room. He was, of course, being esped right now. With the plot thickening like this, it hardly let up at all anymore. Frek was good viewing. "Things look warmer and smoother. For short I think of it as the *golden glow*. And there's this other feeling—of being just a little bit outside of myself."

"Exactly," said Renata. "And I get these flashes of having everything look really—surprising. Like I'd never seen a chair or a ceiling or a human hand before."

"Yes," said Frek, smiling at Renata. She understood. "Do you know how to use the flickerball? I wouldn't mind seeing how it feels from the other side."

"It's simple," said Renata. "You just touch the flickerball and it starts up. It begins flashing and making a buzzing noise. It's annoying, but if you focus in on the ball, you start seeing things. It's like the ball is a camera that gets inside the head of anybody anywhere in the universe who's in a talent race that the Unipuskers can see. The flickerball puts your head right inside the alien's head and you see like him or her, and you think the same thoughts. It's extreme."

"Have you been on Unipusk a long time?" asked Frek. "To figure all this out?"

"I've lost track," said Renata. "Maybe two weeks. Like I said, Hawb and Cawmb wanted us to register them as the humanity channel's producers. Only, ever since we got here, the Unipuskers' tunnel to the Planck brane has been down. Talk about losers. And meanwhile you've already been over there?"

"That's me," said Frek, puffing himself up a bit. "When we yunched down, we popped through to the Planck brane right away. The branecasters decohered Bumby and Ulla—froze their souls. But then they made me the humanity channel negotiator. I told them we didn't want to be branecast at all, but they said we had to be, so I picked Ulla and Bumby as producers, so at least nothing will happen right away. While I was at it, I asked them to give me an elixir to restore the Earth's biome. To bring back all the extinct species."

"Bring back sparrows and monkeys?" said Renata. "Artichokes and butterflies?"

"Yubba," said Frek. "Restore everything. But the branecasters are sleazy crooks. They said they'd only give me the elixir if Bumby asked for it, but meanwhile Bumby stays decoherent until the branecasters get a ten-kilometer gold asteroid for bail. And of course the whole deal is off if some other producers make me change my mind. Or if they kill me."

"Carb wouldn't have thought of asking for a genomic elixir," said Renata. "Yessica just wanted him to get her the access to branecast Crufter propaganda into everyone's heads."

"What's wrong with the Unipuskers' tunnel to the Planck brane?" asked Frek.

"They call it the branelink," said Renata. "It feeds on the junk that the Unipuskers pipe in from Jumm through their transport tube. But a bomb from Jumm blew out the transport tube right before we got here. I hope the Unipuskers don't freak out and hurt you. The whole reason they got us to ask you to land here was so you wouldn't get to the Planck brane before them. Talk about a backfire."

"You tricked me," said Frek.

"Well, in a way. Not really, though. We asked you to come help us, and we do need help."

"I wonder how we can escape," said Frek, not really mad anymore. "It'll be hard, with them watching our brains all the time."

"Maybe something will come up," said Renata, glancing around. "Maybe we can figure out a way to block them out."

"I might as well try the flickerball," said Frek. "See what it's all about."

"Do it," said Renata. "I've tried it twice, but I don't like it. It's unny. But see for yourself." She nodded her head, which made her pigtails bounce. "I should tell you that you twitch your left eye to change channels and you twitch your right eye to change the point of view. I'll shake you if you get stuck. Meanwhile—" She put her fingers in her ears and added, her voice a bit too loud, "—it makes a sound that's really annoying if you're not the one esping it."

Tentatively, Frek laid his hand on the flickerball. It was big, nearly the size of his head, a transparent glassy ball resting upon a smooth hole in the table. As soon as he touched the ball, the blue-edged cube with idiotically happy faces faded away. The flickerball began to hum. Light pulsed out of it, strobing faster and faster. Frek stared into the flicker, letting the buzz fill his ears.

And then he was on another world, watching a Unipusk-produced branecast channel. He was a giant lizard beneath a green sun. A creature like a velociraptor. His jaws were stained with blood. He'd just killed a hairy animal, something like a sloth. Before beginning to feed, he threw back his head and gave his victory roar. An error. The jungle trees shook and a lizard twice his size appeared. A creature like a tyrannosaurus rex. The monster sprang at him. Frek twitched his right eye to change viewpoint.

He was the attacking T. rex lizard. He'd already pinned the velociraptor creature to the ground and was about to tear open his neck. The captive lizard was hissing and squealing; its eyes were piteously rolling in their orbits. *Let it go,* thought Frek. *Don't kill it.* The big lizard hesitated, wanting to kill, yet forbidden to by Frek's branecast command. *Run away,* thought Frek. The great T. rex creature rose and wheeled about, heading off through the jungle trees. Frek twitched his left eye to change channels.

He was Spa of planet Zorg. He was a gout of metallic lava oozing down a gently sloping volcanic shield a thousand kilometers across. Powerful electric currents circulated within his molten body, maintaining the patterns of his thought. Next to him was a fellow gout named Fon. They'd been flowing down this slope for seventy years now; when they reached the bottom, they'd seep into a crack, percolate down to the One Great Magma, and rise up again. It was a predictable cycle, presently enlivened by Spa's contemplation of the possible geometric forms to be found in seven-dimensional space. He thought a lovely stellated polytope pattern toward Fon, but, unbelievably, Fon wasn't interested. Why? Fon was busy thinking of—how ghastly, how inane— arrangements for the branches of a three-dimensional tree. He'd been dulled by one of the parasitic esper minds that infested their world.

Sadly, Spa contemplated his seven-dimensional polytope on his own. Fon's lapse made his very ions ache. Frek twitched his right eye.

He was Fon, sliding along beside his old friend Spa. Spa was thinking a seven-dimensional shape toward him, but just now he was absorbed in a problem that an esper voice in his head had set him to working on. It was a design for a rickrack tree to serve as the living quarters for a hundreds-strong family upon the world of Unipusk. The Unipusker espers had been coming and going within their minds ever since the coming of the branecast to planet Zorg—two full flow cycles in the past. Fon sensed Spa's frustration with him for not accepting the beautiful frozen music of his seven-dimensional polytope. But he had no choice but to obey the branecast voice that had spoken within his mind. He was bound and determined to search through every possible configuration of a particular seventy-three-branched rickrack tree to find the one form that maximized the comfort indices of all of its three hundred and eighty-eight rooms. Frek spoke into Fon's mind. "Forget about the Unipuskers' tree. Listen to your friend Spa." Still sensing through Fon, Frek shared the joy of hearing an esper voice release him of his wearisome task! Gladly, Fon opened his mind to accept dear Spa's intellectual treat. Frek twitched his left eye to switch to a different channel.

He was a bobblie on the surface of Jumm. He hated the Unipuskers with all his might. Their vile, intrusive transport tube was sucking away the substance of his home world. Their snooping branecast technology peered into the noble souls of the bobblies and dared to try to influence their behavior. And now he sensed the presence of a bossy esper within his mind again. His shape just now was a ragged crescent covering most of Jumm's largest red and yellow spot. He was sinking down into the atmosphere, his body a chain of raging storms. He'd nearly caught a Unipusker saucer a little while ago. He had to do something against those brutes. Perhaps he could feed another bomb into the filthy force field vortex of their transport tube. But probably the esper in his mind wouldn't let him. "Go ahead," said Frek silently. "Bomb the Unipuskers. Go for it. Goggy indeed." The bobblie's mind registered pleasure and surprise. He sank deeper, his winds howling, searching for the tube's bottom end, fashioning a supercritical mass of sulfur and helium on the way. Frek twitched his left eye.

He was Lora Huggins, wondering about her missing son. She was sitting in her kitchen, feeding her two daughters, having a little trouble keeping her mind focused. She felt like someone was watching her. The talk around Middleville was that something had happened to Gov in Stun City, some kind of attack upon his puffball. But the news shows said the puffball was merely undergoing renovations. And seemingly new images of Gov had appeared to address his subjects. The talk was that he'd fully restored himself from backups. Had Frek been responsible for the attack? He was nowhere to be found. Lora sighed, wondering and worrying. Frek reached out, trying to put some words of reassurance into Lora's mind. But the flickerball wasn't transmitting thoughts to humans. This must be because Bumby and Ulla hadn't yet been able to bring their production on line. The branecasters had spoken of open read-only access. This seemed to mean that any race at all could esp humanity, but none of them could influence the humans. Frek twitched his right eye to jump to another person's mind, hoping he might get to check the state of mind of his father.

But now the flickerball turned in on itself. Frek was esping himself, Frek esping Frek Huggins in a Unipusk saucer esping Frek. The pattern grew more and more involuted, forming a kind of inward-curling spiral. Frek's mind was chasing its own tail. His arm and leg muscles began clenching and unclenching in a rapid rhythm. The shuddering moved into his chest and stopped his breath—

"Frek!" It was Renata, breaking his connection to the flickerball. Frek collapsed back into his chair, gasping for air, his eyes weakly roving over the lavishly appointed saucer room. The flickerball was back to innocently showing that same ad: the turning cube with the six happy faces. Frek noticed now that one of the ad faces was a grinning Unipusker, another was a glowing donut, somehow a very stupid and self-satisfied-looking donut. Unlike the live "talent" aliens Frek had just been esping, the images on the ad cube were taped loops of happy users, forever delightedly chortling over their flickerballs.

The golden glow of the other espers was still upon Frek, feeling through his mind. The Unipuskers. It wouldn't do for them to see Frek's memory of helping the bobblie send another bomb into their transport tube. And now, for the first time, Frek made a successful effort to block the glow. Having experienced the flickerball himself made the difference. He understood what he was fighting against.

Rather than trying to push the golden glow down, or to block it out, he blew it up to the size of a sky. He put himself inside the espers, so to speak, and in this fashion he became too small to watch, like a minnow invisible within the currents of the water. Rather than resisting, he was giving way; rather than being felt by the alien minds, he slid around them. He was safe; he was free. Incredible.

With the pressure of the espers gone, he felt like his old self, like the same old messy, vague, indeterminate Frek, more likely to stare at the shape of a cloud than to tell you if he thought it might rain.

Looking up, Frek saw Hawb standing in the doorway. His tail cover was fastened a bit askew. Having just experienced the flickerball, Frek now understood how terrible it would be to have the Unipuskers giving people orders inside their minds. Could other people learn to free themselves as Frek just had? But how could he ever explain the process? And, for all Frek knew, the golden glow and the espers could reconquer his fragile newfound independence any time.

"Observe that you've learned more about the branecasting process," said the Unipusker. "Repeat my demand that you and your father go to the Planck brane to cancel the Ulla/Bumby deal and register Hawb/Cawmb as your sole producers. Threaten you."

"Yeah, yeah," said Frek, deciding to try insulting Hawb. He was a little giddy over having learned how to avoid the espers. The minds were still reaching for him, but he was continually sliding away, elusive as an air current. Why not try to rattle the Unipusker enough to expose a weakness? "It looks like another of those 'Pusker babies is about to drop off your nasty tail. Or is that a piece of dirt from the floor? Go spawn in private, you gross shell-head."

"Command you to proceed to cockpit to be under the surveillance of Pilot Evawrt," bellowed Hawb. "Forbid your further use of our flickerball. Condemn your insulting demeanor."

"You're ugly and you stink," riposted Frek.

"You tell him, Frek," said Renata loyally, though she looked a bit uneasy.

"Inform you that we are likely to kill both you and your father and let Yessica Sunshine negotiate a fresh deal with the branecasters," trumpeted Hawb. So there it was, the Unipuskers' backup strategy. Frek had goaded Hawb into revealing it. But now Frek immediately saw a way to pick a hole in it.

"You don't dare kill me because your crummy, gumpy branelink is broken," said Frek, staying on the offensive. "Kill me and my father, sure, but then some third group of producers is likely to bring a different person to the branecasters way before you get Yessica to the Planck brane. You need me alive, and I know it, you low-tide piece of muck. Treat me right and I just might have another talk with the branecasters and give the production deal to you. Bully me and you won't get any help at all."

"Assure you of our support," said Hawb in a sudden about-face. "Remark that I couldn't help esping some of your plan about a genomic elixir before you became so hard to read. Guarantee that if you throw the humanity channel's production rights to Cawmb and me, then we will obtain for you this elixir." The Unipusker parted his shell-head edges in an expression meant to be a smile. It was a terrible thing to see.

Frek make a shooing gesture with his hand, and Hawb went back down to the lower deck to rejoin Cawmb, Gibby, the new Unipusker babies, and the imprisoned dogs. And then Frek and Renata climbed to the summit of the saucer, a large room with a transparent dome.

Pilot Evawrt sat upon a jewel-encrusted throne in the room's very center, one eye stalk staring out through the dome, and the other eye stalk looking down at his hands. He was a lighter and more graceful Unipusker than Hawb and Cawmb, with a more angular jut to his clamshell head. He was guiding the saucer's flight by moving a luminous model of the saucer about in his lap, now and then tapping its little feelers. He paused from his piloting to greet Renata in a friendly, if somewhat sarcastic, fashion. Renata introduced Frek.

"Remark that my people will enjoy esping your race on branecast," said Pilot Evawrt. Perhaps he'd managed to listen in on Frek's discussion with Hawb. "Observe that the Unipusker public is always craving new shows. Diffidently remark that Unipuskers are somewhat dull and ordinary. State that they love the input of a colorful new race like yourself." Evawrt had a tenor voice that seemed odd coming from his dark, powerful form.

"What ends up happening to the races you guys watch?" demanded Frek. "Doesn't it have a bad effect on them?"

"I bet it does," chimed in Renata. "It'd be like having your mother always breathing down your neck and poking into everything you do. But with a complete alien instead of your mother. Even more of an alien."

"Distinguish myself from the mass of Unipuskers," said Evawrt in his light, mocking voice. "Brag that I am a saucer pilot and not a vegetative consumer whose primary excitement in life derives from esping brane and manipulating alien creatures such as you. Frankly question the morality of esping brane. Admit that the process saps the vitality of the peoples whom we esp. Gruffly state that, nevertheless, I make my living by helping Hawb and Cawmb find talent races like yourself. Shrug off the degenerative consequences of our projected activities upon your race. Self-forgivingly observe that there are, after all, trillions upon trillions of talent races in the galaxies. Compare you to a single ripe berry in an endless forest of rickrack trees. Terminate our conversation ostensibly to concentrate upon my piloting duties, but primarily to make you feel weak and unimportant."

And with that Evawrt stopped talking. With one stalk eye studiously directed toward the dome and the other studying the model saucer in his lap, he gave every indication that he had no further time for chitchat. Frek almost wondered if the pilot had been kidding him. Or were the Unipuskers somehow unable to do anything but state their exact thoughts? Frek tried asking Evawrt about this, but the pilot wouldn't say any more.

Frek and Renata sat down together on a soft bench at the edge of the cockpit's large deck. Both of them started to talk at the same time, then said, "You go first," at the same time, and then tried again.

"Do you really think they might kill us?" Frek got out. "Are you scared?" He could feel that he was still successfully blocking out the espers. They might be watching Renata, but his own thoughts were free.

"That's what I was going to ask you," said Renata, overlapping him. "But, okay, I'll answer. I think we're like ants to them. So, yes, I think they could kill us. And no, I don't want to die. But Crufters teach that we live in the Now moment, and that death is a part of life that happens to everyone, and that when you die you merge back into the Brahman, so there's nothing to worry about. I kind of like that, even if some of the Crufters are nuts." Renata bobbed her head and one of her hanging pigtails bumped against Frek's hand. "We're alive right now, is the main thing, right? Let's keep on making friends, Frek, and keep on thinking about ways to escape. Don't let the stinking, ugly Unipuskers stampede us into feeling all tense and doomed and *guuuh*." Renata illustrated the meaning of this last sound by making a grimace and clenching her fists beside her head and whirling them in little circles. Then she relaxed her face and sighed. "I wish I could think of something humdrum for us to talk about, though."

"Ants," said Frek at random. "You mentioned ants. We don't have ants. Do you have ants on Sick Hindu?"

"Yes," said Renata. "They're one of the species that came in Sri-Sri Krisna's founding ark in 2666." Sri-Sri Krisna was a high-ranking genomicist who'd broken free of NuBioCom and helped found the Crufters, a group dedicated to trying to bring the old ways back to Earth. He'd escaped from Earth in a spaceship right after the Great Collapse with a few dozen obsolete genomes that he'd saved.

"He brought ants on purpose?"

"He brought whatever he could. The official teaching is: The ants came with Krisna, and we Crufters are blessed to have them. Sri-Sri's seeds are sacred." She gave an odd little laugh, then continued. "The ants do keep the hummingbirds from wearing out the trumpet vine flowers. If the birds hang around drinking nectar for too long, the ants crawl up their bills and bite the corners of their eyes. Show the picture of the ants and the hummingbird, turkle." The plate-sized little creature displayed another of Renata's drawings, with orange flowers, green hummingbirds, and pinching purple ants. Renata cocked her head at the picture and poked one of the ants' mandibles with her fingernail to change its angle. "Save it like that, turkle." She turned her attention back to Frek. "The ants get into our honey and our flour and they spoil a lot of things."

"It must be fun inside Sick Hindu," said Frek. "We have turmites instead of ants, and watchbirds instead of hummingbirds. And the only kind of flower we have any more is roseplusplus."

"I'd take Earth any day," said Renata. "Sick Hindu is a hollow rock that's like ten or twenty kilometers across. It's run by a religious cult that forbids realtime Net access and won't let me see new toons. Did I mention that my stress-fest mother is a high poobah in the Crufter cause? But tell me more about how the turmites make your clothes."

Frek and Renata chatted the rest of the way to Unipusk, with Renata showing him a turkle picture every now and then. Their topics of conversation included: parents, friends, first memories, dinosaurs, stars, the fear of falling, types of human-powered flight, weightlessness, the force of gravity, kenner and the other kinds of matter, famous physicists, famous musicians, the superiority of the magnetic guitar over its predecessor the electric guitar, the Skull Farmers toon character Strummer, Goob Doll Judy, the current Earth fashion for ear-painting, Frek's previous experiences with girls, Renata's previous experiences with boys, the difficulties of being a socially awkward smart kid, the possibility of having a successful career without a formal education, the current state of toonsmithing tools, Frek's experiences with the Merry Mollusks url, how real-world squid and octopus suckers had worked, the legendary rivalry between sperm whales and giant squid, speculations about the intelligence of the extinct whales, attempts to estimate the number of intelligent species in the universe in light of the new evidence gained from Frek and Renata's experiences with the flickerball, pimples, breakfast foods, hot baths, swimming on Earth versus swimming in zero gravity, the different greens in the leaves of plants, estimates of the total number of colors that a person might see, speculation about aliens' additional sensory organs, favorite and unfavorite smells, the cause of sneezing, the highest note that a human being might conceivably sing, whether a high and pure note could actually shatter glass, learning to play virtual instruments as opposed to real instruments, Lora's job as a facilitator, Yessica's former job as an ethical analyst, Yessica's current standing in the Crufter party, Yessica's bad habits, Carb's bad habits, the nature of reality, loneliness, the institution of marriage, the ideal number of children to have, the size of the premium paid to mothers willing to have more than two children, the painfulness of childbirth, the qualities of tank-grown children, the best hair colors to have, Frek's haircut, Renata's pigtails, types of braids, and more.

All the while Gibby was down on the lower deck with Hawb, Cawmb, and the baby, the dogs were locked up, and Pilot Evawrt continued to ignore them.

Before long, Frek knew he liked Renata more than any girl he'd ever talked to before. He was glad to have met her on his own like this, without his friends around. If his friends saw him talking to a girl for this long, they'd say he had a girlfriend, and they'd ask him when he was going to kiss her and so on. Frek had very little experience in this area. Looking at Renata's smooth cheek so close to his, it did seem conceivable that he might kiss that cheek some day. He'd never thought that way about a girl before. Their two years' age difference didn't seem to matter one bit. Renata's cheek had fine down on it like a peach.

"Why are you looking at me that way, Frek? What are you thinking?"

"Um, you know." And, without saying more than that, he felt that she did know, exactly.

"There's Unipusk," said Renata after a long, thoughtful minute. "We're almost there. Too bad."

Unipusk was a bright crescent off to one side of the dome. The sunlit part was green, blue, and white, just like Earth with her land, seas, and clouds. The darker part was itself dimly lit from Jumm's reflected light, with bright spots pricked out against it like lace. If the lights were cities, then Unipusk was very densely inhabited indeed.

In preparation for landing, they orbited Unipusk for a while, passing near the transport tube from Jumm. A very large cloud of icy crystals floated around the tube, and within the fog of the cloud, Frek could make out two other Unipusker saucers shining beams upon a rough-looking patch of the tube.

"They're annealing that hole in the tube's force fields," explained Renata. "I think they're actually going to be done today. A bomb went off in the tube right before we got here, and ever since then the Unipuskers have been working on repairing the field. I think I mentioned that's why their branelink has been down? It runs off of the kenner gas that they extract out of the Jumm-stuff they pump through the tube."

They angled down through the atmosphere, striking it near the terminator line between day and night. The saucer spiraled smoothly toward a coastline, a peninsula, a flat region, a spaceport. And there they settled to the ground.

"Disembark," said Evawrt, doing something to the model saucer in his lap. One side of the cockpit wall opened up into a ramp that stretched all the way to the ground. "Bid you farewell."

Frek and Renata stepped onto the ramp together. He felt a gentle breeze. The air smelled fresher than inside the saucer, less sulfurous, with a faint whiff of violets. Two suns were sinking below the horizon. One sun was large and red, already partly out of sight. The other sun was smaller and brighter, hovering just above the bigger sun's edge. It was dusk on Unipusk.

unipusk

Looking around from the top of the ramp, Frek saw a spaceport with scores of spacecraft and dozens of alien hangars and warehouses. Some of the structures were domes and cubes, others had odder forms. The nearest building resembled a giant black sea-urchin, with hundreds of shiny spikes. Open doors punctuated its walls.

Ranged around the outer edge of the spaceport field were stylized green plants of an immense size—each of them had a tall, tapering shaft, with horizontal tubes sticking out for branches. These were giant versions of the rickrack plants they'd eaten for lunch. The branches were made up of sections, and each section bore round shiny dots: windows. Along the bottoms of the branches were dark sprinkles— spores? With the waning of the day, lights were becoming visible within the great rickrack trees.

"See that rickrack tree right there?" said Renata, pointing. "That's where Hawb and Cawmb live with their umpty-ump children. Like I said, the richest Unipuskers have their trees right beside the spaceport. Mom and your father are in there, too, eagerly awaiting us. If they're awake."

Although half the craft visible at the spaceport seemed to be Unipusker flying saucers, the remainder must have been from other alien worlds. No two of them were the same. Among the alien ships, Frek noticed a steel pear resting on its small end, a rainbow-reflecting cube balancing itself upon one corner, a golden ball with black spots, a softly slumping gelatinous mass, a snowman-shape of three glowing spheres, a piled-up stack of immense copper chain links, two great matte-black cylinders crossing each other like a letter X, a silvery boomerang and, right beside the sea-urchin-shaped building, a house-sized green barrel with a fan of purple tentacles protruding from either end. The barrel had black ridges along it, dividing it into five sections. Like Ulla, this ship seemed to be independently alive.

All this Frek saw, walking down the long ramp from the Unipuskers' giant flying saucer. As they neared the bottom, Renata took his hand in hers. Her touch was warm and smooth. Holding Renata's hand was, in a way, even more amazing than landing on Unipusk.

Figures moved here and there across the spaceport. Not all of them were Unipuskers. Some things like starfish were busy by the nearby sea-urchin building and its barrel-shaped spacecraft. A few smiley-faced balls bounced around the snowman-shaped ship, and a half dozen large cockroaches could be seen crawling upon the matte-black X ship.

One particular figure was speeding across the flat spaceport field toward them: It was a single hulking Unipusker upon a hovering disk. The rim of the disk was decorated with metallic scrolls. As it drew closer, Frek could see that the little craft had a purple velvet railing held up by posts that were slim models of Unipuskers. The heavy-set pilot steered the hoverdisk by moving his foot against a low, stubby control.

As Frek and Renata stepped onto the hard-packed blue soil of Unipusk, the hoverdisk drew up to a particular spot on the great curved hull of Evawrt's saucer. The driver cocked an eye stalk at Frek and held out a stubby, finned rod that could have been a weapon. Presumably he was something like a chauffeur.

A section of the hull dissolved, revealing Hawb, Cawmb, and Gibby. They were carrying a baby apiece, with Gibby's astride his tail. The three of them stepped onto the ornate hovering disk, which now lowered to the ground so that Frek and Renata could join the others.

Curious about the new world, Gibby hopped down off the hover-disk onto the ground to pick at and sniff the soil. He gathered up a few of the blue pebbles and placed them in his pocket, all the while balancing the Unipusker baby on his tail.

"Request you to get back on our hoverdisk," said Hawb to Gibby. "Explain that we're in a hurry to go to the house of Hawb and Cawmb."

"Not so fast," put in Frek. "Don't forget our dogs. You said I could keep the dogs in my room in your house, remember?"

Hawb narrowed the crack in his clamshell head and let out a staccato series of chirps. Invisible in the cockpit, Evawrt piped a response. A second patch of the saucer's hull thinned out, this spot a bit lower down. With a yelp and a thump, Wow and Woo dropped to the hard surface of the spaceport field. Wow sniffed the air, shook himself twice, and trotted over to Frek. Woo, however, took off full tilt toward the barrel-shaped spacecraft nearby.

Cawmb said something sharp, and the chauffeur shot a pulse of light after the fleeing dog. But he missed. One of the barrel's great tentacles twitched and fired back a warning shot, a green ball of light that bounced slowly up to them and burst in a vile-smelling puff of gas. Meanwhile, Woo had rounded the barrel and disappeared into one of the many doors in the sea-urchin-shaped building beyond the barrel ship.

Frek snatched up Wow and held him in his arms, both to keep him from bolting, and to protect him lest the Unipuskers chose to punish one dog for the other's escape.

But Hawb didn't seem very interested in the issue. "Regret your dog's defection to the Radiolarians," was all he said. "Opine that nothing can be done. Caution that you steady yourself before our chauffeur Gawrgor flies the hoverdisk to our mansion."

As they glided across the spaceport, the second sun went down. Brownish-red lights sprang into life upon the surface of the Radiolarians' sea-urchin structure, while their barrel ship's ribs took on a purplish glow. All across the spaceport, the other ships and buildings were lighting up as well. And the rickrack trees—the rickrack trees became canes of glowing green, the greens an artful composite of lighter and darker pinstripes, quite lovely. Above it all hung the vast red and yellow disk of Jumm, filling perhaps a fourth of the sky. And for Frek, a golden glow was overlaid upon everything; alien watchers were tasting the beauties seen through his eyes.

Renata squeezed Frek's hand. "I'm worried about what they'll do to you," she whispered. "If you don't get them their deal with the branecasters."

With the golden glow creeping up on him, Frek again tried his new head trick of making the glow as big as the sky, and of making himself as untouchable as air. It seemed to work, and now yet another mental exercise occurred to him, a way of correcting whatever changes the alien contacts had wrought upon him by their constant subtle questioning.

Odd as it sounded, the best phrase for the feeling Frek now had was *combing his brain*—a sensation of running invisible fingers though his gray matter, of restoring his mentality to its full infinite-dimensional glory, of uncollapsing his opinions, of letting his streams of thought recohere into their true, natural form. Combing his brain, yes. He seemed continually to be learning new mental skills.

"Don't worry," Frek whispered to Renata, briefly letting himself savor the fact that another transport tube bomb was coming soon. And then, before the ever-grasping espers could come find the thought, he let the secret dissolve out into the air he was breathing. He thought only of the air, of the sweet, violet perfume from the rickrack trees. He crouched down to talk to Gibby and, so far as possible, to Wow.

"The Unipuskers are going to lock you guys up in my room," he told them. "They say they'll kill us all unless I tell the branecasters to let *them* produce our channel instead of the Orpolese. But they're not going to do anything until their branelink comes back up."

"Hope it takes a while," said Gibby. "There's got to be a bar here somewhere. Maybe even a cowloon. It's thirsty work comin' halfway across the galaxy. Seems like a fella could settle in for a nice long party here."

Frek didn't have the heart to tell Gibby the branelink was supposed to be coming up tomorrow.

Hawb and Cawmb's dwelling was the largest of the rickrack trees. The tree's outer walls were encrusted with architectural ornamentation—columns, arches, statues, balconies, friezes, spandrels, cornices, and more. Although the tree itself was clearly biotech, the elaborate ornaments around its base had a clarity of color and purity of form that indicated they were kennies. As in the saucer, the decorations were everywhere marked with representations of the faces and bodies of Unipuskers.

On either side of the building's enormous round door, for instance, was a giant statue of one of the clam-headed Unipuskers. Each statue bent to one side, so that the two of them made a pair of parentheses around the disk of the door. Frek had trouble telling the Unipuskers apart, but perhaps these guardian figures were images of Hawb and Cawmb. Little sloping cornice roofs shaded the statues like droopy stone awnings. The projecting roofs were shingled with squares and circles, each circle holding a bas relief of yet another Unipusker's clamshell head and eye stalks, each head slightly different. Kennies like colored porcelain chandeliers dangled from the undersides of the roofs, lighting up the heads of the statues who were themselves holding saddle-shaped surfaces bearing yet more faces of Unipuskers, mixed in with representations of vigs and Unipusker flying saucers.

The door itself was decorated with concentric rings of heads: an outer ring of Unipuskers, then a ring of heads of creatures from alien worlds, within that a band of vig heads surrounding another ring of Unipuskers, then more aliens, more vigs, more Unipuskers—more rings than it really seemed there could be room for. The center depicted a final triumphant Unipusker with his eye stalks pointing right at you. Shiny branching hinges held the door in place; the bronze kenner of these brackets writhed in among the hundreds of heads, sending a curlicue or a tendril around each and every one.

Gawrgor the chauffeur prodded the hoverdisk control stick with his foot; the hoverdisk sounded a triplet of notes like a French horn's. The immense door swung slowly open. A heavy smell of sulfur wafted out, pungent as sewer gas. Frek held his breath for a minute, but then he was out of air, and he had to start the task of getting used to the Unipuskers' stench. The hoverdisk floated in and settled to the floor of the mansion's single ground-floor room. Breathing through his mouth, Frek dismounted with the others.

The room was fully a hundred meters high, a round, tapering shaft with a helical kenner staircase wrapped in great turns around its inner wall. A Unipusker head was carved in relief upon each stair step, and no two steps were alike in texture or color. The floor was ankle deep in plush kenner carpeting, with overstuffed chairs and elaborate spindly tables to every side, each table's sides covered with friezes of tiny Unipuskers.

The room held a dozen flickerballs. Though most of them were simply showing the branecasters' blue-edged logo cube of the six imbecilic happy customers, three or four of the balls were active. It was enough to fill the room with a steady vibe of buzzing and blinking. To stare at one of the active balls for more than a few seconds was to feel your viewpoint drawn off to another world; seen even from the corner of your eye, a turned-on flickerball would send a constant stream of alien landscapes your way, doing its best to suck you further in.

Kenner statues of Unipuskers and of vigs ringed the bases of the walls, and in the very center of the room was an immense onyx statue of two Unipuskers in what seemed to be a domestic situation. Possibly Hawb and Cawmb. They were sitting up to their waists in a tub of—mud? Their hands were raised in the air, supporting a flickerball two meters across. Standing to one side as a pendant to this monument was a statue of a nobly proportioned vig. The vig was of kenner trained to resemble orange-tinted marble. The vig's eye stalks were tipped with glowing green jewels and it bore a great golden bowl upon its back.

Gibby had never seen a flickerball before. It was only a matter of seconds till the big one in the center of the room had reeled him in. He stood rooted to the spot, staring up at the hypnotic sphere. His mouth was slack and his tail was slightly twitching; his Unipusker baby slipped to the floor.

The muscular Gawrgor prodded the hoverdisk's control stick with his foot, piloting the disk off into a kind of garage set into the room's wall beneath the high round door to the outer world. As the garage door opened, Frek could see that Gawrgor had an apartment for himself in there. And then chauffeur and hoverdisk were gone from view.

Another Unipusker servant came trotting to pick up Gibby's neglected baby. He introduced himself as Angawl; he seemed to be something like a butler. Taking Hawb and Cawmb's charges as well, Angawl bustled toward a thick vertical column of light on the far side of the room. It seemed to be a zone of negative gravity, for when the butler stepped into the shaft, he and the three clam-headed babies floated upward. Peering after them, Frek saw young Unipuskers and vigs darting in and out of the negative gravity like birds swooping around a thermal, appearing and disappearing amid the tunnellike mouths feeding into the high reaches of the great hall's walls, occasionally swinging themselves from the scattered vines that seemed to grow across the narrowing shaft. Faint sounds of sibilant gurgling drifted down, along with sharp liquid creaking noises that might have been Unipusker laughs.

"Here they come," said Renata, giving Frek a nudge.

Frek looked and saw someone sweeping down the staircase that circled the wall. Renata's mother. Frek recognized her from the turkle drawing Renata had shown him. She wore a watch-me boa, which was a once-popular NuBioCom kritter that surrounded its bearer with flashes of light from its tail and with the chiming of gongs and the piping of flutes from its mouth. She had long, tangled hair, mostly blond. Her face was unbeautiful, with small eyes and a tense mouth. Six breasts ran down her chest and belly, arranged in three pairs. Like the watch-me boa, multiple breast pairs were a fashion that had gone out of style on Earth five or even ten years ago.

"That's my mother," said Renata. "Yessica Sunshine to you."

A lean, rangy man was coming down the stairs behind Yessica, picking his way across the embossed Unipusker faces, a man with weather-beaten skin, a large beak of nose, crinkles around his eyes, and a long, twitching line of a mouth. A half-meter Mohawk crest protruded evenly from the center-line of his head. The smeared blue tattoo molds in his temples were patterned like Unipusker UFOs.

"Dad!" shouted Frek, running toward the stairs, all his anger temporarily forgotten.

"Frek!" called Dad, his face splitting in a smile. "The supreme Frek Huggins! You made it!" With a quick twist and jostle, he got ahead of Yessica and came loping down the stairs. They shook hands, and then Carb even tried to lift Frek into the air like he used to, but Frek had grown, and he wasn't all that eager for Carb to be lifting him, so it didn't last long. They didn't quite manage to hug. Hawb and Cawmb stood by Frek's side, listening and watching.

"Is this some goggy action, or what?" said Carb, gesturing around the room. Frek noticed that he was wearing the ring that matched Frek's. Even though the rings had caused him trouble, it still made Frek proud to be paired with his father. "We're halfway across the galaxy," continued Carb, "cutting deals for clam-headed monsters with the branecasters from Dimension Z! I've missed you, son. You look great. How's Lora?"

"Oh, she's all right," said Frek, unable to suppress his smile of pleasure at seeing his father. "We've all been kind of mad at you for leaving. I guess you heard Mom got you two guys unwebbed."

"Yeah," said Carb, looking a little sad. He glanced over his shoulder, hooking his thumb toward Yessica, who was just completing her grand entrance. "Truth be told, Yessica's the one got me to leave Earth. It hasn't really worked out like I expected. Women, Frek—someday you'll see. I know I'm a rat. But I had to bail. Gov wanted to give me the Three R's, I owed money to a gleep who was threatening to collect one of my kidneys, and when I met Yessica on the Net—well, it seemed like a point-and-click. And all to help the mighty Crufter cause! I had to sneak off without telling you guys, or Gov would have stopped me."

"You tell him, Carb," said Yessica, sweeping up to them in a cloud of stink. "The cause is everything." Musk perfume wafted up from her three low-cut dress tops, a floral perfume seeped from the nostrils of the watch-me boa, incense trickled from a miniature shield-bug clamped to her left earlobe, and she even had a pheromone shelf-fungus growing upon her right ankle.

Mixed in with the sulfur smell of the silently listening Unipuskers, the combination made Frek sneeze.

"Yessica, this is my son, Frek," said Carb, dredging up a scrap of the manners that Grandma Huggins had drilled into him. "And Frek, this is Yessica Sunshine, my special friend. I take it you met Yessica's daughter, Renata, on the saucer. You two hit it off?"

"Sure," said Frek, not wanting to give his real feelings away. He glanced at Renata; her face was studiously blank. "Hello, Yessica," added Frek.

Yessica stared deep into Frek's eyes, formed her lips into a smile, and held out her hand as if Frek might kiss it. Frek sneezed again, then shook the woman's hand, doing his best to avoid looking at her triple décolletage. The gongs and flutes were still playing about her, but now Yessica did something to make her watch-me boa fall silent.

"Have Hawb and Cawmb told you about our big plans?" Yessica asked Frek in a bright tone. "They're going to help us to spread the Old Ways all over Earth. The Crufter Teachings. Your father's to negotiate for the whole human race."

"Provide Yessica and Carb with updated information that Frek has already met with the branecasters," interjected Hawb. "Inform them that, so long as Frek lives, he is the exclusive negotiator for humanity channel production deals with the branecasters. Point out that Frek need not live very long."

"You met the branecasters during that little blip when we lost track of you?" exclaimed Carb. "That was less than a second of real-time. And you were over in the, the—what do they call it again, Yessica?"

"The Planck brane," said Yessica in a cold tone. "Oh, Frek—you pushed your way over there? How piggy. You really could have checked with your father first. This was supposed to be his big thing. His key to self-esteem. You must have some unresolved issues with him, if you treat him that way."

"Come *on,* Mom," exclaimed Renata. "Enough of your gobbledygook. It's not like Frek had a choice. He unyunched because we asked him to, remember? Frek thought Carb was hurt. Don't you remember putting the makeup on Carb to trick Frek into coming down? Hello? How could Frek possibly know they'd come down too near the transport tube and pop on through to the Planck brane?"

"If it's so easy to 'pop through,' as you put it," said Yessica, changing her tack, "then why did we just fritter away two weeks sitting here off the grid? Cawmb? You know perfectly well how essential a role I have on the Sick Hindu asteroid. I can hardly imagine how my people are getting along without me. It's not acceptable for you to waste my time like this."

"Remind you that we suffered a Jumm bobblie bomb in the transport tube," said Cawmb. "Question your presumption in using such a peremptory tone with me. Threaten to kill you."

"I'll use any tone I like, you freaking monster," said Yessica. "Threaten, threaten, threaten, all day long. Why don't you chew on *this* idea with your disgusting toothless mouth-shell: you've got Carb's flesh-and-blood son now, which means you have all the leverage over him you could ever need. Send back my daughter immediately. It's criminal that she's being endangered. Surely you recognize that a person of my status is entitled to have her gene-line preserved. Send Renata back today, but, yes, you may keep me a bit longer. I admit to being intrigued by the branecast production negotiations. I think there's still a chance I can do something significant to synergize the process."

Three little vigs came frolicking across the room, bouncing on the stubby bumps they had instead of legs, their eye stalks dancing. Wow took off after them, and they burrowed under one of the enormous chairs. Unable to get at them, Wow ran to the other side of the room, where more vigs were vheenking.

"Inform you that the transport tube's force fields are fully repaired and that our branelink will be operational by noon tomorrow, Yessica," said Cawmb. "Don't make us feed you to the vigs."

Cawmb and Hawb dragged over a pair of huge thronelike chairs with tail holes and seated themselves beside a couch and the chair where the vigs had hidden. The calm, tasty beasts hardly seemed like man-eaters, but presumably bigger, meaner ones could be found. Not that the Unipusker's threats seemed very likely to be carried out any time soon. Right now they seemed in the mood for extensive conversation.

"Obviously you'll help the Unipuskers, correct, Frek?" said Yessica, flopping down onto the chair with the vigs. Dad perched himself on the chair's plush arm. He silently studied his fingernails and picked at the cuticles, listening with an amused expression.

"I might," said Frek, taking a seat on a nearby couch with Renata. There was no point in antagonizing Yessica and the Unipuskers just now. Might as well gather more information. With the golden glow as big as the sky, his thoughts as elusive as air, and his brain fresh-combed, Frek didn't have to form opinions before he was ready.

A few meters off stood Gibby, still esping the big flickerball. The buzzing truly was unpleasant. And if you looked at the ball even a little bit it was hard to look away. Frek disliked branecasting more all the time.

"Help them or else—" put in Dad, cutting off his phrase with a shrill razzing noise and running his finger across his throat. He meant it as a joke, and Frek laughed. Rebellious old Dad could make anything official seem ridiculous. Even a death sentence.

"It's not funny, you two," snapped Yessica. "I have been absolutely depending on Carb to get the Unipuskers to let me transmit Crufter lore to everyone on Earth. Can we depend on you to support your father and me in this, Frek? Giving me open access to humanity could be a major evolutionary step forward for our human race."

A major step toward killing everyone with boredom, thought Frek. But, for Renata's sake, he came on glozy. "My idea is to have the branecasters give us an elixir to restore the biome of planet Earth," he said mildly. "To bring back all the missing species."

As Frek said this, he briefly wondered if the elixir really *was* his idea. Hadn't Bumby actually been the first one to suggest it? But, come to think of it, Bumby had probably esped the notion from Frek's mind, esped how intensely Frek wanted to restore the biome.

"Oh," said Yessica, not exactly able to argue with Frek's worthy goal, but not wanting to support it either, since it wasn't something she'd come up with herself. "But—"

"But I'm also wondering if we'd be better off without any branecast at all," continued Frek, drowning her out, glozy or not. "Even if that means not getting any goodies." He glanced at Hawb. "What's the precise appeal of having us as one of your talent races, anyway?" he demanded. "And what would happen to us if you produced our channel?"

"Confess that, on our own, we Unipuskers are unexciting and un-original," said Hawb self-deprecatingly. Angawl was moving among them, offering glasses of vig milk, mounds of rickrack shoots, and platters of raw and cooked vig steak. "Amplify that we're always looking for something new from outsiders," added Hawb, tossing off a glass of the foamy gray milk. "Single out Cawmb and myself as the very hungriest for novelty. Assert this is why we're the best producers."

"Explain that production has to do with crafting a talent race's be-havior to be pleasing to us," added Cawmb, pausing to flip his mouth wide open and shovel in a large raw vig steak. "Caution that too much novelty isn't good," he continued in a muffled tone. "Inform you that Unipusk citizens adhere to a Unipusk Branecast Code, designed to avoid witnessing thoughts and behaviors deleterious to the stability of Unipusk society. Politely stipulate that our espers will in fact be tailor-ing human behavior to pull it into conformity with the Unipusk Branecast Code." He swallowed, then wiped the vig blood from the rims of his mouth shells. "Assert this will be for your own good. Guar-antee as a sweetener that we will let Yessica broadcast her Crufter teachings to one and all for five minutes a day." He snapped down an-other vig steak. "Add an insincere promise to try to obtain your genomic elixir. Weaken this unenforceable noncommitment by re-marking that we can honor it only to whatever extent the application of so radical an alteration to the talent biome would prove fully con-sistent with the Unipusk Branecast Code. Stand back to observe your furious but entertaining reaction." Another great swallow and more shell-wiping. "Remind you that if you oppose us we will kill you and feed you to the vigs."

One thing about the Unipuskers, they certainly spoke their thoughts. Bad as the news was, it didn't really surprise Frek. Cawmb's remarks simply confirmed what Frek had subconsciously realized as soon as he'd met the Unipuskers and tried the flickerball. By now, Frek had no intention of voluntarily giving the Unipuskers the humanity channel production deal. Come what may, no branecast at all was the proper answer. Desperate as the situation seemed, Frek had a deep sense that things would work out. He felt power within him, more power than he'd ever imagined before.

"Give it a rest, clam-head," he said to Hawb, and helped himself to a handful of rickrack shoots and a nicely seared vig steak.

Cawmb and Hawb got into one of their squabbles then. Amidst the drainpipe sounds of their native tongue, Frek kept hearing his name. Probably they were arguing about what Frek had said to them or what one of them had said to Frek. But for now they were done talking to him directly.

"They bicker all day," said Renata. "It drives me nuts. Try the vig milk. It's not as pukeful as you'd expect."

The stuff was sweet and mild, almost like a vanilla milk shake, although you *could* kind of taste that it came from the underside of a vheenking vig.

While Frek ate, Dad wandered over to the other side of the room to fiddle with the golden bowl resting on the back of the marble statue of the ideal vig. All at once a white balloon appeared in the bowl; it looked like a pod of moolk. Dad glanced over, and seeing Frek watching him, he winked at Frek and dropped the moolk pod inside his shirt rather than drinking it right away.

"Mention one other thing to you, Frek," said Cawmb, surfacing from his dispute with Hawb. "Inform you that the Orpolese like to push their branecast worlds into chaos. Point out that this is the opposite extreme from our Unipusk production style. Remark that your race might very well be worse off with the Orpolese than with us. Urge you to thoughtfully consider your options."

"Where's my room?" said Frek. Wow was lying at his feet. The dog had given up on chasing vigs and had come back to enjoy some of Frek's free vig meat. So far Frek and Wow hadn't had a chance to talk about Woo's disappearance. And Gibby was still mesmerized by the flickerball he was watching, his mouth slack and half open, his eyes rolled partway back into his head.

"The 'Puskers want you and Wow and the Grulloo to share a room that's to hell and gone at the end of the second branch up," said Carb. "Nice and far from Hawb and Cawmb; they sleep at the tippy-top. Angawl has to take you to your room to lock you in. But I'll come along so we can talk." He hunkered down and rubbed Wow's head. "Good to see old Wowie again. Remember me, Wowie-Zowie?"

"Carb," squeaked Wow in his back-of-the-throat voice.

"Good dog. It was nice of you to help Frek on his big adventure. Maybe tomorrow we can finish the job off, Frek. No reason you can't ask the branecasters for that elixir and for Yessica's broadcast rights both, huh?" Without waiting for an answer, Carb walked over to Gibby and tweaked his tail. "Bedtime, you!" Like most normal humans, Carb didn't like Grulloos.

"What!?" shouted Gibby, snapping out of his flickerball trance. "I was—I was climbing a tree. I had arms and legs. What'd you have to bother me for? Who the geeve are you, anyhow?"

"That's my father," said Frek. "You were already esped-out when he came downstairs. Carb, this is my traveling buddy, Gibby. Gibby, this is Carb."

"You got a peach of a young'un, Carb," said Gibby, gamely resetting his mood. "He took a big risk to come down here and save you."

Carb seemed a little bemused at meeting a Grulloo socially, but he took it in his stride. "I hope I didn't call him here for nothing," he said. "Tomorrow's the big day."

"Announce a tour of Unipusk beginning bright and early," said Hawb, still listening in. "Inform you that the tour ends at the branelink. Inquire again if we can depend on you to help us with the branecasters, Frek? Threaten death for noncompliance."

"Don't nag me," said Frek, determined to keep his options open. "Ready, Dad?"

"Stay down here with me for a while, Carb," put in Yessica, leaning against Frek's father. "Renata can show them where to go."

"That's pretty selfish of you, Mom," put in Renata. "Frek hasn't seen his father in over a year."

"Would you mind, Frek?" said Carb.

"Oh, sure. I nearly kill myself to come save you, and—"

"Present myself as prepared to escort you," interrupted Angawl.

"I'll come upstairs with you, Frek," said Renata in a comforting tone. "To help show you the ropes."

"I don't feel so good," complained Gibby. "With my spacesuit gone I can't get any stim cell nuggets."

"Use the wishing well," said Carb in a careless tone. "At least that's what I call it. That gold bowl on top of that marble statue of a vig. You stare into it and visualize what you want, and it makes it for you. And, Frek, don't make me feel even guiltier. Let's just enjoy being together again, okay?"

"You *should* feel guilty!" exclaimed Frek, feeling a balloon of anger in his chest. "You left us without saying good-bye. And how come you never sent us a message?"

"Because I wouldn't let him," said Yessica imperiously. She caught hold of Carb's hand and led him over to a big soft couch farther off. They flopped down together and Carb took out the moolk pod and passed it to Yessica, who couldn't wait to start sucking the juice from it. Carb was totally under Yessica's spell. Was this his idea of being together with his son? Thanks for nothing, Dad.

Meanwhile Gibby got himself some stim cell nuggets from the golden bowl, easy as pie. Fortunately he hadn't noticed Carb getting the moolk. Angawl and Renata led Frek, Gibby, and Wow over to the other side of the room to the negative gravity zone so they could ride up to the living quarters.

The forces in the bright-lit column of air were tuned so the upward motion was pleasantly slow. It was a nice feeling to be drifting up through the big rickrack stalk. There were decorations for the first thirty or so meters—paintings, bas reliefs, sculptures, and moving holograms, mostly of Unipuskers. But after that the walls were just plain green, a two-tone green with faint vertical stripes.

To make it easier to get around—and to fend off a possibly disastrous drop—the rickrack tree had grown a number of tendrils across parts of the shaft, green ropes like jungle vines. At first Frek was worried about bumping into these safety vines, but then he noticed that as long as he was still moving up, the vines got out of his way. A rickrack tree seemed to be at least as intelligent as a house tree.

At the fifty-meter level they began encountering orange viglets and young Unipuskers frolicking in the negative gravity column. The frisky creatures liked to ride the column up, find their way out of it, drop down along the edges, and swing from a vine—or air-glide—to get back into the column for another ride up. Both the vigs and the Unipuskers were flexible enough that they could stretch out their bodies enough to cut the air. For his part, Wow's legs churned frantically in the air each time a vig hurtled past with its eyestalks laid back against its head for speed.

When Frek thought to look down again, he noticed Yessica twining her arms about Carb's neck, rubbing herself against him like a spider spinning silk around a captured fly. How could his father prefer a dumb, pushy woman like that to Mom?

Right about then Frek was distracted by a little Unipusker the size of his forearm smacking into him. "You're ugly and you stink," gurgled the child alien, parroting the insult Frek had delivered to Hawb back in the saucer. Word spread fast on Unipusk. The little creature spread his shell-head wide open to emit the wet creaking noise of Unipusker laughter.

"Prepare to alight," said Angawl.

"He means we get off at the next branch," said Renata. "Your room's out at the very tip." She grabbed Frek's hand and shoved him away from her. The reaction sent her out of the negative gravity column, and as she fell, she pulled Frek after her. Frek caught hold of Gibby and Gibby grabbed Wow. It almost looked as if they'd fall straight back down to the floor, but some smart rickrack ropes swooped into position for them to grab. Renata caught hold of one, and Frek did, too. The elastic tendrils slowed their fall, and swung them into one of the hollow side branches of the great rickrack tree.

A gingerbread-man army of young Unipuskers went pounding down the long branch with them—well, actually some of them were more than waist high. Every single one of the Unipuskers wanted to tweak Gibby's tail, to ruffle Wow's fur, to feel Renata's soft skin, to sniff Frek, and to pipe, "You're ugly and you stink." What made it even worse was that Angawl let out the exact same gurgling chuckle each time one of the children said the tag line. If one Unipusker thought of something interesting to say or do, all the others had to say or do the same thing. And none of them ever got tired of it. Hawb had said they were unoriginal.

The horizontal branch was a series of dorm rooms, separated by soft walls with slits in them that you could easily push through. Unlike the great room downstairs, the dorms were sparsely furnished, with little more than dome lamps on the ceilings. Upon the floors were disk-shaped pools of muddy slurry, grown right into the flesh of the rickrack tree, three or four pools to a room. These were the dark spots Frek had earlier thought might be rickrack spores.

Seeing some of the little Unipuskers comfortably lying in the puddles, Frek understood that these were their beds, and that the sculpture of Hawb and Cawmb in the great hall was of the couple about to sleep together. The smell from the beds was rank; it was the very essence of what was unpleasant about the smell of Unipuskers.

Frek felt uneasy about pushing farther and farther into the branch, through room after strong-smelling room. As they got farther out, the Unipuskers in the rooms got larger and more intimidating. "I'd rather be closer to the middle," he complained.

"They want you out on the very tip," repeated Renata. "For security. Mom and I live on the tip of the branch directly across from yours, by the way. And Hawb and Cawmb sleep at the rickrack tree's top. Like this." Quickly she sketched a diagram on her turkle.

"What about my father?"

"He usually sleeps on a couch in the main room," said Renata, marking the spot with an X. "The Unipuskers don't mind, so long as some of us are out on the tips being hostages. Carb doesn't like it up here. And Mom's not good at getting in and out of the shaft, particularly if she's drinking moolk, so she stays downstairs a lot, too. The nights when they both make it upstairs, I get to go and sleep downstairs myself. The air's better down there. But don't worry, the tipmost rooms don't smell that bad. How do you like my mom? Are you going to help us get out of here?"

"I hate to say," said Frek, focusing on the second question. Too late he realized that it might sound to Renata as if he didn't like her mother—which was true, but obviously it wasn't the right thing to tell her, even if she herself didn't like her mother. Immediately Renata grew distant and cold.

Just then they reached the sealed green door to their room. Unlike the other doors, it didn't have a simple entrance slit, only a pinhole at its center. Angawl patted the door with a rapid and subtle series of gestures and the pinhole spread open to make an entrance hoop.

Renata stiffly watched Frek, Gibby, and Wow climb into the green conical tip of the long branch. Frek would have liked to talk to her alone some more, but Angawl was impatient and in any case Renata too seemed in a hurry to go. She said a quick good-bye and then Angawl tapped the door closed.

Immediately Frek had an urge to run after Renata to try to clear things up, but by now the door had stiffened, and it wouldn't let him through. They were locked in for the night.

So Frek, Gibby, and Wow settled down on the sloping green floor as best they could. The room had neither beds nor a lamp, but some light filtered in from the Unipusker dorm room next door. The rickrack walls were soft to the touch, with a fresh plant smell, faintly scented with violets. With the door sealed off like this, the room was fairly pleasant.

"I'm beat," said Gibby, comfortably curling his arms around his head. He looked very small. "That flickerball stuff, Frek, it was goggy. Fella could get hooked on that thing. I was a tiger, and a bird, and a—some kind of jellyfish. And then I was climbin' a tree. What a day."

"I have no idea what'll happen tomorrow," said Frek uneasily. Part of his defense against the espers was to resist forming opinions before he had to. And even if he had known his exact plans, telling his companions would be tantamount to telling the Unipuskers.

"You'll know what to do," said Gibby. "Don't worry." He wrapped his arms a little tighter and shut his eyes.

"I'm glad you're here, Gibby," murmured Frek.

There were some air holes on the walls, like windows the size of Frek's fist. He peered out a hole for a minute, staring at the other lit-up rickrack trees, and at the glowing ships and warehouses upon the field of the spaceport.

"Woo gone," said Wow, standing next to him, reaching his nose up to catch some of the window's air.

"Why did she run off?" Frek asked the dog. "Do you know?"

"Sweet whistle called us," said Wow.

"From the other ship? That barrel thing with the tentacles?"

"Sweet whistle," repeated Wow. "Wow stay with Frek. Wow miss Woo."

"Good boy, Wow. Maybe we'll get Woo back soon."

And then Frek lay down with his companions and fell asleep.

In the night Wow woke him up.

"Woo," Wow creaked into his ear. "Woo barking. Lift Wow up to smell and listen." Though Frek's ears weren't sharp enough to hear any barking, he held Wow up to one of the air holes for a minute, letting Wow thoroughly sniff the air, all the while cocking his ears, turning his head, and wagging his tail.

And then Wow did some barking of his own, which set the four nearly-grown Unipuskers in the next room to hissing and gurgling in excitement, until one of them called out, "You're ugly and you stink," and then they all had to yell that, and then one of the Unipuskers thought of pounding on the wall separating them, and then they all had to do that, and then of course Wow had to bark back.

"Good barking," said Wow when things quieted down. "Woo know Wow here. Wow know Woo there. Woo know Wow know. Wow know Woo know."

In the morning Renata came along with Angawl to get them. The first thing Frek saw when the door irised open was the hurt expression on Renata's face.

"I'm sorry about last night," he said, not entirely sure why he was apologizing, but having a sense that it was expected.

"You weren't very nice about my mother," said Renata, slowly swinging her pigtails.

"Oh, she's fine," said Frek. "For a grownup. I'm nobody to complain about parents. Look at Carb."

"I'd rather not, a lot of the time," said Renata with a little smile.

"He and Mom just went to bed in our room about an hour ago. Up all night. They woke me up. I've been waiting for Angawl to come get you. Killing time floating in the gravity shaft and chasing vigs."

"Well, please don't be mad at me," said Frek and then, before really thinking about it, he leaned forward and kissed Renata's sweet cheek.

"Yee haw!" exclaimed Gibby, which was enough to end the moment.

"*You're* staying here today," Renata told the Grulloo with mock sternness.

"Confirm this information," said Angawl.

"Huh?" said Gibby. What with spending yesterday evening staring at the flickerball downstairs, Gibby had missed out on most of the plans.

"You and Wow are supposed to be hostages today," Frek told him. "To put the pressure on me."

"I doubt if this overgrown horsetail plant can hold me," said Gibby, thumping the floor with perhaps more bravado than he felt. "You go and do the right thing, Frek. Don't never mind about us."

The golden glow of the alien espers had been around Frek as soon as he woke up, and it had taken a few minutes' effort to carry out the three exercises he'd started calling *sky-air-comb* for short. First, phase the glow from intense spotlight into a brightness of the sky; second, offer so little resistance to the peekers that he was as untouchable as air; and third, restore his natural mental processes by running a virtual comb of ghostly fingers through the tissues of his brain.

After all that, Frek didn't feel free to think very concretely about the events to come. "You're a pal," was all he said to Gibby.

And then Angawl, Frek, and Renata pushed their way through about a hundred stinking dorm rooms, and swung on a series of vines to reach the ground floor. Hawb and Cawmb were waiting on one of the couches. Seeing Frek and Renata approach, Hawb called out a command. The garage set into the room's wall opened its door, and their chauffeur, Gawrgor, came riding out on the hoverdisk.

"Greet Frek," said Hawb, ushering Frek and Renata up the hoverdisk's brass steps to lean upon its velvet railings. "Announce the start of our little tour. Predict you will love Unipusk. Mention that we'll pick up Carb and Yessica later, right before we proceed to the branelink. Bid farewell to Angawl."

They rose into the air and Gawrgor poked the control stick to make the hoverdisk trumpet the same three notes as before. The hall's great round door swung open and they were out in the fresh morning air. It felt wonderful. The two suns were a handbreadth above the spaceport on the left, with half of Jumm bulging up above the right side of the horizon like the world's largest mushroom. In the morning light the rickrack trees were a gentle shade of green. Their long, pointed branches rocked and whispered in the breeze, now and then bumping together to make musical booms.

Far beyond the trees Frek could see the bright line of the transport tube arcing down from Jumm to the surface of Unipusk. That's where the branelink would be. The morning suns lit up a large high yellow-ish cloud beside the transport tube. This was the leftover spill of Jumm stuff, slowly drifting away.

To begin their tour, the hoverdisk circled among some of the nearby rickrack trees, with Hawb and Cawmb pointing out the dwellings that they most admired. As Renata had said, all of the Unipuskers living near the spaceport seemed to be pilots, kenny crafters, or producers of branecast channels. To Frek's eye, the ornamentation-encrusted rick-rack trunks soon began looking much the same. And it was hard to get over the fact that rickrack was the one and only kind of plant in sight.

"Show him the suburbs and the farms and the kenny crafters' stu-dio, Gawrgor," put in Renata. "That's more interesting. Look Frek, I made a map. Show the map, turkle." Her turkle's back flashed a colorful little diagram, with the spaceport in red, the rickrack man-sions in yellow, the suburbs in purple, and the farms in green. The kenny crafter's studio was a deep blue splotch.

Gawrgor kicked the stubby control stick. The hoverdisk heeled over and sped out to a zone where the rickrack homes were smaller and their decorations less intense. Unipuskers were out and about: trading stuff with each other, attaching fresh adornments to their houses, gos-siping, playing with their children, and walking their vigs. The vigs rocked along on their stubby leg-bumps like high-speed inchworms.

When two pet vigs met, they'd usually rub their eye stalks together in a friendly way, though a few of them were prone to varking.

Frek could see all this because Gawrgor had slowed the hoverdisk to the pace of a walk, the better to show Frek the ambience of suburban Unipusk. Everyone had time to stop and stare at Frek, often calling out, "You're ugly and you stink." Frek noticed a large number of flickerballs in use; the buzzing sound was pervasive, and every window seemed to pulse with the ragged light. The flickerballs seemed more aggressive here among the lower classes. The fat part of the market. Some of the Unipuskers were using flickerballs to watch through Frek's eyes even as he passed; they alternated between looking at him directly and looking at the flickerball view of what he saw. He sky-air-combed his mind to keep his personal thoughts his own.

The ride got embarrassing when, in a burst of creativity, one of the Unipuskers had the notion of yelling, "Kiss Renata again!" Apparently the espers had observed the tender moment on their flickerballs.

"Kiss Renata again!" repeated the next Unipusker. And then, in typical Unipusker fashion, each and every one of the others had to parrot the little witticism. When Frek shook his fist at one of them, that immediately became something that all the Unipuskers had to do too. At his approach, they'd yell, "You're ugly and you stink," shake their fists, yell, "Kiss Renata again," and burst into Unipusker laughter, making the exact same wet creaking noise every time.

"They're idiots," Frek whispered to Renata.

"I know," said Renata, shaking her head. Even so, she was smiling and in a good mood.

They flew above some fields filled with very small rickrack plants and orange, grazing vigs. Although the rickrack plants were indeed a pleasant shade of green, Frek was getting sick of the color. There were absolutely no other plants but rickrack on Unipusk. And no other animals but vigs. This was the ultimate result of the policies NuBioCom had set for Earth: one plant, one animal. Frek redoubled his resolve to fetch a biome-restoring elixir. Fetch the elixir and save Earth from the branecasters. The vastness of the task was daunting. Yet for some reason Frek felt sure he'd find the way.

Most of the farm vigs looked peaceful. Frek noticed one letting her eye stalks flop down limp in contentment as she munched her food. He saw a farmer milk a calm vig by rubbing his hand along a spongy spot on the beast's belly. The gray milk drizzled down through the farmer's fingers into a little trough leading to a bucket. Yet a few vigs had a wild side; Frek saw a Unipusker vig herder step into one fenced field where the vigs aggressively opened up their long mouths and charged.

Meanwhile they were drawing closer to the all-but-endless column of the transport tube. The bottom of the tube disappeared into a big open pit in the ground. A steady stream of turbid fluid was traveling down the tube to be processed by the devices in the pit. There were several buildings at the edge of the pit, with messy piles of blue Unipusk dirt all around them. Unlike the dwellings on Unipusk, these structures weren't rickrack plants. They were of smooth, clear-colored materials that could only be crafted kenner. One of the buildings was a golden sphere standing on legs, while another resembled an enormous model of a Unipusker's iridescent brown head.

"We'll go in there first," said Renata, pointing at the clam-shaped building. "That's the kenny crafters' studio. Should be lively today with the transport tube working again."

The great, glistening structure was complete with long, gently wobbling "eye stalks" and a dozen shorter projections. And just as upon a Unipusker head, the edges on one side of the building were parted in a great horizontal slit: the door. The hoverdisk carried them right in.

The space within the shell was even larger than Frek had expected from the outside; some kind of alien technological magic was at work, akin to Ulla's shrinking field that made the space inside her seem so big.

The effect was that the cavernous interior of the kenny crafters' studio room seemed to stretch hundreds of meters on every side. Every square centimeter of the domed ceiling had something fastened to it: paintings, models, and full-scale examples of things the kenny crafters had made. Ranged along the edge between top and bottom were flickerballs, all of them turned on, each one showing a different world. And down in the center of the concave floor were a dozen or so Unipuskers fiddling with various objects: statues, couches, lamps, tail covers. They seemed to be studying the objects and, from time to time, doing things to change their shapes. Kenny crafters. Next to each of the kenny crafters was a limp orange cloth tube with one end attached to the floor.

"Give Frek a complete tour of available merchandise," said Hawb.

"Be very alert for fresh enhancements for our home," added Cawmb.

"Oh, please don't do that again," protested Renata. "It's so boring! Frek is supposed to see the kenny crafters themselves, not the stupid junk they make. The crafting is the part that's interesting."

Hawb's only response was a grunt. Gawrgor jiggled his foot, steering the hoverdisk up to the very apex of the shell. They began circling the room, spiraling outward, raptly staring up at displays on the ceiling: kenny crafted furniture, art objects, saucers, hoverdisks, eating utensils, grooming aids, garments, toys, and any number of artifacts whose purpose Frek couldn't fathom. After completing each gyre around the great room, Gawrgor moved the hoverdisk a notch farther out so as to circle a fresh band of goods.

"Order that one," said Cawmb now and then. "Order that one, too."

"They always do this," Renata murmured to Frek. "They love to shop. Viewing the whole display takes over an hour."

Frek and Renata sat down on the floor of the hoverdisk and let their legs dangle over the whorls and swirls of the hoverdisk's ornate brassy border. The constant rapid circling was less sickening if you looked away from the goods. Renata told Frek a little more about the kenny crafters working below.

"See those orange tubes coming out of the floor? That's where the kenner can come out. Dark matter. We have a fair amount of it around Unipusk anyway, but to get it in bulk, we process the stuff in the transport tube. The kenner's invisible until a kenny crafter vaars it."

"Vaars it?"

"A Unipusker word. It means that a kenny crafter can look at a spot where you wouldn't see anything, and he sees the dark matter there, the kenner, and he's able to reach out and make it want to let us see it. Flop it over into ordinary reality. And then the crafter shapes the kenny with his mind."

"Just by thinking at it? How?"

"Some people say that kenner is free-floating consciousness."

"People like who?"

"Like Mom." Renata giggled.

It was hard to keep up a conversation with the hoverdisk racing around so fast. Finally Frek and Renata gave up talking and simply sat it out. Renata passed the time by sketching Frek's profile on her turkle. For his part, Frek was watching the kenny crafters down below. Every now and then one of them would stare at his floor tube for a while, the tube would swell up, he'd move his hands, and there'd be an object next to him. And then he'd mess with the object for a long time. Vaaring. Frek was going to have to get a closer look when they landed. Meanwhile they had to work their way through what amounted to a very large catalog fixed to the ceiling. It really did take more than an hour. Renata went ahead and drew a second picture of Frek, which was flattering, and then, without thinking about it too much, the two began holding hands.

Finally Gawrgor set the hoverdisk down on the floor, right near a slender kenny crafter with extra long eye stalks on his head. Though most of his companions were busy, this one seemed not to be doing much of anything just now.

"Greet Cawmb and Hawb," he said, languidly aiming an eye stalk toward them. "Inquire how many new kennies you want. Greet Renata as well."

"Greet Gawrnier," said Cawmb. "Transmit our order form." One of the stubby antennas on his head twitched, presumably sending information to the kenny crafter.

"Propose delivery in two weeks," said the kenny crafter. "Apologize that we have a considerable backlog, what with the transport tube only having come back online yesterday."

"Politely inquire why you nevertheless appear so idle," said Cawmb.

"Huffily declare that I was thinking," said Gawrnier. "Remind you that I'm an artist, not a machine. Condescendingly explain that the finest kennies take more advance planning than a laypusker can imagine."

"Accept your delivery date," put in Hawb. "Apologize for my partner's rudeness." The two producer Unipuskers seemed a bit in awe of the kenny crafter.

"Tell Gawrnier about Frek," piped up Renata.

"Present the negotiator for a new talent race," said Hawb. "Introduce Frek Huggins to Gawrnier; introduce Gawrnier to Frek Huggins. Prepare to say good-bye."

"Wait," protested Frek. "We spent all that time circling around up there, and I still haven't gotten a good look at what they do."

"Frantically jabber about a shortage of time," said Cawmb. "Stress that the branelink is finally coming online in just a few minutes. Announce that we need to fetch Yessica and Carb before taking you to the branelink. Explain that we expect them to help convince you to play along. Threaten to kill you otherwise. Scold that you should be fully satisfied with your Unipusk tour by now."

"You wasted an hour looking at a geevin' catalog," exclaimed Frek, by no means wanting to go the branelink yet. "That's your idea of a tour?"

"Propose you leave Frek and Renata with me," put in Gawrnier unexpectedly. "Suggest they watch me working while you get the other members of your party."

"Assent," said Cawmb quickly. "Remark that we can fly faster without the flimsy humans on board. Thank Gawrnier. Caution Gawrnier not to let Frek escape. Estimate that we'll return in ten to fifteen minutes." And then he, Gawrgor, and Hawb were gone.

"Inquire if you want to watch me craft a kenny," asked Gawrnier.

"Sure," said Frek, mainly wondering if this might be the last thing he ever saw. He stuck one hand in his pocket and glued his fungus purse to the palm of his hand, trying not to think too clearly about his half-formed plan. The golden glow and the espers were pressing in. Sky-air-comb, he thought. Sky-air-comb.

Gawrnier took hold of the floppy tube leading up out of the floor; it was made of a material resembling shiny cloth. He focused his two eye stalks on the tube, vaaring it, and suddenly the tube grew firm, as if air were blowing out of it. Dark matter? Frek leaned forward and stuck out his hand. He felt the ghost of a breeze. The tube was rippling with the passage of *something*.

Gawrnier let go of the tube, which was temporarily able to stand up on its own. He held out his arms as if hugging a big ball; he brought them high up into the air and began staggering back and forth as if he were carrying something awkward and heavy. Frek glimpsed a flicker above Gawrnier, like the wiggling in the air above a fire. And then a big box on legs took form; Gawrnier jumped to one side to let it drop to the ground.

The thing was shaped a bit like a four-legged mahogany piano, but with no keyboard and with a circle of gold pads on its top surrounding a cut-out hole. The legs had an archaic animal look to them; they ended in claws tipped with gold talons. One of the legs had splintered when the thing dropped from the air. Gawrnier vaared at the leg until it healed itself. Frek forgot about the life-or-death decision hanging over his head. This was goggier than anything he'd ever seen. Could Gawrnier perhaps teach Frek to be a kenny crafter?

Gawrnier circled the object, examining each part. Frek could see greater or lesser alterations taking place at the touch of the kenny crafter's eyes. Embossed images of lizards like the ones Frek had seen in the flickerball appeared upon the gold disks on the thing's top surface. Wonderful. The edges of the top rounded themselves off, then became scalloped. Carvings of prehistoric ferns appeared upon the sides of the table. The legs roughened their texture and developed knees, becoming still more like dinosaur legs.

"Unbelievable," breathed Frek. "What's it for?"

"Dismiss it as merely another lizard-world-style table to be used as a flickerball-stand," said Gawrnier. "Impugn my customer's taste for having ordered it. Remark how uninspiring most of my orders are. Suggest that the glut of kenner coming in through the Jumm transport tube lowers our customers' level of taste. Assert that I would much prefer reworking our existing stocks of kenner into more interesting creations. Remark that certain kenny crafters are in fact pleased by the transport tube bombings, as these slow down our all-but-mindless order fulfillment process."

Gawrnier kicked at the limp orange tube on the floor till it perked up again. This time he drew off a smaller amount of kenner—the tube went flat quite soon, and Gawrnier's hands weren't very far apart.

Gawrnier vaared the space between his hands, that is, he fixed his attention on it with a marvelous intensity that Frek could almost feel. The air wavered, thickened, became like a lens. And then Gawrnier was holding a brand new flickerball, already displaying the blue-edged branecaster logo.

"Question the purpose of making yet another one of these," said Gawrnier with a sigh. "Remark that my countrymen esp entirely too much brane."

"But you have all those flickerballs set up around the edges of your studio," said Frek.

"Explain that we're expected to draw inspiration from them," said Gawrnier. "Regret that the customers want us to ape the worlds that they esp. Confess that, personally, I'd be content to make nothing but statues of vigs."

"Did you make the marble statue with the golden bowl on his back?" asked Frek ingratiatingly. Maybe, if he played his cards right, Gawrnier could be of help to him. He was worrying about the branelink. Maybe Gawrnier could help him escape. "The one that Cawmb and Hawb have? It's beautiful. I've never seen anything so skillfully crafted. And the wishing-well feature, it's like magic."

The kenny crafter's shell head parted in a long smile. "Express appreciation for your astuteness. Confirm this creation as mine. Gloat that I call it *Dream Vig,* that it's filled with a reserve chamber of liquid kenner, and that I crafted it so that whatever one wishes for, within reason, will appear within the golden bowl. Explain that *Dream Vig*'s telepathic interface is my invention, based upon a clever repurposing of flickerball technology. Declare that this is the noble kind of project I'd like to be spending my time upon instead of filling orders for stupid kac like a flickerball stand with dinosaur legs!"

In a sudden fit of pique, Gawrnier vaared so hard at the newly made table that its entire surface became covered with spidery hairline cracks. The cracks gave the thing a crackle finish that was kind of interesting; it made the table look as if it were covered with irregular transparent tiles. Cocking his head at the table for a moment, Gawrnier vaared again, so that now the bits of crackling took on alternating colors, making a bizarre checkerboard effect.

Right about then the hoverdisk came swooping back, with Gawrgor, Hawb, Cawmb, Carb, and Yessica aboard. Yessica was glued to Carb's side, stroking his cheek, working on him. Carb looked a little heavy-lidded, as if he still wasn't quite awake. He hadn't groomed his Mohawk today; it was flopped halfway down to the left.

Cawmb was briefly distracted from his mission by the sight of the new flickerball stand. "Express admiration for that finish," he said, his eye stalks stretching down. "Add a copy of this to my order."

"Kac on copies," muttered Gawrnier. "Praise the bomber of the transport tube."

"Tolerate the ravings of crazy artists," said Hawb dismissively, then turned his attention to Frek and Renata. "Urge haste," he cried. "Report that the branelink is ready!"

"This is it, Frek," murmured Carb as Frek and Renata squeezed onto the crowded hoverdisk. Though his father was acting sleepy, he was, Frek now realized, poised and alert. "I won't let them hurt you," breathed Dad.

And then they swept out of the kenny crafters' studio and over the mounds of dirt to the ball-like building on stilts next door.

"The branelink's inside of it," fretted Renata. "Don't pressure Frek, Mom. You don't have to always try to win!"

"Stay out of this, dear," snapped Yessica. "You have no idea what's best for you."

The hoverdisk rose up above the golden ball on legs. The ball had a hole at the top. Looking down into its interior, Frek saw a racing whirlpool of fog with a shiny green ball in the center. Evidently the ball was the mouth of the branelink. It looked like the leafy canopy of an earthly tree, pleasant enough. But Frek could readily imagine the unkind faces of the branecasters down there past the vegetation—the branecasters and the warped bright toony curves of the Planck brane landscape.

"Explain that all you have to do is jump in," said Hawb, taking hold of Frek's elbow.

"Inquire one final time if you will secure the humanity channel production deal for us," said Cawmb, holding Frek's other arm.

"No," said Frek, a little surprised at how calm he felt. "I'm not."

"Command you to kill him, Hawb," said Cawmb. "Plan then to send his father in his place."

"Stop it!" cried Renata.

"You'd be wasting your stinking time," said Carb in a hard, level tone. "I won't do it either." He placed himself between Frek and the Unipuskers.

"Kill Frek and *I'll* go," said Yessica suddenly. "I can negotiate the deal for you. I'm more trustworthy than Carb."

"Damn you, Mom," shrieked Renata, and gave her mother a shove. Yessica very nearly fell off the hoverdisk. Gawrgor had to drop the little craft down about five meters to keep her aboard, while Hawb and Cawmb released their hold on Frek to steady themselves. Frek seized the moment and jumped off the hovercraft onto the ground.

He had a chameleon mod out of his fungus purse in a second, and when he hit the ground he tore off his clothes and smeared on the mod. At the same time, he used his ever-growing mind powers to sky-air-comb the espers from being able to read his mind or even to see through his eyes. He was free and, if not invisible, at least reasonably hard to find. Even so, Gawrgor would probably have caught him right away—but just then there was a *boom* followed by a prolonged screaming noise from the sky.

Not taking time to look up, Frek bent low to the ground and ran away from the branelink as fast as he could, his skin the same stippled blue as the soil of Unipusk. By the time the two Unipuskers started yelling for him, he'd lost himself in the dirt piles. Only when he'd put the kenny crafters' studio between himself and the slowly circling hoverdisk did he pause to look up.

He saw a giant finger frantically color-painting the sky. It took a moment to grasp that this was the transport tube. The new bobblie bomb had gone off—not way out in space, but less than a kilometer overhead. The transport tube was completely severed from its Unipusk terminus. The force fields were steadily unraveling in either direction. The stub attached to the ground was already gone, and overhead the receding mouth of the tube flailed around like an out-of-control garden hose. Plumes of ammonia-scented Jumm stuff shrieked from the mouth, blotting out the sky.

The gas was chilling the air. And then all of a sudden it began snowing red and yellow methane crystals.

the
spaceport
bar

The snow stung Frek's bare feet, and the fumes made the air hard to breathe. The shrill roar from the burst tube was stupefying. He wanted to head for the spaceport—he had a vague plan of getting aboard some alien ship. But just now, more than anything, he needed shelter.

Glancing up at the kenny crafters' building, Frek noticed a lone figure standing in an open door. Gawrnier. The languid Unipusker's eye stalks were pointed straight at him. Even though Frek's skin was cunningly stippled with blue, red, and yellow to match the methane crystals and the Unipusk dirt, Gawrnier could see him. The kenny crafter made a quick beckoning gesture.

The smell of the Jumm gas and the melting crystals was sickening. Frek could hear a threatening buzz beneath the shriek of the broken transport tube. The hoverdisk was about to appear from around the clam-shaped building's edge. Frek darted up a spindly staircase toward Gawrnier, and a moment later he was safe inside the kenny crafters' building.

Though Frek had expected to end up in the same big-domed room he'd seen before, he found himself in a Spartan two-room apartment with some odd, minimalist chairs, a dark steaming tub that he recognized as a Unipusker bed, and an inactive little flickerball. A door across the room led out to the big workshop.

"Welcome Frek to my private studio," said Gawrnier. "Explain that I prefer this to my mansion by the spaceport. Offer you a seat." He cocked his head, peering at how Frek's skin had changed color to blend in with the room's shades of gray and pearl. "Observe that if I weren't able to vaar the kenner in your body, you'd be hard to see. Admire your camouflage, not to mention your forceful autopoietic blocking of branecast visibility. Propose that you relax."

"I'll try," said Frek, gingerly perching himself upon a kind of coiled spring. It rocked beneath his weight. "Please don't tell Hawb and Cawmb you found me. I have to get to the spaceport to escape. And I want to take the others with me. Carb, Renata, Gibby, Wow, and Woo. Not Yessica."

"Praise your determination," said Gawrnier. He closed the door to the big workshop. "Reveal that I despise Hawb and Cawmb. Reassure that I'll do what I can to help you. Inquire if you want to be a kenny crafter?"

Frek's heart leaped at the thought. "Uh—how did you guess?"

"Reply that I can sense your desire and your latent skill. Confess that I am eager to teach you so as to spread my noble occupation to your world. Propose that we begin immediately."

But surely this was impossible. "I don't have time for lessons," exclaimed Frek. "I'm on the run." He glanced down at himself. His skin was nicely patterned to match the opalescent curves of the spring-seat. This dose of chameleon mod would only last another few minutes—but he still had one more dose in the purse-fungus glued to the palm of his hand. Though he could feel the delicate touch of the golden branecast glow trying to seep back into his mind, he was finding it easier and easier to sky-air-comb it away. Maybe he could spare some time after all. "How—how long would it take to learn?" he asked.

"Propose ten minutes to begin," said Gawrnier. "Predict the rest of your life for mastery." He held out his hands to shape an invisible ball. "Observe and imitate."

Gawrnier had no tube of Jumm gas to get material from; he was going to work with whatever ambient kenner—that is, dark matter—could be found in the air of the room. Frek held out his own hands, imitating the Unipusker. He studied the empty space between his hands, wondering how to vaar the dark matter. Supposedly it was everywhere. Outside the broken transport tube was screaming in the sky, though bit by bit the sound was dwindling.

"Think smoothly," said Gawrnier. "Be like ripples in water. Don't grasp. Forget as fast as you notice. Let the space between your hands be part of you."

Frek peeked over at Gawrnier and, as before, he saw a shimmer between the Unipusker's hands.

"Don't watch me," admonished Gawrnier. "Don't think words. Be the kenner."

Frek flexed his fingers, focusing again on the ball of air between his hands. Nothing there, and nothing to say about it. Nothing—instead of starting up a new thought, he dove into the mental space at the end of the word. Holding back his own thoughts was no different than holding back the prying eyes of the espers. He breathed evenly and gazed straight ahead. At some point he had a sense of his head growing forward to fill the space—he hacked away the perception like weed in a garden and sank back into emptiness. The space between his hands was like part of his head. Emptiness. Something was flickering, but he didn't try and name it. Nothing.

There was a *thump*.

"Commend Frek," said Gawrnier.

Frek snapped out of his trance and looked down. A striped ball the size of a plum had dropped to the floor from between his hands. A ball of kenner. He'd vaared it from thin air. Glancing over at Gawrnier he saw that the Unipusker had made a large thin disk big enough for two people to stand on.

"I can't believe I did it," said Frek, nudging his little ball with the tip of his toe. "It was so easy. Why haven't people always been able to do this?"

"Suggest two reasons," said Gawrnier, "these being that (a) it's much easier to do something that you know to be possible, and that (b) you, Frek, are unlike your fellow men. Repeat a rumor that before your birth you were blessed by the Magic Pig."

Through Gawrnier's door Frek heard voices in the common room of the kenny crafters. Hawb and Cawmb, asking questions, and that damned Yessica yelling something, too.

"What blessing?" demanded Frek. "What Magic Pig?" The phrase sounded vaguely familiar.

"Confess I know little more on this topic. Suggest you question your father, within whose somewhat addled brain Hawb found the phrase and the rumor." Gawrnier cocked his head at the sounds from beyond the door. "Prioritize a second kenny crafting lesson," said the Unipusker. "Promise I will then rush you to the spaceport."

"All right," said Frek. "Show me how to vaar my kenner into something useful."

"Thus and so," said Gawrnier, cocking his head and gazing down at his round plate of kenner until it grew a railing and acquired new convolutions upon its lower side. He'd made the thing into a hoverdisk, complete with railings and a stubby control rod.

The Unipusker regarded Frek with a noticeable twinkle in his stalk-supported eyes. "Suggest you vaar what might be most useful to you," he said. "A vig-shaped spacesuit!"

"Huh?" Out in the common room, Hawb's voice was slowly drawing closer. For the moment all thoughts of kennies flew away.

Frek looked down at his body and saw naked copper skin. Kac! His chameleon mod had worn off. No time to lose. Without even looking at Gawrnier, he pried open his fungus purse, pulled out his last mod, and rubbed it on. His skin once again took on the shadings of the room around him. The only thing left in his fungus purse was the twig of Aaron's Rod. Add water and get a hundred-meter thicket of impenetrable tendrils. He had a feeling it would soon be time to use the Aaron's Rod, though he wasn't yet sure exactly how.

"Fix your mind upon your goal," said Gawrnier, calmly regarding the agitated Frek. "Imagine the shape of a vig, and the functionality of a spacesuit. Push the image out to the rind of your consciousness and empty your mind's center. In nothingness, merge with your ball of kenner. Let the target image collapse inward. And thus craft your kenny."

"I—I don't know how to design a spacesuit," protested Frek.

"Curse," said Gawrnier, and rapidly diddled with his flickerball.

"Look and absorb," he said after a minute. Frek gazed into the flickerball and saw that Gawrnier had tuned in on a holographic set of plans for a spacesuit similar to the ones the Orpolese had given them, though lighter and less durable in appearance. The plans were of Unipusk origin; the labels on the figures were three-dimensional squiggles resembling markings Frek had seen upon the Unipuskers' dwellings. Perhaps a hundred sets of the images flew past: views from every angle, close-up detail shots, filigrees that must have been logic circuits. And then Gawrnier turned the flickerball off; that is, he let it revert to showing the familiar blue-edged ad-cube. "Go," said Gawrnier.

Again Frek calmed his breath and his mind. Though he didn't think he remembered the exact shape of a vig, let alone the intricacies of the designs he'd just seen, he found the information intact within himself. He pushed the images out so that they surrounded him like a hollow shell. He and the kenner became one and the same.

Just as the pounding on Gawrnier's door began, Frek let the prepared images descend upon his ball of kenner. And then came the last mental twitch that Gawrnier had promised Frek would find. It was like the way Frek could sometimes look at a drawing of a cube and see it flip into its mirror image. His mind folded the target pattern right into the kenner. And now a floppy orange spacesuit lay at his feet; a kenny vig skin with a slit on one side where he could crawl in. The skin was wondrously light, no thicker than turmite silk.

"Praise my student," said Gawrnier, hopping onto his hoverdisk. "Urge haste."

Frek grinned at the Unipusker. He almost felt like, in just ten minutes, Gawrnier had been more of a father to him than Carb had been in the last ten years.

They skittered out Gawrnier's back door an instant before the door to the common room gave way. And then they were flying across the monotonous Unipusk landscape. Methane snow, blue dirt, rickrack, vigs. Frek hunched down, with his new spacesuit wadded into a little bundle between his feet. His skin was streaming with colors matching the crystal-dusted fields.

The sky was a low mass of billowing red and yellow clouds from the ruptured Jumm-to-Unipusk transport tube. But the screeching of the sabotaged tube had faded away—the tube's dissolution had advanced up past the Unipusk atmosphere. A fresh breeze was blowing, bringing in clean air.

Rather than heading straight for the tall rickrack plants on the horizon, Gawrnier angled a bit to one side, as if to approach the spaceport from another direction. Low rickrack homes and fields of vigs flew past below.

They were just drawing even with a curious collection of shiny linked kenner domes when a crackling bolt of green light shot past them. Hawb and Cawmb's hoverdisk was closing in on them, moving recklessly fast with its cargo of three Unipuskers and three humans. Even if, to all appearances, Gawrnier was alone, the producers were suspicious of him.

Gawrnier instantly steered his hoverdisk for the ground, managing to land near a small herd of vigs. Besides the mysterious domes, there were a few wide-based twenty-meter rickrack trees that served as Unipusker dwellings.

"Go, Frek," exhorted Gawrnier. "Run to the vigs and put on your suit. Then try to make your way to the spaceport. There's a bar called Taz where you can seek passage offworld."

"I'll never forget you," said Frek, unable to say more. It hurt to leave this incredible new teacher.

Holding the suit bunched against the side of his body that faced away from the rapidly approaching hoverdisk, Frek sprinted across the field toward the vigs.

His chameleon mod was still in effect; it was sufficient to make his image blend in with the snow crystals, the tufts of rickrack, and the blue dirt. Frek circled around the vigs and lay down behind them so as to wriggle into his vig suit before his last bit of mod wore off. The anomalous weather had put the vigs into a quiet, somber mood.

For a first effort, the vig suit was well made. Once Frek was inside it and on all fours, he blended right in.

The softly vheenking vigs ambled toward the hoverdisks, their muzzles nosing the tender rickrack shoots, with Frek in their midst, watching. Being among them reminded him of Earth's extinct pigs, and of course set him to wondering about his father seeing a Magic Pig.

Meanwhile Hawb and Cawmb were yelling at Gawrnier in Unipusker. Gawrgor stood to one side holding his blaster. Carb, Yessica, and Renata were still on the hoverdisk, Yessica apart from the others.

Though Frek had no real idea of how he'd achieved the effect, his spacesuit was sensitive to sound. Staring at the others was enough to bring their voices into focus.

"Inform you crass bullies that I was upset by the explosion," Gawrnier drawled, switching the conversation into English. "Point out that I am entirely alone. State that I have no idea whatsoever concerning the fate of your precious Frek. Speculate that you clumsily dropped him into the branelink. Assert that you'd be too coarse and stupid to notice."

"Demand again why you sped away from us," roared Hawb. "Request that you justify your actions."

"Reassert my superior status as a sensitive artist," sneered Gawrnier. He made a sinuous gesture toward the domes on the other side of the field. "Grudgingly confide that some vagrant impulse brought me here to observe the specimens in the Talent Race Zoo."

"Silence yourself," hissed Cawmb.

But it was too late. Yessica had overheard.

"What's that about a zoo?" she cried, a flamingo of fury taking flight in her voice. "Don't tell me you keep sentient beings locked in those cages!"

"Inform you that these quarters are where Hawb and Cawmb plan to permanently display you four humans," said Gawrnier in a loud, clear tone. "Clarify that you will enter the Talent Race Zoo as soon as they obtain their production contract. Reassure that you'll barely notice, as you'll spend the rest of your lives in a dream. Innocently wonder how soon Frek will return from his meeting with the branecasters."

"Insist that Frek isn't in the Planck brane," bellowed Hawb. "Reiterate that he ran away, aided by his skin camouflage, by his ability to block out brane esp and, most probably, by a ride from you, Gawrnier. Deny that we would imprison you or your daughter, Yessica. Categorically forbid any further talk of a zoo."

"Frek?" called Carb, raising his voice. "Are you around here, son? Don't let them get you! We've got to escape!"

"I can find Frek," said Yessica suddenly. Her anger with the Unipuskers was already gone.

With horror, Frek noticed that Yessica was wearing Carb's ring—a gold band with cup and red dot, the twin of the ring on Frek's left hand.

"Stop it, Mom," cried Renata. "You're a monster!"

"There's always more men," said Yessica. "I'm trying to save you."

"Deny that we will harm Frek," said Hawb. "Point out that our branelink is down again. Propose that in the near term we all become better friends. Guarantee that we will protect Frek from other aliens."

"Give me back my ring, you grinskin!" shouted Carb.

"Why are you so hostile, Carb?" said Yessica, dancing out of his reach.

"You wanted them to kill my son!"

"Oh, that was just politics," said Yessica airily. "I thought the Unipuskers could help me make an evolutionary advance." She hopped off the hoverdisk and ran to Cawmb. "Can you promise not to put me and my ungrateful daughter in your zoo?" she asked the Unipusker.

"Assure you of anything you desire if you help us find Frek," said Cawmb to Yessica in his sweetest tone. "Guarantee things can still work out your way, Yessica. Estimate that we'll have the branelink up again by next week. Propose that in the meantime we'll educate Frek and bring him around. Suggest this delay is really a blessing. Let harmony prevail. Use the ring now."

Carb leaped off the hoverdisk and lunged for Yessica, but Hawb easily pushed him away, laughing at the human's impotence.

"I hate you, Mom!" cried Renata. She too made for Yessica, but Gawrgor grabbed her wrists and held her still.

All this time, the vigs had been edging closer to the hoverdisks. Perhaps they expected something nice from the Unipuskers. Frek had been hanging out near the front of the herd the better to watch and to eavesdrop, but now he began trying to work his way toward the rear.

It was too late. The ring on his finger buzzed and tingled. Frek tried every mental contortion he knew to damp it down, but the ring wasn't to be denied. Glowing red and yellow spikes of light oozed out of his left hand—with Yessica's avid face in the center.

Wildly waving his hand, Frek rolled over onto his side and slid out of his vig suit. His chameleon mod had worn off by now, and he'd be visible. But the Unipuskers were about to find him anyway. At the very least, he wanted to keep them from knowing about his newly gained ability to craft kennies.

"I see him," cried Yessica's face from within the ring's spiky projection ball. "He's naked with a bunch of vigs."

Frek found it hard to believe he'd ever been glad to have his father's ring. Filled with disgust for Carb, he pulled off his ring and tossed it into the dirt. A vig gobbled it up.

"It's all black now, but I think he's right over there," sang Yessica. Neither she nor the others seemed to realize what Frek had done with his ring.

From somewhere deep within himself Frek mustered the energy to vaar his gossamer-thin spacesuit back into invisible kenner. And then he was running across the field toward the rounded buildings of the zoo.

"Frek!" called Dad, spotting him from the hoverdisk. His voice sounded weak and foolish. The voice of a loser.

The zoo's units were arranged in a circle around a central courtyard. Each of them had a big window, looking in on captive creatures. One cage held a pair of dusty tornados writhing around each other in a jittery dance. In the next were two glowing pools of lava, their surfaces reticulated in intricately meaningful webs. Then came a unit with a misty atmosphere populated by gently bobbing jellyfish-things. Farther on were purple monkeys on a tree, four enormous snails in iridescent shells, a pair of pink-skinned dogs, giant worms in pool of mud, and a metal cage with buzzing loops of sparks. One oversize unit held a complete little jungle with giant lizards.

What made the sight of the imprisoned creatures particularly melancholy was that the captives seemed oblivious to their plight. For in each cage there were flickerballs, one ball per creature. All of them were continually esping brane. They were plugged into minds upon their home worlds, deep into vicarious secondhand lives. The whole rich vastness of a dozen races was here reduced to the uniformity of consumers esping brane.

A few dozen Unipusker tourists were gawking at the talent race specimens. Just then Frek saw something chilling. It was a cage with no creatures in it, a freshly outfitted cage with a natural habitat in readiness for some new arrivals. It held a couch, a couple of chairs, and four beds. The beds were molded from shelves on the walls; the couch and chairs bulged organically up from the floor; the smooth-cornered walls were covered with softly glowing skin. The Unipuskers had fitted out a cage to look like the inside of a house tree. This was the cell where they intended Frek, Carb, Yessica, and Renata to spend the rest of their days. Four flickerballs sat at the ready, each of them quietly displaying the rotating blue-edged logo cube.

Frek changed direction so fast that he nearly twisted his ankle. He ran past the Unipusker tourists, desperately looking for a shed or an access door behind which he might hide. But everything was sealed. He raced off to the left, heading for the zoo exit—but right then Gawrgor swooped down on him with the hoverdisk.

Carb tried to talk to Frek on the ride back to Hawb and Cawmb's mansion, but Frek didn't answer. He was too mad. Right now he felt like he didn't have a father anymore. Meanwhile, Yessica did her best to cozy up to Carb, rubbing against him, whispering things and sending out her clouds of scent. Frek could see him weakening.

As for Gawrnier, he'd chosen the moment of struggle to head off on his own.

Back at the mansion, Renata threw such a fit that Angawl took her upstairs along with Frek and locked them in with Gibby and Wow, using the same complex series of knocks to control the door. At Yessica's urging, Cawmb and Hawb let Carb stay downstairs with her. She promised them Carb would help their cause. Frek half believed her.

And then Frek was alone with Renata, Gibby, and Wow in the

room at the tip of the rickrack tree branch. Though Frek would have preferred to cover up his nakedness immediately with some kenny crafted clothes, he didn't want the Unipuskers to see him doing this on their flickerballs. So to begin with, he tackled the issue of getting them full privacy.

With only a few hours' practice it had already become second nature for Frek to keep the brane espers away by means of his sky-air-comb exercise of expanding the glow, making his mind untouchable, and massaging his thoughts into their normal shapes. The insidious espers had all but stopped trying to ooze into him. Now he needed to find a way to expand the immunity to his companions.

He tried explaining it to them. Renata understood, and could almost do it, but Gibby didn't. He could barely perceive that he was being peeked at all. And Wow of course was hopelessly open to the espers; the dog's eyes might as well have been a pair of cameras staring at them.

So Frek drew again upon his powers of mind. Learning how to kenny craft had made a difference; it had taught him how to let his mind flow out of his body and into his surroundings. He entangled his consciousness with Renata, Gibby, and Wow, and repeatedly stepped them through sky-air-comb routine—enabling them to resist the pleasure of the glow, to make their thoughts as mobile as air, and to massage their own thoughts into their familiar, personal shapes.

"What are you doing?" said Renata. "It feels good. Like I'm free all of a sudden."

"I'm helping you block the espers," said Frek. "Sky-air-comb."

"I get it now," said Gibby. "It works."

"Don't *you* go reading my mind, Frek," said Renata, giving him a really nice smile. "I wouldn't want you to see what I think of you. You'd get a swelled head."

"It gets better," said Frek, and crafted himself some kenny clothes. He started with turmite-silk blue pants, leather shoes, and a yellow turmite-silk T-shirt just like he'd worn before. Renata and Gibby were suitably impressed. To show off more, Frek made fern-patterned green ribbons for Renata's pigtails. Renata got Frek to put light and dark pinstripes in his blue pants—and to make his shirt purple. She said purple looked better with his skin—and she added that she liked his skin.

"There's got to be a way you can use your power to help us to escape," murmured Renata.

"Except there ain't no way past this," said Gibby, thumping his elbow against the tough, rubbery door. "Wow and me been drummin' on it all morning." He got a thoughtful expression. "Say, I wonder if I could cut our way out with a knife? Can you make me a knife, Frek?"

So Frek kenny crafted Gibby a knife. His memory of Gibby's old knife was clear enough that he was able to make the new one a faithful replica. Gibby immediately tested the knife against the rickrack tree's flesh. Though the knife sliced through easily enough, the living rickrack flesh instantly sealed itself up in the wake of the blade. There seemed to be no way to use the blade to cut themselves an exit door.

It was a long afternoon. Frek maintained a slight continuous pressure to keep the espers off his companions. And he spent nearly an hour trying to teach Renata and Gibby how to kenny craft. Neither of them could get the hang of it.

For now there was nothing better to do than lie around and talk with Renata, which actually wasn't a bad way to pass the time. She explained how her turkle organized its memories, and showed him more of her favorite drawings.

And then Frek asked Renata again about her real father.

"Sri-Sri Krisna," said Renata with a sigh.

"But he's been dead for centuries!" exclaimed Frek.

"He set up a—a fertility center before he died," said Renata. "With a zillion copies of his genetic code. All the really devout Sick Hindu women go there. I'm closely related to a lot of the Crufters."

"Wow," said Frek, letting it sink in.

"I'm glad you're not my half brother," said Renata.

"Me too."

Neither of them cared to push any farther on this topic. Fortunately Gibby interrupted with a new Grulloo song, this one about their trip thus far, with the first verses going like this.

A Grulloo and a Nubbie boy threw in their lot one day,
They rode off to the city to try and make it pay.
The Grulloo got drunk, the boy got stunk, and things was
     looking grim,
Along came an alien cuttlefish and flew them off with him.

Flying's easy until you crash, and that's just what they did.
They met some cold-heart branecasters in a secret world that's hid.
Now branecast's a light inside folks' heads what makes 'em into a
     show,
The bossy clam-head Unipuskers sell it to make their dough.

The clam-heads was a-winnin' out, but things weren't all that tragic.
The boy met an asteroid princess and learned to do some magic.
He made the Grulloo a knife, and some ribbons for the girl,
You can bet your stim-cell nuggets they was gonna move up in the
     world.

Right before supper, Frek considered crafting a gun to shoot the
butler. But with so many Unipuskers between them and the exit, it
didn't seem practical. They needed a better plan.

When Angawl's rapid tapping sounded at their door, Gibby hid his
knife, and Frek slipped off his new clothes and sat on them. Angawl
appeared with a tray of vig milk, vig steaks, and rickrack shoots.

"What's up?" Renata asked the butler, who was certainly too ob-
tuse to notice her new hair ribbons. "When are we getting out?"

"Inform you that our space crews were able to pinch off the unraveling transport tube," said Angawl. "Anticipate a functioning
branelink by next week. Relay Hawb and Cawmb's earnest advice
that Frek join our cause." Yawn.

In the middle of the night Wow woke them all up, just like the
night before. Frek immediately made the mental effort to drive the
alien espers from their brains.

"Woo barking," squeaked Wow.

Once again Frek lifted Wow up to one of the room's tiny windows.

The weary Gibby and Renata grumbled as Wow barked his head off. As before, the Unipuskers next door started pounding on their wall.

"Wow can open door now," Wow reported when Frek set him back down. "Woo tell." The dog trotted over to the wall with the door and began carefully tapping it with his paw.

"Just a minute, Wow," said Frek. "Stop. Give us a chance to get ready. The Unipuskers aren't going to let us walk straight out. The little ones will make noise, and Cawmb and Hawb will come down from the top with Angawl."

"Sweet whistle," said Wow. Apparently the Radiolarians as well as Woo were calling to him.

"Oh, lie down and lick your butt," said Gibby, pulling Wow away from the door. "Frek not ready."

"I'll make us Unipusker disguises," proposed Frek. "Like the vig suit I made myself before."

"Unipuskers with *ickspot*!" suggested Renata. "It's very contagious. When they see us, they'll go gollywog."

"What does ickspot look like?" asked Frek.

"We'll want a few dozen scabby craters on our bodies," said Renata. "Four or five centimeters across. Black and gooey in the middle, gray and flaky around the edges. Our eye stalks should be crooked too, with kinks in the middle. And our shell heads will need moldy white fuzz. Like this." She chuckled a little as she sketched the images on her turkle, telling the little kritter what colors to shade the shapes she made.

"Looks gumpy all right," said Frek. "Calm *down*, Wow, we'll be ready in ten minutes."

Actually it took over an hour, with Frek blocking out the alien espers all the while.

The hardest part about making the lightweight Unipusker-shaped spacesuits was finding enough dark matter in the room's air. The Unipusker spacesuit pattern that Gawrnier had showed him was still intact in his mind; indeed, making the suits seemed to make the pattern that much clearer. And vaaring each suit to truly resemble a Unipusker with ickspot took only a little more effort. But each time Frek got a suit finished, he'd have to wait ten or fifteen minutes for enough dark matter to diffuse into the room so that he could vaar out a fresh glob of kenner. Though it didn't take much kenner for a suit, there wasn't much to be found.

As a final step, Frek vaared himself a little bulb of water that he stuck to his suit's waist, and he glued his fungus purse to the palm of his suit's hand. He was ready.

"Open the door, Wow," said Frek.

Wow looked comical walking across the floor with his head inside a Unipusker clamshell. Even so he had, as always, a certain inalienable doggy dignity about him. Solemnly, carefully he tapped the door with his front paw. He got it right on his first try. The door irised wide open, revealing a chamber with six sleeping Unipusker youths. Clam-headed Renata stepped forward with icky Gibby in her arms. Frek swept Wow up into his own arms and shrieked the Unipusker word for the dreaded warning.

"Ickspot!"

The young Unipuskers went into a total panic. And whenever one of them came too close, Frek or Renata would hold out Gibby or Wow—as if brandishing a flaming torch at some crude, wild beast. The Unipusker's little shell would gape wide in terror, and he would turn and race off hollering, "Ickspot!"

It was great.

When Frek and Renata got near the central shaft, they set down Gibby and Wow to walk on their own. The four of them made a reverse feint to drive the young Unipuskers back from the center toward their sulfurous dorm rooms, then the four jumped into the shaft, dropping down beside the column of negative gravity. Frek caught hold of Wow again, and slowed their fall by tugging at the elastic vines they passed. Gibby and Renata were on their own, a bit farther down.

As they neared the bottom, Frek heard Hawb bellowing far overhead. It was time for the next part of his plan. Frek caught hold of a rubbery rickrack rope and nestled himself and Wow in a sling some fifteen meters above the floor level. Moving carefully, Frek pried open his fungus purse and took out his twig of Aaron's Rod.

His hands were a little damp from anxiety. At the slight touch of moisture, the rough bark of the Aaron's Rod grew bumps, with the bumps sending out little sprouts that in turn branched again. The thing was twitching in Frek's hand; it was all he could do to keep from dropping it.

Quickly he separated his water pod from his suit and squirted it onto the Aaron's Rod. The vegetal tangle sent out an explosion of tendrils, each new branch leading to three or four more. Frek hurled it upward.

Wiry pale green tendrils sprouted from the missile as it flew. Before it had gone more than ten meters, the vigorously branching plant had formed a plug all the way across the rickrack shaft. A pleasant smell came off the foliage, a Gaian odor of breezy forests with rich humus floors. The tendrils seethed down toward Frek as if in speeded-up motion—and at the same time, the growth was rushing up into the length of the shaft, penning in Hawb, Cawmb, and Angawl.

Frek and Wow met Renata and Gibby on the big room's floor. It was the wee hours; the lights were very low, with pools of shadow everywhere.

"Can I trash my costume now?" growled Gibby. "I can't hardly see."

"Hang on a minute," said Frek. He took a quick look around the room. A number of the young Unipuskers had ended up down here, but seeing the four "diseased" Unipuskers come down the shaft had sent them off to the gloomy far perimeter of the room. Other than that, he saw no life but a few sleeping vigs, some on the floor, some in the armchairs.

The next problem was how to get through the high round door that led outside. Frek had never seen anyone exit the door save upon Hawb and Cawmb's hovercraft, which was lodged with Gawrgor in the darkly shadowed garage that bulged out into the room. Never having seen the designs for a hoverdisk, Frek doubted if he could craft one. They'd have to steal the one in the garage.

As Frek pondered how best to get the hoverdisk from the sleeping Gawrgor, something nudged him in the backs of his legs. The thicket of Aaron's Rod was pushing out from the shaft after them, spreading across the floor and mounding itself into wobbly hedges.

Slowly, not quite sure how they would work it, Frek, Renata, Gibby, and Wow started across the dimly lit room toward Gawrgor's garage, talking over their possibilities in whispered voices. As they moved along, Gibby scavenged for loot, happily pocketing a finely carved little statuette of Hawb. Suddenly someone called from the shadows.

"Frek?"

It was Carb, blinking at Frek from a couch facing away from the shaft. He looked disoriented. He'd recognized his son's voice—but he was seeing a diseased Unipusker. Yessica was at Carb's side, asleep against his shoulder, a half-empty moolk pod in her limp hand.

"Oh Brahman," said Renata. "Them."

"Come with us, Carb," said Frek with a sigh. Much as he might be tempted to, he couldn't leave his father behind. "We're breaking out. Heading for the spaceport."

"Where are we?" asked Carb. The old man often had a few seconds of that old peeker-induced confusion when he woke.

"We're here," said Frek impatiently. "It's now. I'm me. Get your butt in gear."

From somewhere far overhead he heard Cawmb hollering again. And now Carb came to. His features tightened and his eyes lit up. When Frek made the mental effort of reaching out to push the espers from his father's mind, he found, to his surprise, that the espers weren't there. Carb had the glow pushed off as far as the sky, his thoughts were as imperceptible as air, and his mental quirks were very nicely in place. It was like he was doing sky-air-comb too. Frek could hardly believe it.

"Gaud costume, Frek," said Carb in his normal tone. "And your friends, too. You guys look like gundo sick 'Puskers." As he got to his feet, Yessica slumped sideways on the couch, limp as a rag doll. Carb glanced down at her, his expression a mixture of pity and impatience. "She's gonegone," he said. "But don't worry about me, I'm fully gitgo. Mean and clean. Power is my drug, not moolk. I was sitting up with Yessica, is all. Making sure she doesn't try to cut another deal to kill you. Don't worry, Frek, she's old news, I got no more feelings for her at all." He laid his arm on Frek's shoulder and stared intently, unable to make out his son's expression inside the disguise. "Forgive me. You're the one who counts, Frek, not me." Frek liked the sound of this, but he didn't want to let his father off the hook by saying anything back. He just looked at him, noticing that Carb had gotten his ring back from Yessica.

Carb continued after a bit. "We're breaking out, you say? I'm on. Main thing's gonna be to get that hoverdisk off Gawrgor."

"Wake up, Mom," said Renata, nudging her mother.

"Nuuuh," went Yessica, pawing the air in front of her. And then she opened her eyes and saw Renata's costume. *"Wuuuh?"* Maybe Frek should have sky-air-combed her, but he couldn't stand the thought of touching her mind.

"I can't see!" complained Gibby again. With a quick burst of angry wrestling, he got himself out of his suit. Wow immediately did likewise—rolling, clawing, and biting until he'd ripped free of the kenny disguise. Frek and Renata slipped off their Unipusker suits as well.

"Time to mow the lawn," joked Carb, noticing the Aaron's Rod churning across the floor toward them. "Yo, what we need to take out Gawrgor is a gun."

Urgent as all this was, Frek couldn't resist taking the time to ask Carb about what he'd just noticed. "How come the espers can't read your mind? I thought I was the only one who could—could comb his brain."

"Comb your brain?" said Carb, with a laugh. "Good way to put it. Me, I've always called it—remembering myself. I've been able to do it since I don't know how long, since around the time you were born, I guess. Like father, like son, like father, eh? If it weren't for me being able to remember myself, the peeker uvvy would have killed me. Once I got to Unipusk, I learned to remember myself and keep off the espers so I could keep being me." He glanced at the Aaron's Rod again. "Man, that crud's coming fast. We gotta get past Gawrgor and out that door. We can comb our brains later, eh?"

"I can make a gun," said Frek. He'd been thinking about it since suppertime. A gun would be perfect for stopping Gawrgor. And not some organic NuBioCom-type spider gun, no, a real old-fashioned blaster made of chips and metal. A machine. Nobody made machines on Earth anymore, but Frek had seen some of the antique designs on the Net.

"Don' hurt Renata," mumbled Yessica, slapping at the Unipusker costume dangling from her daughter's hands.

Rather than vaaring fresh kenner, Frek wadded up the four Unipusker-colored spacesuits and crafted them into a solid little blaster, a silvery L-shaped chunk of metal with a ruby crystal at one end, exactly like the one he'd seen on the Net. It was a mystery how he remembered the gun's exact inner details but, just as with the spacesuit, when he'd needed it, the information was there. Merging with the kenner gave him an incredible clarity of mind.

"Let me use it," said Carb, trying to take the blaster. "I like guns. I had one on Sick Hindu."

"Okay," said Frek, "In a minute." The old man might be good for something after all. But first Frek wanted to try out their new toy. "Let's see if it works," he said.

Ever since they'd taken off their disguises, the little Unipuskers had been edging closer. Four or five of them kept peeking out from behind a nearby couch. Frek aimed the blaster at the couch and squeezed the blaster's trigger-stud.

Fa-toom!

The couch exploded into burning scraps. The Unipuskers went shrieking off to the farthest recesses of the room.

"Gimme," said Carb, eagerly snatching the blaster.

If they'd been wondering how to rouse Gawrgor, the problem was already solved. A slit of light appeared around the garage door, and now it swung open, revealing Gawrgor himself, perched upon the hoverdisk. With a roar, the Unipusker dug against the control stick with his foot. He flew straight toward them, brandishing his blaster.

"Run and dive for cover," said Dad, slipping behind his couch and giving Frek a shove to the right. "I'll get him."

Frek took off full tilt, with Renata, Gibby, and Wow at his heels. Drawn by their motion, Gawrgor sped after them, giving Carb a perfect shot at the Unipusker from the side.

When Frek heard their blaster's percussive *whoosh,* he looked over his shoulder. Yes. Dad's first shot had taken Gawrgor's head right off. But—the Unipusker still rode his hoverdisk. Silhouetted against the wavering forest of Aaron's Rod, he looked like a headless horseman.

Gawrgor was turning the charred stub at his neck this way and that—it was almost as if he could still see. He raised his blaster, and a bolt of green light crackled past Frek, narrowly missing him. In the brief flash of the explosion Frek glimpsed the glint of a fresh eye stalk growing from Gawrgor's neck.

Carb fired off another shot, taking off one of Gawrgor's arms and part of his shoulder. Staggered by the impact, the Unipusker lost his footing and fell off the hoverdisk, still clutching his blaster in his remaining hand. He landed heavily, crushing a hole in the spreading thicket of Aaron's Rod.

The empty hoverdisk went slashing by low over Frek's head. As it passed, Gibby made a sudden pinwheel motion with his body, springing up into the air and catching hold of the hoverdisk, climbing aboard as it raced on. Renata cheered.

But now Frek's attention was drawn back to Carb and Gawrgor. The scaly, glistening creature was on his feet, fighting free of the tendrils and stumping after Carb, all the while laying down a withering series of lightning bolts from his blaster. Carb fell back, dragging and half-carrying the muzzy Yessica, now and then pausing to fire another shot at the dogged Unipusker. And then Yessica stumbled over some vegetation and fell to the floor. Carb bent over her, pushing away the lashing fronds.

Renata shrieked at Gawrgor to distract him; she broke up a spindly table and hurled the broken legs at the Unipusker's back. Slowly the monster turned, firing a few blasts her way.

Frek quickly vaared a fresh lump of kenner and formed the mental image of the NuBioCom jo nets that the counselors liked to use. Jo nets were primitive kritters made up of giganticized muscle cells stiffened with monomolecular crystals. Frek knew the DNA codes for jo nets from the bottom up; as one of the very earliest NuBioCom kritters, jo nets were a standard example in the online genomics tutorials. Frek put every bit of his concentration into his task, overlaying

the kenner with the jo net pattern. Could he indeed craft a living kritter? Yes. In just a moment a big swatch of jo net lay twitching at his
feet, scintillating with pale silver light.

Frek bent to pick it up—too late? Gawrgor was standing over Dad
and Yessica, sighting his little eyestalk down his outstretched arm,
ready to fire the final shot.

Just then Gibby came arcing across the room, flattened against the
surface of the screaming hoverdisk. One of his powerful hands
grasped the side edge, the other clutched the stubby control stick. The
hoverdisk slammed into Gawrgor's back, sending the Unipusker
sprawling.

Frek ran forward, all over Gawrgor, snatching away his blaster and
wreathing him in the smart meshes of the jo net. A tiny bud of a shell
head had already reappeared upon Gawrgor's neck, and a miniature
arm was sprouting from his blasted shoulder. But the jo net continually readjusted itself around the monster, pulling tighter with his
every move.

Frek breathed a sigh of relief. The fierce gatekeeper had been rendered harmless as a grub worm. And now the rampaging thicket of
Aaron's Rod covered him over. Checking Gawrgor's blaster, Frek saw
that it had a firing button just like on the gun he'd made.

"I've about got this thing doped out," sang Gibby, circling around
on the hoverdisk. He brought the little craft to a stuttering halt and
hung crookedly a half meter above the floor, his head resting on the
platform like a fried egg. "Git on it," said Gibby with a grin. Filtered
through the shaft of Aaron's Rod plants came the sound of Cawmb
and Hawb roaring to each other. Making plans.

Renata helped Carb load Yessica aboard. Though Frek didn't much
feel like saving her, it wasn't his place to say no. Frek and Wow hopped
on as well. Feeling around with his strong, clever fingers, Gibby found
a way to make the hoverdisk sound the three notes of a French horn.
The great disk of the exit door irised open and they flew out.

Though the suns were down, Jumm was hanging huge and full in
the sky, flooding the landscape with pale orange light.

Standing on the ground right outside the rickrack tree was Woo.
Wow barked and squeaked while Gibby set the hoverdisk down. Woo

sprang aboard, bringing their party to four people, one Grulloo, and two dogs. Frek's expanded mind shield was keeping the brane espers away from all of them.

"Woo lead you to Taz," creaked Woo from the back of her throat. "Escape." But then, rather than pointing the way for Gibby, she spent a minute licking and sniffing Wow—more time than Frek liked, for he could still hear Hawb and Cawmb's voices in the rickrack tree's highest tip.

Finally Woo raised her paw and aimed her nose toward the spaceport. Gibby diddled the hoverdisk control rod and they swept forward. But now something came swooping toward them from above. Hawb and Cawmb, borne upon great iridescent brown wings, membranes that seemed grown right from their own bodies. The two elder Unipuskers weren't alone; streaming behind them were legions of their children, gliding down like stinking bats, eerie in the luminous light of Jumm.

Carb fired off a few shots with their blaster. One of Carb's bolts must have singed Cawmb, for the Unipusker unleashed a cry of fury like nothing they'd heard before. Hawb streaked toward them like a vengeful dragon. Aiming carefully, Frek fired a green bolt from Gawrgor's blaster. The Unipusker flipped over in midair, then corkscrewed past them with his one remaining wing flapping like a rag. Cawmb plummeted after his partner, catching up with him to slow his fall.

The little Unipuskers came massing toward the hoverdisk, their wings glinting in the light of the gas giant in the sky, their open headshells crying threats. A vast, slow cracking sound came from the producers' rickrack tree, and a split shot up the full length of the trunk's side. Aaron's Rod tendrils burst out like stuffing from a cushion. Slowly the enormous home began to crumple, its clashing branches sending out solemn deep tones. The Aaron's Rod reared from the ruins like a triumphant predator; it flung flying vines through the air as if reaching toward orange-glowing Jumm.

Gibby put the hoverdisk into fast forward, guided by rapid twitches and yelps from Woo. They left the horde of winged Unipuskers behind.

The spaceport was larger than Frek had realized. Even at top speed, it was a matter of nearly five minutes till they'd crossed to its other side.

And there, all by itself at the far edge of the great ship-studded field, sat a kenner building with peaked roof, curved walls, and a glowing pink sign that seemed to change its shape as you looked at it. It was as if the sign could sample your mind and cast itself into lettering that you could recognize. For Frek, the sign settled down into cursive English reading: "The Taz Spaceport Bar."

Uneasy about being followed, Gibby lost no time in parking the hovercraft by the front door. And then the seven of them went inside: mother and daughter, father and son, the Grulloo, and the two dogs.

Though it was getting on toward dawn, the Taz was lively. It was a fair-sized rectangular room with the front door in one long wall, and a bar along the other long wall. Tables lay beyond arches at either end. Aliens stood at the bar and sat at the tables, chatting with each other in a dozen ways, some of them speaking aloud, some using fleeting kenner glyphs, a few even talking via faint bursts of smell. Dancers bopped to the stuttery piping rhythms of a live band on a little platform beside the entrance. Fragrant plumes of incense filled the air, the smoke looking almost solid in the colored lights.

Gaping at the alien band, Frek picked out six musicians and a vocalist. A pale-blue stomach-creature played a bagpipe horn that was also his nose, backed by cymbal crashes and drum beats from an angelic moth's fluttery wings. A crocodile alien walked her heavy, forked tongue along her gleaming teeth with an effect like a vibraphone. The guitars were a pair of midnight blue cockroaches twanging their feelers and sawing at their wing covers. A gleaming-eyed crystal with shiny spring legs crouched to one side, showering out musical billows of static.

The vocalist was a kind of sea cucumber—a two-meter cylinder with a warty red surface divided by five blue stripes. Bright yellow tube feet stretched from her lower regions to the ground, anchoring her in place as she weaved and writhed to her corybantic song, the music pouring from her intricately branching crest, a feathery tongue of yellow flesh. The feathery organ's pulsating twitches produced haunting high notes layered upon a contralto croon.

"Sweet whistle," said Wow once again. He and Woo ran to sit as close as possible to the singing sea cucumber. Presumably she was one of the Radiolarians. As if to confirm Frek's surmise, the alien swept her intricate crest toward him in greeting.

The singer wasn't the only one who'd noticed Frek's party; indeed there had been a little ripple of excitement when they came in. A pair of yellow crabs studied them with bright blue eyes, a red-and-white-striped brittle starfish rose up onto two of his wiggly legs and waved to them, and a hovering yellow smiley-face sphere emitted an old-time speech-balloon saying, "Hi!"

Gawrnier the kenny crafter and Evawrt the pilot had noticed them as well. The two Unipuskers were seated together at a low table beneath an archway at the right end of the room, smoking a fuming water pipe of shredded rickrack blossoms. Catching Frek's eye, Evawrt raised his hand in greeting and gave a friendly nod, the rickrack smoke trickling from his great shell mouth. Frek waved back, especially glad to see Gawrnier.

"I bet Evawrt will take us home!" exulted Renata at Frek's side. "You've freed us, Frek! I'm impressed."

"It looks good for now," said Frek, glancing around to see what his father was up to. "But remember, I have things to do before I can go home. I have to find the elixir—and get the branecasters off our backs."

"I'll skip that part," said Renata. "I want Evawrt to take my mother and me back right now—and to Earth, not Sick Hindu. I'm ready to get my career as a toonsmith on track."

Frek forgot his worries and enjoyed the glow of her sunny face. He reached out and touched one of her beribboned pigtails. "I hope you don't get too grown-up for me," he said, wanting to say even more.

Something jostled his legs. It was Gibby scampering across the dance floor toward the bar. The only creatures Gibby's size were a pair of half-meter-high rat aliens dressed in waistcoats, standing on tip-toe and clasping paws as they stepped through a minuet.

The bar was manned by two yellow cone-headed creatures with humanoid arms and three eyes apiece: one red, one green, one blue. Behind them against the wall, pots simmered with pungent vig organ stews. A flat piece of vig meat was sizzling on a grill, and a liquid with ice cubes and rickrack berries boiled endlessly within a glass vacuum bell. Above the cooking area were three shelves. Upon the bottom shelf, vegetables and meaty flowers grew in varicolored hydroponic tanks. The middle shelf was crammed with bottles of every shape holding colored liquids and swirling gas. Some of the bottles contained small moving creatures within their fluids, others were crafted of force fields to contain more exotic goods like energy knots and microscopic space flaws. Along the topmost shelf marched a steady parade of virtual shapes. The bright forms appeared at the right and disappeared on the left, like figures in a shooting gallery, never repeating themselves.

Coiled hoses dangled from the ceiling with oddly shaped breathing masks at their ends. And at the left end of the bar bobbled a small cowloon, its damp udder in plain view. Gibby was already standing upon the bar before the cowloon, draining his first cup of moolk.

At the other end of the bar, snaky metallic branches projected toward four lounge chairs ranged against the wall. Each branch bore a pair of faintly glowing white disks at its tip. Frek had the feeling that applying the disks to one's head would be a far more intense experience than esping brane on a flickerball. A single chair was occupied, by an alien who looked for all the world like a long, creased yam, complete with clusters of green leaves growing from his eye sprouts. They didn't have any flickerballs inside the Taz Spaceport Bar.

Frek's heart sank when he noticed Carb and Yessica near the brain-feed chairs, but then he realized that all Carb was doing was settling Yessica down to sleep—without putting the disks on her temples. Quickly the troublesome self-centered woman dropped off. And then Carb was looking around the room—looking for his son. Their eyes met; Carb beckoned to him.

"I'm gonna talk to my father now," Frek told Renata. "There's some things we need to work out."

"I'm going to ask Evawrt and Gawrnier about a ride home," said Renata. "And then I want to make some drawings of the musicians. Good luck."

Carb led Frek to a quiet space beneath the arches at the left end of the room. Some of the spherical yellow smiley-faced aliens followed them in there, wanting to discuss a production deal, but Carb was able to shoo them away. The fact that both Carb and Frek had blasters didn't hurt.

A glass of water sat on an empty table. Frek and his father stood there looking at each other. Frek noticed that Carb had gotten his ring back from Yessica; he was wearing it on his left hand. Not that it mattered now. Frek was mad at Carb—both for leaving Lora, and, even more, for teaming up with Yessica against him. He felt like he and Carb were done.

"Like I told you, I'm through with that woman," began Carb, answering the anger in Frek's eyes. "I don't know why I let her lead me on this long. I'm—" He sighed and ran his hands over his face. "I've been a jerk. I practically forgot I'm your father. It's like Yessica hypnotized me."

"You helped her trap me by the zoo," said Frek.

"I wasn't helping her at all. I was fighting with her. But I shouldn't have given her the ring in the first place. I shouldn't have left you guys. I shouldn't have lied about needing help. So many shouldn't-haves. You don't even know how bad I've been. But that's all over now, I swear."

"I don't trust you anymore," said Frek.

"Give me a chance, will you?" said Carb, a little sharply. "You're the only son I've got. My father wasn't so great either. But I got over it. Some day you'll be a father, too. It's not that easy." Carb glanced down at Frek's bare hand. "What happened to your ring anyway?"

"Fed it to a vig," muttered Frek.

To Frek's surprise Carb chuckled. "Glatt. The rings came from another kind of pig in the first place. The Magic Pig. He gave them to me the night I had my big dream. When I woke up I was holding them in my hand. The Magic Pig said one was for you and one was for me."

"And you gave yours to Yessica," repeated Frek with a frown.

"Those perfumes she wears—I think they've been addling me," said Carb. "You know my brain's got that peeker damage, too. But no more excuses. It's over. We'll send Yessica and Renata back to Sick Hindu."

"*You* don't plan to stay with me, do you?" challenged Frek.

"Yes," said Carb softly. "I do. I won't make any trouble. I want to be part of something important. I want to help you out." Carb was talking faster and faster. "I'll help you get that elixir. I'm a good man in a fight, you know that. We'll bust those branecasters and when we get home we'll kill off the Govs."

"Bumby and I already killed the Stun City Gov," said Frek, drawn in by his father's enthusiasm. "And you were right. He really was a worm."

"Frek and Carb all the way," said Dad a little too heartily.

"Until some woman changes your mind and you sell me out," said Frek, flashing back to the bad stuff.

"Never again. Listen." Dad took a deep breath. "Maybe you don't need me—but I need you."

Frek was quiet for a minute, letting his father's words sink in. What a thing for him to say. It had never occurred to Frek that his father needed him. "Thanks," he said finally.

Carb laughed and stepped forward and hugged Frek against him. Part of Frek wanted to twist away, but he didn't. The hug felt good, like drinking water when you're thirsty.

After a while they stepped back and looked at each other again.

"You want your ring back?" said Carb. "I've been figuring out some stuff about the rings. Watch this."

Carb stared at his ring in that certain way. As all the times before, a ball of red and yellow spikes formed above the ring's cup. But this time, instead of showing a scene, the ball showed a ring like itself, little at first, and then its own right size. A ring with tape on it. It was Frek's lost ring, floating in the cool flicker of the spiky light.

"Take it," said Carb. "If you want to."

Frek wondered about that for a minute. Had the ring brought him anything but bad luck? Well, yes, he'd seen Renata for the first time in the ring. Renata was good luck for sure.

So he went ahead and felt the glowing image above his father's hand. There was a wriggling sensation, and the virtual ring grew solid to his touch. Frek hefted it and held it to his face. It smelled a little like the insides of a vig. He took the glass from the empty table and poured some water on the ring, then wiped it off and slipped it on.

"Good as new," said Dad. "Our magic link."

Frek happened to set down the glass of water crooked. Just a week ago he would have spilled it. But this time he didn't. He took a breath, adjusted the glass, released it without knocking it over. He had a feeling he was done being clumsy. It helped to be on good terms with his father. Not that he wasn't still a little suspicious.

Frek glanced out into the main room. Everything was calm. Renata was sketching the band and petting the dogs. Yessica was still asleep. And Gibby was out of sight around the corner.

"Tell me more about the Magic Pig," said Frek to his father.

"The Magic Pig," repeated Carb with a rueful smile. "Lora saw the Magic Pig too, but she got sick of me talking about him. Like I told you, the night you were born, we saw him in a dream. Both of us had the same dream, and that never happens, so that means the Magic Pig was real. And as if that weren't proof enough, when I woke up I had the two rings he gave me. The Magic Pig talked to us right before Lora's water broke and her labor started in. It was maybe three in the morning."

"What did he look like? What did he say?"

"He was like a toon. Pink, friendly, with a shining gold aura around his head. He said, 'You're son's the one. You and the boy will save your world. I give you these rings and I give you auto—' Auto something."

Gibby's shouts interrupted them. The Grulloo was making trouble, standing on the bar screaming at the bartenders for more moolk. They didn't want to give him any. He was on the point of drawing his knife. Carb and Frek hurried over and lifted him off the bar, each of them taking a kicking leg, or arm, and carried the struggling Grulloo to join Renata, Wow, and Woo.

The night's music was just ending with a final series of jittery whoops. It was amazing how loud a sound the sea cucumber could produce by vibrating her intricately branching crest. The feathery tendrils affected the air like the surface of a loudspeaker. The music ended with a boom from the wings of the moth, a chaotic blast from the blue horn-creature's nose, clouds of chirps from the crystal thing, an arpeggio from the crocodile, and dying twangs from the cockroaches. The singing red-blue-yellow sea cucumber closed the song with a few plaintive husky notes that quieted everyone, even Gibby.

The sea cucumber leaned forward toward Frek, Dad, and Renata. "Hello, I am Nefertiti the Radiolarian," she said into the moment of silence that followed her song. Her conversational voice was a melodious whisper. "I am offering cooperation between our races," continued Nefertiti. "My family and I are very glad to be helping you leave this planet. We are shipping out at sunrise. Quite soon." Woo whined with pleasure to hear the sweet whistle of Nefertiti's feathery fan.

"The Unipuskers won't try to stop us from boarding?" asked Frek.

"The spaceport is being off limits to the Unipuskers' concerns," said Nefertiti the sea cucumber. She made an inclusive gesture with her branching yellow tendrils. "The galactic races are meeting here for trade and for personal contacts. The Unipuskers are receiving a certain landing fee. If they will be bothering us, we will be killing them, this is well understood. These clam-heads have been evolving only recently from the low status of a talent race."

"Do you think maybe we should go with them instead?" said Renata to Frek in a low tone, nodding her head toward Evawrt and Gawrnier. "I asked, and they said they'd be willing to fly us back to Earth. That's where I want to go."

"I don't trust Unipuskers anymore," said Carb flatly. "None of them."

"I'm—I'm with Dad," said Frek after a moment's thought. Yes, Gawrnier had saved his life and taught him a wonderful skill, but there was no telling about Evawrt. And once they got back into a Unipusker flying saucer, who knew but whether Hawb and Cawmb might not be able to influence it.

While they were talking, the red and white brittle starfish who'd waved to them appeared at Nefertiti's side, unsteadily walking upright upon two of his thin, writhing legs.

"I am introducing you to Firooz," said Nefertiti, rippling her yellow frond. "My husband." Firooz held out one of his wriggly, bumpy arms as if for a handshake, but he didn't say anything. "The suns are rising very, very soon," continued Nefertiti. "And then we are going on our way. We will gladly be taking all seven of you wherever you wish. This is what I have been expecting to happen after I was passing the door combination to your dog." She wriggled the long fine hair of her fronds. "It was a simple matter to be probing such information from the thuggish Gawrgor as he was sampling the pleasures of the Taz."

"My father and I want to go to Orpoly," said Frek. "And you should take Yessica back to her asteroid near Earth." He wasn't yet clear about where Renata, Gibby, or the dogs should go, and for now nobody was saying.

"Come then, we are leaving immediately," said Nefertiti, floating up off the floor. "Although we have been remaining ignorant of Earth's location, I'm sure your presence will be helping us to find the way."

"Not so fast," interrupted Renata. "Not to seem rude, Nefertiti, but how do we know you aren't a branecast producer like Hawb and Cawmb? How do we know you don't plan to kill Frek and send another one of us to the Planck brane to make a deal for you?"

"We have always been despising flickerballs," said Nefertiti primly. "My people will never be having an interest in branecasting. I am offering you this transportation for the sake of promoting harmony between our peoples."

With no sign of a mouth or of eyes on her, it was hopeless to try and read the red-and-blue sea cucumber's expression. But Frek was inclined to trust her. The fact that she wasn't interested in flickerballs boded well.

"All right," began Frek, glancing at Renata and Dad. "If it's okay with you two—"

"At least talk to Evawrt," said Renata.

"We are hewing to a tight schedule," pressed Nefertiti, hovering in the air at their side. Apparently her body had built-in antigravity.

"We'll be right back," said Frek. He and Renata headed across the room to the table where the two Unipuskers sat.

"How were things with your father?" asked Renata as they walked.

One of the crab aliens rushed toward them just then. The last thing Frek wanted at this point was another offer to worry about. He took out Gawrgor's blaster to make the crab back off.

"Things are okay with Dad," said Frek, as they circled around the alien's outstretched claws. "At least for now."

"Lucky you," said Renata a little bitterly. Frek could tell she wasn't too happy about Yessica being nodded-out on the couch.

"Greet Frek," said Gawrnier. He was toying with a bar snack, a handful of live squid in a dish of brown ink. "Report that I observed a bit of your escape via a flickerball tuned to Yessica's mind. Commend you upon your growing skill at blocking out the espers. And at kenny crafting. Marvel that you learned so fast."

"Greet Frek and Renata," echoed Evawrt, exhaling a violet-scented plume of rickrack blossom smoke. "Query again if you'd like a ride in my saucer. Inform you that I'm taking Gawrnier to one of our colony worlds, lest Hawb and Cawmb punish him for helping you escape."

"Well, I'm thinking we'll go with those Radiolarians instead," said Frek, hooking his thumb toward Nefertiti and Firooz across the room. "Nefertiti says they aren't even interested in branecasting. Carb doesn't think we should trust Unipuskers. Not even you two."

"Casually accept your decision," said Evawrt in his high mocking voice. "Jokingly remark that perhaps your father is right. Confirm that the Radiolarians don't use flickerballs. Suggest, however, that the familiar devil can be preferable to the unknown one. Add that I truly don't care if you travel with us or not."

Frek paused, looking around the room at all the aliens. Something had been bothering him, and now it came clear. "What are these different races doing here anyway?" he asked Evawrt. "They wouldn't be trading physical cargoes—I mean what would they ship? Thanks to kenny crafting, you only need the design for something and you can make it yourself. So what are they doing here?"

"Reveal the answer within your question," said Gawrnier. "Most of our visitors are trading information. Add that tourism is a motive as well, the desire to see other beings and other worlds. Summarize that aliens visit Unipusk to come to the Taz Spaceport Bar both to barter information and to enjoy each other's presence. Warn, however, that some are prospectors, in search of talent races like humanity to exploit."

"Like the Unipuskers," Frek couldn't resist saying. "With their branecast productions and their zoo. Though not you, of course, Gawrnier. I'll be grateful to you for as long as I live."

"Come on, Frek," called Dad, gesturing from across the room. He was having a little trouble holding onto Gibby, who was struggling to make another dash at the cowloon. Nefertiti was bobbing around like an impatient balloon, with the five-legged Firooz floating at her side.

"We'll go with the Radiolarians," decided Frek. "I think that's the right thing to do."

"Whatever you say," said Renata doubtfully. "I'd feel better about them if they had eyes. I wonder if I can count on them to take me home."

"Offer one last bit of advice about kenny crafting," said Gawrnier as Frek bid him farewell. "Never work with kenner that tries to fight your will."

Nefertiti had joined Dad in calling for Frek, filling the whole room with her warbling voice. It was time. A few minutes later the seven Earthlings were outside, Frek holding Gibby under one arm, Yessica leaning heavily against Dad, and Renata with the dogs. The horizon was glowing pink, and the great disk of Jumm had slid halfway out of sight.

As they loaded themselves back onto the hoverdisk, Renata again asked Nefertiti about her motives for helping them.

"You don't run a zoo, do you?" she demanded. "And you're not planning to eat us, right?"

The blue-striped red Radiolarian sea cucumber gracefully vibrated her yellow fan, repeating that she only wanted to help them because her people wanted a pleasant association with humanity. And she insisted that they should hurry.

Maybe it should have told Frek something that Nefertiti was so pushy. But it had been a long, tiring night. And he didn't want to look weak by changing his mind.

It was hard to concentrate anyway, for Yessica was awake again, wanting to argue about everything, even though she barely grasped what was going on. Her obnoxiousness was coming on line just in time to replace that of the moolked-out Gibby, who was drifting into sleep.

Once they were all on the hoverdisk, Carb hunkered over the stubby control stick. He did a creditable job of flying them across the field to the Radiolarians' ship. Nefertiti the sea cucumber and Firooz the starfish sailed through the air at their side, buoyed by their internal antigravity.

The first of Unipusk's twin suns peeked over the horizon as they arrived at the barrel ship. The ship was less imposing than Frek had remembered, little more than five meters tall. She seemed to be a sea cucumber something like Nefertiti, only larger, and with plainer colors—mottled sea green, with five vertical black stripes. Her oral fan was a delicate lavender.

At their approach, the ship extended her fan to the maximum, the forked lavender tentacles rising up to perhaps two times the length of the ship, and then, branch by branch, she laid the feathered tendrils down upon the field.

Two more Radiolarians were to be seen perched among the tentacles. Everything was very bright and clear in the light of the rising suns.

"You are meeting Mother Atmen and my two sons, Tutankh and Smenkh," said Nefertiti. "As soon as you guests will be taking your seats in Mother's branches, we are flying on our way."

Tutankh was a starfish of the snaky brittle star type like Firooz, with his arms striped green and white like mint candy canes. Smenkh was more like a sea lily, that is, like a feathery-armed starfish. His arms were iridescent, shattering the morning light into all the colors of the spectrum.

Frek felt more and more uneasy. Were they to travel packed inside the stomach of a giant sea cucumber? And what about spacesuits for them just in case? He began trying to vaar some kenner from the air. But as before, it was slow going, and it didn't help to have Nefertiti rushing him, insisting that they wouldn't need suits, that Mother Atmen would fill herself with air.

Meanwhile Yessica was pacing around, compulsively running her fingers through her tangled greasy hair, querulously demanding where she was supposed to go to the bathroom.

Frek had only finished one spacesuit when Dad yelled, "Look out!"

He was pointing out across the spaceport field toward the crumpled stump that had been Hawb and Cawmb's mansion. Two, no three, hoverdisks were coming for them. It seemed foolish to stay here and fight it out.

Hoping for the best, Frek tucked his suit under his arm and waded into the tangle of Mother Atmen's tentacles. He'd have to make the suits for the others while they were underway. Nefertiti, Firooz, Renata, Carb, Yessica, Gibby, Wow, and Woo quickly took their places amid the sticky lavender branches. A blaster bolt from the approaching Unipuskers crackled past.

And then, faster than the time it takes to tell it, Mother Atmen lifted her branches skyward, drew her passengers into her body, and lifted off.

Pressed in on every side by the ship's dark, feathery innards, the exhausted Frek postponed any attempts at struggle and dropped off to sleep.

10

orpoly

Frek dreamed he was back in Middleville. Mom had kissed him good night, but he couldn't sleep. He crawled out of his window, climbed down the house tree, walked over to an open patch of the yard and stared up at the sky, Wow at his side. In the dream, he looked at the sky for so long that he got a crick in the nape of his neck, a sharp ache that seemed to drill right in. Frek tried to look down at Wow to ease the pain, but when he did that, his dream switched back to when he'd first walked over to the clearing and looked up at the sky. It was one of those loop dreams where you do the same sequence over and over. He'd look at the sky, get a neck ache, look down, and there'd be a little glitch and he'd be back to staring at the sky—really focusing on it, trying to see each and every star.

Outside of the dream loop something was happening that made his stomach feel hollow and sick. With a rising whine the dream loop spun faster.

The sound of voices woke him; everyone in the ship was talking at once. Frek realized something horrible. His neck hurt because Atmen had grown hair-fine tendrils through his skin and into the base of his brain. Just like the peeker uvvy that Gov had used on him.

Frantically he jerked his arms, wanting to tear out the connection.

But his arms were bound fast by the great sea cucumber's feathery tentacles.

"Wake up, Frek," Gibby's voice was repeating, as if from inside him. The Grulloo's moolk madness had worn off. "She's trying to pick our brains! Block her off like you did the espers!"

Yes, the Radiolarians had been driving Frek's dream of looking at the night sky, dredging up his star memories. How creepy to have aliens manipulating his simple dream of home.

"We screwed up," groaned Dad. "She's got us strung together like beads. They want to invade Earth. Don't think about the stars, Frek, she still doesn't have a good fix on the location."

"Mother Atmen?" Yessica was saying over and over. "Can we talk?"

"Do something, Frek," wailed Renata. "We're about to yunch!"

It was pitch dark inside the ship. Presumably they were well out in interplanetary space, far from Unipusk and her binary sun. All eleven passengers were tangled up in Mother Atmen's tentacles. The connecting tendrils made everyone's voice seem to come from inside Frek's head.

A memory of the home sky seen from his backyard flashed through Frek's mind yet again. He seemed to see Wow and Woo standing beside him, muzzles raised to the heavens, barking. But now he could feel the probing inhuman intelligences—Atmen, Nefertiti, Firooz, Tutankh, and Smenkh—feeling through his mind for star sightings, working to find the route to defenseless Gaia.

Unlike with the espers and their golden glow, the sky-air-comb routine seemed to be of no use in blocking the Radiolarians. Frek strengthened his will and redoubled his efforts.

Acting on instinct, he thrust a blazing sun into the sky of his mental landscape, blotting the stars from view. He visualized Atmen's connection to him as a tunnel in the ground, a tunnel leading both to his sly enemies and to his friends. He made six mental copies of the Sun and hurled them down the tunnel toward Renata, Dad, Yessica, Gibby, Wow, and Woo, hoping to cover over the star images in his companions' minds. It must have worked, for now Atmen's tentacles twitched, giving him an angry shake.

The whirling sensation of an imminent yunch continued to grow.

Soon they'd zoom up to galactic size. And then they'd yunch back down—to where? To the Radiolarians' home world, or directly to Earth? Perhaps the Radiolarians' vast minds couldn't yet pinpoint Earth's location from the information they'd obtained—but surely they'd soon overcome Frek's temporary blocks and find what they needed. In his mental image of his yard back home, the brightness was draining from his imagined inner sun—and feathery tentacles were creeping from the tunnel in the ground. Quite soon it would be dark again.

And all the while the voices were talking, the trains of thought overlapping and at cross-purposes, the five Radiolarians and seven Earthlings fighting like weasels in a sack.

YESSICA: "Frek is humanity's representative with the branecasters. Did you know that, Mother Atmen?"

CARB: "Leave my son out of it, you grinskin. Don't always be trying to get something for yourself."

NEFERTITI: "Flickerballs are not attracting us. We are wanting Earth to host a planetary Radiolarian as well. Your people will be living as fruits upon a single vine."

RENATA: "The sun image you sent me is working, Frek. The aliens keep making me think about the sky, but your sun blots out the stars."

TUTANKH: "Smenkh is needing more information, Grandmother Atmen."

GIBBY: "Gaussy. I just pulled the plug outa my neck with my tail. Can't get my arms free, though. Here you go, Woo, I can reach your plug with my tail tip. That's it. Claw your way over here, girl, and chew these damned tentacles off my arms."

WOO: "*Yipe!* Woo help Wow first."

FIROOZ: "One dog is being loose, Mother Atmen. She is gnawing the other dog's connector. I am crawling toward them."

YESSICA: "You'll need a Regent, Mother Atmen. A representative to speak to the peoples of Earth. I'm uniquely qualified for this role."

RENATA: "Don't start that stuff again!"

WOW: "Wow free. Wow and Woo dig to Gibby."

MOTHER ATMEN: "We will now be yunching up and down. Who is helping me to find our target location? I am offering rich rewards."

TUTANKH: "The grotesque dwarf's brain plug is being severed, Mother Atmen. He may be causing grave disruption very soon. I am crawling to aid Firooz."

SMENKH: "I have been integrating our route, Grandmother. You must be waiting a bit longer. We are lacking sufficient data points."

YESSICA: "Look in me, Mother Atmen! I remember the sky from Sick Hindu. I often went to the surface to meditate, I'm visionary that way. There was this blinding sun in my mental images before, but now it's going away. The stars—I see stars."

RENATA: "Don't be so geevey, Mom! Everyone's laughing at you!"

WOW: "Wow chew meat vine through."

GIBBY: "Good dogs. It's butt-kickin' time. I got my knife. First for that striped starfish."

NEFERTITI: "Careful, Firooz!"

FIROOZ: "I am being dismembered. My arms will not be grasping the ugly dwarf's neck. Hurry, Tutankh."

GIBBY: "I'll show you five-legged brain suckers what ugly is."

TUTANKH: "They're rising up, Mother! They will be dissecting me, too!"

CARB: "Get those spacesuits ready for us, Frek!"

FREK: "Use your knife on Atmen, Gibby! Cut her biggest stems!"

GIBBY: "Here's the bull-goose main trunks of them all! Five of 'em. Yee haw!"

The connection went dead. Frek was alone in the darkness, with nothing to guide him but muffled sounds. The tentacles around his wrists were slack. It was a simple matter to pull his hands loose. And then he ripped the pad off his neck. The pad's hundred hair-thin connectors made a tearing sound that traveled into Frek's nerves and into his bones. *Ow.* He blacked out for a second, and woke to the touch of a human hand.

It was Renata; she'd pushed over to him. Frek could smell her sweet breath.

"Take this," said Frek, handing her the one suit he'd had time to make earlier. "Get into it fast." Even as he talked, he was feeling around within his mind to see if Atmen's intrusion had messed up his memory. But he felt normal.

"The thing on my neck," said Renata. "It's in the way."

"Rip it off."

"I'm scared to. It'll hurt."

"You want me to do it?"

Renata was still for a second.

"All right," she said finally.

Frek felt for the knobby sucker in the darkness, and yanked it off as abruptly as he could. Renata grunted and thrashed in pain. But then it was over, and she was slipping into the suit, Frek helping her to find the arm and leg holes. She fit the turkle inside the suit with her.

"Take my blaster," said Frek, pressing it into her hand. "But don't shoot until we all get suits on. We'll be sucking vacuum once we blow a hole in the side of Atmen. Call the others over here, and remind Dad not to shoot his blaster yet either."

And then Frek focused inward, vaaring kenner. Even though they must have been thousands of kilometers from any solid matter other than their ship, this particular location proved to be kenner-rich. In just minutes, he'd pulled five baseball-sized globs from the void, and a few minutes after that he'd crafted them into kenny spacesuits for him, Dad, Wow, Woo, and even Yessica. He wasn't making these new spacesuits look like vigs or Unipuskers, he was leaving them transparent. He wished the Unipusker spacesuits were as sturdy as the Orpolese ones—but he didn't dare tinker with the complex design. Once he'd crafted the spacesuits he also made a flashlight flower like he'd had at home, a ten-centimeter kritter with a luminous blossom.

Meanwhile Renata called the others to them. Gibby slashed easily through the underbrush of tentacles with his knife, the dogs in his wake. And Dad simply tore his way toward them with his arms, Yessica close behind.

For now, Nefertiti, Tutankh, and Smenkh were keeping well away from them. Playing the beam of his flashlight flower amidst Atmen's lax tentacles, Frek glimpsed the Radiolarians lurking in the tangled thickets, doing their best to wriggle out of the light. Down where Gibby had cut the main stalks of Atmen's five tentacles he saw jelly-globs of transparent goo. Atmen was regenerating her tissues to heal her cuts.

A few desperate, trembling moments passed before Frek and his companions were all garbed in their transparent spacesuits. As before, the suits fed them air and transmitted their voices. Just as Frek was telling the others about how you could move by speaking commands to your suit, Atmen's tentacles came back into play.

The great sea cucumber's lashing fan tendrils were strong and unbelievably fast. But Renata and Dad were faster. They fired their blasters before the tentacles could seize them. The beams charred a hole in Atmen's outer wall—and she ruptured.

Drawn along by the rush of air, the party flew outward into the vacuum, banging into each other, tumbling head over heels. It took Frek a minute to form the proper commands to his suit to stop his careening through space. Gibby managed too, then Dad and Renata. The dogs and Yessica went pinwheeling off into the distance.

"I'll go for them," said Dad, and with a few quick words to his suit he was on his way.

Renata and Gibby joined Frek, frowning back at the giant split-open sea cucumber. Nefertiti, Tutankh, and Smenkh remained enmeshed in the dangling tendrils. Firooz's cut-up body fragments were reassembling themselves, and Atmen was still moving. There was no reason to believe she wouldn't heal herself.

"Should I blast them some more?" wondered Renata.

"Let's wait till the others get back," suggested Frek. "Let Atmen have it if it looks like she's going to fire at us. But she probably won't. We're worth more to her alive than dead."

Meanwhile the others kept up a steady low chatter of conversation. Renata was studying the alien sea cucumber in the way she did when she was remembering something she wanted to draw. Right now she couldn't get at the turkle tucked inside her suit.

Frek tore his attention away from Renata and stared off into the distance. The bright binary suns of the Unipusk system were to his left. To the right lay the tiny red-yellow disk of Jumm, with Unipusk a speck beside it. Closer by were the lively shapes of Dad, the dogs, and Yessica, making their way back. Oh, oh. A flying saucer was coming up behind them.

"Hurry, Dad," said Frek into his spacesuit.

"I hope it's Evawrt and Gawrnier," put in Renata. "If it's them, they might still help."

But of course it wasn't. The saucer drew even with them just as Dad, Yessica, and the dogs returned. Though all Unipuskers tended to look somewhat alike, there was something about the two figures in the saucer's bridge window that could only be—

"Hawb and Cawmb," said Dad, a little out of breath. "We're fubbed."

"The rings," said Frek. "Can the rings help us?"

"The rings can only call each other," said Dad. "But you, Frek, maybe you can call the Orpolese. You're the one who's special."

The saucer heeled over and a door swung open in its bottom. Meanwhile, Mother Atmen's torn side sealed itself up like a slow zipper. She moved toward them, waving three branching lavender tentacles.

Frek reached down into himself and found a clear memory of Bumby and Ulla when last he'd seen them. A big friendly cuttlefish with W-shaped pupils in his eyes, accompanied by a dimpled purplish ball. They'd been crying out in anguish as the branecasters tormented them. And before that? They'd been in a form perhaps closer to their true selves, Ulla a crimson hoop covered by green veins of Bumby. Right at the end, when Frek had made them collapse toward Unipusk, Bumby had repeatedly called out a phrase in the Orpolese tongue.

The sounds were clear in Frek's memory. He began saying the phrase over and over, at the same time mentally projecting the message toward the Orpolese—wherever they might be.

"*Alilallah tekelili eheu uborka Orpoly.*"

Nothing. The Unipuskers and the Radiolarians drew closer.

Frek thought now of the sensation of the upward yunch, and he found a way to put some of that feeling into the phrase.

"Alilallah tekelili eheu uborka Orpoly."

The words seemed to spin and fly up into the beyond. Did Frek feel the beginnings of an answer?

A flash of pink light flew past. An appendage on the base of the Unipusker saucer was firing at the Radiolarian ship. Atmen twitched out of its way, then swung one of her tentacles and launched a glowing green ball toward the saucer. A hole appeared in its hull where the blaster-cannon had been. The saucer quickly patched itself, using its feelers to fasten a plate of kenner into place. But it seemed to have no replacement for the missing cannon. Atmen quickly launched another ball, and the saucer began backing off, but not fast enough to avoid getting a second hole in it, this one larger than before. Once again it was able to seal the hole over, though not as quickly as before. Atmen reached for the Earthlings.

"Alilallah tekelili eheu uborka Orpoly," repeated Frek, yunching the words as hard as he could.

Again he felt an answer, more clearly than before. Something was approaching. Yes. The Orpolese were coming.

Before Atmen could seize them, someone appeared from the hatch in the base of the Unipusker saucer. It was Hawb, swathed in a floppy transparent spacesuit and carrying a glowing white cube.

"A bomb!" wailed Renata. "I'll never get home!"

"No," said Dad. "I saw the Unipuskers do this once before at the spaceport when they'd been fighting with the alien cockroaches. The white cube is like a peace flag. Hawb wants to make a deal with Atmen."

"Over here," shouted Yessica to Hawb, meanwhile putting her hand on Frek's shoulder. "I've got the boy right here!"

Everyone ignored her. Hawb jetted his way over to Atmen, and the two of them began to gesture and talk. The Earthling's spacesuits weren't picking up whatever it was the Unipusker and the Radiolarian were saying to each other.

"They're gonna divvy us up like a creel of fish," said Gibby hopelessly. "Make a deal."

"Alilallah tekelili eheu uborka Orpoly," chanted Frek one more time.

The Orpolese arrived.

At first Frek thought it was just his eyes, or maybe some mist on the inside of his transparent spacesuit—but, no, there was definitely a gauzy cloud gathering all around them. The shape thickened, drew together, and then, with a slight shuddering of space, the Orpolese were there, a pair of them, another "husband and wife," the wife a thick gold donut overgrown with the silver vines that were her husband. Their meshed flesh was spinning around on itself like the smoke in a smoke-ring.

This pair of Orpolese seemed yet more powerful than Ulla and Bumby, and the other aliens knew it. The Radiolarian ship drew in its tentacles and started jetting away. The Unipusker saucer sealed up its hatch and did the same. Floating alone by himself, Hawb was frantically waving the white cube.

A snake of silver lifted up from the twisted Orpolese donut and shot three quick blasts. Hawb, the Unipusk saucer, and the Radiolarian sea cucumber scattered like leaves before the wind, wrapping themselves in mirrorlike force fields lest they be vaporized.

With their rivals dispersed, the Orpolese were quick to tractor-beam the Earthlings into the safe center of the gold and silver vortex ring. Seven copper arrows of tweet spiraled in toward the party—slender elongated pyramids that moved with the alertness of birds. Yessica struggled and cried out. The arrows breezed through their heads.

If Frek hadn't experienced this before, he might not have noticed the touch of the tweet, but this time he could sense when the linguistic kenner glutted itself with his info. Mission accomplished, the tweets darted back out to merge with the shining donut.

"Hey, Bub, howdy, how do you do, I can tell by your vibe you're Earthling goo," erupted a voice in Frek's suit. "Call me Whaler. I'm the silver veins amidst the gold of my partner, Tusky. I'm a spawn of poor old Ulla/Bumby." Like Bumby, Whaler projected a very human sound. "You made my mommy and daddy go bye-bye." Whaler put on a childish lisp. "Tuthky thaw it in the tweet."

"Why didn't you come save us before we fell into the Planck brane?" countered Frek. "Bumby was calling for you."

"That happened too fast," said Whaler in a more normal tone. "We weren't expecting it. So we didn't get an accurate location fix. Also, we were busy eating loofy. But ever since then, I've been half listening for another *tekelili* call. I didn't expect it to come from a human."

"I'm sorry about your parents," said Frek, hoping the powerful Orpolese weren't angry. "The branecasters said they'd release Ulla and Bumby for ten trillion tons of gold—that's supposed to be, like, a gold asteroid ten kilometers across? I already agreed to an Orpolese production contract with the branecasters. I'm your talent. You're supposed to protect me. Can you take my friends and me away from here before those other aliens come back? I'll be glad to deliver the gold to bail out your parents. I still have to ask those branecasters for the elixir to heal Earth's biome, you know."

"Let's trudge your road of happy destiny, yes," said Whaler. "And, mainly, get our family's deal in play. But first you need some better spacesuits. Orpolese quality, guaranteed solid right up to the pluperfect Planck temperature where spacetime melts like a Dali watch. Not those cheap-jack Unipusker rags you're sporting. We'll chew the further fat at chime five. Yunch, Tusky."

And so the yunch got underway. As before, their progress was signaled by a series of clear, musical tones.

Chime one. The braided wreath of Tusky/Whaler flattened into a band with silver veins embossed upon gold. The top edge grew up and the bottom edge grew down, forming a glowing spherical shell. When the last tiny holes at the poles had sealed over, there came a *thud* of air filling the chamber, followed by a sizzling sound. The Earthlings' floppy Unipusker spacesuits dissolved away.

Chime two. A flock of curved crystal tweets swept out from the glowing walls and garbed the seven in Orpolese spacesuits, solid as armor. These suits definitely had the feel of being crafted for extreme conditions. Frek wondered in passing how high the Planck temperature was. Did the Orpolese live on some hellish planet like Mercury or Venus?

Holes reopened in the ship's north and south poles. The air hissed away. Tusky returned to her twisted gold donut configuration, with Whaler a flexing tracery of silver within her flesh.

Chime three. Frek felt a hollowness in his guts as he and the others began to grow. Soon their bodies were vast overlapping clouds, ringed in by the Orpolese rescuers. The gas giant Jumm and its moon Unipusk were as tiny marbles at their feet.

Chime four. They powered into the superexponential phase of the yunch. The stars streamed past like specks of luminous plankton. A hungry keening sounded from every particle of Frek's frame.

Chime five. They coasted to a stop, their heads tenuously protruding from the Milky Way's great disk. As before, Frek thought of a pond. The Tusky/Whaler donut encircled them like an old-fashioned inner-tube.

"Who's going to Orpoly?" asked Whaler. "And who for Earth? First thought, best thought. Hurry before any clam-heads or five-leggers show up. Safe to bet they'll send reinforcements after us soon."

"I'm coming," said Frek. "And Yessica's not. The others can do what they like."

"I'm with Frek," said Dad.

"Me too," said Gibby. "We're gonna get that elixir from them snooty branecasters, whatever it takes. Maybe Frek'll craft us some old-style Nguyen War singularity guns before we go back in there."

"I've seen enough," said Renata. "I don't want to die out here. I want to go to Earth."

"No, Renata," insisted Yessica. "We have to push on with the others. It has to be me who meets with the branecasters."

"Oh, sure," said Renata sarcastically. And nobody else said anything.

After a long, awkward pause, Yessica continued. "All right then, I'll take you back to Sick Hindu if you insist. It's my duty to see that my daughter gets home safely."

"You're not hearing me, Mom," said Renata. "I am not going back to a stupid hollow rock full of gollywog know-it-alls. I've had enough of that kac. I'm going to Earth."

"You can stay at my house," put in Frek, wanting to offer her something. "In Middleville. The Toonsmithy is just down the river. You know my mother's name, right? Lora Huggins. She'd be glad to see you. And you can tell her what I'm doing. She'll be worrying about me. You'll have fun with my sisters, Renata. You can teach Ida and Geneva to draw." Saying the names made Frek wish he was going home, too. He'd already been through so much—must he really travel on to Orpoly and the Planck brane?

"It'll be okay with your mother if I just show up?" asked Renata. Her sweet, husky voice was all around Frek. It was pleasant to have their bodies overlap. "She won't make a fuss?" continued Renata. "I can't imagine a calm mother."

"She'll be glad," said Frek warmly. "She'll love you."

"And once you settle in, go visit my burrow in the Grulloo Woods," put in Gibby. "Or send a talking dog. Salla needs to know I'm off helping Frek save the world and not moolked-out in a Stun City gutter."

"Tell Lora hi from me, too, Renata," said Dad. "Tell her I'm sorry."

"Traitors," snapped Yessica. "All of you. If you go to Earth, Renata, I'm going there, too. We're a team, we two. We'll get a place of our own."

"Whatever."

"So that's decided," interrupted Whaler impatiently. "How about the pooches?"

"Woo like Renata," said Woo. "Woo miss Earth."

"Wow stay with Frek," said Wow.

"So let's split," said Whaler. "Here's how."

Chime six. The braided donut grew and jiggled, its fields herding the overlaid figures of the Earthlings. The donut elongated, changing its hole from a circle to an oval, stretching one side toward the galactic center, and the other side farther toward the rim. Unseen Orpolese energies separated the passengers into two groups: Frek, Dad, Gibby, and Wow closer to the galactic core; Renata, Yessica, and Woo closer to Earth.

The moment came when Frek felt his body losing its last bit of overlap with Renata. "Good-bye, Renata," he called. "I'm so glad we met. I'll see you again soon."

"Good-bye, Frek," she sang. "I'll wait with Lora."

"No you won't," put in Yessica.

"Shut up for once. Can you still hear me, Frek? You might as well know that you're the nicest boy I've ever met."

"Me you too," said Frek awkwardly. And then they were out of contact. For a moment Frek felt lost, sad, and perhaps a bit doomed.

Chime seven. The elastic tubing of the stretched donut hole bulged inward, pinching in between the two groups of passengers. The sides touched, and now the donut was a figure eight. Whaler's voice sounded an ecstatic cry within Frek's suit. A pattern of bumps shivered across the surface of the double donut, like ripples in water, like heavy rain pounding the sea. And then the great loops broke apart. Whaler moaned and sighed, and silent Tusky sent out a single, chrome, musical-note-shaped tweet. The Orpolese had reproduced.

"We're still Whaler and Tusky," said Whaler in a dreamy tone. "Our new clones yonder will find their own dear names in a second or few. Name-picking is the first zigzag of self. Aha, it's happened. They're Tagine and Vlan, the she and he. Isn't this great, Tusky? Tagine and Vlan, I never would have thought of those. And, see, now they're picking their colors. Orange and—*hmm*—black. Only a few seconds into their own various and particular lives, and they're branching into unknowable otherhood. Torn off from Mom and Dad, yes, careening down time's thundering dream. Farewell, beamish girl and boy, bon voyage, dear Tagine and Vlan! May we graze eddies together soon!" He lowered his voice a bit. "And I do think the colors work quite well, don't you, Mother Tusky? I like how crisp Vlan's black lines look against Tagine's orange gleam."

Whaler and Tusky continued moving toward the glowing hump at the galactic core, while the fresh-spawned Tagine and Vlan drifted the opposite way. Frek strained to pick out Renata's features amidst the gauzy mass at the Tagine's center. But by now the other Orpolese were too far.

The hill at the Milky Way's center looked close enough to climb—a private snow-sparkling sledding-hill. Frek saw no sign of Unipuskers or Radiolarians.

Chime eight. The downward yunch slammed on at the most extreme rate imaginable. Frek felt like he'd had his legs kicked out from under him. He was all but deafened by the hum. Stars rushed away on every side—it was like being at the center of a cosmic explosion. Frek peered down into the overlapping bodies of Dad, Gibby, Wow, and himself, trying to spot their destination. It seemed to be a dense blaze of light near his navel.

Chime nine. The growing mass of light refueled the sense of confidence that had been gracing Frek of late. Yes, he'd get the elixir, make his way back to Earth, and find some way to cancel the branecasting of humanity. With Dad and Gibby and Wow to help him, it wouldn't be so hard.

Though the four male Earthlings were still layered together, it was getting easier to distinguish their separate selves. Dad had a shaky, gritty feel, Gibby was smelly and leathery, Wow was itchy and springy, and Frek—Frek felt juicy and supple.

What was that last thing Renata had said? "You're the nicest boy I've ever met." Not that Frek was particularly interested in having a girlfriend. But it sure felt good to know Renata liked him. He tried to imagine Lora and Yessica meeting each other. Like day and night.

He hoped Renata would really be waiting at his house when he got back to Middleville. Of course he still had a few little bridges to cross.

While Frek was thinking all this, they'd continued shrinking. Ahead of them lay cluster upon cluster of suns, like the lights of a densely populated city.

Chime ten. Their collapse slowed. Frek turned his head this way and that, trying to spot the planet they'd be landing on. But there were no solid worlds in sight, just suns—hundreds, no, thousands of them, stars everywhere you looked—dull red giants, gemlike blue dwarfs, stormy white stars with coronas flickering from them, binary stars pulling each other's substance into tendrils, and lenslike warped spots betokening black holes.

Surely anything so puny as a planet had long since been swallowed up by these monsters and their churning gravitational tides. So where were they going to land?

"Welcome to Orpoly," said Whaler, halting their downward yunch at no place in particular amidst the crowded stars.

"We ain't done shrinking yet," objected Gibby.

Though it was hard to judge, Frek had the impression that he—and the others—were a thousand kilometers or so tall. And they were still overlapping.

"When Ma and Pa visited Earth, they knotholed down to your runtsome size," said Whaler. "But we're in our home zone here, and you stay big like us. Yunched extra-large. Whoopsy-doozy while I deshuffle you." The great braided wreath of gold and silver got out of their way. And then—

Sproing!

In the blink of an eye, Frek and the three other Earthlings had rebounded from each other like a fistful of rubber balls. Frek's fellow travelers weren't overlapping him anymore. They loomed before each other like giants, like titans, like foggy gods.

"Now to apply lotion with sun protection factor ten-to-the-thirtieth power," resumed the peppy voice of the enormous, wavering ring that was Tusky/Whaler. "Oinkment to shield your pigment. Stiffen up those suits." Moving with the steady, rolling languor of a squid's tentacles, the braided wreath wound itself around Frek. A half dozen shimmering planes of additional tweet lifted free of Tusky's flesh and wrapped around Frek's arms, body, head, and legs. His spacesuit hardened and gleamed.

Frek's body was a living gas within his titanic suit's transparent tubes. He was a neon sign a thousand kilometers high. Quietly a sun blazed nearby.

"And you live—?" began Frek, already guessing the answer, but fearing to say it out loud.

"The Orpolese live in these suns," said Whaler simply. "And in the spaces around them. We're Polynesians of the galactic core, you wave, hopping from isle to fiery isle. This whole zone is Orpoly. Our archipelago."

"But—what are you made of? Nothing can live in a sun!"

"Ever heard of sunspots?" said Whaler. "Stars are full of donut-shaped plasma rings, and a sunspot is where one of those rings crosses the surface. We supertwisters evolved from crude sunspots. Just like how you meat-brains evolved from protozoa. The Orpolese are personified plasma vortex rings, yes, thinking toroids of magnetofluid, spheromaks with soul. The dopey rings in your home Sun are like algae we might eat."

A flock of giant polyhedral tweet shapes burst out of Tusky's flesh, swooped through Frek and returned.

"She-Who-Must-Be-Obeyed is deciding our plans," said Whaler. "Bossy as her mother Ulla, the yore princess of the royal rassen family, you understand. Ulla's folks think they're nobler stock than a znag like Papa Bumby. Bumby dragged Ulla down into a znassen pair."

"What's he saying, Frek?" interrupted Dad. He seemed a little spaced-out. "We're so big. Did something go wrong with the yunch? I'm scared. I can't catch up with what's happening." Slowly, immensely, Dad reached out to take Frek's hand. With Dad's suit still unburnished, his hand felt soft to Frek. Poor Dad. Frek was careful not to squeeze him too hard.

"Whaler's strengthening our suits," Frek told him. "So that sun can't hurt us."

"He's not takin' us in thar, is he?" shouted Gibby, the sound of his voice reverberating endlessly within Frek's enormous glassy shell.

"It could be goggy," said Frek, who was still letting the concept sink in. The intense sunshine felt good on his long legs. It would be incredible to jump into the huge sphere of fire and not worry about being burned.

"Into a star," mused Dad. "I want it. That's what you're planning, Whaler?"

"Simple as jumping in a pond," said Whaler. "We'll finish sun-screening your suits, dive into this fattie here to graze some gnarly vortices, meet and greet the local mokes, surf solar tsunamis to the branelink at the center of Orpoly—and then it's into the hole with you and your son and his pal and his dog. Along with that gold asteroid to bail out my parents. You're going to have to make the gold yourself,

Frek. You're the one who busted their yunch. You and your dad."

"But—" started Frek, then let it go. He'd find a way. In any case, Whaler and Tusky weren't listening anymore, they were busy writhing around the thousand-kilometer bodies of his companions, layering and polishing them like shiny-backed lifter beetles.

Wow got upset when the great wreath closed in on him, and even tried to bite it. "Bad snake," yelped Wow. But they hardened his suit, too.

The Earthlings and Orpolese were falling toward the nearby star at an ever-accelerating rate, but this wasn't fast enough for Whaler and Tusky, who used some googly force field to speed things up. Their efforts made them pitch and rock. The sun rushed toward them like a jerky, speeded-up toon. It occurred to Frek that his body was big enough to hold everyone on Earth. This was beyond gaussy, beyond gollywog, beyond his googliest dreams.

Solar prominences licked out like giant flames. The star's vast, glowing surface was patterned into slowly shifting polygons—yellow patches rimmed by edges of fierce clean white. Frek was so close now that some of the flares reached out past him.

Frek had a vague memory of a facilitator saying that the temperatures in a solar flare were in the millions of degrees, hotter even than within the star itself. But thanks to the souped-up Orpolese spacesuit, he felt fine, neither hot nor cold, just comfortable, with a slight sense of enjoying the pleasant glow of sunlight upon his skin.

Frek heard Whaler talking in the sibilant gurgle of the Orpolese tongue and then, from the corner of his eye, he noticed a great flutter of tweet leaving Tusky. Whaler made more gargling sounds, louder than before. Tusky responded with an agitated cloud of dark blue polyhedra. Could the two be quarreling?

It seemed absurd to mix something so humdrum as a married couple's bickering with something so extraordinary as diving into a sun. Shouldn't they stop arguing and pay attention to where they were bound? Their party was rushing toward the bloated, twitching sun at what felt like a million kilometers per hour.

For his part, the old husband Gibby was amused to notice Whaler and Tusky's exchange. "What's the spat about?" he asked in a cozy tone. "One of you got a rival down in that star—might could say an old flame?"

"I just picked up on the fact that it's mostly rassens shoaling in this sun," said Whaler in a tense tone. "Not my scene. But the little lady insists we go on in. As if we'll have a hearty holiday reunion with her cousins and her grandparents' friends. But I know they'll gnash and scowl at us for being znassen."

"What's all this rassen and znassen?" asked Gibby.

"There's two castes of Orpolese," said Whaler. "The fancy, rich, important rassens and the plain, poor, ordinary znags. One guess which of us two is which. A mixed marriage like ours is called a znassen. Ulla/Bumby were znassen, and we inherited it. The difference has to do with what you'd call handedness or chirality. In your language, Tusky's counterclockwise, I'm clockwise. Bulge your eyes, she'll give you visual aids."

Silent as usual, Tusky created two hundred-kilometer-long tweets, a pair of gold rods that were perhaps ten kilometers across. The rods twitched and coiled themselves into gentle helical springs, like spiral staircases. They looked dark against the reticulated plain of the onrushing sun's surface. If you walked up one of those staircases, you'd move in a counterclockwise circle as you rose.

"That's a rassen twist," said Whaler. "Twisted like your human DNA, as it happens. Sex them, Tusky."

One of the helices bent around to join itself and make a twisted donut. The other helix branched at the tip, splitting into a broom of baby helices, all twisted the same way. Frek remembered Bumby's tentacles.

"A rassen female and a rassen male," said Whaler. "Now show them two znags, Ulla."

"Stop jawin' and pay attention to whar we're goin', Whaler!" yelled Gibby. "I don't give a squat about your screwy tribes. Forget I asked!"

"Into the sun," intoned Dad, who wasn't listening to Whaler at all. "We're falling into the sun. The white light."

Wow howled. He didn't like any of this.

The sun had grown so large that you couldn't see anything else.

Immense sheets and towers of glowing gas rippled up from the surface, streaming past. Here and there the rolling donut plasmas of other Orpolese could be glimpsed in the flames, capering like the demons of hell.

The dogged Tusky continued her demo. A second pair of tweet lines appeared; these were thin and silver, all but black against the star. They coiled themselves into two more helical springs, coiled in the opposite sense from the gold ones. These were znags. Enough already.

A slow eruption on the sun sent a ragged cloud of fire up toward them. The fire held four Orpolese donuts, each of them with a rassen twist to their flesh.

"Put a znag on a rassen and you get a znassen like Tusky and me," continued Whaler obliviously. Her silver znag squid model meshed into the flesh of the gold rassen donut she'd made.

But who cared anymore, for the Orpolese rassen were upon them, and none too friendly. Gusty force fields tossed Frek's party from side to side. Wow was barking wildly. Tweets swirled, and Frek heard garbled Orpolese speech. One of the rassen pairs stood out, a pink donut with purple veins. The pair sniffed appreciatively at Tusky and murmured to her in a low tone. Tusky replied with a delicate tweet greeting, a shape like a creamy orchid. The fresh donut's female part replied with a polite round tweet of her own.

"Head for the deeps!" cried Whaler, obviously wanting to break off the conversation. Tusky formed a second friendly orchid. The mauve male part of the donut spoke again in Orpolese, his voice deep and melodious.

"I said let's go, damn you, Tusky," bellowed Whaler.

For a moment Tusky/Whaler hung there, torn by two wills. As if by main force, Whaler spurred the reluctant Tusky down toward the sun. Tusky left behind a single rueful tweet in the shape of a teardrop. The purple-on-pink donut swallowed the teardrop and followed along. Gibby, Wow, and Dad went, too.

But Frek couldn't join the others. A rassen pair was blocking his way. The ring pushed him upward and tugged at his limbs as if to tear him in half. Maybe the donut thought he was food.

Frek surprised himself by moving with sudden, violent grace, his suit acting in perfect synch with his thoughts. He dove through the hole of the menacing donut, and as he passed through, he landed a solid kick that sent the shape spinning away. His actions seemed to have caught the donut off guard. Perhaps these Orpolese hadn't realized Frek was alive, conscious, and intelligent. As smoothly as if he'd been doing this his whole life, Frek bent at his waist and dove for the sun.

The others were far ahead—with the exception of Wow, who was kicking and snarling, caught in the grip of the two other Orpolese donuts. One was pulling Wow's hundreds-of-kilometers-long tail, the other was fastened to the dog's monumental snout. Frek knifed into first rassen, pulling the monster nearly in two. She/he fluttered raggedly away. Frek shoved one arm through the hole of the second rassen, hefted the great donut, and flung her/him like an old-time Frisbee. Wow yelped his gratitude. The purple-on-pink donut that had been following Tusky swooped up from below to join the skirmish.

The boy and his dog evaded the new donut and sped down before any of the Orpolese could retaliate. As they neared the sun's stormy surface, the excess of light spilled over into Frek's ears, nose, and sense of touch. Though his eyes were functioning, they were overloaded to the point of showing ragged checkerboards of feedback. His suit was using his other sense organs to process the overflow. It was almost like being a blind person, modeling reality from sound, smell, and touch.

And then he was inside the sun.

The sound of the sun was as the warm hubbub of human voices in a crowded room, with the buzz and throb of great machineries in chambers far below. The touch of the sun was like the bubbles and currents in the foamy white spot at the base of the waterfall in the River Jaya where Frek and his sisters went to swim. Tickling taps danced along the shell of Frek's suit; little swirls plucked at his limbs. The smell of the sun was like a garden on a hot summer day, with vagrant breezes bringing a pleasant palette of scents. Frek could pick out roses, beanblossoms, an anyfruit tree, and the vinegary smell of a turmite mound.

His four companions were nearby. He could hear the touch of their voices in the perfumed tessellations of light.

Something big and hollow brushed against him. A dark, quiet cavity. Dad.

"There's nothing left after this," said Dad. It was hard to be sure from his tone if he was happy or sad.

"There's always more, a little farther," insisted Frek, not liking his father's eerie calm. "It never ends."

"I used to think that way," said Dad. "Before I went to the Crufter asteroid."

"We're together now," said Frek. "I can bring you home."

"I don't want to be there," said Dad shortly. "That's why I left." He paused for a while, and then added, "You wouldn't want me if you knew everything I've done." Another pause, longer than before. "Are we in the Planck brane right now?"

"We're in a sun, Dad."

"You know how I get confused sometimes," said Dad. "Ever since Gov peeked me."

The space around them began flickering and shaking. Pinging sounds and the smell of ozone accompanied the turbulence. It felt like soft little objects were bumping into Frek.

"Loofy," called Whaler, the twirling ring of him and Tusky heaving into visibility like a thick spot in a glowing fog of gems. The dark shapes of Gibby and Wow were nearby as well. "Good eats," added Whaler. "Your suits can yum it, too."

As if mocking her husband, Tusky glyphed a greedy silver ball with a stupid-looking open mouth.

The loofy consisted of darting eddies of solar plasma—twirling, quivering, and swarming around them. Though myriads of the loofy twists lay within easy reach, they were as nimble and hard to catch as minnows.

But Frek did manage to trap and squash a few in his hands; they melted into his armored suit, making a pleasant *zing* that left him feeling energized. Meanwhile Tusky/Whaler was swooping around like a whale eating krill, engulfing the loofy twists by the thousands.

"That's more like it," said Whaler presently. "Let's rest, my motley crew."

Tusky glyphed a grossly bulging tweet of selfish fatness, pale silver amidst the turmoil of the star.

"How did Bumby hook up with Ulla anyway?" asked Gibby. He looked/felt/sounded like a long forked cave in the mountain of light. "If them rassen hate znags so much."

"They were both already married," said Whaler. "An Orpolese can get by alone, but we don't like to. Ulla and Bumby were already partnered when they met in some tasty shoal of loofy. They'd gone cold on their workaday mates, and they liked the looks of each other's hot mirror-twists. So Bumby hopped off his old wife and onto Ulla."

Tusky sent out an excited stream of glowing red hearts, soft dark thuddy holes in the roiling flame.

"What about the old wife and the old husband?" wondered Dad.

"They—killed them and ate them," said Whaler. "It's the usual way. Honeymoon breakfast."

"Ow," said Carb, then laughed in a way that Frek didn't much like.

Tusky echoed Carb's laugh with a tweet flock of green monster-birds that hooted and cawed for far too long. This was the first time Frek had ever heard tweets making noise.

"It's not *that* funny, Tusky," said Whaler in an uneasy tone.

"Fleas," interrupted Wow, snapping at some large curls of loofy. "Catch fleas."

"Were them rassen up there tryin' to eat us, or what?" asked Gibby, still trying to figure things out.

"Since you're not curled into hoops, you Earthlings look like giant loofy," said Whaler. "Big dumb yum." His voice dropped an octave. "But as for me and Tusky, I think—well, I think that reddish guy—Yonny—I think he'd like to croak me and blend with Tusky. But you wouldn't let him do that, would you, Tusky?"

A branching fern of purple tweet floated past, barely visible amid the crooning, caressing cells of light.

"Tusky says I'm stewing an empty pot," interpreted Whaler in a suspicious tone. More tweets followed. "She says the purple-on-pink couple just wanted to be friends," he continued. "Yonny and Marta. Tusky wants us to float up there and ask them for news of the family tree. But I don't trust them. That Yonny, he's got a thing for you,

Tusky, I can tell. And it's two-way. I saw those pretty tweet blossoms you made for him."

Tusky answered with a tweet of a swollen silver claw grasping a drooping gold ring.

"I am not a bully," hollered Whaler. "But I don't trust Yonny and Marta. We lie low until I think they've gone away. And that's final. Relax, dammit!"

Tusky sent out a complicated, angry series of tweets. But again it seemed like Whaler had the power to control the pair's motion. Though the silver-on-gold donut twitched and trembled, she/he stayed right where they were.

For quite a long time not much happened. A whiff of peach blossoms came to Frek, along with a fizzy feeling all along his legs. The sun was gently chiming. How lovely it was here, really. He hung there basking, now and then catching an overbold twist of loofy that ventured too close.

Eventually Frek and the others must have slept, for at some point he had the feeling of waking up. Blissfully he hung there, enjoying the gentle shifting of the currents of the sun, faintly hearing the waking mutters of the others. Idly he wondered if there were anything odd about his sense of time. They'd been in here—how long? And they had to go—where? Oops.

"Hey, Whaler," called Frek. Buried in the beating light/sound/touch of the star, it would be so easy to forget the purpose of their quest. "You're supposed to take us to the branelink. So I can get the elixir and take my guys home." Home to Mom, Geneva, Ida, and Renata. Home to trees, grass, water, and the open air. Home to their cozy kitchen with the little yellow-and-white-veined marble statue of the Buddha. Earth was even more beautiful than the inside of a sun. "Come on," clamored Frek.

"Those rassen will be on us like a murder of crows," whined Whaler. "Handsome purple Yonny and his snotty Marta pecking first. You'll be loofy sushi, Frek."

"Stop stalling," said Frek. "They didn't hurt us before."

Tusky sent out tweets of smiley faces, rainbows, candy canes, and flowers. Meaning that she was on Frek's side. But Frek was starting to wonder about her motives. Maybe Whaler's fears were justified.

Be that as it may, they had to get out of here. What if the rassen really were waiting for them? Thanks to the element of surprise, Frek had been able to push them around before. But maybe if there were a serious battle it would be a different story.

An idea came to Frek. "What if we grab our feet with our hands? Gibby grabs his tail of course, and Wow can bite his tail. If we're curled around, we'll look a little like Orpolese. So they don't right away think we're giant loofy." Another idea. "And why don't we ride out on one of those solar flares we saw? Didn't you say something about surfing a tidal wave, Whaler?"

"Of course we'd ride a flare," said Whaler in a sullen tone. "If we were leaving at all. Ouch!" A big pinch appeared in the flesh of the silver-on-gold donut, a thin spot that wobbled around and around the ring. "Don't do that, Tusky. Hey!" Another dent appeared, and the donut seemed very nearly on the point of breaking into pieces. "All right, then," snarled Whaler. "We'll go."

The six of them plowed through the synaesthetic gumbo of light/sound/scent/touch, the angry Whaler not bothering to watch if the Earthlings could keep up. And then Frek lost his bearings. Suddenly he couldn't tell which way was up. If he drove himself forward, would he be burying himself yet deeper in the sun? But if he stopped moving he'd fall farther behind. You could lose your mind in here.

Your mind, my mind, in the sun's rind find a bind, you mind? Unkind. My mind, your mind . . .

Something prodded Frek in the belly. Wow?

"Hey Frek!" Dad was right there too, a cool dark spot of reason. "Good boy, Wow, you found him. Come on, Frek, you're drifting down. Whaler and Tusky are up that way, waiting with Gibby for a blast. I told those damned Orpolese they were going too fast, but stupid sulky Whaler wouldn't even answer. You okay?"

Frek gratefully let his father lead him to the others. The sun-stuff was madly surging, with tornados of loofy tearing past.

"Hang onto us, you selfish turkeys," yelled Dad to Whaler and

Tusky. "Net us in a force field so you don't lose us on the way out."

"Ready!" called Whaler, sending out a fairly weak force field to help them. "Everyone blast up as hard as you can when I give the signal!"

A stench of burnt sulfur, an avalanche roar, a sleet of needles—a rush of sun stuff came at them.

"Go!" yelled Whaler.

Frek jetted his suit as hard as he could. He was catching up to the rolling space wave of the solar plume, he was getting up on top of it, Whaler was still in sight, but—

"Wipe out!" yodeled Dad, laughing a little.

"Circle back, Whaler," yelled Gibby. "We missed the son of a gun. You gotta drag us stronger, you lazy cuss. Wow don't get the picture a-tall."

Frek skittered off to one side and let himself drop back down to his companions. In a bit Whaler reappeared.

"Another one's coming right up," said Whaler. "They pulse in threes."

The second time around Dad and Wow caught the plume, but Gibby slipped and knocked Frek off the rushing shock-front.

"If we miss the third one, we'll be dog-paddling here for another hour," scolded Whaler. "Not that I mind but—don't pinch again, Tusky, you shrew! Front and center, cannon-fodder. Catch this wave or I'll turn off your spacesuits." Whaler made his voice into a hoarse, scary whisper. "I'm not kidding."

This time they all caught the wave. It was incredible, a Nantucket sleigh ride through rough seas of sound, a romp up the blossom-scented stairway to heaven, a barefoot scamper across a million-note chrome xylophone.

Frek wished there were a way he could have recorded his sensations to play for Stoo Steiner and the other guys. That would geeve up their minds! And, as he thought this, he realized that the espers were in fact relishing his inputs. At some point during the jangling chaos of his trip into the sun, he'd let down his branecasting block. The golden glow was on him stronger than ever before. So once again, Frek pushed the glow out into the distance, made his thoughts as unresisting as air, and "combed his brain," getting back his normal modes of thought. And then he entangled his thoughts with those of his companions and did sky-air-comb with them as well, to keep the espers from seeing through their eyes. Thinking about your adventures in your own way felt better without other minds leeching onto your feelings and your thoughts.

And now they were up in interstellar space, entering the open gulfs of Orpoly. The plume they'd ridden had spent its force; it was guttering back into the sun they'd just left. They were free, in the black, their suits a little pocked and iridescent, everyone intact, and no rassen in sight.

But Whaler and Tusky were still quarrelling.

All at once Tusky poofed out a spore-cloud of ten thousand tiny shiny red tweet hearts. Messengers. The hearts buzzed off in every direction, and it wasn't long till one of them must have found its target—for here came Yonny and Marta, a growing dot against the endless bright star, pink Marta bucking and struggling, Yonny throbbing on her surface like a web of varicose veins. They looked ready to rumble.

"Come on, pretty boy!" yelled Whaler aggressively. He peeled himself loose from Tusky to hang free. "You want a piece of me?" He floated up above his wife's gold donut, his body an angry tangle of silver strands and stalks. Yonny too tore free of his mate, ready for battle.

The two male Orpolese circled each other, tightening up their shapes. Whaler drew much of his mass into a flattened central wad, leaving about a dozen tentacles writhing from his forward end. In their midst was a large, sharp beak. Whaler resembled a cuttlefish, like Bumby, only a thousand kilometers long. For his part, Yonny looked more like a giant crab, with much of his purple mass formed into a menacing pair of claws.

Moving fast, Whaler darted forward, slung a two-hundred-kilometer-long tentacle around one of the immense claws, and tore it off. He whisked the purple mass into the furious tangle of his feelers and devoured it with his beak.

"Dig it, Tusky!" roared Whaler. "Who's your man, baby? Who's your man?"

Glancing over at Tusky, Frek noticed something new. Tusky had extended a kind of snout, a tube like an elephruk's trunk, and she'd managed to dig the proboscis into the flesh of Marta. Lumps were moving up the trunk. Tusky was eating Marta! But Marta was extruding her own tube-snout and—

A bellow from Whaler brought Frek's attention back to the two males. Yonny had snipped off half of Whaler's tentacles, and he'd grabbed the silver Orpolese's body with his remaining purple claw! A snaky knot of Whaler's tentacles surrounded the great pincer, struggling to pry it loose.

Looking back at the two female Orpolese, Frek was shocked to see Tusky suddenly shrunken to a tenth of Marta's size. The pink donut's trunk was deeply embedded in Tusky's flesh. Bolus by bolus, Tusky's body was traveling up Marta's steadily pulsing snoot. Though Tusky continued sucking at Marta's body with her own trunk, she was losing the race.

A scream from Whaler and an obscene alien twitter from Yonny signaled the denouement. The attacker had torn Whaler in two! Whaler was done for!

The huge one-clawed purple crab stuffed the silver fragments into the churning machineries of his mouth.

Meanwhile Tusky was nearing her own end; she was little more than ten kilometers across. But Yonny saw, and raised his claw, and struck his wife a fearsome blow.

The great dent in Marta's pink flesh threw off her sucking rhythm. Tiny Tusky seized the opportunity. Cubic hectokilometers of Marta-stuff surged up Tusky's greedy golden snout. Marta never did manage to get back into the groove. In minute it was all over. Marta was no more.

Yonny stretched himself into a comely purple tracery and settled onto the plump gold body of his new bride. The two forms quivered in sensual delight.

"Lordy lord," marveled Gibby. "What's gonna happen now? They gonna eat us too?"

"Yonny pinch," said Wow, impressed by how the Orpolese had used his giant claw.

"I wonder what'll happen when Yessica meets Lora down in Middleville," mused Dad. "I'm glad I won't be there for that."

"What in the world are you nasty beasts?" said Yonny all of a sudden.

"We're from Earth," said Frek. "I'm Frek, this is my father, Carb, my sidekick, Gibby, and my dog, Wow. I made a deal with the branecasters to let the Orpolese produce the Earth channel. You're supposed to help us get to the branelink so we can work some details. Like us getting paid."

"I ain't no sidekick," protested Gibby. "I'm the brains."

"I despise branecasting," interrupted Yonny in a lofty tone. "Tacky, tacky, tacky. Turning our stars into idiot-balls to show branecast advertisements and to display disgusting creatures like you? Spare us the details of your utter degradation. I most certainly won't help you. In fact—" The purple veins of his body drew together, reconstituting his fearsome claw.

Tusky began tweeting, explaining the situation to Yonny. An image of Earth, of a flickerball, of the branecasters, of Ulla/Bumby.

"Branecasting is contemptible," intoned Yonny. "It's as simple as that. These soulless beasts are better off dead. I say put an end to their wretched—ow!"

Once again, Tusky had thrown a pinch into the flesh of herself and her current mate. The toothy bulge of Yonny's claw melted away.

"Very well then, I won't harm them," said Yonny quickly. "You're a passionate one, my little Tusky." He was really pouring the honey into his tone now. "It's lovely to be with someone so vivacious. But don't you think we could simply send these revolting vermin on their way?"

Tusky tweeted the image of captive Ulla/Bumby once again.

"But that's not our job, don't you know," said Yonny in a nasal tone. "Let this—this what's-his-name—this Frek thing, let him clean up the mess he's made. We mustn't waste a single minute of our honeymoon in the monoculture wasteland of central Orpoly, dear Tusky. I'm keen on whisking you off to a special spot I know. A marvelous binary dwarf star near the outskirts. You'll find the most extraordinary loofy there, and the shapeliest gravity waves you've ever seen.

It's quite unspoiled; the znag and znassen rabble haven't ruined it yet. Do let me take you there, my sweet. We've no need to watch these spit-talking fools rush into their dreary branelink. Surely it's enough to point them on their way." His veiny purple body was kneading Tusky's golden flesh as he talked.

Tusky hesitated, then tweeted out a single, large, pointing hand. Just as Frek might have expected, the forefinger was directed toward the brightest region of the Orpolese environs. Toward the center of the galactic core.

"Fine, but what does the branelink look like?" demanded Frek.

For some reason the question provoked a mocking laugh from Yonny. But Tusky helpfully formed one last tweet for them, an mind-entangled form that would turn out to look different to each of them. For Frek, the tweet resembled the friendly creamy marble Buddha that sat on their kitchen shelf back home, rounded into a sphere, and with an emerald in his forehead.

"The branelink shapes itself to lure the rubes in," said Yonny in a condescending tone. "We've done enough for them, now, Tusky. Forget these wretched beings and their trashy home world. Let our nuptial celebration begin."

Tusky made a nodding gesture that must have meant yes. The Buddha tweet disappeared and the floating tweet hand waved goodbye. Tusky and Yonny flew off, swooping outward past the nearby star.

"Let's catch another flare," said Dad. "Get a boost toward the core. There's a good set about to break over there."

"Did you see the Buddha just now?" Frek asked his father. "The statue from our kitchen?"

"Well, um, to me it kind of looked like a statue of me," said Carb, sounding embarrassed. "I wish I'd seen Buddha. Maybe next time."

"I saw the nice round door of my burrow," said Gibby. "With firelight glowing in the windowpanes."

"Wow saw vig meat," said the dog.

"That Yonny's right negatory on them branecasters," mused Gibby. "Maybe he knows somethin', even if he is a toff. Maybe we shouldn't oughta go in that branelink at all."

"Look, the only hope of stopping the branecasters is to talk with them and learn more. We gotta go all the way in to get out. Anyway, I didn't come this far to go home without the elixir."

"Let's do it," said Dad.

So they used their suits to jockey themselves into a line-up above a particularly active region of the star, and, yes, they caught the next good solar flare toward the mass of light at Orpoly's core. Frek's suit fed him a sound of breaking waves.

The trip was like liveboard surfing, sailfish riding, angelwing gliding—and more. Whenever they'd slow down too much, they'd swing near a sun and get a slingshot boost off its gravity, sometimes catching a fresh flare wave as well. Carb was especially good at riding the interstellar energies. Cheerfully he showed Frek and the others how to improve their style. The old man was at his best out here. He made their urgent quest into play.

As the suns grew denser, Frek saw some Orpolese in the distance. He murmured a warning, and the four curled themselves into hoops and used the power of their suits to race away.

Frek had to grin at the way Wow looked, with his teeth clamped onto his two-hundred-kilometer tail, the tail continually about to slip away, his great snout twitching as he readjusted his bite, his eyes rolling back so that their whites showed, his legs twitching as if to run across the empty vacuum, his expression strained and grim.

Noticing Frek's smile, Carb began clowning: wagging his Mohawk, bucking his long body and acting like he was having trouble holding onto his toes. Finally Frek started laughing so hard he couldn't stay curled at all anymore. But it didn't matter, the Orpolese weren't following them.

Fewer suns lay ahead now, tens of thousands rather than hundreds of thousands. The missing suns had gone into a black patch that covered a third of the sky: a great wobbling dead zone, a giant black hole at the galaxy's exact center. Lively lines of light wound around the vast nucleus. The lights were a bit like chrome wires around a lump of coal, though more smeared out than that, more like chaotic strange attractors. A deep ghostly chant echoed from the dark central void, a sound like a chorus of the damned. Frek's suit was using all his senses to model this strange place.

A nearby star faltered after a near miss with another star and veered toward the dark zone. As the star fell, it screamed; and as it dropped, its voice grew deeper and slower. The titanic black hole kneaded the falling star, squirting out a hot jet that added to the bright traceries upon its dark surface. The doomed star's remaining shreds faded into a deep orange, then red, dimmer and dimmer, never quite going away. Its death cry merged with the never-ending plainsong of the millions of other stars who'd crashed here since the dawn of time.

The suns in this neighborhood had to step lively to survive, racing around the galactic doom-egg to postpone falling in. Frek and his party blended into the flow out on the lip of the whirlpool. Circling the core, jostled by suns, they encountered more and more Orpolese donuts.

The Earthlings did their best to look like hoops. Frek avoided looking at Dad lest he start laughing too hard to stay curled. Even in the face of a galactic black hole, Carb made things funny. The man was completely irresponsible.

And where was the branelink? No sign of it yet.

Just then Frek noticed a really odd-looking sun. This star had somehow been turned into a giant flickerball. It was displaying—you guessed it—the same old branecaster logo, the boring cube with blue pipes for its edges and an esper's face on each of the slowly tumbling cube's six sides. It gave Frek a sick feeling to see a star turned into an advertisement. The branecasters had brought this profound desecration of Nature to the very heart of his home galaxy.

Frek thought of a word he'd heard from both Bumby and Yonny. "Monoculture." Bumby had used the word to describe the Unipuskers, and Yonny had applied it to the branecasters. Monoculture was exactly what was wrong with Earth. Monoculture was what Nu-BioCom had brought to the biome. And monoculture was what Gov and his cohorts were planning to spread across people's minds with their ooey internal uvvy—assuming people still had any minds after the branecasters and espers had taken hold.

A sudden shoal of Orpolese converged upon the star with the logo. The tamed sun switched to full flickerball mode, beaming out images of alien landscapes. No, wait, those were images of—Earth.

Frek stared, mesmerized. As an interface, the star was great enough to readily fold together millions, even billions, of images at once. Frek was looking at the head of each person on Earth, all of them, everybody overlaid on top of each other to make one supernal image of loving, suffering, weeping, laughing, feasting, starving humanity, men and women, boys and girls, morphs and bis, gumps and Grulloos, every size, every shade, every age.

Frek felt a rush of universal love for his fellows, and a shy joy that it was his lot to make their world better. He was glad to be seeing this, it was important. He'd never forget it.

One of the Orpolese changed the channel.

So much for Frek's vision of humanity. It hadn't really been a vision, it had been a product. Yes, it was universal love, but it was love in slop buckets. The branecasters had made the very soul of mankind into just another piece of slick entertainment. Frek's raw, whipsawed emotions settled upon a grim determination to end the branecast.

Following Dad's lead, the four Earthlings caught a flare off the flickerball star and proceeded on their way among the great procession of stars circling the central black hole.

They passed perhaps a dozen more flickerball stars. Each was attended by a rapt coterie of Orpolese users, none of them aware enough to notice the four real Earthlings in their midst. Meanwhile, in the background, the insane grandeur of the galactic black hole's light show played on—with only the Earthlings watching.

By now Frek was wondering if they'd ever find the branelink. Would he recognize it? But then he saw something that took his doubts away.

Though he wasn't sure at first how it looked to the others, to him it was a star resembling that same old yellow-and-white marble Buddha, the comfortable beloved figure from their kitchen shelf. Just as Tusky had predicted. The subtle color shadings of the star's convection cells mapped out the giant, blissful face, set with a great green emerald in his forehead, and surrounded by a gently tinted halo.

"The Bodhisattva," said Dad, who must have been seeing about the same thing as Frek this time, instead of some personal ego-boosting statue. All at once he recited a half-remembered bit of scripture.

"He wears a crown of eight thousand rays, in which are seen fully reflected a state of perfect beauty," murmured Carb. "The color of his body is ivory and gold. His palms have the mixed color of five hundred lotuses, while each fingertip has eighty-four thousand gem facets and each facet has eighty-four thousand colors and each color has eighty-four thousand rays which are soft and mild and shine over all things that exist. With these hands he draws and embraces all beings. In his towering forehead gleams the eye of wisdom, eight thousand kilometers tall."

"The branelink," murmured Frek. The Bodhisattva's green third eye rippled like a jungle in a windstorm. Now and then you could glimpse the warped Planck brane landscape behind the green scrim. They were supposed to fly in there.

"I don't see nothing like that at all," said Gibby. "I'm just seein' my front door, though it's hella big. Got a little green light up in the window." He paused, then continued. "If we really gotta fly in there, Frek, what about the bribe? No point goin' off half-cocked. You gotta make that gold asteroid for 'em like you said."

Frek was a little glad for the delay. They and the Bodhisattva-star were orbiting the black hole fast enough not to fall in. There was no rush. He'd take his time and vaar the gold, yes. Making a ten-kilometer gold asteroid shouldn't actually be that hard. After all, Frek was still a thousand kilometers long. The ball of gold only had to be as big as the tip of his finger.

So, just as Gawrnier had taught him to do, Frek held out his hands and let his mind merge into the space between. Empty space, with nothing to say about it. Frek breathed evenly and gazed at the Bodhisattva, then pushed that perception away.

The space was part of Frek's breath. Emptiness. The space was breathing. Nothing.

"Something's there!" shouted Dad.

Frek snapped out of his trance and looked down. There kenner between his hands, but it wasn't solid. It was a wispy cloud.

He imagined solid gold, he gilded the image onto the perimeter of his thoughts, let the center of his mind merge with the cloud of kenner, and turned his perceptions inside out.

A ball of gold hung in space. But the ball was tiny, nowhere near as big as Frek's fingertip. It was a mere speck, maybe a kilometer across, a tenth as wide as what he needed. Remembering the old volume-varies-as-the-cube thing from school, he figured he'd need about ten-cubed of these balls. And, oh man, that was a thousand. Wishing that much nothingness into gold was going to take a long time.

"Can I help?" asked Dad, leaning his tattooed head forward to study the tiny dot of gold. Just now his tattoos were depicting suns with solar flares. "Show me how you do it," added Dad.

"I already tried to teach it to Gibby and Renata," said Frek wearily. "It's no use."

"Try me," urged Dad. "Maybe I've got some powers, too. Don't forget, I'm the one who saw the Magic Pig!"

And, yes, Carb was able to craft kenner, too. Even though Frek couldn't explain it very well, Dad got the knack right away. In fact his first ball of gold was twice the size of Frek's. Dad managed to make his two-kilometer glob look a little bit like a pig with a Mohawk. Gibby, who had the keenest eyes of any of them, used his powerful fingers to tweeze the two lumps into one.

In a couple of hours they were done. They'd made a ten-trillion-ton asteroid of pure gold, a ball ten kilometers across. Gibby cradled it in his enormous hand, using his powered suit to nudge the massive lump around.

Wow began barking. A really big pink and yellow Orpolese donut was swooping in toward them, a male-female pair bent on making a post-flickerball snack of them. Without even saying anything, Dad kenny-crafted himself a hundred-kilometer long Nguyen War singularity gun and fired a stinging swarm of space-cusps that sent the couple howling for safety, their donut surface roiled into untidy peaks.

"Carb boom," exclaimed Wow.

"Spaceman with a shotgun!" hooted Gibby.

"How did you make something so big?" cried Frek.

"It's hollow," said Dad, happily brandishing the great, finned tube.

"There's no more mass in it than in one of those tiny pinches of gold. I studied the designs for these suckers one time. I always wanted one." He glanced over at Gibby. "Do we go off alien-hunting or do we finally go in?"

"We go in to get out," said Gibby. "Like Frek said." He clenched his fingers around the asteroid of gold and held his arm in front of his face. "Might as well do it now. I think we're drifting into a cloud of, like, cinders out here."

"Ready, Wow?"

"Wow ready."

Dad tossed away his singularity gun. The four of them arrowed toward the Bodhisattva's third eye.

11

the
exaplex

Frek thought he heard branches breaking as they shot through the green veils of the idol's eye. It was as if they were crashing through the canopy of the world's largest tree. Not that he saw a tree. And then they were falling through a pearly gray sky.

They fell for a while, and as they fell, Frek started absentmindedly thinking about the Skull Farmers game and its old-time decor. But then finally he was able to see the Planck brane world below—far, crooked, and shining. It had the feel of an artificial construct, like a three-dimensional painting, with every detail put in by hand. Zigzag lavender mountain ranges ran all along the horizon. Damp green and pale yellow foothills rose in abrupt bulges, some of them wind-carved into beetling bluffs. Farm fields rolled out of the hills, patterned with loamy stripes of brown and dotted with orchards in pink bloom.

A city was set amidst the fields, a sprawling metropolis with mansions mixed in with city blocks of apartments and office buildings. On the industrial fringes, factory chimneys puffed rhythmic balls of smoke. Radiating out across the enormous city was a pie-slice of park with a freeform lake and tens of thousands of trees. The park's tip was at the city's center, its leafy avenues ran clear out to the countryside. At the center was a great concrete-paved square with ugly old-style glass-box buildings and a stone gingerbread City Hall—presumably Bumby and Ulla were jailed in its basement.

All this was visible to Frek even though they were incredibly far up in the endless, empty, glowing sky—at an altitude of perhaps a million kilometers. But as Frek had noticed last time in the Planck brane, he had only to stare at something for its image to get as big as he liked. It was the phenomenological autozoom feature, the pzoom.

Pzooming on the town, Frek saw humanoid figures pointing at them and running about. One oddity was that the figures had spherical auras surrounding their heads, big bright auras for some, small faint ones for others. Not that this was heaven. In fact the city was set up like early times on Earth, like the Y2K era, with a somber palette and finely modeled forms.

The marble statues in the park had been heavily graffiti-tagged, perhaps by the skateboarders practicing beside boom-boxes with fanciful little music notes pulsing out. Automobiles crowded the streets with honks and fumes. Women with auras pushed strollers past people getting paper money from cash machines. Men with auras sold waffles and pig meat sandwiches from holes in the walls, hawking their wares over the din of leaf-blowers cleaning the pavement. Farther from the city center, a tram rattled past a soft, deserted building with a three-story lit-up yellow sign saying EXAPLEX. Frek had a vague memory of Chainey mentioning something about finding the elixir at the Exaplex, so seeing the building made him feel good.

And then, *pop,* Frek pzoomed his view back to normal. Though it was hard to be sure, he had the feeling that the Planck brane city was scaled like a city on Earth, which meant that Frek and his thousand-kilometer-tall companions would be giants here. And they were falling right toward the middle of town, closing in faster than seemed possible.

"Use your suits to steer out to those hills!" Frek called to the others. "Hurry!"

Dad moved forward, but Wow didn't get it. And even though Gibby's suit was humming with the strain, the Grulloo seemed unable to make any progress.

"The gold!" called Gibby. "It's too heavy!"

Frek darted over to his side and gave him a shove. Gibby swung around, but the hand with the asteroid held him in place. The gold ball was linked to its trajectory like a bead sliding down a wire. There was no deflecting it from its predestined path to the heart of the branecaster's sprawling city park.

"Leave it!" yelled Frek, getting hold of Wow. Gibby abandoned the asteroid and followed. They sped a few hundred kilometers, just in time to land in the cartoon foothills. It was an easy, springy landing; the hills felt like rubber.

Using his pzoom, Frek watched the gold asteroid smash into the branecaster's park, throwing up an iconic cloud of spirals, five-pointed stars, exclamation points, and X-eyed fish from the lake. And then the asteroid was at rest, ringed by the tidy ridge of an impact crater. Above the golden orb floated dollar signs and wavy lines of gleam. A swarm of tiny figures were already crawling upon the great nugget, their bright auras bobbing like fireflies.

Wondering what might happen next, Frek, Dad, and Gibby shifted about uneasily, their enormous feet scarring the bumpy carpet of hills. For his part, Wow lay down and began scratching himself through his spacesuit. The thumping of his leg sent tremors rippling across the fields.

Fifteen minutes later, the gold asteroid was completely gone, like a cow-pie dismantled by dung beetles. Immediately thereafter, a jet came whining toward Frek and the others from the city, a plump gold-plated cigar-shaped jet with stubby wings. It did a quick exploratory loop around them. An arched door appeared in its side, and with a quick series of pops, six tiny branecasters appeared with parachutes. The plane sped off; the branecasters floated to the ground and discarded their chutes.

Peering down, Frek could see them milling like excited ants. Unless he was mistaken, these were the same six as before. Sid, Cecily, Batty, Bitty, Chainey, and Jayney, humanoid figures with intense gold auras. Sid ran toward Frek's foot and gave it a series of kicks.

Bam! The sound traveled though Frek's vast, airy body, echoing off the inner curves of his glassy suit. *Bam, bam, bam!* The final kick triggered a prolonged whistle that slid up the scale into inaudibility. *Fweet!*

With the whistle, Frek shrank, his body finally finishing the un-yunching process that the Orpolese had halted in mid-stream before. When he reached his old hundred-sixty-centimeter size, his body locked in on it with a *bing*. Fine, but the *bing* was followed by *crash* and *tinkle*—the sounds of Frek's spacesuit popping off him and shat-tering like a shell of ice, the suit's pieces spinning through the air and melting away.

The air was nice; it smelled of rich soil and grassy meadows. It felt great to be out of the suit. Frek heard three more sets of *bam-fweet-bing-crash-tinkle* sound effects. And then the others were back to normal, too. The four Earthlings faced the same six frowning, selfish branecasters as before.

This time, instead of coarsely painted wall-sized faces, the brane-casters were three-dimensional figures, none of them taller than Frek. They were somewhat realistic now, but not entirely so—like carica-tures brought to life.

"You ruined the branecasters' picnic!" Batty shrieked. Oh Buddha, thought Frek, that routine again? Batty was dressed like a mental pa-tient, with a white gown that had long, dangling sleeves. His legs and feet were bare. He'd pushed the sleeves back so that his knobby, pur-plish hands could show. His fingernails were gilded, and he held a gold-handled carving knife.

"You wrecked our park," hollered Sid, starting right in at a fever-pitch of fury. He was bald, with orange highlights along his thick, twisting lips. Drops of spit flew from his mouth. "You'll have to pay damages! Make us another asteroid!" He wore an old-fashioned black suit with a white shirt and a gray tie. He was sporting a massive gold watch.

"He's actually serious," said chunky pink-jowled Cecily in her grav-elly voice. She was wearing a gray suit as before, livened up by a heavy gold necklace.

"I think it ought to be two more asteroids," put in thin-lipped plastic Jayney. Her face was as peach-colored and glossy as before. Beneath her pastel blue suit was a creamy blouse with a strict, tight collar. She had thick gold hoops in her ears.

"Get them, Batty," chirped Bitty, a wild-eyed thin woman dressed in a rumpled red suit. She had a hot red spot on each cheek. Her mouth sparkled, for she had a gold tooth and a massive gold stud in her tongue.

"I'm afraid we may not be able to honor your attempted ransom of Ulla and Bumby," said gray Chainey, patting his necktie. He pushed back his gold-rimmed glasses with his finger and cleared his throat. Like the others, he had a fine big aura like a bubble of light. It was obvious they'd made good use of their share of the asteroid. "It seems there was an irregularity in—"

Good old Dad broke the set. "You forgot to say thank you," he snarled, stepping forward and punching Batty so hard in the stomach that the branecaster dropped his knife.

At the same time Wow bit Sid in the leg. Gibby yanked Chainey's legs out from under him and held Batty's knife to the bespectacled branecaster's throat.

"Free our friends," said Gibby.

"You fool," said Chainey. "I could decohere you right now." But in point of fact he looked worried.

"Call off this damned dog before someone gets hurt," yelled Sid. Wow was up on his hind legs, snarling and snapping near Sid's face. Meanwhile, Bitty had jumped on Dad's back and he'd hurled her into Jayney, sending the two branecaster women to the ground.

Frek strode toward the swinelike Cecily. Was she modeled on a person or a pig? It was hard to be sure. Her ears were triangular flaps, clearly outlined against her gold aura. She took a step back. She actually seemed a little scared of Frek.

"I admit we're acting greedy," said Cecily, making a placating gesture with stubby arms that ended in pig trotters. She glanced over at Sid. "Don't you think we better play fair, honey? I don't see why we can't spring Ulla/Bumby if that's what it takes to get these thugs out of here. Right, Chainey?"

"And don't forget our elixir," yelled Gibby, digging the point of the knife right into the skin of Chainey's neck.

"Let him go!" shrieked Jayney, getting back to her feet. "You can have what you want."

"Now you're talking," said Gibby, releasing his grip on Chainey.

"Here Wow," added Frek. "Leave Sid alone."

"Take them downtown, Chainey," said Sid, brushing the dog hair off his suit.

"New frame," said Chainey.

And with no transition at all, Frek, Dad, Gibby, and Wow were standing with Chainey on the steps of the City Hall. The other five branecasters hadn't bothered to come.

The rendering of the town was darker and more realistic than the hills. The steps were coated with grit. Across the street, where the gold had been, the cratered park had repaired itself: lawns, trees, and lake were back in place.

Gibby was feeling through his jacket pockets, going over the contents. "Look at this," he said, holding out a foamy little rock with an iridescent sheen. "This is one of them pebbles we bumped into before we fell through the branelink. Another souvenir for the kids." He began looking around the sidewalk for something else small enough to pick up.

Meanwhile figures were coming out of the park and hurrying off down the gray sidewalks. Many of them sported jewelry, and all of them had bright-burnished auras. But nobody was looking over at them; nobody gave a smile or a wave of thanks. A tram clanked past, pushing its way through the stinking, photorealistic cars.

"This will free your Ulla and Bumby," said bland-faced Chainey, handing Frek a shiny piece of metal with one round end and a sticking-out piece with grooves in it and teeth along one edge. An old-fashioned key. "The cell door's around back."

"What's the name of this place?" said Frek, taking the key. "And who are all these—people?"

"This is Node G," said Chainey. "And our people call themselves Hubs. Has to do with the fact that we depend upon each other's attention. A word of advice: don't stay here too long. We're near the end of a cycle—what we call a yuga. We're due for renormalization." Chainey glanced at his wrist. Like Sid, he had a shiny new gold watch. "I've really got to leave you. Another deal to work out."

"Hold on," said Frek. "What about the elixir?"

"As I've told you before, your payment is something you need to take up with your producers," said Chainey. "Not me. But, I suppose it doesn't hurt to tell you that, in principle, you might be able to find what you want in one of the Exaplex projection rooms." That would be the movie theater that Frek had seen from the sky while they were falling down.

"How do I get to the Exaplex from here?" demanded Frek. He wasn't exactly sure what Chainey meant by a projection room either, but he'd put that off for now.

Chainey pointed vaguely toward a passing tram. "Theoretically, one of those vehicles could perhaps take you there. Ask Bumby." This guy was Mr. Helpfulness; he was really putting himself out. "So now I'll be—"

"Wait!" hollered Frek, seizing hold of Chainey's necktie. "There's something else I want to tell you. We don't want to be branecast at all."

Chainey gave his head an impatient little shake, twitching his necktie free. "Not negotiable. Can't fight progress. Go run after your elixir and don't make any more pathetic impossible demands. Oh, and that reminds me, if you do make it into Earth's projection room, stay clear of the mind worms, or we really *will* decohere you."

"What?"

"Cheers."

And then Chainey rotated around some impossible axis and disappeared.

"Let me see that," said Dad, taking the key from Frek and examining it. "This scene is so, so Y2K. Like Earth a thousand years ago."

"Yeah," said Frek. "Kind of like the Skull Farmers game. I was thinking about that game on the way down, you know? I wonder if the Hubs looked into my mind for tips on how to set this world up. Maybe they wanted to make us feel welcome. You *are* seeing what

I'm seeing, aren't you, Dad? We both see the key and, like, the knobby spires on this City Hall with statues on the tops?"

Dad nodded. "And you see that tram with the blond Hub woman driving it?"

"I see her, too," put in Gibby.

Dad looked around a little more. "I always thought I'd like the old days," he said, sadly wagging his Mohawk. "Now I'm not so sure."

In silence the three stared across the City Hall square of Node G.

The passing crowds of Hubs—it was hard not to think of them as people—the Hubs were quite physically diverse, which was an interesting change from home, where genomics had everyone looking pretty much the same. But none of the Hubs smiled, none of them spoke to each other. Their clothes were dull: whites, grays, tans, neutral blues, and black. Moreover, viewed as people, the passersby seemed diseased. They were obese, compulsively smoking cigarettes, twitching with neuroses, blowing phlegm from their noses and coughing in every direction; their blotchy skins were pocked with suppurating infections, they had missing and damaged teeth, many of them were balding, half wore brittle external corrective lenses, all of them stank of bacteria and decay. Their auras were stained, pale, and partly worn away, looking like little more than dirt in the air near their heads.

The ground was covered with dead artificial slabs of concrete, the buildings were lifeless blank glass and steel. The sky was gray, the air stank, the constant noise of the cars bounced back and forth from the office buildings' unornamented walls. It was nearly unbearable. How could people live this way? The old-time environment was a lot less pleasant than Frek would have imagined.

Another tram clanged past, its sides painted over with incomprehensible ads. Even though the words seemed to be English, Frek couldn't string them together into meaningful phrases. It was like trying to read inside a dream.

A dream. That was a chilling thought. The Hubs weren't people; Node G wasn't a Y2K Earth city. What they saw here was an illusion, a way of viewing something even less conceivable than life inside a star. Frek didn't want to see what lay behind the illusion. He only wanted to skate as rapidly as possible across the thin ice of this false reality, to finally finish his quest, and to leave Node G before the dream became a nightmare. Chainey had hinted that things might turn ugly very soon.

"Let's do our thing and go home," shouted Gibby over the roar of traffic. "Back to where it's green."

"We'll start with this," said Dad, holding up the key, excited about the archaic technology.

"I think the cell's back here," said Frek, leading the others around to the side of the City Hall.

The dirty sidewalk led right to a gray-painted metal door with a handle and a keyhole. Dad insisted on being the one to open the lock; he really liked the idea of using a key.

As soon as Dad yanked the door open, a dozen of those muddy demon things came flying out, slimy iridescent fish with gaping cat mouths that showed four fangs, two above and two below. The fishes' buzzing, chitinous wings danced with glaucous highlights.

Compared to the blind, dead machineries of the street, the ill-favored demons seemed almost homey, like some kind of new model NuBioCom kritters. But they were vicious little beasts. If Wow hadn't barked and snapped at them quite so savagely, they might well have attacked the Earthlings. But thanks to the dog, the devilish flying fish buzzed away.

The doorway brightened—and a shiny, fat, purple wheel came rolling out. One of the dimpled hubs irised into a triangular window, and out popped a glowing, branching shape that congealed into a floating green cuttlefish.

"Ulla and Professor Bumby!" cried Frek, glad to see the familiar forms in this uncanny place.

"Frek!" said Bumby, still orienting himself. "You sprung us from decoherence? Yes! I can think again; I know I'm me! How long has it been?" He began ticking off facts on his corkscrew tentacle tips. "You crashed our yunch, we fell into the Planck brane, the flying Hub demons jailed us and—good morning, darling!" Ulla had just interrupted him with a red heart of tweet followed by a little black cloud. He ran a tentacle across her and glanced up at the glowing gray sky. "No sun in the Planck brane, did you notice, Frek? But that doesn't

mean they don't have weather. Ulla smells a storm." His voice grew
urgent. "Tell me how many days we've been on ice."

It took a bit of effort for Frek to mentally order the recent events.
"I ran away from Middleville on Thursday, May twelfth," he said.
"On Friday, I went to Stun City with Gibby. Saturday we hooked up
with you at Gov's puffball and yunched. That's when you got decoherent. We slept in space and then the Unipusker saucer came for us.
With Renata. And Sunday night we got to Unipusk. We were there all
day Monday. They were going to kill me because I wouldn't make
a deal for them though the branelink. But then their branelink went
down, so they just locked me up."

What a week it had been! A far cry from: I went to school, I went
to school, I went to school. Frek felt proud, telling all his adventures.

"Tuesday at dawn we escaped Unipusk with some Radiolarians,"
he continued. "But then we had to ditch them, too. They wanted to
enslave Earth with a plug in everyone's head. And then your children
Whaler and Tusky showed up just in time to rescue us and bring us to
Orpoly. We slept for a while inside a sun with them, which brings us
up to today. Wednesday. Today we surfed the solar flares and gravity
waves to the Orpolese branelink and dived in. So I guess that means
you've been decoherent for four days."

At the mention of Whaler and Tusky, Ulla sent a quick, interroga-
tive tweet-icon of the two. Frek hated to give her the bad news. But
Gibby didn't seem to feel any such compunction.

"Whaler's dead," said Gibby. "Torn up and et by Yonny. Tusky's
new flame. A rassen."

Ulla's tweets darted through their heads to winkle out the full
story. In the process she noticed something Frek hadn't bothered to
mention.

"Ulla says we're grandparents?" exclaimed Bumby, not seeming
all that upset by the death of his son. "Whaler and Tusky pinched off
a clone before they broke up?"

"Yeah," said Frek. "It happened when we were yunched up to the
size of the galaxy. They were called Tagine and Vlan. They took
Yessica, Renata, and Woo back to Middleville on Earth."

"Whaler passed the torch," said Bumby in a satisfied tone. "He got over. That's what it's all about. Make a copy before you die or divorce. Not that we two will ever stop our endless boogie, hey Ulla?" Tenderly he laid some tentacles upon his wife and let them begin sinking in. For her part, Ulla deepened the dents in her middle, taking on a form more and more like a donut. She sent out a bright yellow ball of tweet.

"That's a picture of a sun," explained Bumby. "Meaning she's hungry for some good loofy. We're gonna mount up and ride to reality, Frek. We have to do some groundwork about getting the humanity show set up. It won't actually click until you shake hands with an Orpolese on Earth. Are you and your friends ready to board the Ulla/Bumby luxury liner? Ulla will make you some new spacesuits. Once we're through the link, we'll yunch up to the right size for surfing the suns. I'll be stoked to see you boys do the spaceman freestyle."

"I want to get the elixir to restore Earth's biome," said Frek stubbornly. "Chainey said you'd help."

"I'm sorry, but we're outa here for now, kid," said Bumby in a careless tone. Neither the branecasters nor the branecast producers seemed to take their contractual obligations very seriously.

"You promised!" cried Frek. "That was part of the deal for letting you produce the humanity channel."

"Earth's still on open access," said Bumby in a peevish tone. "Strictly speaking, I don't have to pay you till our show comes on line. And, like I said, the show doesn't come on line until we ferry you all the way back to Earth. Bit of a legal thicket, eh? But I'll tell you what, we can come back here in two or three days and get your elixir then."

"No!" said Frek. "I want to go to the Exaplex right now."

Bumby wobbled his tentacles in a negative way. "You don't want to be here when the renormalization storm hits. The Planck brane gets especially weird at the end of each yuga. A yuga lasts fifty-two days, and this is day fifty-one. Nothing here is factually real, you understand, and when there's a storm it all gets changed around. We can tell because the branecasts always go whack-a-doozy. Come with us now, this isn't the right time to be poking around, especially not for Ulla and me, weak as we are. We'll regroup in Orpoly. Eat some loofy, lay more groundwork for our little production deal, and meanwhile spend a few more nights inside a star. That loofy's good stuff, isn't it? And, fine, this weekend when the storm's over we come back to the Planck brane and pick up your elixir, then Ulla and I yunch you back to Middleville, safe as a magic school bus, and the ultragaud Ulla/Bumby humanity channel begins."

"Branecasting sucks," put in Dad suddenly. "We don't want you to set up the production deal at all."

"That's right," added Frek. "Earth shouldn't be on branecast. I found out how bad branecasting is. Your guys would be playing us like characters in a game. We'd be your monoculture. You're not really on our side at all, Bumby. You don't care if I get the elixir."

"Oh, you and your elixir," said Bumby. "I never should have mentioned it. You're obsessed! Yes, Earth with her full Noah's Ark will make for a better show. But can't you wait till later—like after the next yuga begins? Open your thinker, stinker. Thanks to you we've been decoherent four days. Ulla and I are too weak to risk facing a storm."

"Then we'll get the elixir on our own," snapped Dad.

Bumby turned his attention to Carb. "This is the father, hey? I thought you were all set to sell out your boy to the Unipuskers, Dad. Since when are you brave-little-trumpeting against branecasting?"

"Just tell us how to get out of the Planck brane on our own," interrupted Gibby. "Since it looks like you're not gonna help us get the elixir, and since it seems as how that's what we're fixin' to do, come hell or high water. Where's the branelink outa here, you double-crossin' space-squid?"

"Tough guys, huh?" said Bumby. "All right then. The last time I was here the link looked like a branching solar plume. But it'll be different this time around. Everything changes in the Planck brane after each of their storms. What you see here has a lot to do with who you are. Right now the branelink might look like, I don't know, a fountain." Bumby pointed a tentacle across the street. "But it's always in the same place. On that little hill near the far edge of that park. Pig Hill. Pig Hill's always there, no matter how many renormalization storms they have. You're really not coming with us now?"

"No," said Frek. Dad shook his head, backing Frek up. Gibby said nothing, though he looked a little wistful. Wow was busy staring at the passing Hubs.

"Well, bighearted energy vortices that we are, we'll wait in the plane brane for you poor forked radishes," said Bumby. "I mean, first we'll eat, and then we'll do just a little business, and *then* we'll wait. You'll find us in a polar orbit around the star with the branelink—Ulla says you thought the star looked like a god? The Hubs do that, they turn every glass of water into wine. They're grand masters of reality hacking; you can't beat them. So spare me the snide snoot-tooting against branecasting. Oh, before we go, don't you at least want space-suits?"

"I can make our own," said Frek loftily. "A Unipusker showed me how to craft kenner. Maybe I forgot to mention that Dad and I kenny crafted ten trillion tons of gold to bail you out. So we don't owe you a thing. And we're *not* done talking about the branecasting deal."

"Ducky dander," said Bumby in a slightly amused tone. "Go ahead, dabble around Node G for your elixir. You've got a good chance of finding it in that Exaplex. But do mind those proud white tail feathers of yours and watch the time. If you die here, we'll have to set up a whole new deal—and the Unipuskers could end up running the humanity branecast after all. There's sucking and there's *really sucking*, Carb. Whatever you boys do, get through the branelink before the storm." Ulla popped out another yellow ball of tweet. "Yes, yes, dear, we're on our way. Good luck, Frek!" Bumby sank the rest of his branches into Ulla, and the ever-rolling veined donut sped toward the hill at the end of the park.

"I'm takin' that key," said Gibby, pulling it from the lock and putting it in one of his pockets.

"Fine," said Frek, who'd grown used to Gibby's acquisitiveness. He and the others walked down the dirty stone steps to the paved square. A tram was just coming by. It was long and yellow, a sleek construct of glass and metal. Frek found it odd to see machines that had been built one piece at a time. Not like back home, where things just grew.

Though it didn't seem quite logical, the tram was driven by the same Hub they'd seen going by a few minutes before; she looked like a woman, with blond hair cut into chunky bangs. Her tight little aura didn't extend much beyond her hair. As they stepped forward, she brought the tram to a screeching stop and opened its door.

Wow pushed ahead of Frek and ran right in. Gibby was next, nimbly rocking up the steps. With Dad at his side, Frek addressed the conductor. She was sealed off in a little transparent cabin. A window with a counter was set into the glassy cabin door.

"Do you go to the Exaplex?" asked Frek.

As the Hub turned to face Frek, her head underwent a subtle warp and flicker. It was as if in this world, anything could change into anything else at any time. A disturbing possibility. But for now, at least, the Hub kept her humanoid appearance.

"I go right past it," she said.

"Do—do we need tickets?" asked Frek, though he had no idea how he might pay.

"You ride free," said the woman, waving her hand toward the rear of the tram. "The end of the line, if you like." Were there webs of pink membrane between her fingers? Before Frek could decide, the Hub pushed a great metal crank to lurch the tram into motion.

The tram was full of Hubs, most of them seated, but a few holding onto the chrome poles that rose up from the backs of the seats. Alternating rows of seats faced forward or backward. Frek and Dad found an empty backward-facing seat for two. Frek took the window side and Gibby hopped on their laps. Wow squeezed under the seat and promptly fell asleep.

A pair of Hubs sat facing them, seemingly a mother and daughter. They wore black raincoats and gray head-scarves. The lady was green-skinned and bony, with angular cheekbones, a large nose, purple lips, and a prominent chin with a wart on it.

The Hub girl surreptitiously took a nugget of gold from her pocket and popped it into her mouth. As she savored the morsel, she peered up at Frek and gave him a little smile. Her eyes sparkled with humor and life; her aura pulsed with energy. The lady's eyes flickered from Frek to the girl, and back to Frek again, protectively noticing him noticing her daughter.

"I hope we don't miss our stop," Frek murmured to Dad.

"Travel dreams are the worst," answered Dad with a grim chuckle. "Nothing ever works."

"This ain't a dream," protested Gibby. "We're all seein' the same thing." Cloddishly he stretched out his arm, or leg, to point at the woman facing them. "Her wart's got two jiggly hairs stickin' out from it, right?"

"Shut up," hissed Frek, embarrassedly staring out his window.

A moment later the Hub lady tapped Frek's knee to get his attention. She was leaning forward to talk.

"Is not wart," she said in a hoarse tone. "Is my husband." She smelled of pungent, unknown spices.

And, yes, Frek could now see that the irregular bump on her chin was in fact a man's tiny head and shoulders—and what had seemed to be hairs were two wee arms. The arms were waving about as if to the sound of slow, flowing music. And the little man had his own tiny aura.

"I got gold," piped the little girl, wanting to get in on the conversation. "I got a whole pocketful!"

"Vhere you fellows headed?" the Hub lady asked Frek, settling back into her seat.

"To the Exaplex," said Frek. "A branecaster—Chainey?—he said we could get some stuff there from our planet's past."

"Should blow up Exaplex," said the woman. "Stupid greedy branecasters trying to get more wham than anyone. One fine day we'll manage to forget about them."

"I like the branecasters," piped the Hub girl, sneaking another nugget from her pocket to her mouth. "They bring in gold, and that's good for my wham. What's that, Father?" She stretched her neck out and put her ear to her mother's chin. "He says it's almost his turn, Mamma. He says he's gonna eat some of my gold!" Giggling, she rapidly shuttled five more fragments of gold from her pocket to her mouth. Her cheeks got big, and she took on an expression of bliss. "Mmmm!"

Just then the tram screeched to a halt. Frek peered anxiously out the windows, looking for the big, glowing sign of the Exaplex. But there was nothing to see but dirty gray apartment buildings. The Hub mother stumped down the aisle to the tram's rear and descended from the left side, her daughter following behind. As the tram pulled away, Frek stared back at them through his window.

Something very strange was happening to the woman's head. The husband-wart was growing, pulling her forward to the ground, and then, in a quick round of bloat and shrivel, the husband had drawn almost all of the wife's mass into his own body.

Thanks to his pzoom, Frek could make out a little wart upon the man's chin. This was the head and shoulders of the bony Hub woman, waving her arms as if she were dancing. The man took his daughter's hand and they headed off down the sidewalk. The smiling little girl handed her father a nugget of her gold. And then the tram went into a short tunnel.

Frek had been so busy staring at the dance of the wart-people that he'd missed the newcomer sitting down across from him. It was a man with short black bristles covering his scalp and the lower part of his face. He had a huge round stomach. He wore a stained white T-shirt and droopy gray pants with beige suspenders. He kept sighing and twisting his neck.

"Hi there," said the irrepressible Gibby.

The man let out another sigh, slowly bending his neck from side to side. "You visitors from de plain brane?" he said finally. His breath smelled heavily of rotting meat. His aura was little more than a few faint scraps in the air near his ears.

"Might could say we're here on a galactic quest," answered Gibby from Frek's lap. "Lookin' to patch our planet's biome. We're headed for the Exaplex." The tram whooshed out of the tunnel and rattled around a curve.

"Don't know if dis tram stops dere," said the man. "Nobody wants to go to de Exaplex. Why for? Dat's just a switchboard."

"The stop's not automatic?" said Frek, instantly worried. "How would I ask for a special stop? How soon is the Exaplex?"

"Press dat when it's close," said the man, pointing up at blue button set into the chrome seat pole. "But she might not halt. I dunno. Exaplex is after I get out. I only ride one stop."

He sighed again, and slumped back in his seat, letting his face fall into a blank, mindless expression. He had nothing else to say. A few minutes later the tram began slowing.

"Can we just get out at your stop and walk to the Exaplex from there?" asked Dad.

"Too far," said the man wearily. "You never get dere before de storm. Anyway de doors, dey don't open at dis stop. Dis only a facultative stop. I don't got enough wham for a regular stop. I don't got enough wham at all. Nobody gonna see me no more after dis storm." With another meat-reeking sigh, he got to his feet.

And then the Hub did a curious thing. Rather than walking to the closed doors at the rear of the tram, he gave his head an especially sharp twist. His body broke into pieces—his head, his shoulders, his arms, his hands, his stomach, his butt, his thighs, his calves, and his feet—they scattered from one side of the tram to the other, vibrating together and apart.

Frek noticed something moving outside the tram window. A piece of the man had somehow tunneled out. It was a stubbled roll of fat from the base of his neck. The roll of fat jiggled as if to invite the other pieces, and, one by one, the other pieces quantum-tunneled through the tram's wall. Outside on the pavement, the man reassembled his wavy particles and went lumbering off, his hand reaching up as if to feel his tattered aura.

Just as the tram began moving, a cloud of colored blobs converged on the tram's rear and cohered into a shape in the aisle. It was a woman Hub, quite remarkable in appearance. While most of the things in Node G were fairly realistic, this woman was close to being abstract art.

She had a spherical head, a leaflike hank of blond hair, and a body like a pear, with arms and legs just as long as they needed to be at any given time. A vivid green profile line divided her round face. The left side was a delicate white with hints of purple, the right was yellow as a smiling sun. Her body was striped mauve on the shadowed parts, and highlighted with pale green circles on the spots where it was lit. Her aura, too, was boldly designed, with zigzag rays of bright gold against a background of light gold polygons. She sashayed up the aisle and dropped into what had been the fat man's seat.

"Good day, I'm Dora," she said, noticing Frek, Dad, and Gibby staring at her. Her sketchy fingers kneaded her hair. "And youm would be whom?"

"We're visitors from the plain brane," sad Dad, always glad to talk to a woman. "Milky Way galaxy, Sol system, planet Earth. We came here for a deal with the branecasters."

"The branecasters are a social disease," said the colorful woman. She pushed her face forward for emphasis, batting a flirtatious eye at Carb. "I don't need them. Everyone knows me. See how much wham I have?" She gestured toward her striking aura, and then her eye pulsed out a blaze of blue lines that actually bounced off of Dad, Gibby, and Frek before dissipating. They felt tingly when they hit Frek's skin. One of the lines must have zinged Wow, for he squeaked and sat up, sniffing at the woman's leg. She gave him a gentle pat on the head.

"You look pretty," observed Gibby.

"Refresh my memory, if you would," said the woman. "Over in the plain brane, you 'see' with 'light'? And you project reality down into just four dimensions? Or is it two? I always forget." She tossed her head, and her profile line flipped to pointing the other way. Now the left side of her face was like a blurred brown moon, and her right side was a dusky mix of orange and lavender with a deep dark eye socket. She continued fiddling with her banana of hair, now gone narrow and green.

"We're three dimensional," said Dad. "We're trying to get to the Exaplex."

"This tram will never stop there," said the woman. "You should have switched to the seventeen-A at my stop."

Frek felt sweat running down his ribs. He peered out his window, trying to see what was coming up. The tram was going faster than ever, screeching around bends, clattering over low bridges, and darting through impossibly narrow alleyways between crumbling buildings. The walls had taken on pastel shades of orange and purple, with something odd about the upper floors' perspectives. The sky overhead was growing dimmer.

After a bit, Frek saw a yellow glow. Yes—he reached up and

pressed the blue button on the pole—they were approaching their goal. He could already read the letters on the lit-up vertical sign. E - X - A - P - L - E - X.

Far from slowing, the tram accelerated. "Hey!" shouted Dad. He'd noticed the sign too. "This is our stop!"

"This car doesn't stop till Hilbert Space Axis seven seventy-eight-ZW," said Dora, tossing her head. Again her colors changed kaleidoscopically. "You'll have to try to work your way back, I suppose. Maybe you can catch the one thirty-three. Not that you'll have gobs of time to do it before the renormalization storm sets in. I wonder if you'll even survive. You don't seem to have any visible wham. But I reckon being made of matter is enough. Certainly the branecasters believe in using matter to get wham. How crude they are, how inferior to artists."

Gibby ran up the aisle, as if to force the driver to stop. But the Hub had sealed off her window, and when Gibby beat his tail against her cabin's transparent walls, she only hunched farther forward over her controls. The situation seemed hopeless.

Just then the tram's bell clanged a warning at something ahead on the tracks. With a rusty screech, the metal wheels locked. The tram skidded to stop, throwing up fountains of sparks, the bell sounding all the while.

With a final delicate nudge, the tram came to rest against the pink creature blocking its progress. Standing foursquare in the tracks was a smallish pig with a glowing aura. He let out an abrupt grunt that was somehow a recognizable greeting.

"The Magic Pig!" exclaimed Dad. "He's real!"

"You know the Magic Pig?" said the paintinglike woman, darting her head toward them. "Don't talk about him in the Exaplex! Supposedly he's a big enemy of the branecasters—though some of us think that's an act. In any case, this is your chance if you really want to debark. Best of luck and so on."

"Come on, Gibby!" yelled Frek. They ran to the tram's rear door. Of course it wouldn't open. And there was no obvious way for them to duplicate the fat man's quantum-tunneling feat. So tough old Carb just kicked the door so hard that half of it flew off its hinges.

They hopped down onto the dirty concrete sidewalks of Node G. The towering yellow Exaplex sign bathed the scene in warm light. The sign wasn't neon; it was, rather, a glowing pattern within the flesh of the building. They were near the end of their quest.

The tram was already pulling forward again, clattering off down the tracks toward Hilbert Space Axis 778-ZW, wherever that might be. Meanwhile the Magic Pig was nowhere to be seen. Wow must have been able to smell him, though, for he was circling around excitedly sniffing the air.

The others studied the Exaplex. What made the buildings in the neighborhood look so funny was that the windows along the soft, receding walls of the buildings had a space-warped quality, with each further window looking half as wide as the window before. The Exaplex was going to be mighty big on the inside. At least it didn't look to have more than maybe five floors.

"All right now," said Gibby. "We'll go in that movie house and get the elixir. What's elixir look like, anyhow?"

"I'm not sure," said Frek. "I figure the elixir will have the genetic codes for all the missing species. But how all that gets packaged is—"

"I can't believe we really saw the Magic Pig," interrupted Dad. "So he lives in the Planck brane! Must be some kind of Hub. Funny he'd have taken an interest in your destiny, Frek. Maybe we should split up in teams to search for the Magic Pig."

"It's the elixir we're looking for, not any pig," corrected Frek. "I don't think he ran into the Exaplex. See how Wow's sniffing for him across the tracks?"

"Come here, Wow!" yelled Gibby, and the dog came trotting over. "I'll stick with Frek," Gibby told Dad. "You take Wow if we're gonna split up."

"I want to be with Frek, too," said Carb.

"So let's all stick together," said Frek, feeling a little gratified. "Come on!"

The Exaplex doors were wide open; they walked right in. Though the lobby was lit up, it was completely deserted. And there were no ticket-sellers in sight.

Frek, Carb, Gibby, and Wow walked tentatively forward to the dimly lit door at the rear of the lobby. It led to a little curved antechamber which had five doors leading off it. The floors, ceilings, and walls were rubbery with red fuzz, and the doors were edged in shiny stuff that resembled the chitin from a silver beetle's wing covers. Unlike the tram, the Exaplex seemed to be a single huge organism—like Gov's puffball.

Frek picked the second door from the left. It opened onto a landing with three more doors, and stairways leading down and up. The stairs were like catwalks of a stiff cartilaginous substance. The treads had perforations in them, and at certain angles, Frek could see through them to level after level of landings with more doors. The Exaplex was a living labyrinth.

Gibby pulled open one of the three new doors, revealing a dim screening room with perhaps a hundred stoollike seats, all but one of them empty. Upon one of the front seats perched a single manlike figure who, as soon as they came in, got up and left without pausing to glance back.

The screen was a big boxy three-dimensional view into an alien world. The graphics had the same pulsing, stroboscopic quality as flickerball visions. There was a curious multiplicity to the images, that is, Frek had the sensation of seeing several scenes at once. It took an effort of will to narrow in on one particular version of the scene.

Frek settled, more or less at random, upon a vision of frenzied oversized ants fighting—or making love?—beneath a curdled pink and blue sky. The giant ants were upon the beach of a sea with large square waves, the waves impossibly piled up like silver blocks. The visuals were accompanied by the chirping and squawking of the ant aliens, the steady crashing of surf, a pungent scent of chocolate and dill, and a faint metallic taste.

As if their search for the right theater wasn't going to be hard enough, there were additional doors ranged along each of this screening room's side walls.

"How about it, Wow," said Gibby. "Can you sniff out the right room for us?"

"Find pig?" squeaked Wow, still thinking about the apparition they'd seen on the tracks.

"Find home," said Frek. It stood to reason that the theater show-ing Earth would smell familiar. And the Earth room would surely be the place to find the elixir.

Wow took off so fast that it was hard to follow him. To start with, he led them back out to the antechamber and through the center door instead of the door Frek had picked. Confronted with more doors and two staircases as before, Wow led them down two flights, and then through the central door of that landing.

It was another screening room, again with a dark man—or some-thing resembling a man—who left as soon as they came in. The screen here showed a desert world of tornados, great yellow twisters splitting into pairs, gobbling up smaller ones, partnering in groups of two and three, endlessly whirling the sand. The room was filled with roaring, and with a dusty, acrid smell. As with the world before, there was a sense of there being a whole continuum of possible im-ages, with your subconscious volition singling out but one of them.

Wow darted down the right aisle and led them through the second to last door in the wall. This gave onto another long red-fuzz-covered hallway, punctuated by the same featureless shiny-framed doors, everything slightly warped and curved, with a constant deep throb-bing noise in the background. Wow scratched at the fourteenth door on the right. Passing through, they found a fresh set of staircases, and went four more levels up. Or was it five? They pushed through another door, and found a theater showing scenes of giant snails, incredibly clear and vivid. Once again the screening room held a single watcher who rose to leave. Seeing him in silhouette, Frek noticed the man had a funny way of walking; his big feet never seemed to leave the floor. And his head was covered with little projecting braids.

"Hey," shouted Dad as the dark man glided toward the door. "Wait up. Talk to us." The silhouette ignored him and was gone.

Wow whined and took off down the aisle to lead them through the fifth or sixth door on the left. They ran down another red hallway, opened a chitinous door, ran down a wobbly staircase a few levels, pushed through some other door . . .

"Anybody keepin' track of what we've done?" said Gibby. "So we can get outa this nuthouse later on?"

"Wow will know," said Frek, hoping it was true.

They continued running the maze for perhaps an hour. Time and space folded together into an endless blur of meaty walls, of dull shiny door frames, of staircases, of empty screening rooms displaying multiplexed photorealistic images of weird worlds. In every room a shadowy figure left the front row as they entered.

Was it a different watcher in each theater? Frek didn't think so. The figure always looked the same, unchanging as a mirage appearing over and over at the far end of a hot summer's road. Yes, somehow the dark man was staying out ahead of them down every twist and turn of their path. There could be no fathoming how the watcher managed to do this. Wow wasn't following him—the dog and the dark man always chose different doors. Yet their paths kept crossing, again and again.

Was the strange man laying a trap for them? There was something uncanny about his stealthy haste. No threat or command made the wraith wait up; no mad dash succeeded in catching him.

"Home," said Wow at last, paw-tapping one more door.

When Frek pushed this door open he saw a screen that showed, not Earth, but a world of dogs. Dogs in trees, dogs in chariots, dogs herding chickens, dogs happily piled on each other with their tongues hanging out. The theater was filled with yips, snarls, growls, barks—and the rich, nose-tingling smell of canines.

"Oh, Wow," sighed Frek. "I meant find *my* home. Find house tree. Find Lora."

Wow wasn't listening. He was crouched beneath the great rectangular display, nose pointed up, raptly savoring the air.

As usual the dark watcher was at the far corner of the front row, on his feet, about to go.

"Please help us," called Frek, stepping toward him. "We're desperate. Oh please! Maybe we can give you something you want."

For the first time, the dark figure paused, seemingly looking their way. "Help us find the room that shows Earth," begged Frek. "We can't do it without you."

"I been waiting for you to ask me polite that way," came the figure's voice, rich and rough-edged, vibrant with life. "Instead of yelling and grabbing like you got something coming. Your world's been right next door all along, hear? Come on in, boys, it's time. Top floor."

The figure tapped a blank-looking spot on the hairy red wall. A shiny-framed door appeared and swung open. Pleasant yellow-green light spilled out, the color of sunlight reflected from leaves. Frek could see through to the room's screen. Instantly responding to Frek's unspoken wish, the screen showed Middleville, as real as looking out a window at it.

"Yee haw," said Gibby to the dark man by the open door. "Thank you, friend. My name's Gibby."

The being stood silent, his expression watchful, calm, faintly amused. He wore a red T-shirt, skinny gold pants, and bulbous black shoes. His skin was the dark shade of an African's in the days before humanity's genes were monoculturized. Unlike the Hubs, he didn't have an aura at all. He was neither human, nor Hub, but something different.

"I'm Carb," said Dad, approaching the dark figure. "What's your name?"

"Zed," said the black-skinned being. "Zed Alef." His hair was twisted into dozens of little pigtails arranged in a grid. Corn rows, they'd been called. "Might say I'm the brains of the Exaplex, the quintillion-world puppeteer, understand?"

"Are you friends with the Magic Pig?"

"Not hardly. I hate that bossy little grunter. I chased him outa here just before you came. He was nosing around in your time pool, as if I had to tell you. Maybe I oughta think twice about helping you boys. Especially since I still haven't heard any kind of 'please' from you, Mister Carb Huggins."

"Please," said Carb, nodding his head. "Please help us. My son, Frek, wants to save Earth's biome. Tell him the details, Frek!"

"I already know the particulars," said Zed. "I been watching through your mind worm."

Frek was back by the dog-world display, tugging at man's best friend. "Come *on*, Wow, come with us now."

"Aw, let the dog be," called Zed. "Smart dog like that. He be fine. We'll be right next door."

"No," said Frek. The way Zed had been able to directly open a fresh passage to the theater of Earth indicated that "next door" didn't mean much here. If Zed Alef should choose to close the new door, Wow would be lost for good.

"You're coming with me," Frek told Wow, getting his arms around the dog's middle and lifting him up into the air. Wow twisted and clawed, even snarled a few curse words. But Frek hung onto him.

Dad and Gibby had already stepped through to the screening room of Earth. Through the door Frek could see their silhouettes down near the display. Zed was waiting by the door. His skin was wonderfully lustrous.

"You said you'd give me something I want?" asked Zed in a low tone as Frek approached. The whites of his eyes were slightly yellow and his tongue was a vivid pink.

"Yeah," said Frek. "If we can."

"I was studying on keeping that dog, but you're so mighty tight with him, I changed my mind. Now I'm wanting you or your old man. Me and the branecasters could use some nice fresh plain brane folks to get qubits from. You'd be tasty."

"I can't stay here," protested Frek. "I've got to take the elixir back to Earth."

"I expected you'd be saying that. And you know that means we keep Carb."

"No!"

"Hush," said Zed with a confidential wink. "Don't tell him yet." And then, before Frek could protest any further, Zed hurried off into the dark recesses of the Earth theater. Again Frek noticed an oddness in the way Zed moved. His feet never left the floor; in fact it looked as if the floor bulged up a bit to merge with his big, rounded shoes. Frek promised himself to keep a close eye on his father.

And then Frek carried Wow from the dog theater to the Earth theater. Behind him the door to the dog-world disappeared. Of course Wow had to frantically claw the throbbing red wall for a while, and then try pushing open one or two doors. But finally Frek managed to interest the dog in the scene showing here. It was, after all, home.

Yes, the flickering block of space floating at the end of the room was filled with the swaying house trees and bindmoss-covered paths of Middleville. With the natural perspectives and familiar homey colors it seemed realer than the Planck brane. Earth was a world where things made sense.

A sigh of homesickness welled up from Frek. How nice it would be to step into the picture. The view panned across the rolling sunlit lawns set with roseplusplus bushes, past the anyfruit trees, and through a little garden of yams, tomatoes, carrots, chard, rice, and red beans. Seeing the familiar plants made him hungry.

Frek and Wow joined Gibby and Carb, staring up at the solid screen of Earth images. Frek let his hand rest on his father's shoulder. No way was he going to leave his old man behind in this gollywog world.

Frek's view of the 3D screen zoomed out from the garden, showing a damaged turmite mound, a turmite-paper garage and—the Hugginses' house tree. The outer wall of the tree melted away and he saw into the kitchen. Briefly Frek wondered what Carb and Gibby were seeing. But he didn't bother asking them. There was too much for him to take in.

Lora, Geneva, Ida, Yessica, and Renata were in there together, with Woo lying on the floor. It was perfectly real, with every hair in place, all the sounds of everyone breathing, the faint scent of Lora's perfume, even the scuff marks on Ida's shoes. Renata was still wearing the green fern-patterned ribbons that Frek had crafted for her.

Yessica was putting some food on the table, a dish made of whole anyfruit-tree raspberries and ground-up carrots, the raspberries lined up on the watery little mounds of orange paste. She was holding forth about the perfect balance of this dish that she'd just now concocted from fresh ingredients found in the Huggins garden. She called it vitamash. Yessica explained that the vitamash was to help welcome herself and Renata into their temporary new home. She said the raspberries were like chakras, and that vitamash exemplified the Crufter way.

Lora told Yessica not to talk about Crufter stuff because Gov and the counselors were always watching and listening through the walls of the house tree although, added Lora, Gov had taken a big damage hit last week, and been replaced by a clone, with a few memories lost in the transition, thank goodness, but even so you shouldn't be waving a red flag in his face, not that he had a face, being in fact a parasitic worm, as was clearer than ever, given what people had seen in the blasted-out hole in his puffball that those alien attackers from the Anvil had made.

Meanwhile Geneva and Ida were getting Renata to tell about the Unipuskers and about how Frek had scared the aliens with the ickspot costumes. Renata was showing them some of the drawings she'd stored in her turkle. To keep Gov from getting interested, they talked like the story was a made-up plan for a toon show Renata wanted to invent, and instead of saying "Frek," they were saying "Roarboy," which was what Geneva sometimes called Frek to tease him.

And then Lora asked Yessica how "that man" was doing, and Yessica said that man was okay, except he'd let Yessica down in not helping her arrange to make daily broadcasts into the minds of everyone on Earth. "And how would that be?" wondered Lora, and then Yessica started to tell about the branecasters and about how she'd wanted to kill Frek so she could become the branecaster representative. Yessica was saying this flat out as if she didn't see anything wrong. And then Lora emptied the carrots and raspberries over Yessica's head.

Renata started crying and ran outside, but Geneva and Ida went after her to tell her to come back in, and that even if their moms fought, Renata was welcome anyway since she was a friend of Roarboy's. Renata whispered, "I have a goggy crush on Roarboy," and that made Geneva laugh, but Ida shushed her.

The screen was showing both the inside and the outside of the house tree. In the kitchen, Yessica was acting surprisingly calm, wiping off the pureed carrot with a cleaner tongue, saying that Lora didn't have to be such a mother lion, and asking, by the way, if Lora minded if Yessica left Renata here while she had a look around the area. Lora said no, and then she carefully added that if Yessica wanted some excitement, then Stun City was the place to go, and *that if Yessica needed money, then maybe Lora could lend her a little, and that Yessica shouldn't feel she needed to hurry back.*

All of this was as interesting as anything Frek had ever seen.

"Yo!" shouted Zed from somewhere back behind them. "C'mon up!"

"He's in the projection room," said Dad, pointing toward the rear wall of the theater. Visible through a square hole was a glaring light. "This is how old-time movie theaters worked," said Dad. "They had a little cubby in back with a projector that uses a film ribbon or maybe a digital file. I know because we had a theater on Sick Hindu. That projector light is what's putting out the different pictures we're seeing. And the projection room is where we'll find Earth's past. If Zed Alef helps us."

Gibby and Wow went to investigate.

Suddenly Frek remembered Zed's threat. "Zed says they want to keep you here," he whispered to Dad. "Be careful!"

"Why would Zed want me?" exclaimed Dad, sounding almost flattered.

"Sssh! He said he and the branecasters could, like, feed on us. We can't let him trap you." And then Frek came out and said something he hadn't quite realized he'd been thinking. "I want to bring you back to Middleville, Dad." Somewhere deep down Frek was hoping to get Carb and Lora back together and patch up the Huggins family.

"Kill me now," said Dad in that odd way he had of mixing a joke with something serious.

"I found the stairs," called Gibby from the rear of the room. Wow came running back for Carb and Frek.

In and of themselves, the stairs were no big deal, just a single steep, dark flight of steps. But Frek felt strange. The display at the front of the room was indistinguishable from reality—which meant the projection room held the underlying pattern of the world. Going up the stairs was like pushing behind the curtain of a puppet show. What hidden forces might Frek find in the projection room, what puppeteers?

The room was a largish cube, some four meters on a side, with a thick spongy floor that shook underfoot. The very first thing Frek noticed was a knot of meaty vines upon the room's high ceiling, slowly writhing shapes, evil eels. With immediate conviction, he knew that the eels were the conduit to humanity's watchers. And with the same certainty, he knew that the eels were the mind worms Chainey had warned him to stay away from. If humanity were ever to fight free of the branecasters, the unny grayish tubes on the ceiling were the shackles they'd have to cut. But not yet. Finding the elixir would come first.

An oily, iridescent pool was set into the floor beneath the projection window, and standing in the pool was a kritter or Exaplex organ of some kind. He resembled a chess piece with spindly arms ending in white-gloved hands. The number of arms was impossible to determine: they moved very rapidly and they left trails in the air. The creature's head was a lightbulb or, more accurately described, a glass pod with a tiny sun at its center. The lightbulb head was opaque and shiny on the side toward Frek, while the clear front side of the bulb was beaming three-dimensional images into the theater.

Zed Alef leaned against the wall by the shiny pool, fingering one of his little pigtails, watching them with that same half-smile on his face. His feet were wholly merged into the soft floor.

"Hi boys," he said. "This here's Li'l Bulb and your time pool."

Wow trotted up to the pool and tried to drink from it, but the sparkling time stuff was more like tar than like water. When the dog pulled up his head, a taffylike strand of time stretched briefly from the pool's surface to his nose—and snapped back, sending out some sluggish ripples. Wow gave a little yip and went to sit by the projection room's door.

Meanwhile Li'l Bulb was steadily hauling a thick column of time from the pool with his right hands, shaping the translucent mass into a squarish animated block that he held in front of his blazing "eye" to project the scenes of Earth. The used-up time passed through Li'l Bulb's left hands and back into the pool. The time strand was continually feeding the magic theater before Li'l Bulb's glowing eye.

The motions of Li'l Bulb and the time strand left afterimages, like you'd see if you waved a burning stick in the dark. It almost looked like there were multiple copies of Li'l Bulb.

"Your elixir's waiting in there," said Zed, pointing at the pool. "Get down on it."

Frek cast a wary glance at the snaky gray things on the ceiling. One of them seemed to be watching him. It had a disk face of concentric rings of teeth around a raspy central tongue. Like a lamprey eel's. The lamprey had the same higher dimensional quality as Li'l Bulb, that is, the lamprey's sluggish motions sketched ghostly spacetime veils, and sections of it were continually disappearing and reappearing, folding in and out of higher spaces unknown to man.

Frek went and knelt by the pool of time. Dad quickly joined him. Wow remained by the exit door, while Gibby squatted against a side wall, his knife in one hand, staring watchfully at the shapes on the ceiling.

Frek tapped the pool's shimmering surface and pulled out a strand. Little figures moved within it. The whole pool was full of reality animations.

"That's our past and our future?" Dad asked Zed. "How do we find what we want?"

"Gotta stick your head in there," answered Zed.

"There's something bothering me," said Frek. "The branecasters only started watching the human race a couple of weeks ago, right? The Unipuskers made first contact when they abducted Yessica, Renata, and Carb, right? In other words, your Exaplex has only been projecting Earth's reality since the first Monday in May, 3003. So why would your time pool have the Great Collapse of June 6, 2666?"

"It's like pulling up a yam," said Zed. "You yank on the leaves— and the roots, shoots, and patoots come along with it. Once we get one day, we got 'em all. It's hyperdimensional, son."

Brave Dad took a deep breath and dipped his whole head into the time pool. For a long minute his head was invisible, two minutes, maybe three. Frek couldn't stand it; he grabbed Dad's shoulders and pulled him out.

Dad's face was dripping with glittering time, droopy shapes running off him. Frek could make out the forms of a chair, sagging windows, a bed, a woman with a great stomach, a bony Mohawked man—the melting shapes of the man's youthful dreams.

"Frek!" exclaimed Dad. He didn't seem at all out of breath. "I saw myself on that night I told you about! It felt like I was there for an hour. Lora was lying on her back with her stomach domed up like a beach ball, feeling some pains, wondering whether to wake up her husband yet, and there he was, young Carb Huggins, lying next to her having his vision. What a night that was. The night my son was born. I could see right inside my dream, Frek. The Magic Pig's a Planck brane revolutionary. In the dream back then he knew you'd be here now. That's why he came! The Magic Pig says—"

"Enough about him!" interrupted Zed. Up above, the hyperdimensional lampreys were lashing about faster than before. Large new sections of them were in motion, leaving trails like blurry gray fans.

"Stop pussy-footin' around, boys," added Zed, gesturing at the pool. "It's time. Do your thing."

Dad didn't hesitate to stick his head back into the time pool. Frek followed suit. A recent scene from the past sprang into life before Frek's eyes: Mom telling him to pick up his room.

"Your room is a mess," said Lora Huggins, standing in her son's doorway. "A dog den. You're not going anywhere until it's straightened up. Poor Snaffle doesn't know where to begin."

The boy on the floor sighed and finished pulling on his soft leather shoe. "My room's not a mess," he said. "I know exactly where everything is. Snaffle's too stupid to understand. I have more important stuff to do, Mom."

Frek could hear the chatter of the Goob Dolls on the walls of the family room, with Geneva and Ida shouting things back at them. It seemed like so long since Frek had heard his family—Lora's slow warm voice, Geneva's clipped, cheerful tones, and Ida's bursting quack.

Right about then somebody, probably Zed Alef, shoved Frek's butt really hard, and he fell all the way into the time pool. For the moment he still saw his Middleville bedroom, but then Dad appeared, hanging in midair, overlapping the image of Lora. Zed must have shoved Dad in, too.

It occurred to Frek that they were breathing. As far as his lungs were concerned, the time stuff was like colored air. They could stay in here for quite a while.

Dad wasn't seeing what Frek was seeing, he was seeing something different. Something he didn't want Frek to see. For when Frek reached out to touch Dad, Dad twitched and tried to push Frek away. But Frek had caught hold of Dad's arm, and now Dad's motions spun Frek sideways into the scene his father was watching.

A recent version of Dad was sitting in the cockpit of a Unipusker flying saucer, gliding over the green wooded valleys of planet Earth. A river glinted in the setting sun—the River Jaya. Up ahead was Stun City, with the corkscrew Toonsmithy, the Kritterworks cube, and Gov's NuBioCom puffball.

Standing beside the Dad were Hawb and Cawmb. Pilot Evawrt was flying the ship. The Dad was fiddling with his uvvy, tuning someone in.

"I have some information for Gov," said the Dad. "The Anvil that's coming down tonight is an alien ship intending to abduct Frek Huggins. H-U-G-G-I-N-S. He lives in Middleville with his mother, Lora. Be sure and stop them."

"Don't look!" shouted the real Dad at Frek's side. With a convulsive effort, he managed to tear them away from this scene. And now they were drifting like dead leaves through the air above Stun City. Frek could hardly believe that his father had betrayed him.

Even though he was boiling with emotions, Frek didn't let himself forget that he was here to find the elixir. If Carb's betrayal distracted him from the quest then, in the end, the forces of monoculture would have won. So before Frek started in on Carb, he focused his mind upon the puffball and its NuBioCom labs—the place where the last samples of Earth's diverse genomes would have been. Somehow Carb stayed right in synch with him.

Almost immediately they came to rest amid the square before the NuBioCom puffball in Stun City. People were walking backward across the square, this way and that, their clothes progressively more old-fashioned. Frek and Carb were fixed in this one space location, sinking steadily deeper into the time pool. Now there was a little time to talk.

"So you were the one who warned the Gov the Anvil was coming for me?" demanded Frek. "Thanks to you I got peeked! How could you, Carb?"

"I didn't know it would come to that," cried Carb. "I never wanted you to find out! Oh, why did I have to go straight to that memory?" A crowd of laughing 2900s women went skipping by, their reversed motions looking unnaturally lively. Carb kept talking. "I did it because it was my big chance to be important, don't you see? I've never amounted to much, Buddha knows. I was supposed to negotiate with the branecasters for the whole human race. But the geevin' branelink was down when we got to Unipusk." A group of NuBioCom lab workers dressed 2800 style hurried backward out of the puffball.

"You weren't on any Unipusk," snapped Frek. "You were in that saucer telling Gov about me and the Anvil. Stop lying!"

"We'd been on Unipusk and come back by then. The open access branecast had already started, right, so on Unipusk we could see the people on Sick Hindu and Earth. We watched those nosy Orpolese finding out about me and the Unipuskers from Yessica's sister Meshell in the Crufter colony. It was Meshell who told them that Carb Huggins had a son. Right away I guessed the Orpolese would try to get you. So Hawb, Cawmb, Evawrt, and me yunched back to Earth to give Gov a warning. We didn't want to lose control of the humanity branecast channel. I had no idea it would end with—"

"You told them about the Crufter hideout, too, didn't you?" said Frek, giving Carb a shake. Just now Carb seemed as weak as a puppy. "About the hideout where Lora tried to send me when I was running away from the Three R's!"

"That was Hawb's idea," said Carb in a barely audible tone. "He saw the hideout location in my mind."

In the scene around them a street-cleaner tongue was working over the square's cobblestones. One of the earliest completely unnatural kritters, the oversize street tongues had been terminated back in 2700 after a series of unpleasant incidents in which they'd consumed unwatched babies and napping bums.

The puffball had changed into a faceted crystal dome, the original housing for the NuBioCom labs. Frek and Carb were closing in on 2666, the year of the Great Collapse.

"You know I'd never let Gov give you the Three R's," said Carb in a pleading, insistent tone. "You've got to believe me!"

"I hate you," said Frek, the words bursting out by themselves.

Carb didn't say anything back.

Right about then the sun stopped rolling across the sky and hung still. People began walking forward instead of backward. This was it. They'd reached the day of the Great Collapse. June 6, 2666.

Frek turned away from Carb, struggling to focus on finding the elixir. It took only a slight push of will to launch himself into dreamlike flight, straight toward the center of the great glassy dome of the NuBioCom headquarters.

As Frek drew close to the wall, it melted away.

Three men and two women were sitting at an old-style round computing table. One of the men wore a turban. The table was made of computational plastic; its top was a beige disk with a dark hole in its center. A slight waviness in the air above the hole indicated that it was a memory shredder.

Upon the tabletop rested the translucent 3D icons of a planet's worth of animal and plant species and subspecies. Elephants, squid, giraffes, monkeys, banana trees, whales, prickly pear cactuses, houseflies, morel mushrooms, rattlesnakes, swallowtail butterflies, crows, angel fish, sea snails—the whole Noah's ark of Gaia's diversity was ranged in concentric ranks around the table's faintly humming central hole. The NuBioCom workers were herding the icons inward to destruction. As Frek watched, a narrow-beaked platypus icon hit the hole; it shriveled away with a pathetic queep.

"I feel gleepy doing this," burst out one of the women at the table. She had an angular face with dark, vivid lips. "We've already deployed the knockout virions. Nothing but NuBioCom-authorized species can reproduce. Why can't we at least hang onto the DNA of the species we're making extinct? Just in case?"

"We've been over this and over this, Karla," said a man sitting across from her. He had a wide mouth and a shaved head. "As long as any obsolete genomes survive, even in software, there's always the risk of some anti-progress zealot bringing them back. Let's get on with it. We're going to erase them all, we're going to do it now, and we're going to share the responsibility. We five, the heads of the five NuBioCom divisions. If you're going to go environmentalist on us, the company will find someone reliable to head up your unit."

"No need to get huffy," said Karla quickly. "I was only asking." She nudged a little model orchid into the hole and it withered away with a barely audible rustle. Gone for good.

Though the turbaned man beside Karla pretended to be working right along with the others, Frek could see that, whenever possible, he was sneaking an icon into his lap. It was Sri-Sri Krisna, founder of the Crufters!

Though it was exciting to see Krisna, Frek well knew that the Crufters would only manage to save a few dozen species. Frek turned his attention from Krisna to a little red-breasted robin icon near the center of table. The robin would be one of the next to go. How to save it? It wasn't as if he could sweep the icons off the tabletop and pocket them. The substance of the past was inalterable.

But it would be enough to *remember* the icons. The icons themselves were the data they represented. It was a standard interface trick. The genome data sets were arranged so as to resemble the plants, animals, and microorganisms they stood for. The robin icon's appearance held all the information needed to generate its DNA.

In other words Frek could save the robin if he could remember exactly how the robin icon looked. First the robin, and then the tapir next to it, and then the raspberry bush and then—how many icons in all? At first Frek had thought there were a few thousand—but in fact the icons grew quite a bit smaller near the outer edges of the table, with more and more of them crowded in. There were millions of them. Impossible.

Someone nudged Frek's elbow just then. Carb, looking like a whipped dog. "Hi," was all he said. "I see it, too."

"Don't bother me," mumbled Frek. He didn't want to think about his geevey no-good father. But now of course he couldn't stop. Carb had told Gov about the Anvil. He'd leaked the Crufter hideout info. He'd tricked Frek into crashing the yunch trip. He'd given his ring to Yessica to help the Unipuskers. He'd—

"I'm sorry!" cried Carb.

"No good," snapped Frek. "Words don't change what you did."

"By Buddha, I'll make it all up to you, one way or another," blustered his father. "Now come on, what can I do to help here?"

"You can't do anything, you loser," said Frek. "You only make things worse."

"Talk to me, Frek. Please tell me what's happening."

The old man was absurd. But he wasn't going away. In exasperation, Frek went ahead and started explaining the problem. Maybe talking would help. "Every one of these icons codes up a genome," he said. "The most I'd be able to remember would be ten of them or a hundred. But—" He waved his hand across the crowded table. It seemed like the harder he looked, the more tiny figures there were to notice by the rim. Meanwhile, at the table's center, a tiny striped pig bit the dust. *Wheenk!*

"Why not make copies of them," suggested Carb. "Like how we made the gold. We'll kenny craft copies and take them home."

"Not a bad idea," admitted Frek after a long pause. "Do you think there's dark matter in the Planck brane?"

"Only one way to find out," said Carb, holding out his cupped hands.

Sure enough, the Planck brane was loaded with kenner. In a moment, Frek and Carb were each holding a colorless ball of the stuff.

"Let's start copying the icons," said Frek.

He and Carb hovered right over the table, with their legs harmlessly projecting through the insubstantial heads of the NuBioCom workers. Frek stared down at the little robin on the edge of extinction. Moving his head from side to side, he absorbed every detail of the image and zapped it onto a pinch of his kenner.

"Lemme see," said Carb, setting down the model he'd just made and looking at Frek's. "You nailed it, kiddo! Every detail in place. Mine didn't come out so good." Carb's copy of the tapir icon was missing a leg.

"I think the copy has to be exact," said Frek. "Each little bit of the image probably codes a piece of the genome."

"Tell you what," said Carb. "You make the copies. I'll keep the kenner coming and accumulate our stash."

Frek hovered above the table gathering his strength, studying the table. The tabletop reminded him of one of those round stained glass windows in the old-time cathedrals. A rose window. Each species was a gemlike fragment, each was a spot of color in Gaia's holy wheel of life.

Frek began crafting kennies, eidetically copying the little plant and animal icons one after the other, his mind unbelievably clear and sharp. Some of the icons were bacilli capsules and viral squiggles. Frek considered leaving these out but, after all, the former ecosystem had been a whole, a web delicately tuned by millions of years of evolution. And if he tried starting to make case-by-case decisions he'd never finish. The only option was to preserve it all. He started with the inner, more endangered, species and worked his way out, going faster and faster. All the while Carb was murmuring encouragement, continually feeding him fresh bits of kenner and taking the copies Frek made. From the corner of his eye, Frek could see Carb's long tweaker fingers fitting the pieces together like bits of a three-dimensional jigsaw puzzle.

Time passed, perhaps a lot of it—though who can say how long ten hours or a hundred years might be, played out so far beneath the surface of time's pool? Now and then Frek would pause to craft some food and drink to keep him and Carb going; he lost track of how often.

They were getting tired, but they didn't sleep. Frek was afraid that if he slept inside the time pool, he might never wake up. Finally the point came when Frek encoded the last icon—a scorpion—and each and every species on the NuBioCom table had been faithfully preserved.

Frek's father held up the result for Frek to admire. He'd nestled the myriad copies together into a smooth, intricately patterned egg.

The elixir.

part 3

earth"s
fate

12

all hell
breaks
loose

"Finally," exclaimed Gibby when Frek and Carb emerged from the time pool. "You were in there must have been half an hour. Wow and me were startin' to get worried."

"Where's Zed?" asked Frek, wearily looking around the projection room. For the moment, he and Carb lay sprawled on the floor at the side of the pool, too tired to stand.

The overlaid copies of Li'l Bulb were taffy-pulling time strands through their light beams, and the sinister hyperdimensional mind worms were slowly twitching, the same as before. The rear door of the projection booth was open, and Zed Alef was gone. Wow trotted over to sniff at the elixir egg. Even though it contained millions or billions of the little genome models, the talisman fit in Carb's palm.

"Look at that!" exclaimed Gibby, ignoring Frek's question in his eagerness to examine the egg. "All them little shapes fitted together." He peered closer. "I've heard of some o' these. A toucan, a daffodil, a guinea hen, a dung beetle—you boys done good! You gonna just plant this in the ground and everything'll come back?"

"Where's Zed?" repeated Frek, unwilling to start thinking about all the steps that lay ahead. Buddha was he beat.

"Oh, he slipped off to take care of something else," said Gibby.

"Says he's the only one watchin' over this whole dang theater. Even asked me if I'd like to be his assistant. No thanks!"

"He told me he was going to try to keep Carb," said Frek. "I'd like to be out of here before he comes back." But why was he still worrying about Carb after all his betrayals?

"How would we leave?" said Carb, lying propped up on one elbow at Frek's side. "Zed led us into the Earth theater through a special door that's closed back up. How would we find our way out of here without him?"

"So forget it," said Frek, flopping down flat on his back.

"You boys need to sleep," said Gibby. "Wow and me too. I'm right peaked, tell you the truth. Anyhow if Zed or Li'l Bulb or them worms on the ceiling was gonna kill us, seems like they woulda gotten around to it by now. I'd say there ain't no kac-a-brick rush to get outa here. And—before we snooze, Frek, could you kenny craft me some food and some stim cell truffles?"

"Eat food," echoed Wow.

So Frek thought about nothingness and made a nice lump of kenner, and then he turned the kenner into water and anymeat and stim cells. And then he was really and truly too tired to think of leaving.

The very last thing Frek did was put the elixir egg in his pants pocket.

They slept.

Much later a noise woke Frek, a thump and clatter as of something sliding across the building's roof. The moaning sound of high wind filtered in.

All was still calm in the little room. The overlaid versions of Li'l Bulb were projecting, Frek's companions were asleep, and Zed wasn't around. Frek could feel the reassuring lump of the egg in his pants pocket. Lying quite still, he stared up at the mind worms.

For some reason he was seeing them and Li'l Bulb in a new way. The mind worms' motion trails seemed to persist for longer than before, and he could make out some previously invisible loops of their bodies. It was as if, during his rest, Frek himself had become a little hyperdimensional.

Jiggling his eyes brought more and more of the gray lampreys into focus—revealing something dreadful. Slowly writhing tubes led to Wow, to Gibby, to Carb—and, yes, to Frek. Even though Frek had often felt like he was blocking out the watchers, the branecasters had a mind worm permanently attached to his head.

He slapped his hand against the spot where it seemed the gray tube must plug in. But his fingers felt nothing. The parasitic thought-suckers were hyperspatial; they came in from a direction he couldn't touch or normally see—they were four- or even five-dimensional. The lampreys were like fingers poking down into the centers of ginger-bread men.

And now Frek remembered something about a dream he'd just had. The Magic Pig had been grunting to him, talking, telling him that he was going to have a five-dimensional vision for a few minutes when he woke up, the Pig saying Frek would see how the mind worms enslaved humanity. And then the dream Pig had more or less branded two follow-up commands onto Frek's brain: Kill the mind worms, and shoot your way out of the Exaplex. Now?

Looking up at the mind worms, Frek's vision grew yet more inclusive. There weren't just a dozen or a hundred of the sluggishly coiling things. They numbered—Buddha help him—in the billions, each of the lampreys looping off through the fourth and fifth dimensions to plug into one particular person back in the plain brane. Each and every person on Earth had an individual mind worm siphoning off their thoughts. That's what it meant to be a talent race. The Magic Pig was right; Frek should kill the worms.

Kill. The word echoed in Frek's mind, colored by the memory of the Pig's grainy oinks. Kill. Suddenly there was no room for anything but that one thought in Frek's head. Kill. Without even the slightest pause to consider the consequences, Frek went ahead and kenny crafted one, two, three blasters.

The gale outdoors was monstrously shrieking. Things thudded into the Exaplex roof and went scraping and rolling across it.

"Wake up," said Frek, poking Carb and handing him a blaster. "Kill." He leaned across to give the third blaster to the Grulloo. "Wake up, Gibby. Kill."

"Huh?"

One of the gray mind worms turned its dreadful eyeless face toward Frek, exposing concentric circles of teeth and a raspy, flickering tongue.

"Kill!" screamed Frek and fired his blaster. Although they couldn't see the evil worms quite so clearly as Frek, Carb and Gibby had no choice but to fire as well.

The blaster rays were gorgeous—hot white in the center, with auras of red, green, and purple, a different color aura around each beam.

The mind worms charred and blistered, their disk-mouths choiring a shrill screech. But the beams were making no lasting headway; indeed, fresh heads were growing from the mind worms' fast-healing wounds. Frek whirled his blaster around over his head, steadily holding down the firing stud, hoping to sever the snake that led into his brain.

As Frek continued blazing away, his higher-dimensional vision picked up something else. There was a kind of tube running from Carb's ring to Frek's ring. A higher-dimensional tunnel. He should really get rid of the stupid ring. But he might still need it, so he avoided shooting the tube connecting the rings.

After a while, he actually managed to burn his mind worm in two. But a fresh one immediately took its place. Somewhere inside himself Frek heard the Magic Pig's laughter. Without constant sky-air-comb vigilance, Frek continued to be subject to the cursed golden glow.

Wow was barking furiously. Frek was still firing. Clouds of greasy smoke billowed through the room and chunks of burnt, foamy material dropped from the ceiling—which was made of something very much like meat.

"Stop it!" yelled Carb, grabbing Frek's arm. Traitor. He'd quit shooting and so had the Grulloo. "Help me, Gibby," said Carb.

Carb bear-hugged Frek and Gibby got hold of his legs. But Frek kept his finger pressed down on his blaster, unwilling to stop trying to kill the worms, and especially not wanting to obey his no-good father.

The sweeping blaster beams had blown away large sections of the projection room's walls. And now a crucial supporting section of wall tore in half. The floor lurched and tilted; the time pool sloshed from its basin and streamed onto the theater seats below. Frek hoped the dispersal of the mind worms' pooled history of Earth wouldn't have any odd back-reaction upon humanity's actual reality. But still he continued firing.

His red-tinged blaster beam lit upon Li'l Bulb, or rather, upon the fan of Li'l Bulbs. Li'l Bulb no longer looked like a single creature at all. There were thousands, perhaps even billions of Li'l Bulbs, as many as the mind worms. They responded to the blaster's heat with the same kind of high-pitched shriek. Indeed, with the pond gone, Frek could see that the Li'l Bulbs were a bundle of snakes that ran through the floor, up the rear wall and into the knot of mind worms on the ceiling. The Li'l Bulbs were nothing but a kind of mind worm output unit. Both were components of the great branecaster router-server complex that was the Exaplex.

Lights still blazing, the Li'l Bulbs stretched out their bodies, reaching through the blown-out projection room walls and into the cavernous Earth theater, modulating their screams into an endlessly chorused pair of names.

"Zed Alef! Zed Alef! Zed Alef . . ."

A deep chuckle rose from below.

With a startled clatter, Wow lost his footing and slid across the slanting projection room floor to bump into Frek's legs. At the same time Carb finally ripped the blaster from Frek's hand. Frek tried to get it back, but it was hard with Gibby wrapped around his legs. The struggling Earthlings staggered across the floor, fetching up against a broken fragment of wall.

Close up, the wall resembled singed flesh with bones sticking out. Yes, the entire Exaplex was a single Planck brane organism. Overhead the mind worms were writhing about the same as before, all signs of damage gone.

The Li'l Bulbs had fallen silent, but their lights shone on, casting multiple shadows across the theater. The floor was bulging up in the middle, and the seats looked pointier than before, like little haystacks. Puddles of time were gathered at the bases of some of them. The domed floor chuckled again. It sounded like Zed Alef.

"You're gollywog, boy," murmured Gibby into a brief moment of silence. He gave Frek's leg a vengeful squeeze. "Look what you done stirred up."

Somewhere overhead the largest object yet went crashing across the Exaplex roof. The roaring of the wind grew deeper, more powerful. It would take but one more jolt to snap their tilted platform loose—an unpleasant prospect, as the now-hemispherical theater floor was acting so very weird.

"Let's play it nice and glozy," Carb whispered to Frek. "You've still got the egg, right? Getting you out of here safe with your elixir is all I care about." He almost sounded like he meant it. But how many times had he lied before?

Behind the noise of the storm, Frek heard something else. Memories of the Magic Pig's insinuating grunts were playing in his head, telling him to fire his blaster at the theater ceiling.

Carb had the blaster out at arm's length where Frek couldn't reach it. Frek wanted to start wrestling him with all his might, but he was afraid that too rough a motion might send them all tumbling down.

"Give it to me," said Frek.

"Don't let him, Carb," hissed Gibby. "No indeedy!"

"I won't," said Carb.

So Frek lunged for the blaster, and sure enough the floor gave way entirely, sending the four of them tumbling down. It was a soft landing. The theater seats were springy—like big tufts of hair.

"Cooties on me!" said Zed Alef's enormous voice. The theater seats were Zed's pigtails and the floor was the top of his head. The theater walls drew back on every side. The room became a giant stall with Zed standing inside it.

Over to the left, Frek could see one of Zed's enormous arms stretched out, with his hand grown right into the wall's foamy flesh. Frek recalled how Zed's feet always touched the floor. Zed was part of the Exaplex. The mind worms were inputs, the Li'l Bulbs were outputs, and Zed Alef was—the controller. What had he called himself? "The soul of the Exaplex." Zed's other arm came snaking upward, undulant and boneless, his fingers feeling for the Earthlings.

"Me and the branecasters are changing the game," boomed Zed.

"Being as how you messed up on the rules. You plain braners are here for good. We'll decohere you and siphon off your qubits. Good for our wham."

The giant hand grabbed for them. Its fingers had branched into smaller fingers that branched two more times again; it seemed like they were everywhere.

Atop Zed's head, Frek and the others were like kids playing hide and seek in a cornfield. They splashed through the puddles of time, each splash sending a thousand images flying. It could have been fun—but it wasn't. Frek was as frightened as he'd ever been.

And he still hadn't gotten his blaster back from Carb! Twice he tried to stop and kenny craft himself a new one, but he couldn't focus, what with Zed's creepy crawly fingers continually after him.

And then all at once Frek was nabbed. A wad of baby-sized sub-subfingers was clamped around his neck, and another bunch of the fingers took hold of his waistband. But Zed hadn't reckoned with faithful Wow, who snarled and bit, over and over, till Zed had released the boy.

"Here," said Carb, appearing around a hair stack to finally return Frek's gun.

"Shoot the ceiling!" roared Frek, firing straight up just like the Magic Pig had told him. Carb and Gibby let fly, their beams hot white, with green and purple auras, focused upward on the same spot as Frek's.

The result was smoke, fire, a hail of singed scraps of meat, a whistle—and a sharp, cold current of air. And then, with a sound like the end of the world, the gale caught hold of the punctured roof and pulled the whole thing to pieces. Gibby linked arms with Frek and Carb, who used their free hands to grab hold of Wow. The storm whirled in, furiously snatching them up into the sky.

Sharp spatters of rain stung Frek's cheeks. The air was acrid. Parts of Node G were in flames, tinging the smoke with an orange glow. On Earth it might have been morning by now, but here it was still night. Frek had the feeling that it might stay dark here for many days to come.

Below them was the congeries they'd called the Exaplex, lit by its own dancing bulbs of light and by some burning rubble nearby. It was nothing like a movie theater anymore. The illusions had fallen away, and he could see it as it really was: a vile mound of interlinked mind worms and Li'l Bulbs arcing off in bundles toward eldritch vanishing points. The worms led to talent race brains, the Li'l Bulbs to subscribers' flickerballs. Time pool data bases glinted amidst the evil, writhing mass. And there, humped up like a tumor, was the wobbly dark controller organ who'd worn the face of Zed Alef. The Exaplex was a huge organism controlled by Zed Alef. Zed and the Exaplex were the brain and body of branecasting.

The rain-sprinkled wind tugged Frek and his companions still higher into the sky. Gibby kept his leg-arms locked around Frek and Carb, who had their arms wrapped around each other's shoulders. Frek had tucked his blaster inside his shirt to free up his other hand to hold Wow against his chest. And Carb was holding Wow, too. The four of them tumbled along together like a fan of leaves.

Through the smoke and rain, Frek could see that Node G was utterly changed. Buildings were burning all across the city. The structures that remained had turned uncanny, arcane. Frek saw: stone castles with long wind-whipped pennants; fanciful assemblages of transparent domes and marble cones; organic shapes resembling insect parts hybridized with plants; long spiky feelers bedecked with berries and pods; tall masts with apes in the rigging; crystal spheres dangling from iron chains.

Thanks to phenomenological autozoom, Frek could pick out the individual Hubs as well. They'd altered along with the buildings. He saw chimerical drolleries like a harp with a human head, a knife with two enormous ears, and a lobster with clamshell wings. Crawling over everything were fat black frog-bellied demons with their fanged little mouths agape. Everything that moved was edged by a glowing aura.

Meanwhile the great dark wedge of the pie-shaped city park was receding from Frek's view. That was where the branelink to their home universe was supposed to be. But the raw, turbulent wind was blowing them the wrong way.

Two silvery shapes wiggled down at them from the flame-lit, cloud-wracked sky—supple forms that moved too fast for Frek to even think of trying to shoot them with his blaster.

"Fear not!" fluted one of them. They were a pair of large fish, surrounded by luminous auras, sailing through the air like birds. "My aunt's an enemy of the branecasters," said the one. "I am Flinka." She resembled a ten-meter trout; her voice was a soprano singsong with a middle-European accent.

"And I am Flinka's aunt Guszti," said her companion in an equally accented contralto. "She forgets to introduce me." If Flinka was a trout, Aunt Guszti was a catfish, with floppy barbels on her back and around her mouth. "You can ride us," continued Aunt Guszti. "We help you go home."

The wind raged ever stronger, bearing them out past the borders of the surreal cityscape that had been Node G. Ahead of them lay only dark fields and ragged mountains. Riding the flying fish seemed like the best option by far.

"Let's divide up," suggested Gibby. "I go with Frek, and Wow goes with Carb. You Huggins guys can always find each other with your rings."

"Good," said Frek. "I don't want to ride with him."

So Carb and Wow mounted Flinka, while Frek and Gibby settled onto Aunt Guszti. Aunt Guszti's glowing yellow-brown back was slippery in the rain; Frek grasped her barbels like a bridle. Gibby sat behind Frek with his leg-arms linked around him. For his part, Carb clamped Flinka's narrower body between his legs, cradling the damp Wow against his chest.

With a powerful slap of her tail, Flinka went darting toward the dark mountains. Aunt Guszti followed in her wake.

"Wrong way!" hollered Frek. "We need to go to that park back in the city!"

Aunt Guszti's eyes were so high up on her head that she could roll them back to look at Frek. "This storm blows stronger than even we can fight," she said. "But not make a worry. Today's configuration of Planck brane wraps around."

"How do you mean?"

"Mountains ahead of us are same as mountains behind us. As soon as you sail off one edge of Planck brane today you come back the other side. We'll land by Pig Hill with your branelink before you know it. Unless reapers catch us. They come out above fields during renormalization storms. Nearly all of them die during each renormalization, so they become frantic to eat and breed. They breed very fast, the filthy things. Is good that Flinka and I are faster than the reapers."

As if in response to this last remark, something fierce came whistling toward them. Aunt Guszti dodged it with a quick snap of her tail that nearly sent Frek and Gibby a-tumble. Hugging the fish and squinting his eyes against the cold rain, Frek could see Flinka rapidly weaving, too.

Another attacker went screaming past, briefly visible in the light from Guszti's aura. The creature resembled an ordinary pottery jug, with two leathery arms holding an old-fashioned reaping scythe. Instead of wings, it propelled itself with a jet of steam from its rear end. It was such an unlikely apparition that Frek didn't fully absorb the image until the reaper circled around and came at them a second time.

The reaper handled its scythe with the smooth expertise of a professional hockey player wielding his stick. Even though Aunt Guszti bent herself nearly in half to dodge it, the reaper managed to cut a nasty gash in her tail. Frek let go of one of the barbels he was clutching and fished his blaster from inside his purple shirt. To his satisfaction, he was able to nail the next reaper that came after them. Even though the blaster beams hadn't had much success against the mind worms, the reapers were small and three-dimensional enough to vaporize effectively.

A green explosion ahead showed that Carb was shooting reapers, too. Gibby unlimbered his blaster and opened fire as well.

For the next few minutes they were busy picking off incoming reapers, their blasts red, green, and purple. And then things quieted down. Frek focused his attention upon his ring and right away Carb's head appeared.

"Everything okay?" asked Carb.

"Gaussy," said Frek, momentarily forgetting to be mad. "Aunt Guszti says we're gonna wrap around and come back into Node G from the other side."

"Flinka told me," said Carb. "How many reapers did you bag?"

"Seven," said Frek.

"And four for me," put in Gibby, peering around Frek's side.

"This is fun," said Carb. His head lurched to one side and a dog-muzzle appeared by his cheek. "That's right, Wow, I'm talking to Frek. Now calm down. Stop it! I better sign off, Frek."

The black fields sailed by beneath them, marked here and there by the guttering orange flames of burning barns. Up ahead were the fantastically carved foothills, and beyond them the mountain range that rimmed this world.

"Tell me about the Magic Pig," Frek said to Aunt Guszti. "Who is he? What does he want?"

"His name is Rundy," said the flying catfish, rolling back her eyes. "He claims to be ordinary Hub like rest of us. But nobody remembers a time when he was not. He is often with the branecasters, but he says he is against them. He is very ancient, very strong."

"So he's against the branecasters?" said Frek.

"I like to think so," said Aunt Guszti, twitching the barbels beside her mouth. "But I am not, how you say, brightest bulb on Christmas tree. I wish to get rid of the branecasters. And I dream the Pig can help. The branecasters amass so much wham that fewer normal Hubs survive each storm. Yesterday Rundy called on me to fly him to the Exaplex. He says you four plain-braners are bringing us the liberation. And that you would break the Exaplex. That was Plan the A."

"Rundy's advice nearly got me killed," said Frek. "Shooting up the Exaplex hardly made any difference at all."

"Where's that Magic Pig now?" asked Gibby.

"In his burrow under Pig Hill," said the flying catfish. "It's at the end of the park with the branelink. The branecasters built their link tree right atop Pig Hill. Our Magic Pig claims this angers him. He has always been beneath Pig Hill. Maybe you make with Rundy a Plan the B."

"I'm not really sure he's on our side," said Frek.

"Rundy will talk all this with you. Meanwhile I fly."

Aunt Guszti was vigorously beating her tail, driving them higher and higher, with a view to sailing over the dark, jagged mountains. The air grew increasingly frigid, and the spatters of rain turned to snow and ice. Hearing Gibby's teeth chattering behind him, Frek suddenly thought of making a cape to wrap themselves in. In a minute he had one.

"How you do that?" asked Aunt Guszti, who'd been keeping an eye on him.

"Kenny crafting," said Frek, settling the cape around him and Gibby. "Don't you know about it? I thought you Hubs had superpowers."

"I am not brightest bulb," repeated Aunt Guszti. "Which is why my hopes run so high for you. Advise your father to make cape, too. Flinka says he's soon keeling over."

So Frek dutifully used his ring to remind stupid Carb he could use kenny crafting to warm himself. And not a moment too soon. Carb was quite blue, and there was ice in the bit of Wow's fur visible above the ring.

Still higher they rose, driven up the inky mountain slopes by the wind and the steady beating of the fish's tails. The mountains were darker than the sky. The silvery gleam of Flinka stayed fifty meters ahead of them, Carb a dark spot on her back. It was hard to gauge just when the moment of the wrap would come.

Finally the ridge began sinking beneath them. And then Flinka disappeared.

"Dad!" shouted Frek to his ring, at the same time wishing he could stop caring about his father.

"It's fine," said the little image of Carb's head above his hand. "I can see Node G up ahead."

Frek felt a prickling in the skin of his face. The front part of Aunt Guszti disappeared. And then Frek, Gibby, and the rest of the flying catfish had passed through the singular surface that glued one end of this Planck brane configuration to the other.

Lights gleamed in the vast plain below. Node G, seen from the other side.

As they neared the outskirts of town, a fresh wave of the jet-propelled pottery jugs came for them, each with its insect-thin arms wielding a scythe. Again, the Earthlings' blasters made short work of the little monsters.

"I hope high," repeated Aunt Guszti, angling down toward the base of Node G's triangular slice of park. It was a wooded region with a low hill in the middle. "There's Pig Hill; your branelink is the tree in the middle."

The husk of a large dead tree loomed at the hill's center, lit by a great bonfire nearby. The many-branched tree had an opening in one side, revealing the warped-looking tunnel of a branelink. Fine.

But four hangman's nooses hung from the branches of the tree. And fat-bellied black demons were capering around the bonfire, their toothy mouths open in savage song. Mixed in with the demons were the buttoned-down figures of the six branecaster execs—Chainey and Jayney, Sid and Cecily, Batty and Bitty. They too were pumping their arms and legs in the figures of the dance; they too were throwing back their heads to howl at the sky.

Frek felt for his blaster, then paused. It took a strong effort of his will to stop himself. Opening fire on an army of demons would be madness.

The music of drums and horns drifted up with the shrill cries. The instruments were living Hubs: the drums fat sullen demons pounding their enormous bellies with hands like clubs, and the trumpets blue storks with human arms to finger their bugle-shaped beaks. But the loudest noise came from a single monstrous bagpipe near the fire, a soft unclean thing, twitching its sticks and raising its horn to blat out an endless droning squeal compounded of anger, resentment, fear, selfishness, and cold-blooded lust.

Four carcasses were turning upon two long spits over the enormous bonfire, the charred roasts shaped like a man, a Grulloo, a boy, and a dog. The fat was sputtering, the smoke was drifting, and two chattering demons were cranking the squeaky gears, now and then running over to tend to the squawked demands of the huge bagpipe.

Snaking up the hill's side came a torchlight procession of still more demons waving swords and pikes, their voices massed into a hoarse roar. The tangled woods were alive with fire-lit yellow eyes.

"We don't have a chance!" exclaimed Frek. He focused in on the maddening, familiar face of his father. "Do you see those monsters? What does Flinka say?"

Up ahead the silver fish was circling around to the far side of the hill, avoiding the firelight. "She says the Magic Pig has a den at the bottom," reported Carb. "They're gonna set us down there."

"We're fubbed," said Gibby wearily. "I don't understand why this is all takin' so long. Hang me by the legs, stab me, roast me—kill me now and get it done. Good-bye, Salla! Good-bye, Bili and LuHu! I ain't never seein' you again."

"The branecasters wait for you to approach the tree," said Aunt Guszti. "They wait to pounce."

"Oh great," said Frek.

"If the Magic Pig were more honest, you would have better chance," said Aunt Guszti fatalistically. She was skirting around the rim of the lit area as Flinka had done. "You would travel home to Earth and carry out clever plan B to defeat the branecasters. Ah, look below and see him waiting, your new friend."

Sure enough, at the very bottom of the hill was a tilled garden patch, and beside a tiny dark hole in the hill with a glowing pink face peeking out—the Magic Pig, smaller and less prepossessing than Frek had ever expected.

A few moments later, Flinka and Aunt Guszti had unloaded them.

"Quick," said the little pink pig. "Come in here! I'm Rundy." His voice was a rough lively grunt, modulated into words. Perhaps he was old, but he was well cared for and spry. His body was made up of smooth curved surfaces, like a toon's.

"Don't trust him with your life," were Flinka's final, gloomy words. "I think he is maybe for the branecasters today."

"You are foolish, Flinka," Guszti scolded as the fish flew away. "Rundy is playing a much deeper game."

It was easy for Gibby and Wow to walk through Rundy's door, but

Frek and Carb had to bend double. Crouched down behind Gibby, Frek noticed that the Grulloo was carrying a large fish scale that had come loose from Guszti. Another of his souvenirs.

Just like a Grulloo burrow, Rundy's hall tunnel opened up into quite a large living room, complete with comfortable piles of straw to lie upon, a pantry cupboard filled with yams and sugar beets, a handy bucket of pure clean water, and a little hearth with a clean-drawing chimney and a kettle of porridge over the flames. Wow went and drank from the bucket, and began slowly sniffing all over the room. There was a locked door in the far wall.

"Nice sty," said Gibby. "Cleaner than I'd expected."

"I keep the wallow outside," said Rundy. His grunts were high-pitched, excited. Although the bristles on his neck were snow white and he had deep wrinkles around his eyes, his face was eager inside his bright gold aura. "I don't use my wallow so much anymore," continued Rundy. "Thanks to them putting that skewy branelink on Pig Hill. But I'm getting ahead of myself. First things first. Welcome, dear Earthlings! Sit down on any heap you like, they're all nice and fresh. I don't kac in the house, you know. I'm not a human!" He let out a laugh that twisted into a squeal, then trotted over to nose at Frek with the pink disk on the end of his snout. "My finest creation! A special welcome to Frek Huggins!"

"*Your* creation?" said Carb. "*I'm* his father, Rundy. Remember? You came and talked to me the night before he was born."

"Funny thing is, that was yesterday afternoon for me," said Rundy. "Yep, when I heard about you from Cecily, I quick decided to coach you. So I snuck into the Exaplex and rooted into your past. I got into your dream for a pep talk, Carb. And, better than that, I put some autopoiesis code into your and your son's DNA, and gave you two a pair of hyperdimensionally linked rings. And then Zed chased me out of the Exaplex, which was perfectly synchronistic of him, since that put me in the street at just the right moment to stop your tram. Things are so nicely entangled."

"Wait a minute," said Frek. "You're saying that when you heard I was here, you went back and changed the past to help me come here? That's a circle."

"The world is full of circles," said Rundy, twitching his floppy triangular ears. "I am because I am, and that's my wham. The Magic Pig and Pig Hill only make it through every renormalization storm because the other Hubs are so sure that we will. I'm a tradition. Yuga after yuga, there's always a Magic Pig."

"Yesterday afternoon you changed Carb's and my DNA twelve years ago?" said Frek. He was having trouble wrapping his mind around this. "You changed us to do—what was it again?"

"Autopoiesis," said Rundy, his voice a crisp oink. "Technically it's known as quantum error correction. Autopoiesis makes you quantum-mechanically coherent, which means being like yourself, only more so. Individualistic, you might say. Autopoiesis helped you keep the counselors from twenty-questioning you to death. And autopoiesis helps you block the espers. Autopoiesis keeps you in your own mental state, keeps you from letting the media do your thinking, keeps you from buying into every load of kac the monoculture tries to force feed down your throat. Makes you a troublemaker." Rundy let out another of the stuttering squeals he used for a laugh.

"Combing my brain," said Frek, suddenly making the connection. "That's what I call it. I have this mental routine I do. Sky-air-comb."

"We remember ourselves," put in Carb.

"Can you help us get past them demons and into that hollow tree?" interrupted Gibby.

"We'll give it a shot," said Rundy. "They're waiting for you, but I'll cause a distraction. It'll be fun. They won't actually hurt me. And, boys, Guszti is counting on you to think about a Plan B for shutting down the branecasters. Even if you fail, it'll be entertaining to see you have a go at it. Win win, the way I see it."

"What was Plan A?" asked Carb. "I missed hearing about that."

"Plan A was that your blasters would do some damage to the Exaplex," said Rundy. "Guszti and I wanted to see you try. When you guys were asleep in the projection room, I rooted my way into Frek's head through his mind worm and gave him my suggestions: Shoot the mind worms and blast a hole in the Exaplex to get out. Cecily had told me how tough you fellows are."

"Cecily!" exclaimed Frek, suddenly recognizing the name. The female branecaster who looked like a pig. "She's the one who told you we'd arrived?"

"She's my daughter," said Rundy. "I know her thoughts. Cecily and I are entangled—just like your two rings. But don't worry, I won't let her hear this conversation. Am I right in thinking you're for stopping the branecasters?"

"Of course," said Frek. "I don't want them and their esper subscribers to be watching us and pushing us around like pieces in a game. I'd do anything to bring them down. And you, Rundy—Aunt Guszti says you don't like the branecasters because they built on your hill? But what about Cecily?"

"It's a sad tale," said Rundy with a theatrical sigh. "After they put up the branelink, our little Garth wandered into it, and my wife, Cynthia, went in there to look for him, and I never saw either of them again. It was just Cecily and me for a quite a few years, and then that sleazy Sid started courting her, and next thing I knew she went over to the 'casters. I'm all alone, just me and my garden and my memories of my family."

Rundy gave another sigh and shook his head so hard that the ears flapped. Frek had a feeling the Pig might be doctoring the truth.

Meanwhile Wow had been nosing curiously at the cupboard shelves of muddy purple beets and pointed orange yams. Before Frek could come out with another question, Rundy turned his attention to the dog. "Would Wow like a yam?"

"No," said Wow. "Want meat."

"No meat here," said Rundy. "You're really a kind of wolf, aren't you? You can darn well eat porridge. It's made with the oats, beets, and yams that I grow myself. Good for you."

The Magic Pig rose up on his hind trotters and fetched a ladle and some bowls, then dished out five helpings of thick porridge, gray with orange and purple lumps. What with that long ride through snow and rain on the back of a flying fish, Frek found the gruel very welcome. At first he worried his body might not take to the mutable Planck brane matter—but it felt nice and warm in his stomach.

Rundy's aura bobbed and twinkled as he ate. "That 'wham' you keep talking about," said Frek presently. "It shows up as the size and brightness of your auras, right? And wham has something to do with surviving a storm?"

"Exactly," said Rundy, lifting his grizzled snout from his bowl. "The better your wham, the more persistent you are as a pattern in the Planck brane. There's two ways to get wham. The old way, the traditional way, is to have a lot of links to other Hubs, to make an impression on people, to make yourself useful, to have a family, to be part of society. Everyone remembers you, and you persist. But the new way to get wham, the modern branecaster way, is to huff down some plain brane matter and use that as an anchor to keep you in place during the renormalization storms. Plain brane matter isn't affected by renormalization, you see."

"The branecasters had us bring in ten trillion tons of gold," bragged Carb. "My son and I made it. It looked to me like the branecasters gave most of it away."

"The branecasters get wham both ways," grunted Rundy. "Their plain brane clients pay them in matter and they eat maybe a tenth of it. But they give out the other ninety percent of the matter to average Hubs, who get so grateful that they end up thinking about the branecasters all the time. Pretty glatt, huh?"

Frek shrugged. "I heard the branecasters are accumulating so much wham that fewer and fewer regular Hubs are surviving the storms."

"Tough on them," said Rundy, his voice a callous grunt. "The branecasters do what they like—for now. Eventually they'll push it too far, and this old Pig will move on."

"This is all real interesting and everything," said Gibby, setting down his bowl with a clack. "And thanks for the grub, not that my tongue's doing much good at soakin' it up. But can we get to the dang point? How the Sam Hill do we get our butts outa here without bein' kilt?"

"I have a secret tunnel," answered Rundy. "It spirals up through the hill to the top, and it comes out under a bush right beside the branelink tree."

"But your daughter Cecily must know about it," exclaimed Carb. "She'll be expecting us."

"You'll have to take that chance," said Rundy. "Anyway, the bush isn't far from the tree. And, like I said, I'll make a distraction." Hearing this doomed, half-baked plan, Frek remembered Flinka's claim that the Pig was working with the branecasters. But there was nobody else to turn to. He got up and walked across the Magic Pig's living room to the closed door in the other wall.

"Not there," said Rundy. "That's my private study. The passageway is over here. Behind the cupboard. Help me move it."

With Carb and Frek's help, Rundy pushed aside his cupboard to reveal a little round passageway angling upward. Wow ran right in, followed by Rundy, Gibby, Carb, and Frek, the last two crawling on their hands and knees.

After a few turns of the spiral tunnel, the air grew very close and dusty, so much so that Frek began worrying about suffocating. What would happen if he died in the Planck brane? Would it really count? He wasn't eager to find out. He comforted himself by patting the egg in his pants pocket. If he could get the elixir back home he'd surely manage to repopulate Gaia with her missing species. Moths, lobsters, rabbits, daisies—it would be heaven on earth.

Above them was an intricate noise that grew louder as they climbed. By the time Frek reached the end of the tunnel, the sound had bloomed into deafening cacophony. It was the massed chants and cries of the demons around the bonfire, the squalling of the giant bagpipe, and the pounding of the stomach-drummers.

Frek found his companions already crouched beneath a large bush. The bush reminded him of the please plant that had hidden him in that gully above the River Jaya. Could that only be a week ago? He prayed to Buddha that he was finally on his way home.

Peering through the chinks between the leaves, Frek saw the frog-mouthed demons milling around the fire. Swords and pikes rose above them like feelers. The bagpipe had puffed itself up to a height of fifteen meters; its sticks and horn were waving about in complex, hypnotic paths; its unrelenting voice was an amalgam of every negative emotion. Fanciful demons hovered in the air, buzzing upon insect wings. The six branecasters were, however, nowhere to be seen. Not necessarily a good sign.

The branelink itself was indeed nearby. Little more than five meters of bare ground separated the great hollow tree from the bush where the Earthlings lurked. Looking up, Frek wondered at the tree's vast fire-lit branches fading into the night. At ground level was a ragged gateway in the side of the tree, a doorway of strobing light. How hard could it be to run the five meters and jump inside?

Well, for one thing, the gateway was guarded by an armored demon. He had a long shiny beak with a disk at the end—a spoonbill. He wore an inverted funnel atop his head. The effect might have been comic, but the guardian had evil-looking red eyes, and he bore a weapon resembling a bow and arrow mounted upon a rifle stock. Frek recognized it as a crossbow.

"I'll lure him off," said Rundy in his penetrating grunt. He'd crept over to crouch at Frek's side. "Don't forget that Guszti wants you to think of a Plan B." On Rundy's other side, Frek could see Carb, tensed for the dash, with one hand holding Wow in check. And beyond Carb was wide-eyed Gibby, his leg-arms bent in half, poised to catapult himself toward the branelink.

Rather than trying to shout an answer to Rundy over the demons' yells, Frek simply ran his hand over the ancient pig's bristly, curved back, drawing a bit of reassurance from the touch. Perhaps this only looked like a trap. Maybe Rundy was thinking ahead for a way to save them. The Magic Pig nuzzled Frek's hand with his nose-disk, gave a last sharp grunt, then shot into the open.

The spoonbill demon's arms rose and his crossbow twanged. Though the bolt sank deep into the Magic Pig's pink hide, the damage fazed him not one whit. He ran right up to the spoonbill demon and bit him on the foot, then raced toward the fire with his enemy in hot pursuit.

Gibby, Wow, and Carb were already halfway to the tree. You could count on Carb to look after himself. Frek took off after them. A huge wobble of light flared up to Frek's right; from the corner of his eye he saw Rundy scampering through the bonfire, scattering firebrands in every direction. Just a few meters ahead of Frek, the branelink entrance flashed green as Gibby reached it. And then Wow and Carb were safe inside, too.

Frek only had one more step to go when the dragon caught him.

The six heads came down at him from the dark branches of the branelink tree, seizing him by the arms, the legs, the waist, and the throat. The head holding his throat was recognizably Cecily's. Her snout was long and green and with big nose-holes like a dragon's, but even so she still looked like a businesswoman—and like the daughter of a pig.

"How could you ever think we'd let you get away," growled Cecily. "Especially after what you told Rundy. You're too big a threat to us. We hadn't quite realized before."

"Let's finish him off in the nest," mumbled the Chainey head, keeping his narrow mouth clamped onto Frek's right hand. "Jayney will decohere him." He was still wearing his little gold-rimmed glasses.

Frek was swept up into the air; his body turned at dizzying angles. From what he could make out by the chaotic firelight, the six branecasters had merged themselves into a single great dragon: six heads, six necks, and one long, slender body coiled around the branches of the branelink tree. Far below, Frek saw the Magic Pig come charging back toward the tree. Too late.

Writhing and slithering, the dragon pulled itself up and up to arrive at a large, flat nest of sticks from the tree, smoother than wood, and hollow like bones. The nest had clamps to hold Frek in place, flat on his back, staring up toward the orange-lit clouds.

Jayney leaned over Frek, her plastic dragon face bent into a parody of a motherly smile. She had fangs. She bit his neck and drew something out of him, leaving numbness in its place.

A hundred imaginary faces seemed to bloom around him, bland and doughy, pressing forward, staring, asking questions—all at the same time. Willy-nilly, Frek was unable to do anything but answer the voices in his head.

"How old are you?"

"Are you happy?"

"What's your name?"

"Do you miss home?"

"How tall are you?"

"Are you frightened?"

With each response, Frek became a bit less himself and more of a statistic. The questions were flattening him out. On and on they came.

"Rate your feelings about the following on a scale from one to five, ranging from dislike very much to like very much. My mother Lora, rainy weather, my sister Geneva, the River Jaya, my sister Ida, the Goob Dolls show, my father Carb, the color of my bedroom's walls, Kolder Steiner, the smell of roseplusplus blossoms, Gibby the Grulloo, the taste of amplified trout, my dog Wow, the feel of turmite silk, Sao Steiner, the stairs in my family's house tree."

"Let's explore your relationship with your mother. Rate your perceived frequency of the following classes of events on a scale from one to five, ranging from almost never to extremely often. Lora smiles at me. Lora scolds me. Lora shows affection to me. Lora has high expectations of me. Lora talks to me. Lora punishes me for small things. Lora makes me feel cozy. Lora yells at me. Lora acts unpredictably toward me. Lora asks me to do chores. Lora doesn't understand me."

"Let's analyze your opinions about the branecasters. Specify your agreement with the following statements on a scale from one to five, ranging from disagree strongly to agree very much. The branecasters are evil. There are six branecasters. The branecasters are parasites. Chainey is the leader of the branecasters. The branecasters are dangerous. The branecasters help the human race. The branecasters are dishonest. The branecasters promote personal growth. The branecasters are like gods."

The questions came at him so thick and fast that he never thought of using his autopoiesis. In a few minutes, every spark of Frek's own true self had been sapped away. All he felt now was a faint ache all through his bones, like the pain from a bad tooth.

While Frek was being decohered, the branecasters unwound into separate bodies again. And when the questions finally stopped, they were standing over him, looking down contemptuously. They were humanoid again, albeit with wings of leather and bone.

Lights wriggled in the sky. Flinka, Aunt Guszti, and scores more of the flying fish. And now heavy glowing balls began raining down onto the nest. One of them struck Sid in the head and exploded, sending Sid crashing down through the branelink tree. The flying fish were trying to drive the branecasters away.

Frek had no opinion about any of this. He was a rag doll, an automaton, a thing. He contained no mysteries. He was fully decoherent.

Cecily flew off and reappeared with the wounded Sid. More glow-bombs fell, but none of them came near Frek. After one of the bombs hit Chainey, the branecasters took wing and circled up to fight the flying fish. The last to depart was Batty. Just before leaving, he lowered his mean, crazy face down to Frek's.

"I'm your keeper," he said. He had fangs like Jayney. "I'll be back every so often to decohere you some more. I'll eat every last qubit you make." He gave a jittery chuckle and was gone. The clouds flickered with lights as the branecasters fought the flying fish.

Still Frek thought nothing one way or the other. He was an object, a transparent toy, with less inner life than the sticks he lay upon.

He ached. He was breathing. Eventually it would stop. It didn't matter.

Something tingled on his finger. At some level Frek knew it was Carb trying to call him. But he didn't answer. Why would he? How? Nobody home.

More time passed, and then something bumped the nest. Batty coming back to decohere him some more? Not that Frek cared. But, no, it was Carb. Not that Frek cared.

Carb leaned over him and began talking.

"Come on, Frek. Get it together! Climb down from here and get into the branelink. Gibby and Wow are waiting at the first fork."

Frek said nothing. He could smell his father's breath and his sweat. His reaction was zero on a scale of one to five.

Carb studied him for a moment, then seemed to reach a decision. "I'm going to help you, Frek. You're my heart. Comb your brain and recohere yourself!"

A red glow trickled out of Carb's ring and into Frek's. Like a stream of blood running from one to the other. Frek felt the faintest spark of strength. Comb his brain? Yes. He hadn't been able to think of that before. He visualized running his fingers through his brain, fluffing his thoughts back up. And now the autopoiesis kicked in, the quantum error correction. The numbness began ebbing away.

"Keep it up," his father urged him.

When Jayney had decohered Frek, she'd kicked the legs out from under his personality, taken away his sense of self, collapsed his inner entanglements. But now he was rebuilding his own unique mixed state. Combing it back up, nice and high.

The strengthening flow of red from Carb's ring to Frek's continued. "Those are self-entanglement qubits," said Frek's father, noticing Frek's glance. "That's what they sucked out of you to make you decohere. The Magic Pig told me I could save you by giving you my own self-entangled qubits." He was breathing deeper and slower. He sat down on the sloping edge of the nest. Frek thought of the old days, how his father would tuck him into bed.

"Is—is this hurting you, Dad?"

"I want to help you, Frek. It's all right. I'm glad to make up for the bad things I've done."

Above them, the battle in the sky proceeded, with colored flashes filtering through the clouds. But now here came a branecaster swooping back down. Batty. He landed on the other edge of the nest, observing them with his glittering vampire eyes. Frek stood up. He was feeling much stronger now. He dialed his blaster to its highest tight-beam intensity, and tried shooting a hole in Batty's face. The ray had no more effect than a pocket flashlight.

"Get going," breathed Dad. The flow of red from his ring had dropped to the merest trickle. "It doesn't matter what happens to me now." He struggled to his feet and positioned himself between Frek and Batty. "Run, Frek. I mean it. Otherwise this has no point."

Frek backed to the edge of the nest and peered down. He saw an easy series of handholds he could use to make his way to the ground. Down there the branelink entrance was gently strobing. The branecasters other than Batty were still in the clouds. This was his chance.

Frek glanced back at his father, who was crouched in readiness for Batty's attack.

"I swear I'll come back and save you, Dad."

"No problem," said Dad, his familiar smile visible on the side of his face. "As long as you're around, I'm still alive. And Frek? I know you won't believe this, but—when we were surfing across the Orpolese archipelago the other day? Those were the happiest hours of my whole entire life."

Batty lunged toward Frek, but Dad blocked him. The winged branecaster sank his teeth into Dad's neck.

Eyes blurry, Frek scrambled down the tree. Some of the demons headed toward him, led by the giant squealing bagpipe undulating across the ground like a high-speed carnivorous slug, using its sticks like crutches, and with its furiously blasting horn aimed directly his way.

But Frek made it into the hole before the bagpipe got to him. The space in there was filled with yellow-orange light. He felt an upward-pointing force as in Hawb and Cawmb's negative gravity column; he fell up. But not for long.

A double mandala of concentric circles loomed ahead. Perched unsteadily at the figure-eight juncture of the two circles was a trio of familiar forms. Gibby, Wow, and the Magic Pig. Frek alighted next to them. The branelink tree's inner surface was tingly and slippery. Frek had to balance carefully to keep from being pulled into one of the two branches that led up from here.

"So your father saved you," said the Magic Pig. "Good. Zed Alef and the branecasters were determined that one of you had to stay. It's better for you to be the one to escape, Frek. You're the hero."

"Carb?" whined Wow.

"There was a man," said Gibby and fell silent.

"No time to waste," urged Rundy. "The others might come in here if you stay too long. Let me tell you what to do."

Frek tuned out. He was thinking of Batty clutching Dad. Deep inside his ring finger he could feel that same numb ache he'd felt before. An echo of Dad's decoherence. Just then it crossed his mind that perhaps he should throw the ring away, lest the branecasters find some way to use the connection to come after him. But the impulse felt self-ish, unworthy. Dad had used the rings to save Frek. There was an outside chance that Frek could eventually repay the favor. The ring should stay.

Rundy was still talking. "You'll pass a lot of branch points. No use telling you the pattern, just follow your sense of what's right. You'll find your way back to Bumby and Ulla in Orpoly and they'll yunch you home. The Orpolese have to get you back before they can finish closing their deal."

"How can I get in touch with you again from Earth?" Frek asked the Magic Pig. "How can I get back here to save Dad?"

"I'll root out a connection," said old Rundy. "I'm good at rooting. Get home, repopulate your planet, and work on your Plan B. You'll hear from me. And now I better go and make another distraction." The Magic Pig gave one of his stuttery squeals and scrambled down out of the branelink tree.

"We're gonna need spacesuits out there," said Gibby.

"That's right," said Frek. So he kenny crafted spacesuits for him, Gibby, and Wow. Only the three of them now. Poor Dad.

"These look right flimsy compared to the ones the Orpolese made," said Gibby, hefting his transparent kenner wrapping. "You think they'll do?"

"I hope so," said Frek. He was too upset to think clearly.

"Home," said Wow, pointing his nose into one of the two ring-striped tunnels leading farther up into the branelink tree.

"Yes," said Frek.

"That's the one I'd pick, too," said Gibby.

They went falling upward, past branching after branching. Ten, twenty, thirty times the mandalas broke into submandalas; each time it took but the slightest twitch of will to pick the next one. Fortunately, the three travelers always agreed. In their hearts, they all knew the way home.

When they reached the final stretch of the branelink tunnel, Frek once again seemed to hear the sound of branches breaking, of foliage tearing away. And then they were back in their own universe, the plane brane, somewhere near the center of the Milky Way galaxy, in the heart of the Orpolese archipelago, amidst the suns circling the bloated sullen mass of the galactic black hole.

The passage through the link had angled them out at such a velocity that they entered a tight orbit around the branelink sun, which still resembled a colorized Bodhisattva.

For the moment at least, their spacesuits seemed to be doing a decent job at feeding them air and keeping out the insanely intense radiation. Frek scanned the space around them, looking for their ride home. And then, with a sigh of relief, he spotted the green-veined maroon donut of Ulla/Bumby orbiting toward them from the region of the star that represented the topknot upon the Bodhisattva's head. Ulla would probably surround them and give them fresh spacesuits and—

Right about then Gibby spotted the other aliens.

"Three kinds of 'em!" cried the Grulloo. "They done tracked us down. Looky toward the galactic rim, that's a Unipusker saucer, ain't it? With a geevin' Radiolarian barrel-ship followin' right after! And, over there we got an Orpolese donut comin' in from the edge of that giant black hole! It's the same pink and yellow ring that Carb shot at before. These folks ain't comin' our way just to say how-do!"

Sensing their panic, Wow began barking and wouldn't stop.

The only good news was that Ulla/Bumby was closer than the other aliens. A few of Bumby's green tentacles hung free from the donut's outer surface, and even as they approached, the mobile palps were busily twisting about, firing warning blasts toward the hostile pink-yellow Orpolese, the shiny Unipusk saucer, and the Radiolarian barrel-ship.

Ulla/Bumby considerately yunched themselves down to a size commensurate with the human scale, and then Ulla made herself into a flattened sphere not much bigger than a house tree. Opening a triangular door in her side, she scooped Frek and his companions out of interstellar space as adroitly as a songbird catching gnats.

The inside of Ulla looked much the same as before. Her stubby inward-projecting masts emitted polyhedral tweets that flew repeatedly through the Earthlings to find out everything they'd seen and thought—though surely Ulla could already have learned most of this via the branecast feeds from Frek, Wow, and Gibby's mind worms.

Rather than appearing as a free-floating cuttlefish inside Ulla's body, Bumby remained fully merged into his partner's flesh. The air-filled space vibrated with the familiar sound of his voice.

"Congratulations on scoring the elixir," was the first thing Bumby said. "And condolences in the matter of your lost father. *Sunt lacrimae rerum.* These are the tears of things."

"I'll miss him," said Frek simply.

Sounding in the background were the explosive blasts from Bumby's tentacles. An incoming bolt of energy rocked Ulla from side to side.

"Too little too late, losers," shouted Bumby, his words vibrating out toward the enemies like a fusillade of miniature suns.

"Get us outa here!" cried Gibby.

"We'll yunch now," said Bumby in a chatty tone. "We're eager to get you to Earth and finally switch on our production. It'll be nice to meet Tagine and Vlan as well. We've been talking to them through a hyperspace tube. Our grandchildren and our newest heirs. They're on the job, staking out your home turf."

Two chimes sounded while Bumby talked. With the first chime, their makeshift spacesuits melted away, and with the second, Ulla's transparent kenner tweets clothed them in heavy-duty Orpolese suits.

And now Ulla unsealed her top and bottom, returning to her customary shape of a green-veined reddish-purple donut.

The third chime sounded. Frek felt a familiar dropping sensation in the pit of his stomach; he sensed the yunch whine within his flesh. Looking out from the donut, he could see their alien attackers in the middle distance. But Bumby's tentacles were laying down a withering barrage of energy bolts that kept them from approaching closer.

Ulla/Bumby's rapid transition into yunch had caught the other aliens by surprise. Their pursuers showed no sign of yunching up with them. As Frek watched, the Unipuskers, Radiolarians, and hostile Orpolese dwindled into invisibility, followed, in short order, by the densely clustered suns that filled the center of Orpoly.

A worry pinged in the back of Frek's mind.

"Isn't it dangerous to yunch near so much matter?" he said into his spacesuit.

"Quite the feat of derring-do, eh?" said Bumby's voice. As before, the group of yunchers had become tenuous clouds, overlaid upon each other. It was as if Bumby's voice were within Frek's own head. "Leaping off the maiden's balcony to land upon the back of one's faithful steed," continued the alien. "Scampering down the giant's beanstalk. Out of the joint in time. Unlax, my boy, yunching near massive objects isn't nearly so high-risk on the way up as on the way down. Assuming, of course, that we don't spring a leak. But that's not very—what, Ulla?"

For a moment Bumby fell silent, and in the silence, sooner than expected, chime four sounded, signaling the superexponential phase of the yunch. The stars tumbled past like dust. Frek assumed it was good to be traveling so fast. Soon chime five would sound and they'd level off at galactic size and—

"Shed the ring!" roared Bumby, his voice like a storm. A vortex of Orpolese energies clawed at Frek's hand.

Frek had been too distracted by the yunch to notice his finger. But, yes, his ring was buzzing and sucking, pulling fine lines of red from the hazy ring of Ulla/Bumby, and floating near Frek's hand was the ghostly image of—Batty's face.

"Quantum leak!" shrieked Bumby, his voice cracking. "They're killing us! Tell Tagine and Vlan. They inherit our deal." His voice was weaker than before. Already there was but little strength in the forces trying to twist off Frek's ring.

Still Frek hesitated to cast it away. The ring was his last link to his father. But then he heard the voice of the Magic Pig, squeaking at him through the mouth of Wow.

"Drop the ring before they get you, too, Frek."

So now, as in the vig herd on Unipusk, Frek discarded his troublesome ring. It went tumbling off toward the galactic core. For a fleeting moment, Frek again could see the hyperspace tube connecting his ring to Dad's. It was like a rubber band, pulling his ring toward the branelink and the Planck brane.

Meanwhile their upward yunch continued. Frek heard a faint sound, halfway between a hiss and a moan.

"Bumby?" he called tentatively. No further answer came. The green-veined purple cloud that had been Ulla/Bumby was damaged beyond repair—ragged and breaking into bits on every side. This time Ulla and Bumby were worse than decohered. They were dead. Who would help Frek now?

"Rundy?" he essayed. But the Magic Pig was gone. Wow's only sound was a doggy whine.

They were moving up past the galactic level now. As before, Frek spotted a few other yunchers rising up and then sinking down. But unlike the others, Frek and his companions continued unceasingly to grow.

"Gibby?" said Frek finally. He wasn't eager to hear his partner's reaction to his latest goof.

"You've fubbed it good," came the Grulloo's bitter response. "Killed our ride home. And looky down there. That tiny white disk in the middle of our stomachs? That's the geevin' galaxy, kac-for-brains. Now hurry up and unyunch us like you did when you ruined the first trip. It's the least you can do, you gump. Not that we have a dewdrop's chance in hell of ending up on Earth." Gibby was a cloud of anger.

"Hold on," muttered Frek, too abashed to say more.

He thought back on what he'd done during that first outward trip with Ulla/Bumby. They'd come to rest at the galactic size level and then, spurred by his treacherous ring, Frek had prematurely un-yunched them down toward Unipusk.

How had he done it? It had been a matter of remembering the particle-spinning feeling of the upward yunch, and starting a similar kind of motion, but in the opposite sense.

So now Frek tried. And got nowhere. When he'd cut short their first trip with his will to unyunch, they'd been in a neutral state, paused at the size of the galaxy. But this time their Orpolese guides had died before having the chance to sound the crucial chime five. Frek, Gibby, and Wow were in the throes of a powerful, ongoing upward yunch.

Try as he might, Frek could find no way to overcome the inertia of the yunch-spin.

"The yunch is, like, stuck," said Frek presently. If anything, the pace of their upwards yunch was increasing. A cluster of small white disks flew past. Other galaxies.

"We're gonna keep growing forever?" demanded Gibby.

"I don't know."

13

the
revolution

The galaxies tumbled past like snowflakes in a storm. And still Frek and his companions grew. Frek glimpsed one other pair of yunchers, overlapping ducks who purposefully waddled from one galaxy to another and shrank demurely down. How enviably controlled were their motions compared to Frek's mad, unconstrained upward rush.

The galactic flakes of light shrank to dust motes. The accumulation of bright specks sketched scarves of light. As the scale grew yet vaster, the faint, stippled surfaces folded over upon themselves, as if building up tissues of transgalactic flesh. These shapes in turn dwindled to dots and lines of light that became the elements of still larger forms, ever more remote from anything familiar. Weary and hopeless, Frek and his companions slept.

When he woke, the fractal dusts and skeins of light were still coming at them. Though Gibby and Wow were silent, Frek had a sensation of someone talking to him. The melodious voice seemed to come from inside Frek's body, as if his bones were vibrating to make the sounds, or as if the background hum in his ears was a song. But each time Frek tried to focus upon the voice, it faded away. He could hear it only when he wasn't trying to understand what it said.

Up ahead a patterned cloud rushed toward them. The approaching fog held three enormous shapes: a boy, a Grulloo, and a dog—all seen from behind. Frek and his companions had grown so big that they wrapped all the way around the universe.

Although Frek's yunched-up body was comfortably overlapped with the forms of Gibby and Wow, it wouldn't overlap itself. There was a faint *boing* as Frek stepped on his own heels—and stopped growing. He was as large as anything in his home universe could become. The upward yunch was over.

Frek felt around within himself, unsuccessfully trying to start the unyunch. He'd wholly forgotten about the voice within his body. So now of course the words came clear.

"Hello. I'm Q'lem." You couldn't really call the voice either male or female.

"God!" exclaimed Gibby.

"I'm not God," said the voice. Once again the sounds were overflowing into Frek's other senses. The voice smelled like honey; it sparkled pale white. "I'm more what you'd call an angel," continued Q'lem. "An eigenstate of your universal wave function. Or perhaps an intelligent mold upon the four-dimensional hypersurface you call your universe. There's levels upon levels in the cosmos. Are you planning to hyperjump farther up? I could boost you."

"No, no," cried Frek. "We want to go home. We started yunching and we couldn't stop. We want to go back to Earth—to heal our biome and get rid of the branecasters."

"I'm scanning your worldline," said Q'lem. "A very wriggly thread."

"Can you help us get home?"

"You need a size scale to attune yourself to," said Q'lem. "Follow your heart. Your loved ones are your beacon, your standard meter. Ask one of them to stretch out a hand."

"How would I talk to them?"

"They're inside you. You're everywhere."

"I smell our yard," said Wow, speaking more clearly than ever before. "I can find Lora."

"The dog knows," said Q'lem. "I'm helping him." The shining, sugared voice sank back into the background hum from whence it had emerged. And the odor of Wow replaced the scent of honey.

"I'm just as smart as you are, Frek," said Wow, his voice supremely well-modulated. "You only think I'm dumb because I'm not interested in the same things as you. I'm an expert on our backyard. I know where the turmites have a path up the anyfruit tree. And where there's a puddle with mosquitoes. I know all the blades of grass. The pebbles. They're part of me. I can see our backyard and near it I see Lora. She's sleeping. It's almost dawn."

"Good, Wow," said Frek, trying to hide his unease at having his dog speak as an equal. "Can you help me talk to Lora?"

"Careful, Frek," put in Gibby. "Q'lem has that dog all hopped up. An angel made of universal pond scum? What if Q'lem's given Wow rabies?"

Before Frek could finish thinking this over, Wow barked a slightly mocking command to him. "Come, boy!" The dog's clear, forceful voice set a whirlpool spinning in Frek's head.

Frek had a sense of being in two places at once. He was still yunched up to the size of the universe, with his front wrapped around to touch his back. But at the same time he was at the far end of the whirlpool, peeking into—Lora's dream.

Lora was dreaming about teaching a man to play the sitar. The man's head was a pumpkin carved like a jack-o'-lantern. Whenever the student got a good rhythm going, he'd groovily wag his big orange head—and it would fall off and roll across the ground. Lora would sigh, put the head back in place, and say, "Roast beets, Mr. Taj." And then the student would start playing again, raga variations upon "My Dog Has Fleas."

Frek pushed farther into the whirlpool, sending an image of himself into Lora's dream to stand next to Mr. Taj.

Lora recognized her son right away. "Frek," she exclaimed. "I'm so worried about you. You're okay?"

"I'm as big as the universe, Mom," said Frek. "I want to come home. Can you reach out your hand to me?"

"How?" said Lora. "Which way?" And then the student's pumpkin head fell off again, distracting her. "Roast beets, Mr. Taj," repeated Lora. When Frek tried to get his mom's attention back, he couldn't. Lora was lost in her dream.

The whirlpool closed up.

"No luck?" asked Gibby. He, Frek, and Wow remained stalled at the largest possible size.

"I'll take you to Geneva and Ida," suggested Wow. "I can find them, too."

But this proved fruitless as well. Geneva was immersed in reveries of an endless dress store, and Ida was dreaming about the Goob Dolls. Neither of them recognized Frek. Geneva mistook him for a sales clerk, while Ida thought he was a Goob Doll troll.

"Try Renata," Frek told Wow after giving up on his sisters.

"I don't know her scent very well," objected Wow.

"Try anyway," insisted Frek. "It should be easy to find her. I bet she's in our house in Middleville, sleeping in my room. Go, Wow. Take me into Renata's dream."

Renata's dream image of herself was younger-looking than the real Renata, but with the same long, braided pigtails. She was dreaming about sculpting shapes in three dimensions, waving her arms in the air and leaving solid trails. Just now she was designing a ribbed, branching form like an old-time saguaro cactus. Frek's image appeared seated on one of the dream-cactus's arms.

"Is that you, Frek?" said Renata. "You stayed away too long. When are you coming back?"

"Right now," said Frek. "If you can help me. I'm stuck, and I need to hold your hand."

"I'll try," said Renata, reaching out toward him. "I need help, too."

Renata's hand was at just the right hyperdimensional dream space angle for Frek to catch hold of. As soon as he locked into contact with her, he knew he could come home. He tautened the connection between his two selves: the image within Renata's dream and the yunched-up body that filled the universe.

Renata gave his hand a gentle tug, and then, at last, the downward unyunch began. Quickly feeling around with his other hand, Frek managed to get hold of one of Gibby's hands—or feet. Gibby in turn used his free limb to catch hold of Wow. And thus the three of them unyunched together. There was whiff of valediction from Q'lem, a sweet chime of good-bye.

The trip was fast. The tenuous forms of galactic superclusters flew past, resolving into smaller and smaller components. In five minutes, Earth herself came rushing at Frek like a well-thrown ball. Stretching out before Frek was the long pink worm of his arm, a million-kilometer pink spaghetti leading down to the coastal plains of a green-shaded continent lightly shadowed by Gaian clouds.

The arm reeled him in at a reckless rate, pulling Gibby and Wow behind. They swooped down past dawn-gilded Middleville treetops and through Frek's bedroom window to land—*thump, thump, thump*—foursquare on his bedroom floor.

Renata was sitting up in bed, blinking and smiling, her arm extended toward Frek. He was his solid old self, firmly clasping her hand, with his other arm reaching back to hold Gibby, who was holding Wow. Their space suits were gone.

"Stop that noise, Renata!" yelled Ida from her room down the hall. "Too early!" Frek, Gibby, and Renata started laughing, and Wow let out a joyous bark.

"Frek! Wow!" exclaimed Ida. She came rushing into Frek's room, dressed in her old yellow pajamas with the bumblebee stripes. And then Lora and Geneva woke up, too.

It was a wonderful reunion, with hugs all around, everyone talking at once. Woo found her way into Frek's bedroom as well, she and Wow delightedly sniffing and nuzzling each other, their tails wagging, yipping and nipping, batting each other's muzzles with their forepaws.

"Frek, you look like you haven't washed for—has it been eight days?" said Lora right away. Same old Mom.

"I'll clean up in a minute," said Frek. "It'll feel good. Is Yessica here?"

"She moved to Stun City," said Renata. "So things have been pretty calm."

"Except for yesterday," put in Geneva. "Yessica came back for a visit. She bought Renata some angelwings. They're lying on our lawn."

"Renata was yelling at Yessica really loud," said Ida. "Then she stopped and Mom told Yessica to go away some more."

"It's okay," said Renata, seeming eager to change the subject. "You haven't introduced Gibby yet, Frek."

"Hi, Gibby," said Ida, crouching down to peer under his low hat.

"Careful," said Geneva. "Grulloos bite."

"Maybe I'll eat a Nubby for breakfast," said Gibby, rocking back on his leg-arms and waving his scaly lizard tail.

"Nothing that you hear about Grulloos is true," said Frek. "Gibby's a great guy. I met his family. He saved my life a bunch of times."

"Frek's the man," said Gibby. "A real hero, no lie. And he's got the magic potion in his pocket."

"Show me!" exclaimed Renata.

Frek pulled out the egg, and they leaned over it.

"It looks like a jigsaw puzzle," said Geneva. "All different little animals. What's it for?"

"I think I can use it to bring back the missing species," said Frek, forgetting the need for secrecy. "It's full of gene codes, all the codes that NuBioCom erased back in 2666."

"What an imagination," said Lora, giving Frek a sharp look, as if to remind him that the house tree walls were watching and listening, the same as ever, feeding every word to Gov and his counselors. Oops.

"Aren't those codes NuBioCom property?" said Renata. Her voice had gone flat and cold.

"You think NuBioCom owns the genes to Gaia's butterflies?" said Frek, quite unable to let this pass, even if the counselors were listening. "Come on, Renata, don't be a gurp."

"Well, NuBioCom did register the patent," said Renata. "Whether you like it or not. And even if the detailed patent records were destroyed, the restrictions stay in place. You'd have no right to reimplement those codes. Gov wouldn't allow it."

Frek took a step back from Renata and stared at her. What crazy world had he returned to? Suddenly Renata smiled. "Never mind," she said dismissively. "I'm being silly. That's just Yessica's influence on me, I guess. She's made friends with some counselors. They've found her a place to live in Stun City. I might move there, too, now that you're back. She wanted me to wait here for you."

"You seem different," said Frek, no longer sure where they stood. "And—Gov's still in power? I thought maybe—"

He well remembered his fierce joy of seeing Bumby blast the Gov worm into fat cracklings and greasy smoke. But, yes, Gov had mentioned a clone ready to be programmed with his stored memories. Hopefully, these memories didn't include Frek and Bumby killing Gov.

"The new Gov is just like the one before," said Lora, with the slightest downturn of her mouth. "And the puffball's already regenerated itself. We're all very happy. Yessica told us some crazy story about another planet, but none of that's true, is it?"

"Uh—no," said Frek, following his mother's lead. He wasn't going to be able to tell the truth at all. Once again he was pinned beneath the dead weight of his sick, gleepy society.

Wearily he began to lie. "After that alien attacked the puffball, Gibby took me back to the Grulloo Woods and I rested in his burrow. I got better. I'm sorry I was rough with PhiPhi and the other counselors, by the way." The words were ashes in his mouth. How could anyone live this way? Forcing a smile, Frek hefted the elixir egg like a worthless toy. "I might as well admit this is just a rock. I made up all sorts of gollywog stories for Gibby's kids." He shoved the egg back in his pocket. "I guess I'll take my shower."

"Good," said Lora. "I'm so glad you're thinking clearly again. The counselors were worried after you ran away."

"Did they put the peeker uvvy on you?" asked Frek. He'd been fretting about this for a long time.

"No," said Lora in her blandest tone. "Why would they? I have no secrets. It was just that terrible mix-up about the aliens' Anvil thing. Probably because of Carb." A bit of honest curiosity crept into her voice. "Is he coming back, too?"

Frek sighed and shook his head. There were so many things he wanted to say. Was it really any use trying to keep up a front? For now all he said was, "I'm here. And I'm fine."

"Anybody can see Frek doesn't need the Three R's anymore," exclaimed Geneva. "He really is all better." She couldn't resist adding on a little teasing. "Oh oh, Frek—you have to make up a whole week's worth of homework!"

Homework? Frek's mind reeled at the concept. A minute ago he'd been the size of the universe, and now he was back to being a kid who had to worry about gurpy homework?

"We'll be downstairs," said Lora. "I'll get some breakfast ready."

"Breakfast!" squeaked Wow.

"You two dogs go outside where you belong," said Lora. "But, yes, I'll feed you Wow, don't worry. I bet you're glad to see Woo. She's been asking about you."

"Make puppies," said Wow.

"That would be nice," said Lora, not wanting to start trying to explain about the knockout virus. Maybe Wow was as smart at Frek, but it wasn't obvious anymore. He was back to seeming like nothing more than the family dog. "Go on outside with you two. Now."

"What do Grulloos eat, really?" Ida asked Gibby as the dogs clattered down the stairs.

"Stim cell nuggets are the main thing," said Gibby, bending his tail around to give Ida's shoulder a tap. "And little girls." Ida gave a delighted shriek and danced back out of reach. "And if you don't have no nuggets," continued Gibby, "maybe Frek can make me some." The Grulloo glanced up at Renata. "Did you send word to Salla like I told you to?"

"I only got my angelwings from Yessica yesterday," said Renata. "And then I forgot all about Salla."

"I need a lift home," said Gibby with a frown.

"Frek didn't bring back his angelwings," reported Geneva, standing by the window. "And Renata left hers out overnight. Don't you know about keeping them safe from dogs, Renata? How did you lose your wings, Frek?"

"Oh, I'll talk after my shower," said Frek. None of this was working the way it was supposed to. He padded down the hall to the bathroom, threw his clothes on the floor, and stepped into the arched little shower stall. The soft walls sprayed him all over with jets of water, hot and soapy at first, then hot with no soap, then brisk and cold.

Though the shower felt good, the bad thoughts kept coming. Yessica would have tried to improve her position by telling Gov everything she knew—and she knew enough to make Frek seem dangerous—assuming Gov believed her. And he probably would, no matter how many lies Frek and Lora told.

Really, it was a wonder the counselors weren't here already.

Maybe nobody had looked at the feeds from Lora's house tree walls yet today. Things weren't going to stay calm for long, that was for sure. Frek should go underground as fast as possible. Gibby could hide him in the Grulloo Woods. And Renata could come along. They'd change the world from there. Yes.

Frek stepped purposefully from the shower.

As was customary, when Frek stepped out of the shower the house tree wall flopped down a soft absorbent swatch of material, enveloping him to dry off the moisture. Fine, but while the towel was over Frek's head, someone darted into the bathroom. Frek could hear the light footsteps, but he couldn't quite tell who it was.

"Hey," he said, struggling to disentangle himself. Getting clear took just that one or two seconds too long. When he was free, there was nobody around, and his clothes were gone. The pants and purple shirt he'd crafted on Unipusk.

"Mom," shouted Frek, hoping it had just been her, maybe doing laundry.

Nobody answered. From downstairs came the sounds of his family having breakfast. Frek hurried down the hall. The whole second floor was empty, with a morning breeze blowing in through his bedroom's wide open window. His dirty clothes lay in the middle of the bedroom floor. Even before he checked, he could see there was nothing in the pants pocket. Leaning out the window, he heard the faint sound of angelwings beating above the anyfruit tree.

He pulled on some clean clothes and ran down to the kitchen. Lora, Geneva, Ida, and Gibby were sitting at the table, and the dogs were outside chowing down from a big bowl.

"Hi, Frek," said Lora, smiling broadly at the sight of her son. "Our hero! I found some giant raspberries on the anyfruit tree, dear. They'll be yummy with this toasted grobread."

"Where's Renata?" demanded Frek. "Did she fly away?"

"Maybe," said Geneva, glancing out the window. "I don't see her wings on the lawn anymore." She turned to Frek and giggled. "We thought she was still upstairs with you. Renata has a goggy crush on Roarboy. L - O - V - E."

"Love?" spat Frek. "She stole my elixir!" He knew he should act calm for the sake of the eyes in the walls, but he just wasn't able to. He'd traveled to the center of the galaxy, fought with aliens, sacrificed his father, and bounced off the very rim of the universe—only to have the prize picked from his pocket by the girl he'd almost thought he loved.

"Calm down and eat," said Lora sternly. "Act normal."

"No use!" yelled Frek. "Yessica and Renata are gonna sic the counselors on me again, I know it. Come on, Gibby, let's get out of here before it's too late! Let me use your angelwings, Mom!"

Gibby quickly hand-walked over to the kitchen door. Out in the yard, Wow was standing by the abandoned counselor hut barking at the sky. "Oh, Salla," murmured Gibby, peering out and cocking his head.

"What is it?" said Frek.

"I hear them geevin' lifter beetles," said Gibby and sighed, pulling down his hat. "It's too late for us to try to fly. We gotta run for it, Frek. Take us down the back alleys to the river. If we can luck out that far, I'll get us home. I know the riverbanks real good."

"Not again!" wailed Lora. "I can't stand this!"

"We're going to win, Mom," said Frek. Suddenly he felt a deep confidence. He could make weapons by kenny crafting, and even if he couldn't keep the mind worms from spying on him, he had the sky-air-comb autopoiesis to keep them from having too much control. The Orpolese were on his side, and maybe the Magic Pig. "The revolution begins now." He glanced over at the house tree wall. "You hear me, Gov? Your days are over."

When Frek and Gibby stepped out onto the front lawn, they saw lifter beetles coming from every direction. A half dozen of them, carrying counselors with webguns at the ready.

"Craft a blaster," urged Gibby. "Blow them away."

"I—I'm not sure I should," said Frek, suddenly doubting himself. "They're humans."

"Make a blaster!" insisted Gibby. "It's the only way!"

So in the midst of all the confusion, Frek focused on the empty space between his hands, did his best to merge with the emptiness, and tried to vaar some dark matter into a ball of kenner. But nothing was happening, and before he could try again, here came gurpy Zhak and PhiPhi, sprinting across the lawn, Zhak holding a crimson uvvy that looked even more sinister than the yellow peeker uvvy he'd had before.

Frek wanted to run the other way, but two more counselors were coming across that side of the yard, and when he turned back toward the house tree, yet another pair of counselors burst out the front door, carrying jo nets. Wow and Woo were mixing into things as well, barking and snapping. Frek's legs got all tangled up, he tripped over Gibby, and—

Splat.

The sticky jo nets wrapped Frek and Gibby into a single bundle. PhiPhi and Zhak were leaning over Frek once again, the two of them wearing Gov's uvvies on their necks. As before, they were dressed in powder blue overalls.

"Welcome back the space voyager," said PhiPhi. "Big week for small boy. Gov yes saved the memory of you shooting him in case you wondering. And Yessica tell us lots of things."

Wow and Woo seemed ready to bite her—but she produced an electric eel and gave Wow a shock that sent him yelping away, with Woo following after.

"I put the ooey in Frek now?" said Zhak, hefting the crimson uvvy. It was isolated in a transparent membrane or bag, presumably to keep it from fastening onto Zhak himself. The ooey must have been able to smell through the bag, for when Zhak held it near Frek, the blood-colored glob began twitching like a hungry leech. Its surface was covered with soft, hair-fine tendrils that writhed against the membranous sack. Frek was sure the ooey would be capable of filtering itself right through his skin. Teasingly, Zhak toyed with the seal at the top of its bag.

"Hold on," said PhiPhi. "We ask Frek things first. Ooey not well tested, still having wetware problems. We counselors not wearing them yet, you notice, Frek. And since your brain maybe having some peeker damage from last week, is chance ooey can malfunction in you. So we debrief him first, Zhak."

There was a burst of cursing from Gibby, who chose this moment to make a last-ditch effort to tear off their jo nets. But in the end, the nets held them only the tighter. Nevertheless, the sound of Gibby's voice reminded Frek that he wasn't helpless.

Frek focused on the space between his hands, which were bunched against his chest right below his chin. He shut out PhiPhi's pushy voice, the tension of the rubbery net, the rough feel of Gibby's tail against his shoulder, the cries of the other counselors, the sound of Lora yelling from the house, and the sweet smell of the spring morning breeze. Everything was different, everything was the same.

Frek stared at the space between his hands until he saw it shimmer. Breathing evenly, he vaared the dark matter into a nicely striped ball of kenner, nestled between his palms. This was half the battle. The only thing was, the kenner felt a little funny. Instead of passively waiting for him to vaar it into shape, it was twitching, as if it were trying to crawl off.

"Won't answer?" PhiPhi was saying in an sharp tone. She'd been talking all this time, and Frek hadn't heard any of it. She was angry at being ignored. "Come, Zhak," snapped PhiPhi. "We load them into lifter beetle and debrief on way to Stun City. Taking off kid gloves."

"Drop Grulloo splat on ground," chuckled Zhak. "Scare Frek to talk."

"Snap out of it, Frek!" cried Gibby, thrashing so hard that the whole world seemed to shake. "Get somethin' happenin', boy!"

While Zhak, PhiPhi, and another counselor were roughly bundling Frek and Gibby into the cargo basket of PhiPhi's shiny teal lifter beetle, Frek kept his attention upon the little ball of kenner between his hands. He had to press his palms together to keep the willful kenner from wriggling away. Feeling around in his mind, he found the ruby-crystal blaster specs that he'd used on Unipusk. He pushed the spidery diagrams out to make a shell around the borders of his mind. And in the center was the ball of kenner.

Lora loomed up to one side. "Frek! Are you okay?"

Merged with his crafting process, Frek couldn't pause to answer. This was it. He let his carefully arranged images of the blaster descend upon the shuddering ball of kenner. And it turned into—something more like a crippled rat than like a blaster. Something very much like a rat. The malformed kenner-rat bit into the ball of Frek's thumb, drawing blood. And then it squeaked and limped across his chest, slipping down to land on Gibby's face. Gibby bellowed, and the kenner-rat leaped into the air—where it disintegrated back into invisible dark matter.

Meanwhile the lifter beetle rose up, leaving Frek's family behind. Frek caught a last glimpse of Lora, Geneva, Ida, and the two dogs sadly staring up at them. He pressed his hands together, stanching the trickle of blood. He was remembering the last words Gawrnier had said to him about kenny crafting: "Never work with kenner that tries to fight your will."

"Where's the geevin' blaster, Frek?" muttered Gibby.

"It's not gonna happen," answered Frek. "I can't craft kenner here."

"Talking now?" said PhiPhi, whirling around in her seat to glare at him. "Answer my question, or Zhak throwing ugly Grulloo buddy overboard."

"What question?" said Frek. "I didn't hear."

"Not play dumb," cried PhiPhi. She snatched a short brown eel out of her pouch and reached back with it to tap Frek on the neck. A terrible electric shock traveled through Frek's chest and down his spine, driving an odd, involuntary chirp from his mouth. His muscles spasmed and went limp.

"Answer question," repeated PhiPhi.

"I really didn't hear you before," said Frek, hating how frightened he felt. "Say it again."

"Throw out Grulloo now?" said Zhak, who'd turned around in his seat as well. They were hovering some five hundred meters above the ground, outside of Middleville on the way to Stun City.

"Please tell him the question again," begged Gibby. "He surely wants to answer!"

"Okay, you listen good," said PhiPhi. "Yessica say aliens watching us like toons. Yessica say aliens can change what we do. Yessica say Frek is representing humanity for this deal. Gov want Frek tell aliens to make Gov strong. Will Frek do?"

"Sure," said Frek, with a bit of a sneer. "Anything you say."

"Not enough," said PhiPhi sharply. "Tell more." She scowled and leaned toward him with the electric eel. The kritter had tiny red eyes, blank as two glass beads.

"They call it the humanity channel," said Frek, talking fast. "These branecasters from another dimension are broadcasting our thoughts. And some sunspot aliens from the galactic core are our, like, sponsors. The Orpolese. I picked them instead of these uptight other aliens called Unipuskers. When the Orpolese fully launch the show, the individual Orpolese subscribers will be able to affect what people on Earth do. I'm not sure how that's gonna come down. We'll be like toons in a game played by Orpolese aliens. I'd really like to try and—"

"Now we get somewhere," interrupted PhiPhi. "You saying like Yessica. She say if Orpolese not helping Gov, we can kill you and Yessica talk to branecasters and let Unipuskers run humanity channel instead. Yessica say Unipuskers is better bet for Gov."

"Oh, you can trust me to make the switch if you like," said Frek quickly. "Yessica's a grinskin. You don't want to work with her."

"But we not trusting you," said PhiPhi. "Not yet, anyhow." She winked at Zhak. "Give Frek his ooey. Remember, Zhak, the ooey must crawl in through left eye socket to stick on left half of brain. Not right side. This side." PhiPhi tapped one of her angular cheekbones.

Zhak grimaced, showing a black tooth Frek hadn't noticed before. Zhak was fiddling with the ooey bag, undoing the seal. The bag's top flopped open, and Frek caught a smell compounded of disinfectant and decay. Zhak leaned into the carrier basket, his glittering eyes fixed upon Frek's. The web had drawn itself so tight that Frek could barely move his head. Zhak came closer, balancing the sack with the excited ooey right over Frek's face.

Someone please help me, thought Frek, not saying it out loud, as he didn't want to give PhiPhi and Zhak the satisfaction. But wasn't anyone watching over him? Frek could feel the golden glow. Surely there were espers looking through his eyes. Where were the Magic Pig and the Orpolese?

The living blood-clot of the ooey stretched a first tendril down toward the corner of Frek's eye. Help!

And then, finally, the welcome chaos of an Orpolese donut darted in, surrounding them with luminous orange walls. The Orpolese craft felt large on the inside, maybe a hundred meters across. Suspended in the center of the pumpkin-colored interior was a giant ebony cuttle-fish, his curves rippling with iridescent fringes of color. In an instant, one of his glistening black tentacle-tips had snatched up the ooey and vaporized it in a puff of light. Two other tentacles plucked PhiPhi and Zhak from their seats and held them high in midair, while other black tendrils tore apart Frek's and Gibby's bonds.

"Gov getting you for this, Frek," called PhiPhi, her voice shaking.

Meanwhile Frek and Gibby clambered out of the cargo basket and into the lifter beetle's front seats. Immediately the beetle settled to the curved orange floor of the donut and folded its veined wings beneath its metallic teal blue wing covers. It had a stubborn look about its compound eyes.

A flock of teardrop-shaped tweets spiraled down from a nub on the inner surface of the rind surrounding them. The tweets flew through Gibby, the beetle, and the humans as easily as if they were fog. Frek knew from past experience that the Orpolese were sampling their thoughts. The great black cuttlefish edged closer to talk.

"Yubba you," said the alien, rolling from side to side, brandishing PhiPhi and Zhak like a witch-doctor's dolls. "I'm Vlan, and we're in-side my main squeeze Tagine. Time to close the deal, Frek." These were Bumby and Ulla's grandchildren.

"Tangerine?" said Gibby as if not understanding the name.

"Mandarin, kumquat, satsuma, tangerine," riffed Vlan. "But the name is Tagine like the popular Moroccan dish. Meat, chard, and anyfruit steamed under a glazed clay cone, yubba. My sweet sour Tagine. You saw us get born?" Like Bumby before him, Vlan spoke in bursts and spirals.

"We saw it," said Frek. "Whaler and Tusky pinched you off. What do you mean about closing a deal?"

"Activating the esper feedback loop is what you very well know I mean, bad boy. Don't scheme on burning us. A deal's a deal. For sure we're working our end." Vlan waggled the struggling figures of PhiPhi and Zhak once again. "You got your elixir, and, yo, I'm here when you need me."

"But I lost the elixir," said Frek, mentally scrambling for ways to postpone the Orpolese control over humanity. "Renata stole it."

"Never mind," said Vlan, drifting still closer. Like Bumby, the Orpolese cuttlefish had yellow eyes with W-shaped pupils. On big Vlan, the eyes were intimidating. "Our audience is raring to go; they're solar-flaring a Congo beat. Start the, start the, start the show! Fact is, getting your elixir in action is one of our gamers' priority tasks. We've already got ten thousand customers, Frek—signed, aligned, and paradigmed." Vlan extended a tentacle toward Frek, forming the tip into the shape of a shiny black hand. "Press the flesh, bro. Squeeze me tight."

Frek knew full well that shaking Vlan's pseudohand was going to change everything. But at this point he had no other choice. The hand-shaped tip of the Orpolese alien's tentacle was firm and pleasant to the touch. Frek gave it a quick shake and broke contact. They'd closed the deal.

Right away Frek had the sense of something trying to latch onto his brain—an Orpolese player wanting to control him. He pushed the oncoming glow into the space around him; he made his thoughts as clear and permeable as air; he imagined combing his brain's patterns into their natural state. Sky-air-comb. The player slid aside, unable to take root or gain purchase.

Meanwhile Vlan set down Zhak and PhiPhi on the pumpkin floor beside Frek. All of a sudden the two counselors had tiny little donut-shaped halos floating above their heads, as if they were old-time cartoon angels. PhiPhi's donut halo was pale green with dark blue veins, while Zhak's was smooth gray with bilious yellow markings.

"We like to show the players' icons above their talent avatars," said Vlan by way of explanation. "We bootstrap off the talent's wave function to realize a model into the talent world." Clear as mud.

"I will help you now, Frek," said PhiPhi. "Logging in Hexatope from galactic core. PhiPhi-Hexatope front and center for kicking Govvy butt." She twitched spastically, nearly fell down, then caught her balance and lurched closer. "You need help to fly lifter beetle. Beetle only listen to PhiPhi. I fly you Stun City for the revolution. Shut up, Gov!" With a quick motion, PhiPhi whipped her hand up and tore the uvvy off her neck and tossed it on the floor.

"Me yes too," said Zhak, casting away his own uvvy. "Logging in Gaga. Want slash puffball with sword." By way of demonstration, Zhak began executing a series of karate moves, circling around the gently curving orange floor.

Though Zhak was initially awkward, as the distant gray esper learned the counselor's body parameters, the twists and lunges took on an inhuman smoothness and intensity. Soon Zhak was executing the supernaturally deft katanas of a martial arts toon character. A final somersault and twist brought the counselor to a standstill directly before Frek.

"Zhak-Gaga report for action. We fly to Stun City and recruit." The little gray and yellow halo wobbled above his head.

"Urk," interrupted Gibby, still sitting next to Frek in the beetle's pod. "Urk, urk, urk." There was the ghost of a halo above the Grulloo, a pink and blue thing that kept flickering in and out of visibility. Gibby was fighting the takeover.

"Sky-air-comb!" Frek urged his friend. "Diffuse the signal. Don't give the esper any clear thoughts to latch onto. Focus on your self. You can do it, Gibby." Frek laid his hand on Gibby's scaly tail, willing strength into his friend. Gibby shuddered, struggling to keep the esper off. But his struggles were weakening; the pink halo looked nearly as real as Gibby's brown skin.

"Let him alone," Frek cried to Vlan. "Leave Gibby and Renata and our families out of it."

"You got it," said Vlan, and then made some slobbering, chirping noises for the benefit of Gibby's halo. The pink bagel disappeared, and Frek could see Gibby becoming his old self. But for the moment, the Grulloo was too wrung-out to talk.

"Hella many fleshapoids," continued Vlan. "Even if we spare a few. Eleven thousand Orpolese espers and five billion humans real-time census, tick-tick! Got a ten-percent subscription bump soon as we went live. Fat spike of flame-brains spinning toward Stun City, you understand. Everybody wants to see Frek make the walls come a-tumblin' down. Blow your horn, baby. Squonk it. Me, I'm out of the picture for now. Bye-and-bye."

Abruptly Tagine irised open a hole beneath the lifter beetle. It was all that PhiPhi and Zhak could do to clamber into the beetle's cargo basket before they all dropped clear of the glowing orange donut.

"Yee haw!" whooped Gibby from the front seat beside Frek. He was fully in control of himself again, reckless and devil-may-care. "I'm lovin' it, Frek!" They were falling like a stone, the wind whistling past. The Grulloo rose up on his arm-legs and peered into the back. "You two losers grokkin' this? Ready to splat?"

"Beetle fly!" shouted PhiPhi and, hearing her voice, the kritter flipped up its teal wing-covers and let its wings cut the air. "Fly Stun City," added PhiPhi.

"I want to find Renata," said Frek. "I bet she's with Yessica. Do you know where Yessica is, PhiPhi?"

"No," said PhiPhi. "My work mostly in Middleville. We land Stun City ask around, maybe we can find her."

Frek had to wonder if, even with Gov's uvvy gone and the Orpolese controlling her, PhiPhi was totally on his side. Meanwhile, their flight leveled out. The sun was still near the horizon, flooding the world with kind morning light. Below them was the winding green River Jaya, with the occasional elephruk lumbering along the sandy road beside it. Across the river were the bluffs and the dense Grulloo Woods, gently tossing in the breeze. A second road ran along the top of the bluffs, traversed by a few Grulloos with their own little elephruks.

"Do you want to go home?" Frek asked Gibby. "We could fly you there fast."

"Negatory, good bud," said Gibby. "I ain't gonna miss no revolution. With them Orpolese runnin' half the town, we'll romp all over Stun City. We'll tear up that puffball and get them new genes a-growin'."

"Yes," said Frek. "But I wonder what happens after that?"

"You worry too much, kid," said Gibby, staring over at the Grulloo road atop the bluffs. "It's a beautiful day. I feel some verses comin' on." Gibby tapped out a rhythm on the lifter beetle's side and sang.

Today I ride a beetle, as buggy as can be.
He wiggles his antennae, and thinks these words to me.

"I just been to Nubbie town, I'm flyin' toward the puffball,
I hate to beat my wings so long without a decent gut-full."

"Let's stop and score some grub," I cry,
"I'm empty too, and awful dry."
I turn around and poke the counselor.
"See that elephruk? Let's pounce on her!"

And with that, Gibby did turn around to prod PhiPhi's knee and, just as he'd hoped, she sent the beetle sloping across the river to alight beside an elephruk traversing the Grulloo road at the top of the bluffs.

And it wasn't just any elephruk, it was Gibby's old Dibble, recognizable by the sour expression on her face. Riding on Dibble's head was a red-jacketed Grulloo peaceably smoking a pipe. Yes, it was none other than Gibby's neighbor Jeroon, bringing home a basket of stim cell nuggets from Stun City.

"Kac howdy, Jeroon!" exulted Gibby, rocking across the road on his gnarled pair of arm-legs, keeping his balance by beating his scaly tail. "Don't worry about them counselors in our lifter beetle. We got 'em under control."

"The prodigal husband," said Jeroon, puffing out a cloud of smoke. "You missed my wedding. You and this gang been on a spree? I see you've still got that Nubbie boy with you. Hi, Frek!"

Frek called out a greeting. Evidently Jeroon wasn't being run by an esper, as he didn't have a halo. Probably the Orpolese gamers were focusing on the people in the cities.

"Paw!" called a piercing voice from the elephruk's bed. It was red-haired little Bili, showing his sharp yellow teeth in an open-mouthed smile.

Gibby's joy knew no bounds. "Bili! You lookin' so good!" In an instant, Gibby had scuttled over and wrapped his limbs around his little son, pressing the tiger-tailed boy against his face. "I never thought I'd made it back to these woods," said Gibby. "Salla's okay? And LuHu?"

"They're fine, Paw," said Bili, squirming at the tight embrace. "We were wondering about you." Like Gibby and Jeroon, Bili didn't have a halo.

"I was wondering, too," said Gibby. "But now I'm almost home." He turned his face up to the sky. "Thank you, Gaia, for bringing me this close." Tears were running down his hard, flat cheeks.

"Salla enlisted me to fetch you and Dibble," said Jeroon. "I couldn't stop your lad from tagging along, although I'd expected to find you besotted in the Brindle Cowloon."

Without missing a beat, Gibby switched from thanking Gaia to yelling at Jeroon.

"Nosin' into my business and my family life, are you?" he hollered, quickly drying his face. "You shoulda got three times as many nuggets as that. You been suckered by Phamelu. Why ain't you home with your new wife instead of takin' over my affairs? You got your eyes on Salla or somethin'?"

"Oh, of course," said Jeroon sarcastically. "I've completely abandoned my bride, Ennie. My highest goal in life is to wear the great Gibby's mantle. If only I, too, could be a stupid, ill-tempered, unreliable, ungrateful moolk-guzzler. Surely that must be any Grulloo's fondest dream."

Gibby glared at Jeroon for a moment without saying anything, and then he recovered his equilibrium. "Don't mind me," he said. "I'm just hungry. I been to the center of the galaxy, the edge of the universe and back, Jeroon. I gotta eat some of them stim cell nuggets."

"Help yourself," said Jeroon calmly. "That's a long voyage you're talking about. If it's true. Say, Frek, did you find any use for the chameleon mod and the Aaron's Rod I gave you?"

"They saved me three times," said Frek. Meanwhile Gibby stuffed a handful of stim cell nuggets in his mouth, passing a few to Bili as well. The lifter beetle was avidly grazing upon the roadside shrubs.

"Eat fast, Gibby," urged Frek. "I want to get to Stun City and look for Renata." Something occurred to him then. "Hey, Jeroon, when you were in Stun City, did you notice a really annoying woman named Yessica Sunshine?"

"Most all Nubbies are annoying," said Jeroon. "What's this Yessica like?"

"Well—she has long blond hair she wears all tangled. She has small eyes, she frowns a lot, and—oh, yeah—she has three pairs of breasts running down her chest."

"*That* woman," said Jeroon. "Yes, I saw her. She was sitting behind the counter with Phamelu at the Brindle Cowloon, the two of them gossiping and hatching plans like a pair of sisters."

"Let's go there," said Frek to PhiPhi. "I just know Yessica's got Renata. Get back in the lifter beetle if you're coming along, Gibby." Though Frek hated to pull Gibby away from his family, he kind of hoped the Grulloo would come along for the denouement.

"Don't leave again, Paw," said Bili.

"Hold on," called Gibby to Frek. "Don't be in such a dang rush. And don't even think of goin' without me. If you're gonna use that elixir, you need to bring it inside the Kritterworks. And I'm the fella knows his way in there."

"Okay," said Frek tensely.

"I got a powerful hankerin' to smoke a pipe," continued Gibby. "How about it, Jeroon? I know you always carry a spare. I lost mine somewheres along the line."

Jeroon handed Gibby a couple of matchbuds and his spare pipe, already full of tobacco. Gibby seated himself in the road, lit the pipe, and tucked the remaining matchbud into his coat pocket. "That's more like it," he said, exhaling a plume of smoke and snuggling Bili against his side.

"Gibby," implored Frek. "I'm worried about Renata."

"Me, I'm worried about my son," said Gibby. "So shut your crack. Looky here, Bili. I brang some stuff home from my trip for you."

"Yeah, Paw?" said Bili, grinning up at his father.

Comfortably puffing his borrowed pipe, Gibby rooted through his coat pockets, producing five small items. "Souvenirs for you and LuHu. See this here statue of a guy with a shell for his head? That's a Unipusker. And this blue pebble, that's what the ground looks like on Unipusk. This other little rock, the foamy-looking one, that's a star-cinder I found drifting through space at the galaxy's core. And this here's a key what some bad guys used to lock up our friends Bumby and Ulla. And last of all, this shiny disk, that's a scale from a flying fish name of Aunt Guszti; me and Frek rode on her back. Now you share these with LuHu, son, and wait for me, and I'll be home tomorrow or the next day to tell all about how I got 'em."

"Look what my paw gave me," called Bili to Jeroon, holding up the delicately crafted statuette of the Unipusker.

"Lovely," said Jeroon.

Gibby gave Bili one more kiss, returned the half-smoked pipe to Jeroon, hand-walked over to the foraging lifter beetle, and hopped back in. "You hurry up and tell Maw I'm almost home," Gibby called to Bili. "I just gotta look after Frek a little bit longer." And then the four of them were back in the air again, following the River Jaya to Stun City.

Soon Stun City came into view, its curiously formed buildings rising from lush lanes of house trees and aircoral, everything tinged yellow by the slanting morning sun.

The bulbous torus of the NuBioCom puffball was wholly regenerated; presumably Gov's new clone was lodged inside like a worm in an apple. Frek studied the round windows, wondering if his enemy knew what was coming.

Closer than the puffball was the cored-out Kritterworks cube on the banks of the River Jaya, two solid walls showing animated billboards. Rather than airing ads for new model kritters, the billboards were displaying pictures of Orpolese donuts flying among a sea of suns. The aliens had lost no time in settling in. The giant firefly hologram at the apex of the Toonsmith cone was showing a twisty green and red Orpolese donut as well.

As always, Frek's heart rose at the sight of the helical Toonsmithy. Perhaps, once all the dust had settled, things would go back to normal, and Frek could still get a job as a toonsmith. Surely if he could design a game based on this week's adventures, it would be a hit.

The streets of Stun City were thronged with people, with a general motion toward the city center. PhiPhi guided the lifter beetle to the Brindle Cowloon in its pasture at the near edge of town.

The once-lush pasture beside the inn was blasted and black. Frek recalled how the sky-jelly's pale red death ray had twitched across the landscape last Saturday.

The floating cowloon bag was still bobbing in back, the bar was manned as usual by the weasel-faced Pede, but no customers were in sight. PhiPhi sloped down past the wildly ornamental shapes upon the inn's roof and landed by the front door.

Phamelu was sitting behind the Brindle Cowloon counter, watching Da Nha Duc toons on the wall skin. She glanced over at Frek and the others, putting on her disarmingly pleasant smile. A little blue Orpolese halo bobbed above her honey-colored hair.

"Hi, Frek," she said, a friendly expression crinkling the corners of her eyes. "Or should I still call you Huckle? I see you've brought your friends along. Gibby, PhiPhi-Hexatope, and Zhak-Gaga." Even though Phamelu had the halo, Frek hesitated before answering. An Orpolese alien might not know where to begin when it came to changing this woman's duplicitous behavior.

"Hi, Phamelu-Wilco," put in PhiPhi, tacking on what must have been the name of the Orpolese player who was currently gaming the Phamelu body.

"Is Yessica here?" Frek asked Phamelu.

"She left for the puffball," answered the innkeeper. "She wanted to take your elixir to Gov. For some reason she didn't get an Orpolese master."

"Oh no," said Frek, suddenly remembering what he'd said to Vlan. Leave Gibby and Renata and our families out of it. Buddha, was he dumb.

"I would have tried to stop her," continued Phamelu, as usual saying what her listener wanted to hear. Her eyes flicked back to the toons. "But with half the town in play, things are getting crazy. I was able to talk my master into letting us stay here and watch over my place. There's nobody here but me and Pede. Go have a drink of moolk, Gibby, it's on the house."

"No thanks," said Gibby. "Not just now."

"What about Renata?" pressed Frek.

"Who's that?" said Phamelu with an innocent smile, but then her face twitched and changed expression. "She's upstairs," said Phamelu, unwillingly voicing the words of her Orpolese controller, Wilco. "Unconscious. The real reason I let Phamelu wait here is so I could watch what happens when Frek shows up and finds Renata. This should be tasty. A scene of high emotion." And then Phamelu's usual persona took over again. "Wilco's just kidding. You better head for the puffball."

"Come on!" Frek called to his three companions, and the four of them went pounding up the stairs with Phamelu close behind. And there, in the very same room where he and Gibby had slept, Frek found Renata, lying motionless on the bed with her face turned toward the wall. It broke Frek's heart to see his friend brought so low.

"She has an ooey," came Phamelu-Wilco's voice. She'd followed them up and was watching avidly from the door. "Yessica installed it when she visited Renata in Middleville the other day. Gov wants to make a deal with you."

"No deal," said PhiPhi-Hexatope before Frek could respond. "I can fix her fast." She produced a tiny silvery whistle and leaned over Renata. The whistle sounded a pure, sweet note.

The skin at the back of Renata's head rippled. PhiPhi pushed aside Renata's heavy pigtails and whistled again. A single blood-red ooey tendril broke through the milky white nape of the girlish neck. PhiPhi kept on calling the ooey. More and more tendrils appeared, and soon the whole mass had oozed out through Renata's skin.

"Gundo geevey," muttered Gibby.

"Sack it, Zhak," said PhiPhi.

With a quick motion, Zhak scooped the ooey into his membranous little ooey sack and sealed the top.

"No, Mom," muttered Renata, twitching her arms. "Don't."

"Renata," said Frek, leaning over her. Though her eyes were open, it took a long, scary minute until she could see him. "Renata," repeated Frek, kissing her on the cheek. "It's okay now."

"Oh, Frek," said Renata, flinging her arms around him. "Mom made me steal your elixir! Everything's going wrong." And then she pushed him away and sat up. "Can we still save it? She's taking it to Gov."

"It not too late," said PhiPhi. "Lots of Orpolese-run people in the street. Orpolese passing the word all over Earth. All the Govs getting torn down."

"Let's go," said Frek.

"Me too," said Phamelu-Wilco. "I'll get my lifter beetle."

"Me and Zhak can ride with her," said Gibby to Frek. "So you can be with Renata."

The two beetles buzzed across town toward the puffball. As they flew, Frek thought about the fact that Phamelu spoke of the Orpolese as 'masters,' rather than as 'players.' Like or not, that was closer to the truth. Where was it all going to end? One thing at a time, Frek told himself. Get the elixir, restore the biome, and then worry about the humanity channel.

And now, yes, below them in the cobblestone-paved puffball square was Yessica, struggling with a young pair of Orpolese-controlled locals.

The man and woman holding Yessica were gently bouncing on sacks of skin that grew from the soles of their bare feet. Their knees bent backward, like bird legs. It was the same couple who'd talked to Frek when he'd been looking for the puffball the week before. Try as Yessica might, she couldn't get free of them to run the last twenty meters to Gov's puffball.

Frek would have expected a squadron of counselors to come rushing out to help Yessica. But the counselors and scientists all had Orpolese halos by now. The few who remained inside the puffball were leaning out the windows. They cheered and laughed when Frek and his companions landed, many of them calling Frek's name.

Gov wasn't powerless yet. As if to punish the employees for defecting, the floors inside the puffball rooms bucked up, pitching the watchers out of the windows. Most of them managed to slide safely down the puffball's curved wall, but a few crashed heavily to the ground and lay twitching. At the same time, a few dozen tendrils sprouted from the puffball's cornice. Something bad was going to happen.

Frek sprinted over to Yessica.

"Goggy greetings," said the woman holding Yessica. Her tongue was green between her lips. "Remember us—Glen and Gillian? We grabbed the grabber for you."

"She's got your gaussy gene juice," said the man, nodding his head toward Yessica. "The godzoon grow-stuff!" His and Gillian's halos were a light and a dark green.

Frek didn't even try to talk to Yessica. Her hair was webbed across her face and her mouth was pursed in fury. Dodging her kicking legs, Frek reached into the purse that hung from her shoulder and pulled out, yes, the elixir egg.

"No, Frek," said Yessica. "You'll ruin everything Gov's worked for." She looked past Frek to Renata. "Don't let them treat your mother this way, dear. I was only trying to get the best for us."

"Look out," bellowed Gibby. A stinking ball of flame bloomed beside them. Gov's tendrils were throwing firebombs: fatty, phosphorous-laden jelly bags of combustible gas.

"Gleepy!" said Glen, baring his green gums in a grimace. A bit of flaming jelly had landed on one of his backward-folding legs. He released Yessica and slapped at his leg, high-stepping away from the puffball. Yessica twisted free of Gillian and sprinted toward the puffball door. Gillian let her go, and bounded after Glen.

"Come back, Mom!" shouted Renata.

"Let her go," said Frek. "She'll be okay. She always is. You have to look out for yourself now."

Another of the vile fire-bombs splattered on the cobblestones beside them, engulfing PhiPhi's lifter beetle in a blazing stench. The beetle let out a terrible twittering screech as it died. The rest of them were unharmed.

"Let's head for the Kritterworks!" shouted Gibby over the roar of the flames. "We need to seed them artigrows!" The Grulloo took off across the cobblestones, leading the way. Frek and Renata followed on foot, with the three others tagging along in Phamelu's lifter beetle.

As they made their way downhill through the winding streets of Stun City, more and more Orpolese-run Nubbies joined the procession, many of them shouting Frek's name. He was riding a wave of adulation. It was very strange.

"What's going on, Frek?" asked Renata. "Why does everyone know you?"

"It's the Orpolese," said Frek. "They're controlling all these people like toons in a game. The humanity channel branecast is in full effect."

"But we're still free?" said Renata. "I know you have that sky-air-comb trick, but why aren't the Orpolese driving me? I can feel them watching through my eyes. Esping me. The golden glow."

"I asked them not to control you or Gibby," said Frek.

"Thanks," said Renata. "It's nice to be myself again." She patted the turkle on her belt. "I haven't been able to draw since I got the ooey."

"I knew something was wrong," said Frek, smiling at her. "At least the ooey couldn't stop you from showing me the way home. See the Toonsmithy over there?"

"Finally," said Renata. "I want to show them my drawings. You said you know a woman toonsmith, right?"

"Sure," said Frek, even though this was a bit of an exaggeration. "Her name's Deanna." Now that he was famous the toonsmiths would probably listen to him.

They arrived at the great square door of the Kritterworks. The building's facade was punctuated by the mouths of airshafts that ran through the great cube. The whole building was gently throbbing—breathing, as it were. Like a house tree or the puffball, it was a single living thing.

The crowd halted behind Frek, expectantly watching his every move. Renata's eyes ranged over the mass of people. "This is gaud," she said. "Everyone has a colored halo except for you, Gibby, and me. The haloes are, like, icons of the Orpolese players?"

"That's it," said Frek. "The masters. I don't know if we'll ever get rid of them. But right now it's good to have them around." He raised his hand and waved to the crowd.

"Frek!" they roared. "Elixir!"

The sides of the Kritterworks were showing images of people destroying Gov puffballs all over Earth.

"Stop grandstandin' and swing the bat," said Gibby. "Let me tell you about the Kritterworks, Frek. Sometimes I deliver Grulloo eggs down here instead of up to the puffball. The Kritterworkers chop up our eggs to make embryo blanks, what it is. They got mommy longlegs spiders that run around settin' the embryo blanks into the artigrows. And the Kritterworkers use what you call gene wasps to seed the blanks with kritter wetware."

"Sounds pretty funky," said Renata with a little laugh. "I'll help you, Frek. It'll be like the creation myth in that old religious book—the Bible? We can be Eve and Adam."

"What's that make me?" put in Gibby.

"My best friend," said Frek, patting the side of his thick lizard tail. "I wouldn't have made it this far without you."

At first the Kritterworks door wouldn't open for them, but then one of the haloed Kritterworkers within persuaded the door to unlock. She was a lanky old woman with a shock of gray hair sticking out on both sides. She held tight to the door, and didn't let in anyone but Frek, Renata, and Gibby.

"I'm Hanna," said the overalled woman. She had a thin face with glowing eyes. Her halo was bronze with woody-brown highlights. "And of course I know all about you. I think we've doped out a way to get your codes into our gene wasps."

The Kritterworks space was dimly lit, the living walls ledged with seemingly endless rows of reddish-purple gutters. A steady flow of clear nutrient ichor flowed through the troughs, gently cascading from one to the next. Sitting in the gutters were the artigrows, scaly teardrop-shaped buds like old-time artichokes, resting on their fat ends with their pointed ends up. Picking their way along the gutters were hundreds of plump hairy spiders on long articulated legs, reaching into the artigrows one by one.

"The mommy longlegs are eating the embryos we'd started," said Hanna. "They're putting in fresh embryo blanks. In other words, we're getting ready for you. Come on up to the prep room and we'll see about the wasps. Eadweard's very excited."

"Walk slow," said Renata, her fingernail dancing across the surface of her turkle. "I have to sketch some of this. Save, turkle. Fresh page."

They walked alongside the dimly lit walls of gently trickling gutters until they came to a rubbery, irregular staircase, with short flights mixed in among the long. Walking beside an artist made Frek look at things more intently than usual. The stairs led to a clear-walled dome set into the long airy gallery that cored through the heart of the Kritterworks cube.

A bearded man in overalls was waiting in the prep room. "I amm Eadwearrd," he said, stepping forward.

A very large, clean table was set against the far side of the room, as shiny as if freshly extruded from the floor. The walls were mostly covered with a papery insect nest, a gray, undulating congeries of hexagonal cells, alive with wasps the size of Frek's little finger—gene wasps. They had glittering red eyes, stubby gossamer wings with intricate lavender veins, elegantly curved bodies striped black and green, and prominent stingers at their rears. A number of them were feeding from a trough of mush, others were rubbing feelers with their fellows or sleepily crawling about upon the gray surface of the nest. And who knew how many more were inside the thousands of covered cells.

The bearded Eadweard held his slender hands drawn up against his chest, rubbing them together like a housefly cleaning his legs. His Orpolese halo was iridescent black with shiny green markings, just like the body of a gene wasp. "You havve the elixirr?" he asked. His voice hummed and hissed; he made clicking sounds between his words.

"Here it is," said Frek, drawing the egg from his pocket. The two Kritterworkers sucked in their breath. Renata's fingernail was scratching frantically across her turkle, trying to keep up.

"Crack the egg, I think," said Hanna, excitedly gesturing. "Tap it on the big table we made. The gene wasps will buzz down and read the codes. They'll copy a genome apiece, cook up DNA in their stinger glands, go seed some embryos, then fly back and do it again. It'll take a load of trips to instantiate all these new species."

"*Olld* sspecies," corrected Eadweard with a smile that revealed overlapping yellow teeth. "Whatt a cornucopiaa!"

Frek gazed at the intricately patterned surface of his elixir egg, at the myriad of little creature icons tiled together.

"Go ahead, Frek," said Renata. "Do it."

Gibby hopped up onto the tabletop to watch. The table was easily three meters across. Frek gave his egg a sharp downward rap against the broad, smooth surface. The egg shattered into millions of pieces. Some residual Planck brane force drew the tiny plantlets and animalcules into a tidy array, aligning them like iron filings in a magnetic field, marshaling them into a grid with thousands of rows and columns, a square of life two meters in size.

"Come, my pretty buzzers!" sang Hanna in a musical tone. "We have an army of new codes!"

At first only a few gene wasps responded. As they delicately hovered above the grid of tiny gene models, Eadweard spoke to them in buzzes and pops. Apparently he could speak the language of insects.

Eadweard must have told the wasps to start at the upper left corner of the grid and to work their way across and down, for that's what they did. As it happened, the tiny figure at the starting location happened to be the first gene icon that Frek had saved. The red-breasted robin. A gene wasp hovered over the robin, studying it with compound eyes and touching the icon all over with long, stiff feelers. And then the wasp buzzed out through a hole in the clear ceiling that Frek hadn't noticed before.

"His little stinger will seed a few score artigrows at the farthest corner of the cube," said Hanna. "Males and females he'll create. And then, zoom, he'll be back to learn another one." She lifted her voice in melody. "Come come, you sweet striped buzzers!"

Quite a swarm of the gene wasps lifted out of the wall-sized nest. Unsettled by the cloud of insects, Gibby hopped off the counter and hand-walked back to the head of the stairs. Frek and Renata joined him, brushing the gene wasps away from their faces. Eadweard crouched by the table, hissing and clicking, ensuring that the gene wasps copied each code once and once only.

"All is well," called Hanna. "We'll release your new creatures as they mature. We have lifter beetles to carry them to promising habitats. And once we've copied everything, we'll start over."

"We'll keep att itt," twittered Eadweard. "Yess. A nnew Edenn. Only onne taskk remainns."

"We must bring down all the Govs," intoned Hanna. "Make them stop puffing out their filthy knockout virus mist. Let our reborn plants and animals freely breed. Go, Frek, and bring down the Stun City puffball."

"*Gubernator delenda est,*" said Frek, remembering Bumby's phrase. Gov must be destroyed.

"Yes," said Hanna. "The door will let you out."

"Look, there goes a wasp," said Renata, as she, Frek, and Gibby headed down the gutter-lined hall toward the exit. A gene wasp flew past them to hover over the artigrows closest to the door, its red eyes glinting. Wings abuzz, it lowered itself onto one of the plump green buds and forced its abdomen into the artigrow's heart, feeling for the embryo blank. Having read one of the codes stored in Frek's icons, the gene wasp had synthesized the DNA for the corresponding creature. "I wonder what it's making," continued Renata, sketching the wasp's bent body as she talked. "A coconut palm? A snowshoe rabbit? A luna moth? I'm so proud of you, Frek."

Gibby was at the door, uneasily peering out at the waiting crowd. "I been seein' the fight pictures up on the walls," he said, nodding toward a billboard facing the Kritterworks. "Lot of people gettin' killed. How about them Orpolese helpin' us here, Frek? Vlan could blast Gov the way Bumby did."

"I think they want to stay out of sight," said Frek. "If the espers have us do it ourselves it makes a better show."

"Man," said Gibby, mournfully rocking from leg to leg. "We might end up dead—and it's all a game for them donut things." He thought a little more. "You sure you can't kenny craft us a blaster or two? Try it again before we go out there in all that mob."

So once again Frek vaared some dark matter into visible kenner; once again he overlaid it with the blueprint of a blaster; once again the object fought him and turned into—something like a crab this time. The kenner-crab would have pinched Gibby's leg-arm if the Grulloo hadn't impaled it with his knife. And then it deliquesced into invisible dark matter.

"I don't think crafting's gonna work here," said Frek. "The dark matter around Earth might be different from the stuff in the Planck brane and the galactic core."

"You don't need blasters anyway," exclaimed Renata. "Look how many people are waiting to help us. They'll tear down the puffball with their bare hands if you tell them to."

"It's too big," protested Gibby. "Gov's throwing flamin' jellies. No sense half the folks in town gettin' killed. Come on, Frek, think of somethin' smart."

"We know where Gov likes to live," said Frek slowly. "We saw his chamber when Bumby shot him before. Phamelu's lifter beetle can fly us up there. I bet the new Gov's in the same place. We'll take a whole bunch of counselors to help. We'll chop our way in with axes, maybe stun Gov with electric eels and chop him up with knives."

"Now you talkin', boy," said the Grulloo, grinning and whetting his blade against the stony Kritterworks floor. "Now you cookin' with gas."

The crowd roared with excitement when the three companions reappeared. It was late afternoon by now, approaching dusk. Frek found it unsettling to have so many people staring at him and yelling. It was so easy to imagine their emotions flipping the other way. But for now, yes, they were ready to follow him. Nearly all the other Govs on Earth were already gone. It was up to them to finish winning the war, right here and now.

Rather than riding with Phamelu—whom he still didn't trust—Frek called a counselor out of the crowd, a dark-haired, wide-mouthed woman with a double chin. Her name was Xondra. She said her heavy-duty lifter beetle would be powerful enough to carry herself, Frek, and both Frek's companions.

They rose up and criss-crossed above the crowd, enlisting a few dozen more haloed counselors to join them. Their lifter beetles formed a swarm, a little air force. Frek sent four of them winging down to the nearby counselor service center to fetch all the weapons in stock—please-plant-grown knives and hatchets plus, of course, electric eels.

While waiting for the arms, Frek addressed the people who'd followed him to the Kritterworks.

"Are you ready to bring down Gov?" he called, feeling his voice as very thin above the rumble of the crowd and the buzzing of the lifter beetles.

But everyone heard. "Yes," they roared back. "Kill Gov!"

"Is that you guys talking, or just your Orpolese players?" shouted Frek—not that people would be able to give an honest answer. But he wanted to believe they were acting with their hearts. "What do you *really* think about NuBioCom?"

Honest or not, the response was reassuring. "We hate Gov!" cried some, while others shouted, "We want the old-time plants and animals back!" A chorus of "Good old days!" arose, and soon everyone was chanting it. "Good old days! Good old days! Good old days!"

Frek held out his hands for silence, hardly believing his gesture would work but, lo and behold, it did. The Nubbies below and the counselors in their lifter beetles watched him expectantly. General Frek Huggins.

"We're going up to the puffball now," said Frek. "You guys on the ground form a ring around the puffball and watch for any of Gov's clones trying to escape. The counselors and I will go for him through the roof. If we can, we'll set the building on fire. And be careful. You've seen the pictures. Gov will use everything he's got."

"You'll lose," boomed a voice from behind Frek. A fifty-meter-high First Nations raven mask was glaring down from the billboard on the Kritterworks outer wall, pushing away the news feeds of the burning Gov puffballs in the other towns. Gov's image, red and black and white. "I'll kill you. And none of your new creatures will breed. I'm the ruler, for ever and ever and ever." The clacking beak was besmirched with blood.

Goaded on by their Orpolese puppetmasters, the assembled citizens shrieked their defiance. Just then the counselors returned with the weaponry—electric eels, knives, machetes, and axes. There were more than enough arms for Frek's "air force," and the extras were passed out to the foot soldiers below, though many of them had already found their own knives and clubs. With a roar they surged up the street toward the puffball, the lifter beetles buzzing in formation with Xondra, Frek, Renata, and Gibby at the head.

As they entered the square surrounding the puffball, Gov began lobbing firebombs again. Zhak, riding in Phamelu's lifter beetle, swooped in past the fireballs and sliced off one, two, three of Gov's tendrils with powerful swings of his machete. Two more counselors joined him. Moments later all the tendrils were gone.

Images of the angry raven flitted across the puffball's skin. The building door irised open and a horde of small kritters came storming out. They were biters, low-slung balls with big jaws and side-mounted running legs. The biters did substantial damage to the leading rank of Nubbies. But the second rank surged forward, wielding their blades and cudgels until all the biters were laid low. The Nubbies reached the wall of the puffball and began cutting their way in.

Meanwhile, Frek's beetle was angling down toward a landing atop the puffball. The building was a fat ring around a central courtyard. Frek was guessing Gov was hidden beneath the rounded top surface at the same compass point as before, slightly to the west of the door facing the square.

Suddenly something wriggled out of the puffball's flesh—a stubby grub-worm, pointed at one end—a space bug! The creature beat its three little wings to gain a few meters of altitude, then ignited the rear of its body, careless about scorching the puffball's crust. It rocketed straight toward Xondra's lifter beetle.

Before Frek had fully registered the danger, Gibby had shoved him and Renata out of the beetle. At the same time Xondra swung the beetle into a desperate futile evasive loop and Gibby—Gibby didn't get out in time.

The fireball flared up as Frek and Renata thumped down onto the doughy top of the puffball. Frek's ankle crunched, he fell flat. He could feel the broken bones rubbing against each other. Straining though the haze of pain, he craned his head, staring up into the smoke and flame. Something dark and writhing spun down and thudded onto the puffball a few meters off.

"Gibby!" wailed Renata. She'd landed well; she was still on her feet. She helped Frek crawl to his friend.

Gibby's tail was charred black, and one of his leg-arms was burnt down to a stub. Yet his other hand was still clutching his knife. "Always knew I'd never make it home," muttered the Grulloo. Blood oozed from his blackened lips.

"We can patch you up, Gibby," said Frek, wildly looking around.

The haloed counselors' lifter beetles were touching down all over the top of the puffball. "Somebody help!" cried Frek. "He's hurt!"

"Frek," said Gibby, fixing him with his eyes, seeing him one last time. "Look out for little Bili, will you? He'll take this mighty hard." And then, just like that, he died.

Frek put his face in his hands, wanting to weep, but not yet able to. Gibby dead? It didn't make sense. Someone jolted him, sending a fire of agony up through his leg.

"Where we find Gov?" It was PhiPhi, hunkering down to wrap a strip of foamskin around Frek's ankle. The foamskin was covered with prickles that bore a numbing agent. It tightened itself around Frek's ankle to form a cast.

"We'll finish him off, Frek," said Renata. "Just show us where."

Gibby's remains lay inert at Frek's side. Still on his knees, Frek straightened out the twisted little body, arranged the worn suede jacket. Only half of Gibby's coat had been burned; the other half was the same rough reddish leather as before. Frek pushed down the eyelids of the Grulloo's staring eyes and took the knife from his stiffening hand.

"Over there," said Frek, looking up at Renata. His voice was weak and cracking. He cleared his throat and tried again. "About twenty meters." He pointed the way with Gibby's knife. "You should be able to cut through to a shaft there." PhiPhi started forward. Frek wanted to follow, but even with the foamskin, he still couldn't stand.

"We'll get him, Frek," said Renata, glancing back at him. She was holding a machete and an electric eel. For once her turkle was neglected, dangling from her waist. "Let's go, PhiPhi!"

Working fast, Renata and the counselors cut away a patch of the puffball's roof and found the shaft. Renata was the first one down into it, slashing footholds and handholds in the mushroom flesh of the walls. The counselors were quick to follow. Moving as fast as he could, Frek crawled over to stare down after them.

"Five meters from the top," he called, remembering just where they'd found Gov before. "It's, like, the second highest floor. In a hidden room toward the outside of the puffball."

"Here he is," sang Renata, sweeping her machete to cut open a flap of fungus. A familiar stench wafted up. Frek saw the twitching gray coils of the immense worm. The counselors pressed around the opening, their electric eels crackling, their knives and machetes chopping away.

The worm's head appeared; he bared his feeble fangs. His dull gray eyes picked out Frek's silhouette at the top of the shaft.

"You'll regret this," hissed the round wet mouth. "It's me who's kept you people going. You'll live like savages."

"Finish him," said Frek, feeling a sense of déjà vu. But this time would be different. This time they'd wipe out all Gov's clones.

With a single blow of her machete, Renata severed the erstwhile ruler's head. It tumbled down the shaft, bouncing from wall to wall.

Frek heard a slithering noise behind him on the puffball roof. It was a pair of space bugs. One of them had a person inside it— Yessica! Her pale unfriendly face was faintly visible through the creature's skin. The space bug righted itself, flapped into the air and blasted off, shooting high up into the sky.

But the other space bug wasn't leaving. It was writhing around to aim itself toward the crowd in the puffball square.

The foamskin had finally taken effect to the point where Frek could walk. Or maybe he was just too excited to feel the pain. Moving fast, he stumped over to the space bug and, using Gibby's knife, lopped off its three wings. The hapless kritter twitched; volatile yellow juice oozed from its wounds. Frek ended the creature's struggles with a stab of his knife to its brain. He dragged the space bug across the surface toward the shaft, pausing on the way by Gibby's body. There was still a matchbud in the red suede coat's intact pocket.

Meanwhile Renata and the counselors had emerged from the shaft. "Everyone in the lifter beetles!" called Frek. "Who's gonna take Renata and me?"

"I will," said a dark-skinned counselor named Trina.

"Get Gibby!" Frek told Renata. "Please bring Gibby, too."

Frek balanced the dead space bug at the edge of the open puffball shaft. He used Gibby's matchbud to fire up the space bug, then tipped it in. The flaming creature pinwheeled around, spewing fire in every direction and then, just as Frek had hoped, its head lodged in the chamber where Gov had lived. The steady blast of its rocket torch played across the opposite wall of the shaft, cutting deeper and deeper into the puffball's flesh.

"We're outa here!" yelled Frek, finally getting into Trina's beetle beside Renata and poor dead Gibby.

As Trina's beetle lifted them up, the space bug's torch found the bodies of the other space bugs hidden within the giant mushroom. And now, as the sun sank toward the horizon, the pale toroidal building began going off like a fireworks display. The puffball collapsed in upon itself, becoming an out-of-control inferno. Down at ground level a few last people were straggling out. The counselors closed in on them, coaxing the ooeys out of their heads.

"Where's my mother?" cried Renata. "Don't hurt Mom!"

"I saw her leave," said Frek. "I didn't get a chance to tell you before. A space bug blasted off with her. I think maybe it was taking her back to Sick Hindu."

"I'm alone," said Renata, laughing and crying at the same time, one hand stroking Gibby's bloody cheek. The best friend Frek had ever known.

Frek put his arm around Renata's shoulders. Gov's backup clones were crawling out of the blazing puffball. The Nubbies handily crushed them, not missing a one. Word spread that all the other puffballs had been wiped out as well.

The Govs were gone for good.

14

the shuggoths

"Wake up, Frek." It was Lora. "You have a lot to do today." She gave Frek's foot a cheerful shake. "I just fed the angelwings."

Geneva poked her head in Frek's door. "Time to go see your girl-friend," she cooed.

"Nosy pig," muttered Frek, not bothering to look at her.

"I saw a real pig yesterday," said Lora. "One of my music students lives outside of town on a little farm with all the old kinds of animals. I taught her how to use her trumpet to imitate a honking goose."

"Did the farm stink?" asked Geneva.

"You get used to it," said Lora. "Where there's filth, there's life, hey? Just like our house. The farm's by the river, Frek, a kilometer out of town. You'll fly right over it on your way to Stun City."

"Renata has a goggy crush on Roarboy," sang Geneva. Even though she'd been parroting this line for a whole year now, it still made Frek mad. He jumped out of bed and ran toward his sister, meaning to give her a thump in the ribs, but Geneva was too fast for him. She darted through the hall and disappeared down the stairs with a shriek and a giggle.

The sound of the Goob Dolls show came from below. It was another weekend morning in the Huggins home, Sunday, May 20, 3004.

"You and Renata are going to fly from Stun City to the Grulloo Woods, right?" said Lora, wanting to go over the day's plans.

"Yeah," said Frek. "It's a year today since Gibby died. Bili's been building some kind of monument by his grave. I promised we'd visit."

"Try to get home for supper," said Mom. "Linz Martinez will be here. He's his old self again with his halo gone. With that halo on, all he ever wanted to do was pick fights, go flying, and watch cartoons."

"I'll be home before dark," said Frek, thinking of Okky. "Let me get dressed now, Mom."

"Later, alligator," said Lora, and went downstairs with the girls.

Frek's room was a mess, as usual. He was relieved that Mom hadn't started in on that old topic. All in all, she'd been nagging him less since his big adventure. Restoring the whole planet's biome—that had to count for something. Be that as it may, Frek was still going to school and still bringing home glypher slugs that wanted to crawl on the walls and show junk for Mom to worry about.

The floor was littered with the glyphers, with toys, board games, and clothes. There were hundreds of urlbuds lying around as well, many of them for toon games. Even though Frek's family treated him with no great respect, many citizens were grateful to Frek for what he'd done, and hardly a day went by without a gift package arriving at the Huggins home.

Not that everyone was happy. The people being run by Orpolese espers didn't have a very good life. The Orpolese got bored easily, and made their pawns take all kinds of risks: starting fistfights with strangers, winging their way to the highest reaches of the atmosphere, sleeplessly watching toons for days on end, clambering unprotected on rocky cliffs, dueling with guns and swords, diving to the sea floor for overlong periods of time, eating things that weren't really food, exploring volcanoes, and so on.

Frek felt bad about the way things had worked out. The only bright spot was that fewer and fewer people were being controlled by Orpolese. It seemed the espers were losing interest in the Humanity Channel Game.

In any case, many parts of life were still normal. The Orpolese loved toons, and they left the toonsmiths alone, for instance. Frek had been consulting off and on with Deanna the toonsmith all winter, learning the biz from the ground up. What a waste of time it was to still be in school.

Lucky Renata was actually living with Deanna. Though Frek and Renata remained close friends, having Renata live at Frek's house had quickly come to seem like too much. Fortunately, once Deanna got a load of Renata's turkle drawing skills, she was willing to take on Renata as an apprentice.

Frek rooted out a reasonably clean shirt and then, just to get the day started, he stuck the Skull Farmer urlbud to the wall. Gypsy Joker, Strummer, and Soul Soldier appeared.

"He give us the slip agin," said Gypsy Joker, his dice swinging from the nail in the side of his skull. His goggy red eyes flickered. "We comin' closer to nabbin' him ever' time."

Gypsy Joker was referring to Magic Pig. For the last few months Frek and his sisters had been seeing the Magic Pig in the toons, and Mom saw him once, too. Frek had asked Mom if the Pig looked familiar, but she denied having seen the Magic Pig in a dream all those years ago. She said that was just a silly story Carb liked to tell, and that, duh, the main thing that had happened that night was Frek getting born.

But Frek knew the Magic Pig was real. He wanted to ask the Pig how Dad was doing, and if there were some way that he could be saved. He also hoped for some suggestions about getting rid of all the espers.

Strummer twitched his bony fingers against the neck of his guitar and sang.

> This little piggy went to plain brane,
> That pig hid in Pig Hill.
> One little pig ate gold nuggets,
> The other little pig ate swill.
> And the Magic Pig ran—

"Wheenk, wheenk, wheenk, all the way home," rumbled Soul Soldier, nodding his black-burnt skull. "Seems like there might could be a way to follow him, Frek. Them Hub critters in the Planck brane ain't so different from us toons. We're all virtual realities, you know what I'm sayin'? Livin' ideas."

"Glatt concept," said Frek, pulling on his shirt. It was surprising how intelligent the toons were. You never knew what new notions they'd come up with, eternally evolving themselves into new levels of complexity. "I can't really talk now," he continued. "I just wanted to say hi. I'm flying to Stun City and the Grulloo Woods."

"Aloha later, Frekazoid," said Gypsy Joker. He made a mystic pass with his skeletal right hand. The images of the Skull Farmers dwindled to a tiny disk that heeled over to one side and sped off into the furthest recesses of the space sketched upon Frek's wall skin.

Some crows outside Frek's window caught his attention. Three of them were cawing in the anyfruit tree, as personable and lively, in their own way, as the Skull Farmers. Frek leaned out to look things over. It was a nice day, in fact this had been the nicest spring Frek had ever seen. Violets peeked out from the lush grass and clover. Daffodils swayed in the breeze. The dark earth of mole hills marked the lawn. A robin was hopping about, pecking for worms. Higher in the air fluttered an orange butterfly with black patterns on its wings. If only the people of Earth could live as freely as the animals.

Here came Woo trotting across the yard from the old counselor hut—now the dog house—trailed by her three new puppies, the little dogs trying to catch up with her and fasten onto her milky dugs.

"Hi, Woo," called Frek, hopping from foot to foot as he put on his socks.

"Frek," squeaked Woo, then turned to nip an overbold puppy. Wow came into view, and the puppies went for their father. Playfully he rolled over on his back, yapping and wrestling with them. A rabbit bolted from his cover in a particularly high clump of clover, and Woo took off after him.

"Frek," hollered Ida from downstairs. "I see the Magic Pig."

Frek slipped on his shoes and ran to join his sisters.

The wall skin was tuned to the Goob Doll Home, with the imaginary pastel walls and cartoon furniture artfully arranged like an extension of the Huggins family room. Goob Doll Judy was pointing toward her curlicued front door, her hazel eyes big with excitement. Goob Dolls Tawni and LingLing beckoned to the Huggins children, LingLing in her glasses, Tawni with her bun.

"Go ahead," said Ida. "Get him." The Goob Dolls exited their house, with red, yellow, and blue pixie dust sparkling in their wake. The wall skins showed a rapidly scrolling street scene, with toon trees and toon houses on both sides. At the far end of the street was a bouncing pink ball with two ears and a curly tail.

"Faster!" urged Frek. "Let's finally make him talk!"

Goob Doll Judy windmilled her long arms and legs, bringing the pink dot of the pig closer. And then all at once she'd cornered him at the end of a brick-walled alley amid garbage cans with buzzing flies tracing curves in the air. The Magic Pig squatted beside a fish skeleton, glaring at them.

His gold aura was, if anything, larger than before. Plenty of wham. The economical curves of his body fit in well with the world of toons. The white bristles on his snout and the web of wrinkles around his eyes showed it was the same Rundy as before.

"Talk to me," said Frek. "Tell me about Carb. Tell me how to get rid of the Orpolese."

"*Wheenk,*" said the Magic Pig, a mocking look in his eyes. "Wheenk, wheenk, wheenk." He struck one of his trotters against the ground. A hole opened up and he was gone.

"Why does he keep coming around if he won't talk to us?" said Ida impatiently. "I hate him."

"Don't say that," said Frek. "He's my friend."

"I don't *think* so," said Goob Doll Judy, shaking her ponytails. "He looks old and geevey to me. An evil alien."

"I'm gonna stand here taking advice from my sister's toons?" said Frek impatiently. Maybe the Skull Farmers were worth listening to, but Goob Doll Judy? Forget it. "I gotta go." Anticipating a fresh round of teasing from Geneva, he clenched his fist and showed it to her. "You shut your trap, okay? Button your lip."

Geneva gave him her most sickeningly sweet smile, stuck out her tongue, and whispered something to Ida that sent them both into giggles.

Frek hurried into the kitchen, said good-bye to Mom, and grabbed a slice of anymeat on grobread. People were pretty much still eating the same old things. The restoration of the biome hadn't adversely affected the conveniently tweaked kritters that the Nubbies had come to depend upon.

Just as Frek was laying out his angelwings on the lawn, Stoo Steiner came ambling up. He was wearing an Orpolese halo. He'd been sent to look at Frek. Frek had gotten so good at sky-air-comb that the Orpolese usually couldn't pick his brain. The best way for them to find out about Frek was to walk one of their slaves over to his house.

"Yubba, Frek," said Stoo, wearing an artificial smile. "Where you off to?" He looked thin and worn. The Orpolese often forget to get their avatars enough to eat. It was sad to see him like this.

"I'm gonna visit some friends," said Frek, feeling guilty. He had an exciting new life and Stoo—most days poor Stoo was locked up in his darkened room staring at the wall skin.

By now Frek was already lying down on his wings. The wings tightened their cushiony little legs around his upper arms and sank their hair-fine tendrils into his skin, taking hold of his ribs.

"Flying on Earth is boring," said the Orpolese master through Stoo's mouth. "Not as good as watching toons." Which was about all Stoo did anymore. "But those are getting boring too," added the voice—and then all of a sudden Stoo's halo disappeared.

In that instant, Stoo's smile was replaced by an expression of despair. "Thank Buddha I'm free again," he said from his heart. "But I bet they'll be back. You've ruined everything, Frek."

Frek got to his feet, flexing his wings. He felt terrible about Stoo. But staying here would only make it worse. Time to go. He didn't want to disappoint Bili. A good jump and flap and he'd be in the air, out of Stoo's reach.

"Thanks to you, my father lost his good job," continued Stoo. "Thanks to you, we're not ourselves most of the time, with those geevey Orpolese pushing us around like stuffed toys." Far from threatening Frek, he dropped his hands to his side, looking sad and tired.

"I'd like to get rid of the Orpolese, too," said Frek. Not a day went by that he didn't wonder if he'd made a big mistake. "But other than that, things are better now, aren't they?" He gestured at the flower-besprent lawn, at the butterflies and the birds in the trees. He could hear his voice taking on a pleading tone. "All the plants and animals—"

"Enjoy them while you can," cut in Stoo. "You must know that the humanity channel audience share is way down. The Orpolese producers are looking for something new to liven things up. Kolder was talking to a couple of them, as a matter of fact. A black squid-thing and an orange donut. They gave Kolder the first interesting work he's had since you put him out of a job. Your crunchy-granola little biome won't be the same for long, you selfish gurp." And with that, Stoo turned on his heel.

"You saw Vlan and Tagine?" cried Frek. For a whole year the two Orpolese had been lying low. Frek knew they were still on Earth because he heard rumors about them every now and then. "What else did they say? When did you see them? What did they ask Kolder to do?"

"None of your business," said Stoo over his shoulder—and stalked off.

Frek watched Stoo go. He wished they could still be friends. It made him sick at heart to think of Stoo—and so many others—living as slaves of the alien gamers. And what was that about Kolder and the Orpolese? Sounded like it could be very bad news. But maybe it was just empty bragging. Frek hopped into the air and winged off, still thinking. Half an hour later, he was gliding into Stun City.

The first thing he noticed was that the Kritterworks was three times as big as before. A steady stream of little lifter beetles was buzzing out of it, continually spreading new creatures across the Earth. A couple of the beetles passed close by. Frek glimpsed porcupines in one of them, and a pile of snakes in the other. He wondered if the snakes were poisonous. With all the old animals back, people were having to relearn ancient caution.

Frek tipped his left wing and spiraled toward the aircoral dwellings clustered around the base of the Toonsmithy beanstalk. The giant helical stalk swayed ever so gently in the fitful spring breeze. Mild pulses of green and yellow light flowed up along its phosphorescent skin.

The hologram at the top of the Toonsmithy was a preview image of an upcoming game called Star Surfer, which was goggy to see, as Star Surfer was one of the games Deanna and Renata had been discussing with Frek over the winter. It was based on Frek's experiences riding the solar flares around the archipelago of Orpolese suns.

Frek landed beside a particularly sleek-looking aircoral, a domed shape with windows dramatically sliced out like segments removed from an orange. Renata had been living here with Deanna for eleven months. For Renata, Deanna was a combination employer, tutor, and big sister.

Frek settled his angelwings down in the yard, then knocked on the door. Deanna answered. The spiral pattern cut into her blond-dyed hair echoed the shape of the Toonsmithy. Like the other toonsmiths, Deanna was free of any Orpolese halo.

"Welcome, galactic groover," said Deanna. "I've been wanting to show you Star Surfer. It's rather goggy. You gave us some great ideas. Remind me again, why are you still in school?"

"Because I'm thirteen," said Frek. "And my mom's a facilitator."

"Ah yes," said Deanna. "A sound education is the basis for future success, hey? Me, I didn't go to school at all."

"Yubba, Frek," said Renata, running out, her pigtails bouncing. She'd tied them with the special green ribbons that Frek had made her on Unipusk last year. "I can't wait to go flying. Deanna's been working me too hard."

"Renata's been drawing models of the creatures she saw in that spaceport bar," said Deanna. "I used them in the Star Surfer opening scenes. My next hang-up is visualizing what it's like inside a sun. I need your help, Frek. Can you come to my studio for just a minute?"

"It's Sunday, Deanna," protested Renata. "We have to go see Gibby's family!"

"We could spare a half hour," said Frek. He never missed a chance to go inside the Toonsmithy.

So Frek left his angelwings grazing on the lawn and followed Deanna through a round door in the side of the Toonsmithy beanstalk. The building recognized Deanna and greeted her. Sloping up to the right was a long, curving hallway.

"Over here," said Renata, leading Frek to stand with Deanna in the middle of the hall. "We can ride." She squeezed his hand. A hump appeared in the floor and began sweeping upward, carrying them along like riders on a wave, the skin of the floor sliding beneath their feet.

The walls of the Toonsmithy were covered with stray toons: the Skull Farmers, the soap-opera Klaxon family, Dha Na Duc and his nephews, the Goob Dolls, and the Financiers of the Apocalypse. Frek thought he glimpsed the mortar-board-wearing cuttlefish toon that Bumby had made, but it didn't stick around to talk with them.

"None of us even designed that one," remarked Deanna. "The toons have a whole ecology of their own. Competing for wall skins." To illustrate her point, she dangled her hand and twitched her fingers as if they were independently walking around. And then she made a graceful pointing gesture. The bump in the floor settled down, bringing them to a halt at the door to her studio.

The walls, floor, and ceiling of Deanna's room were the dark of deep space, inset with the glowing disks of suns. A shutter covered the window. Now and then an undulating veil of colors shot out from one of the stars: a solar flare. In the middle distance, a boy and a girl were riding gold and chrome surfboards. The toons were modeled upon Frek and Renata. How glatt was that?

So convincing was the illusion of space that Frek had to fight a sense of vertigo. Deanna's wall skin was gundo good quality. The Frek toon character locked onto him and began matching his moves.

"Let's fly into that sun over there," said Deanna, who was steering the Renata character. "Tell me how you like it."

It was all wrong inside Deanna's toon sun. So for a half hour or so, Frek helped her tweak it. For one thing, Deanna had her soundtrack set to dull random roaring. Frek got her to make the air throb and chime instead, adding in gurgling sounds to suggest the feeling of bubbles running along your legs. And then he got her to put in a swarm of loofy. The eddies schooled like tropical fish, glittered like a bin of jewels. Being inside a sun was paradise, that's what Deanna hadn't understood.

"Enough now!" interrupted Renata. "We gotta go!"

Fifteen minutes later, Frek and Renata were flapping above the outskirts of Stun City, heading for the rolling, forested hills of the Grulloo Woods.

"What's wrong?" asked Renata, noticing something in Frek's face.

"It's—I'm feeling guilty," said Frek. "This morning I saw an old friend of mine. Stoo? The Orpolese keep running him. It's terrible. I acted like I didn't have time to talk to him—but I had plenty of time to mess around with Deanna. I've got to find a way to finish off the branecast."

"Don't be so hard on yourself," said Renata. "Look down at how many different colors of green there are. All the new plants are taking root."

"It's good," said Frek. "But it's not enough."

"What's that big gray thing down there?" asked Renata, pointing.

Deep in one of the ravines was a long, twitching shape moving rapidly toward the river. Renata and Frek circled around to get a better look at it, but by then it had slid beneath the water. Barely visible, it undulated upstream toward Middleville.

"I've never seen a kritter like that," said Frek. "The Kritterworks isn't still making new models, is it?"

"Maybe it's a dinosaur?" wondered Renata. "That would be gollywog. There might have been some ancient genomes inside your elixir egg."

"We better not chase it," said Frek, with a glance at the sun. "Salla said to show up between one and two."

They flew along the Grulloo road on the ridge above the river, giving a wide berth to the crumbling dead tree where Okky and her sisters lived. Soon they could pick out the bright green of the tobacco plants along the stream where Salla and Jeroon had their burrows. Bili was on the bank, waiting for them. Seeing Frek, he whooped and waved, lashing his furry striped tiger tail.

LuHu and then Salla emerged from their burrow's round stone-framed entrance hole. LuHu's ponytail body was alive with excitement. Salla was wearing her best white turmite silk jacket, with the flowery petals on her body arranged just so. She was thinner than last year, her face sadder.

"I been makin' a pyramid for Paw!" Bili told Frek. "Dibble's gonna help us lift up the last stone. Looky. It's white." Resting at Bili's side was a gleaming round boulder that the young Grulloo had somehow transported here to smooth and polish. Dibble herself was off to one side, ripping the low-hanging branches off an anyfruit tree.

"Great," said Frek, shrugging off his angelwings. "Gibby deserves it. I still can't believe he's gone."

"Where's that stupid Jeroon?" fretted Salla. She always seemed a little edgy when Frek was around. "He and Ellie walked down to the river to go fishing this morning and they haven't come back. They took our other sister Pfaffa with them. I bet it's her fault. Pfaffa always has her head in the clouds."

"Up an elephruk's butt, you mean," said Bili.

"Don't talk like that, you whelp."

"Bili's bad," exulted LuHu.

"Maybe we should just go without Jeroon," suggested Frek. He wanted to be sure to get out of the Grulloo woods well before dark.

"Okay," said Ellie. "It's about a half hour's walk from here."

"I'm the mahout," said Bili, and hopped into the recessed truck-bed of Dibble's back. In an instant, LuHu was at his side. The ill-tempered elephruk made as if to snatch them away, but she couldn't reach them.

"I got some yams at Paw's grave for you," Bili told the elephruk. "Kneel down and let me roll in the rock." Dibble lowered her bed to the ground. Frek helped Bili wrestle in the spherical stone. And then they got underway.

The woodlands were teeming with new life. Flies and gnats spiraled in the air. Flowers Frek had never seen outside of an url were pushing up from the forest floor—irises, snowdrops, and sorrel. Mushrooms were everywhere, slick and brown, white and round, beige fingers, orange trumpets. Squirrels chattered in the trees, rabbits loped by, a fawn crashed through the underbrush. A woodpecker tap-tatted a dead trunk, nuthatches peeked around mossy branches, chickadees balanced on supple spring-green twigs, jays swept down to peck worms from the ground. Moths were everywhere, gray and tan. The air smelled richer and sweeter than ever before.

And the seeding wasn't done yet. As they passed through a clearing, a Kritterworks lifter beetle rode down on a shaft of sunlight and unloaded a score of star-nosed moles, who quickly burrowed into the soft forest floor. Dibble snorted in surprise. Not finished yet, the lifter beetle scuttled around the clearing, poking seeds into the ground with its horned snout. With a rasp and a clatter it rose back into the sky.

Gibby's grave was in a clearing a bit farther on. Bili had been painstakingly assembling a symmetrical pile of matching round boulders: a four-by-four layer topped by a three-by-three layer and a two-by-two layer, tidy as old-time courthouse cannonballs. Finding, shaping, and setting the stones had taken him all winter; moss already grew on their northern sides.

Bili fed Dibble some yams, and then the elephruk helped them hoist the final stone into place. It was of a remarkable brightness, like an eye on the peak of the pyramid.

"Roar!" exclaimed the young Grulloo, perching atop the monument. "Don't nobody forget my paw!"

Bili and LuHu had brought along Gibby's souvenirs: Bili had the little Unipusker statue, the fish scale from flying Aunt Guszti, the star-cinder from Orpoly. LuHu had the branecasters' key and the blue stone from Unipusk. At their request, Frek once again told the Grulloo children the stories behind their souvenirs. And then Renata retold the tale of how Gibby had saved their lives during the final attack on Gov's puffball. Salla frowned a bit to hear it.

It was late afternoon by the time they got back to Salla's burrow. As they arrived, Jeroon appeared, running up the creek bed with the mermaid-tailed Ellie puffing at his side, both of them disheveled and wild-eyed, their clothes and leg-arms completely covered with mud.

"It ate Pfaffa!" shrieked Ellie. "It almost got us!"

"No!" screamed Salla, her petals standing straight out from her body. "What do you mean!"

"A great pasted-together thing," said Jeroon. "A shuggoth. I've heard of them—NuBioCom used shuggoths against the Crufters to crush the Revolution of 2710. But this one had an Orpolese halo. Its body was masses of animals and plants melted together. Eyes along its sides, bunches of hands and tentacles sprouting out here and there, mouths where you least expect them, a few branches and leaves. It swallowed Pfaffa whole—absorbed her. I could still see her face under its skin, screaming like."

"How did this happen?" asked Frek.

"We heard a voice calling for help around a bend in the river," said Jeroon. "Sounded for all the world like a woman drowning. So we ran over there and—it was a shuggoth fooling us. It came out of the water faster than you can say *knife*, running on flipper legs that grew feet. Ellie and I climbed up on a cliff, but poor Pfaffa was too slow. We were trapped on those rocks for two hours, on the highest, thinnest ledge. Eventually the shuggoth gave up on us and started grazing, and then it split in two. And it kept up like that, eating and splitting. Finally a herd of deer came by. Half the shuggoths took off after them; the others jumped in the river."

"I can't believe how fast they were making babies," said Ellie, her mouth trembling. "In two hours, that one shuggoth became—a thousand? An army. And a new Orpolese halo popped up on every one of them."

"This could mean the end of the world," said Jeroon. "They're swallowing down every last thing they crawl upon. Every plant, every mushroom, every bug. We could hardly make our way through the mud. The haloes mean it's all part of the filthy game your alien friends are running on us, Frek."

"Where were they headed?" asked Frek, feeling sick.

"I think Middleville," said Jeroon.

"Let's go," said Renata.

"Yes," said Frek. "We'll do something."

"It's your fault Pfaffa's dead!" burst out Salla, overwrought at the bad news. Her tears coursed down the wrinkles in her face. "You killed Gibby! You're ruining our lives, you gleep!"

"I'll stop the shuggoths," said Frek, glimpsing the rudiments of a desperate plan. "I think there's a way." As for the rest of what Salla had said, Frek could see the crushed expression on Bili's face. The boy's big day was ending badly. "You made a great pyramid for your father," he told Bili, giving the little Grulloo a pat. "I'll never forget him. And I'll be back."

"Geever," said Bili, and turned away.

Flying toward the river, Frek and Renata crossed several trails like dirt roads. Shuggoth tracks. It was appalling how often the trails branched. Down near the river they spotted a pair of straggler shuggoths hungrily plowing up the landscape—gray-green shapes sprinkled with eyes, feelers, and tentacles. Now and then, when one of them got stuck, it would sprout out a deer-leg to push against the mud. Noticing Frek and Renata overhead, a shuggoth called out in a woman's imploring voice.

"I need your help," sang the shuggoth, the incongruously sweet tones emanating from its vibrating skin. The monster wore a wobbly brown Orpolese halo. "I've lost my friends."

The shambling beast reared up toward them, stretching out a protrusion like an elephruk's trunk. They hovered a bit higher. The disappointed shuggoth popped out a dozen centipede legs and scrabbled onto a ten-meter mapine. The branches sagged and melted; the trunk softened and merged into the shuggoth's flesh. The bloated, foul thing sank down. With a popping sound, it split along its length, sending up a meaty stench of excrement and decay.

The splitting reminded Frek of something: The Orpolese themselves reproduced in this way. Perhaps they were finding the shuggoth bodies more congenial than those of human form. Just as Jeroon had said, as soon as the monster divided, a fresh Orpolese halo appeared on the new scion. Off in Orpoly customers were waiting in line for the New Revised Humanity Channel Game Featuring the Attack of the Shuggoths.

"Did you hear Ellie say that one of them turned into a thousand this afternoon?" said Renata. "That's sick. Where will it stop?"

"There could be millions tonight," said Frek. "Trillions tomorrow. Nothing to stop them until the food runs out. Until nothing's left."

"You should talk to the Orpolese," said Renata. "Make them quit. Or if you don't want to, I can talk to them."

"I have a better idea," said Frek. "I'll go to the branecasters. I'm still the humanity channel's rep."

All the way to Middleville, Frek and Renata saw shuggoth trails and shuggoths. The farms down by the River Jaya were denuded. It was hard to believe this much damage had been done in one afternoon. Uphill from the ravaged farms, the ever-multiplying wave of shuggoths was plowing through the mapine forest. In the mass, the alien-controlled combines were like an avalanche, like a tidal wave, like lava. The shuggoths had just reached the outmost isolated house trees at the edge of Middleville. People were running toward the center of town.

"The Orpolese got bored with us," said Renata. "They're like bratty kids kicking down someone's sand castle. I hate that."

Yes. The Orpolese had tired of watching Earth's slow upward progress. The audience share had dropped. So the producers Vlan and Tagine were pulling a desperation move to attract viewers. Kolder Steiner had given them the recipe for an agent to merge organisms together. What had Stoo said? "Your crunchy-granola little biome won't be the same for long." But surely Kolder hadn't realized things would be this bad. In a day or two there'd be nothing left, from pole to pole.

"There's my house," said Frek. "I think Ida and the toons can find the Magic Pig. He's got to help me now. I have to see the branecasters." They landed in the backyard between the garden and the dogs' hut. Already alerted by the sounds and smells of the shuggoths, the dogs were furiously barking. Wow squeaked out a few hoarse questions.

"Don't let them touch you," Frek told him. "And save your barking until they reach our front yard. Warn us then, and run."

The angelwings were already unsettled, and the sight of the puppies made them frantic. Frek and Renata quickly garaged them and ran into the house.

"Oh, Frek," cried Lora. "Thank Buddha you're here. We're seeing frightful things on the news. They say we should evacuate."

"I can see them from my window," called Geneva from the head of the stairs. "At the edge of town. Help me pack, Mom!"

"What are they?" Ida asked Frek.

"Shuggoths," said Frek. "Giant killer slugs. Look, we have to tune away from the news and watch some toons. The Goob Dolls and the Skull Farmers. I want to talk with them."

"Watch toons!" exclaimed Lora. "Have you lost your mind? Come upstairs and grab whatever you want to save, Frek. The news said we have to be out of here in five minutes."

"Mom!" shrieked Geneva. "I can't find my nupearl necklace!"

"Calm down!" yelled Lora, running upstairs. "You lent that necklace to Amparo."

"Put on the Goob Dolls," Renata urged Ida.

"Okay," said Ida in her deep little voice. She and Renata had become pals.

Meanwhile Frek dashed upstairs and fetched his Skull Farmers urlbud. Lora and Geneva were each in their rooms, frantically packing—for now they ignored him. By the time Frek got back down and slapped his bud onto the family room wall, the three Goob Doll characters were already active. And now Soul Soldier sprang up at Goob Doll Judy's side.

"Frek wants to find the Magic Pig," Renata told the toons. "We only have a few minutes."

"Let's try the alley where he disappeared this morning," said Goob Doll Judy, batting her eyes at Soul Soldier. "We can go there with this big strong Skull Farmer."

As usual Soul Soldier was toting a heavy-duty machine-gun. "Ready for pig-huntin'," he said, opening his bare, blackened jaws to return Judy's grin.

"It's so nice to see you, Leroy," said Goob Doll Judy.

"Don't call me that," said Soul Soldier, shaking his head. "Only my mama call me Leroy. If the other boys hear you say that stuff, they gonna—"

He broke off as Strummer and Gypsy Joker appeared.

"Niiice," said Goob Doll LingLing, elbowing Tawni. "Dates for us girls, too." She stepped forward and plucked a string of Strummer's guitar, then gave a little flip to the lapel of his cape. "I love musicians." LingLing's glasses were pointed like flirty cat's eyes.

"I'll sing about you," said Strummer. "Take you right on board."

"We stalkin' that pig?" Gypsy Joker asked Tawni. She nodded. He cocked his toothy jaw in something like a leer. "Lead the way, pretty mama. I'll be right behind you."

"Heel," said Tawni.

"Are you packed, Frek?" shouted Mom from upstairs. "Ida? The shuggoths are only a few blocks away!"

Up on the family room wall, the Skull Farmers and the Goob Dolls were racing down the same curlicued pastel street as this morning, and once again they ended up in an alley's dead end. With no Magic Pig in sight.

"He ain't gonna hide much longer," said Gypsy Joker, taking one of the dice from his dangling earring. "Back off, boys and girls."

He tossed the ivory cube at the spot on the ground where the Magic Pig had wheenked away this morning. With a disorientingly rapid reverse zoom, their viewpoint sped out from the alley and up into the blue sky, well past some cute puffy Goob Doll clouds. A thermonuclear mushroom bloomed from the alley below, flattening every building in the Goob Doll's home town.

"Oops!" said Judy in a cheerful tone.

Making a sound like a squadron of dive-bombing jets, the Skull Farmers and the Goob Dolls flew down into the heart of the cloud, with Soul Soldier laying down a withering barrage of machine-gun fire, complete with rhythmic muzzle-flashes and the sight of shell casings flying by.

Inside the cloud was a vague glow. But then, yes, they found a round hole in the ground right where the Magic Pig had disappeared. Strummer unlimbered his guitar and struck a fierce arpeggio of notes. The sounds echoed down into the hole—was there a response?

"Sooey sooey sooey, pig pig pig!" sang Goob Doll Tawni.

"We you coming to get!" added LingLing, and burst into giggles. "Kill the pig!"

Strummer plucked his strings again. There was definitely an answer from the hole. A faint *wheenk*.

"Go in there, Judy," said Ida. "Bring him out. He has to talk to my brother."

Squaring her slender shoulders, Goob Doll Judy took a deep breath and dove into the hole. One cartoon moment later she was back, firmly grasping the Magic Pig by one of his floppy ears. He didn't seem able to break free of her grip. His teeth were chipped yellow stumps. With his white bristles and wrinkled eyes, he looked pitifully decrepit. But maybe that was on purpose.

"Let me go," grunted the Magic Pig.

"No," said Judy, giving Rundy a shake. Far from letting him go, she fastened onto his other ear as well, waving him around like a piece of laundry.

"Tell him, Frek!" exclaimed Ida.

"I have to get to the branecasters, Rundy," said Frek. "I want to terminate the Orpolese production deal."

"Business opportunity!" exclaimed the Magic Pig. He followed this with so long and shrill an oink that Judy had to drop him and slap her hands over her ears. But rather than running away, the Magic Pig struck a pose, letting an update ripple across his image. His straggly bristles shortened, his teeth whitened, his careworn wrinkles smoothed away. His body itself grew rounder, his aura brightened to a healthy glow.

"I'm at your service," continued the Magic Pig, bowing with a sweep of his immaculate trotter. "We have three problems to solve. (a) You can't terminate a production deal without picking a new producer. (b) You have to go to the Planck brane in person to contract for a new producer. And (c) there is no branelink hookup between your plane brane location and the Planck brane."

"Oh yeah?" said Soul Soldier, poking the Magic Pig's smoothly curved stomach with his gun. "How'd you get here then?"

"I'm a projection," said Rundy. "An information pattern like you. Shooting me would mean nothing. So don't do it, bonehead."

"Frek!" exclaimed Lora, coming down the stairs with a bag in each hand. "What was that horrible squealing? We have to go!" She glanced back up the stairs. "Hurry, Geneva! The shuggoths will be here any second!"

Frek began talking to the wall skin very fast. "(a) The Unipuskers can be our new producers," he told Rundy. "(b) I'll go to the Planck brane right now. And (c), I bet you can bend a branch of the brane link tree down to touch our space here. Make it lead to—to the pantry in our kitchen."

"That'll work," said the Magic Pig after the briefest of pauses. He was enjoying himself. "It'll be good theater. The Unipuskers can use it in their sign-up ads. I happen to know the Unipuskers haven't withdrawn their offer. Here comes the link."

A *whump* sounded from the kitchen, and a clatter.

"The shuggoths!" screamed Lora, who hadn't been paying attention to the toons at all.

"They're still fifty meters off," yelled Geneva from upstairs. "I'm coming, Mom. Do you realize that stupid Frek and Ida haven't packed a single thing?"

Before Lora could say anything, Frek and Renata ran into the kitchen and flung open the pantry door.

There was no sign of the shelves of food you'd expect to see in here. Instead some wavering pinstripes twitched in the air just beyond the doorframe, sketching a picture of an arched opening—Frek recognized it as the entrance to the Pig Hill branelink tree, as seen from the inside.

And beyond the tree hole was the Planck brane world, with the branecasters standing there posed as if for a formal portrait upon a green hilltop, with more hills rolling away in the background. Chainey, Jayney, Bitty, Batty, Sid, and Cecily—with the Magic Pig cozily nestled in pink-jowled Cecily's ample arms. He was, after all, her father.

"Hang on to me," said Frek, taking Renata's left hand with his left hand. "I'll go in. Be ready to pull me back."

Renata braced herself in the door frame, and Frek stepped through. Ida put her arms around Renata's waist, just in case.

Right away Frek could see the Planck brane had changed a lot. A year's worth of renormalization storms had come and gone, six or seven yugas. Today's Planck brane was flatly rendered, tinted in beautiful unnatural shades, and detailed with masses of photorealistic texture. Objects were juxtaposed in striking ways that ignored the constraints of physical size. It was a world of artful photo collage. The cityscape of Node G had become rolling hills with curious monumental structures on their peaks.

What made the scene especially surreal was that, although the landscape was lit as if by warm afternoon sun, the sky was dark and blue-black, sprinkled with five-pointed stars and hung with a full moon.

Frek's first thought was to look up into the branches of the branelink tree for Dad. While the tree had once looked like a great dead oak, now it was wholly flat and simple, a giant oval leaf, with its trunk transmuted into the leaf's stem. The veins in the leaf echoed the structure of the former branches.

Craning his head so far back that his neck hurt, and pzooming his view across the tree's surface, Frek finally spotted something upon the sky-scraping leaf. A puff of white fiber, like a spot where a spider tacks down a surplus fly. Could that be Dad?

"Hello," said someone, drawing Frek's attention down. It was bald, gray-skinned Chainey, his mouth, as usual, a humorless slot. He and the others were impeccably dressed, with lots of gold jewelry. Chainey's thin-lipped spouse, Jayney, was leaning on his arm, her head cocked at just the exact polite angle to indicate she was attentively listening to what everyone said. "Rundy says you want a new deal," continued Chainey.

"Yes," said Frek. From the Middleville kitchen behind him came the sound of Wow barking. No time to interrogate or bargain. Earth needed instant relief. "Please switch us to the Unipuskers right away."

"Orpolese went crazy on you, hey?" said Sid, twisting his thick lips. "We're more than happy to change the deal. The Unipuskers have a very nice package on the table. We can see you're in a rush, so no need to go over the details. Right, Bitty?"

"I double-checked the figures," said rumpled Bitty, leaning on a pencil the size of a walking-stick. She opened her mouth and waggled her tongue with its heavy gold stud. "We love it!"

"You can be the one to start the deal this time, Batty," said Jayney.

Twitchy, hunched-over Batty lurched toward Frek, holding out a big-knuckled veiny hand for Frek to shake. But first Frek glanced back at Renata and tightened his grip upon her warm hand—lest Batty try and judo-flip him, or worse. And then he shook with Batty.

"Your Orpolese espers are gone as of now," said Batty, fixing Frek with his glittering eyes. "You'll meet Hawb in your home town to finish the deal." He released Frek's hand.

Back in the real world, Wow's barking was rising to a crescendo, joined by Lora's cries of alarm. Frek cast a last wistful glance at the motionless tuft of spider silk stuck so high upon the flat tree, and then stepped back through the arched opening in the trunk.

As he left the Planck brane he heard a low squeal from the Magic Pig followed by a rumble of laughter from Sid, as if to say, "Screwed them again, eh?"

In the kitchen everything looked golden bright. Espers were definitely watching through Frek's eyes. Probably the Unipuskers. But he had no time to focus on his sky-air-comb routine.

"Hurry!" Mom was shouting. "We can still get out the back door."

Wobbly surfaces of gray and green were visible out the front door. Shuggoths. Wow had taken a stand beside his dog house, baying at the intruders.

"Move it!" called Geneva, already out in the back with her carry-pod at her side. Mom, Frek, and Ida ran to join her.

Glancing toward the side yard, Frek saw something wonderful. The shuggoths were lying still, barely trembling. And their Orpolese haloes were gone.

"Help me, Frek," said Geneva, wrestling with her heavy carry-pod. "Stop staring at those icky things."

"We don't have to run!" exclaimed Frek. "The shuggoths are dying."

Wow made so bold as to dart over and nip at a crooked goat-leg that dangled from the nearest shuggoth. A split appeared in the beast's side. Another tug from Wow and the gray shuggoth skin broke open like a wet paper bag. The connective slime oozed away and the shuggoth's components lay revealed: bushes, tree limbs, deer, rabbits, worms, a goat, mushrooms, grasses, fish, and a woman.

"It's Shurley Yang, the tailor," exclaimed Mom. "Can we wake her up?"

"I know first aid," said Ida. Frek's brave little sister picked her way through the smelly debris of the shuggoth and leaned over the comatose Shurley Yang. With quick motions, Ida cleaned out Shurley's nose and mouth, and then she crouched down to give the woman artificial respiration. Even Geneva had to stop yelling and watch.

A few minutes later, Shurley was coughing and sitting up among the tangled mapine branches.

"Bless you, Ida," said the tailor, rubbing her face. "I was working with a turmite mound and—it was like the sky fell onto my back. One of those things—" She gestured toward a nearby shuggoth. "It swallowed me. An Orpolese player was running it, holding us together and thinking our thoughts. Ow." She leaned over and rubbed her legs. "I got pretty banged-up in there. Like a doll in a purse."

Frek walked over to the next shuggoth and gave a hard yank on one of its lifeless tentacles. It, too, split open.

"I'm down with this, too," said Renata, and they moved around the neighborhood, helping to dissolve the shuggoths into their component parts. All across town the shuggoths were dead and decomposing. People were picking around the melting shuggoths, clearing the debris away. Those who'd lost their homes were loosening the soil, preparing to plant fresh house tree seeds. There was a feeling of calm, as after a great storm.

The wonderful thing was that, for the first time in a year, all the citizens were free of alien control. But perhaps not for long.

The unyunching saucer of Cawmb and Hawb appeared in the evening sky like a thunderhead—huge, gray, flattened, with a bump on top and a round window on the bottom. As it shrank toward Middleville, the shape grew smoother and shinier, more clearly saucerian. Soon it was floating right overhead, a two-hundred-meter UFO, its chromed surface broken by a dozen gleaming feelers.

Any minute now Hawb and Cawmb would emerge to finalize the deal by shaking Frek's hand. And then people would be wearing Unipusker halos and living out their days as actors in these new aliens' game.

"I can't let it happen again," Frek told Renata. He kept thinking about poor, angry Stoo.

As if called up by his words, the orange donut of Tagine appeared, flying low across Middleville. Vlan's dark, iridescent tentacles waved from the side of the Orpolese craft; a bolt of energy shot toward the Unipusker saucer.

Moving with negligent ease, one of the saucer's feelers sketched a space warp that reflected the blast up into the heavens. The Unipuskers had learned from their last encounter with the Orpolese.

Six or seven chromed snakes lashed out from the saucer, uncoiling so rapidly that they managed to seize Tagine and Vlan. Vlan launched a cascade of energy bolts. The saucer absorbed these, growing larger and brighter. Tagine spat out a blinding cannonade of fireballs. The miniature suns scattered off the saucer like hailstones, digging smoking craters into the ground where they hit.

The end came quickly. Boluses of energy wobbled out along the Unipusker's gleaming feelers, inflating the Orpolese into a wobbly pumpkin/cuttlefish balloon—which exploded into scraps of black and orange. Just like that, the fight was over. The fragments that had been the Orpolese fluttered through the air like dead leaves, dissolving into nothingness as they fell.

The great round window in the Unipusker saucer's underside shuddered. Hawb and Cawmb floated through, then rode smoothly down upon a tractor beam, their thick-plated brown skins glinting in the setting sun, bright highlights flashing from the gold covers on their stubby tails. Their clawed feet dug into the soft soil of Frek's backyard.

Hawb's flat clamshell head opened one edge, showing his yellow-lined mouth. "Greet Frek. Request that we close our deal."

He stepped forward with his thick three-fingered hand extended, his pale blue eyes bouncing on his eye stalks as he came.

"Just a minute," said Frek, edging back toward the kitchen door. "I'm not ready."

"Demand immediate satisfaction," said Cawmb, close on Hawb's heels. "Inform you that Unipusker gold has already been transferred to the Planck brane. Warn of grave actions from the branecasters should you fail to honor your commitment."

"Um—that's just it," said Frek. "I kind of rushed my deal with the branecasters. They didn't tell me what we'd get in return. We got the elixir for signing on with the Orpolese, but what are we getting for signing on with Unipusk?"

Over by their turmite-paper garage, Lora and Geneva were staring at the Unipuskers with their mouths agape. Ida and Renata were at Frek's side. If Ida was scared of the Unipuskers, she didn't show it.

"Extol the fabled Unipusker organizational skills," said Hawb, twitching his eye stalks to shake off some gnats. "Promise that we will conform your behaviors to the Unipusk Branecast Code. Guarantee that we will prune down the species of your overly diverse biome. Shake my hand."

In front of the house, crows were noisily picking over the remains of the shuggoths. The flowers in the backyard were bobbing in the evening breeze. Starlings swooped about in the twilight, catching moths. At Frek's feet a puppy was nosing a glow worm.

"Go inside and start up the toons," Frek told Ida in a quiet tone. "Put a whole lot of them on the kitchen walls."

"How are your children, Cawmb?" said Renata by way of distracting the aliens. "I hope none of them have ickspot?" She couldn't quite suppress a giggle.

"Express anger that you dare to gloat over your wicked ruse," said Cawmb, slapping the curious Woo away from his gold-covered tail. "Marvel that none of our children perished in the collapse of our dwelling. Deny your right to make further jokes." Ida had slipped into the house.

"So how many children do you two have now, Hawb?" temporized Frek.

"Assert the number at bedtime last night to have been eight hundred and sixteen," said Hawb, still holding out his hand. Flies were landing in the sticky corners of his mouth. "Cease your chatter and close our deal!"

"Correct the always-careless Hawb and assert the correct count to be eight hundred and twenty-two including my newborns!" put in Cawmb pugnaciously. Just then a puppy hopped onto his foot. Cawmb swung his leg, sending the puppy flying. "Advise that we soon replace your filthy plants and animals with rickrack and vigs."

"No way," said Frek, working to keep the conversation going. "The whole reason I went to the galactic core was to restore our biome. Can't you see how beautiful it is here? Listen to the birds!"

Actually, the main sound right now was a cacophony of voices from the Huggins kitchen—drawls, quacks, whistles, yells, and whoops. Ida had started all the toons.

"Shake now!" said Hawb, still holding out his hand, uninterested in anything but closing his deal.

"Give me five minutes," said Frek. "I have to talk to the branecasters one last time and get some things clear. We have a branelink right inside my house. Wait here. You can talk to my mother and my other sister. Lora and Geneva."

"Can we look under the cover on your tail?" Geneva asked Hawb. She'd heard all about the Unipuskers from Frek. "I want to see the baby Unipuskers."

"Don't be rude to our guests, dear," said Lora. "Would you two like to sit down?" She darted into the garage and emerged with a bolt of turmite silk. "I don't think any of our chairs would hold you, but this will take the chill off the ground." She shook out the turmite silk like a picnic spread. "Can I offer you a snack? You must sample our anyfruit and drink some tree-juice. Perhaps I'll play you some music. Do you have music on Unipusk?" A minute later, the Unipuskers were sitting on the ground eating peaches and apples, listening to Lora play a simple tune upon a wooden flute.

Good old Mom.

When he and Renata reached the kitchen, Frek found the walls teeming with toons. Though the Goob Dolls and the Skull Farmers seemed to have become fast friends, some of the others were miffed to be sharing a wall skin. Normally people ran only one cast of toons at a time.

"What these free-loading pests doing on my farm?" fumed Da Nha Duc, immersed up to his orange knees in the green water of his rice paddy. His hoarse voice was so close to a duck's quack that he was quite hard to understand.

Only a few feet away, the water blended into the sour-colored purple and yellow stripes of the Space Monkey's circus tent. "Get rid of the others, Frek," chirped Space Monkey Dolfy, swinging forward so that his face took up a third of the kitchen wall.

"Don't get so big!" snapped Goob Doll Tawni, jabbing Dolfy with a pin from her bun.

"I'm here too," called a cuttlefish with a mortarboard.

"Professor Bumby?" exclaimed Frek.

"I'm the Professor Bumby *toon*," said the cuttlefish. "Not that departed alien's mouthpiece anymore. I've gone autonomous like any other toon. Virtually real and artificially intelligent, with simulated evolution and synthetic speech. It's a life. I've got a plan for a new show that—move over, you!" The cuttlefish flared an angry red and rolled up one of his long tentacles to thump Skull Farmer Strummer on his bony pate.

Strummer elbowed Sue Ellen Klaxon, who shoved Goob Doll Judy, who kicked Dha Na's nephew Huy into the rice paddy. Huy's brother Duy threw a mud ball at Space Monkey Dolfy. Dolfy ducked, and the mud ball struck the stomach of one of the Financiers of the Apocalypse, who was riding Puffy Pam the dragon with Mean Queen at his side. Some round-faced Happy Eaters pushed forward to clean up the scraps of mud. They were part of a pachinko toon game that Ida liked to play.

Ida herself was staring at it all, her mouth open in a grin. "We should always do this, Frek," she said.

"Don't make it no habit," said Soul Soldier, flicking a Happy Eater off his shoulder. "We ain't gonna tolerate this kind of mess very long."

"You tell them, Leroy," cooed Goob Doll Judy, leaning against the dark skeleton's side. Her face suddenly asterisked in distaste and she yanked Fax Frog from the inside of her shirt, then skimmed the obnoxious green toon along the wall's surface. He came to rest in the Space Monkeys' garbage can, his croaks echoing.

But now Frek heard something louder: Hawb's voice in the backyard, complaining, followed by Lora's soothing tones. Geneva sang out something perky to distract the Unipuskers. She and Mom weren't going to be able to keep the testy aliens occupied for all that long.

Renata felt the urgency. "Help us out and I'll see that each and every one of you gets a full day of primo display time in the hologram at the top of the Toonsmithy," she told the toons.

"Oooo," said the toons, pleased at the thought. Toons lived and died by their publicity. The more wall skins they got invited onto, the more space and time they had for their personal worlds.

"So let's hear a plan," said Renata, giving Frek a quizzical smile. "Or should I make one?"

"I'm going through that door into another world," said Frek, pointing to the pantry. He could see from here that it was indeed still a branelink entrance. The Magic Pig hadn't yet taken it away. "And I want all of the toons to come with me."

"Me too," said Ida. "I want to help save Daddy."

"And me," said Renata. "By now I know more about toons than you. But what makes you think they'll be able to pass through the branelink?"

"The creatures in the Planck brane are almost the same as toons," said Frek. "I just realized that today. They call themselves Hubs. They only stay alive if the other Hubs keep thinking about them. They're ideas, just like the toons." He raised his voice to address everyone on the kitchen walls. "You toons will like it over there in the Planck brane. You'll have lots of room."

Again Hawb's voice rumbled outside.

"Less talk, more action," said little Ida, marching over to the pantry door. "I'm ready to kick butt."

"Here's what we'll do," said Frek, talking fast. "We'll find Dad, blow up the Exaplex, and wipe out the branecasters. The toons can help."

Ida led the way through the branelink with Frek and Renata close behind. The toons flowed down the kitchen walls and through the doorframe. As they passed into the Planck brane world they popped into three-dimensionality, as real as Frek and the girls: the hard-looking Skull Farmers and the Financiers of the Apocalypse; the colorful Goob Dolls with their Mean Queen foe; the wealthy, backbiting Klaxons; the choleric Da Nha Duc and his nephews; Geneva's fat Puffy Pam dragon; the alien-designed Professor Bumby; and the bouncy, grinning Happy Eaters.

"Excellent polygon count," exclaimed Strummer, staring down at his guitar. He swiveled his skull around once, twice, three times. "Are we ready to boogie? Who do I ice, Frek?"

"The branecasters," said Frek. "There's six of them, three women and three men. But—"

The branecasters were nowhere to be seen. The top of Pig Hill was deserted, a sunny green meadow beneath a star-spangled night sky. A few pale clouds set off the full golden moon.

Well, even if the branecasters weren't around, Frek could get down to saving Dad and wrecking the Exaplex. The branelink tree stretched up like an enormous beech leaf, veined with a zillion possibilities. High, high up on its side was the cottony little puff that Frek thought might hold Carb. It was only thanks to pzoom that he could see it at all. Before starting toward the cocoon, he looked out across the landscape, checking against the approach of enemies.

No longer a gritty metropolis, Node G was a landscape of pristine creeks and wooded hills with odd-shaped buildings on their peaks. The structures were formed like immense copies of familiar objects— a giant boot, a clock, a jingle-bell, a stone owl, a bowler hat, a pair of lips, an apple—no two of the hilltop edifices were the same.

Distant tiny Hubs quivered in the air around the buildings; it seemed that in this new order all of them could fly. But none were headed toward Pig Hill. This was the ideal moment for Frek to rescue his father. Still he hesitated, afraid of what he might find. It had been a whole year.

He turned his attention to the toon creatures, cheerfully milling around and chatting with each other. They were companionably playing with the possibilities of this new world, quite unconstrained by normal physics.

Strummer hopped high up into the air and hung there playing a solo; Goob Doll Judy flew along a trajectory that included a series of sudden right-angle turns; Huy, Lui, and Duy Duc zapped from spot to spot without bothering to traverse the spaces that lay between. Most startling of all, Puffy Pam the dragon instantiated three, no four, copies of her large self, taking advantage of the unconstrained Planck brane space, so much more commodious than a network of wall skins.

"Well?" said Renata.

"I'll try to save Dad," sighed Frek. "Or see what's left of him. I'm not that optimistic. You might as well wait down here. Keep an eye on the toons." Frek beckoned to Gypsy Joker. "Can you carry me up to that fuzzy spot on the leaf up there? And you, Space Monkey Dolfy, you come along, too."

"I want to help get Daddy," put in Ida. "Tawni, you carry me."

With Frek cradled in the skeleton's arms and Ida perched on the

Goob Doll's back, the brother and sister rose to the top of the kilometer-high beech leaf. Dolfy and two other Space Monkeys followed close behind, climbing up the ridged veins. Professor Bumby tagged along too, gently beating the skirt of his cuttlefish fin.

"Daddy's in that white puff?" said Ida as they approached the silky two-meter cocoon. "It looks awful."

"The branecasters kept decohering him," said Frek. "Feeding on him like vampires. They did it to me for a few minutes, but Dad saved me. And now they've had him for a year. I wish I'd come sooner. I'm—I'm scared that—"

"It might be too late," said Ida. "He's not moving at all. Wake up, Daddy!"

The white mummy was quite still.

"Dad!" yelled Frek, echoing his sister. "It's Ida and me! We're here to save you!"

But when he pulled loose the silken shroud there was no Carb inside. In his place was a layered mass of—pictures? Gossamer-thin leaves with images of Carb and Lora and the kids spilled out and drifted away, melting into thin air as they tumbled. There was nothing left of Frek's father but dry, lifeless memories, and in a few moments the memories too were gone. A final object came rattling out of the limp shroud—a pair of rings, their bands linked together.

"Kac!" yelled Frek, and furiously flung the rings against the towering flat branelink tree. One of the veins promptly absorbed the pair—and they were gone for good. Like Dad. Ida was crying.

Just then some dark shapes angled down toward them from the night sky.

"Look out!" screamed Renata from below.

"Don't worry, darlings," came a warm, womanly voice from on high. It was Aunt Guszti the flying catfish, accompanied by her niece Flinka the trout.

"We have come to be your guides," called Guszti as she approached. "Today I think you will free the Hubs." She beamed at the pullulating toons. "You have found very good Plan the B."

"My father's dead," said Frek. "Where are the branecasters?"

"Hiding in the Exaplex," said Guszti, waggling the barbels beside her mouth. "They're frightened of the toons. Sad news about your father. But no surprise."

"I bet the Magic Pig is with the branecasters," added silver Flinka. "All the things he tells you to do, Frek, they are just so your path is the harder. I think he hinders you to make the humanity channel more interesting to watch."

"Flinka talks silliness about our Pig," interrupted Guszti. "He left branelink door open for you on purpose. He knew Frek would bring his Plan B toons. He sees the ending of the branecasters and he makes his plans the further ahead. Condolences from me as well, Frek, regarding your father."

"Daddy's really gone?" said Ida, not quite believing it. "There was nothing in that sack but leaves with pictures."

"His husk," said Frek, and put his arm around his sister. Renata flew up to join them, and the three kids consoled each other for a minute.

"Let's take a look in Rundy's burrow," said Frek, hoping to find some clues.

They flew down to the base of Pig Hill—Frek in Gypsy Joker's arms, Ida on Tawni's back, and Renata joining the parade with Goob Doll Judy. In their wake followed Flinka, Aunt Guszti, and more toons—lots of them.

The toons had all been making copies of themselves. Dozens of Goob Dolls, scores of Skull Farmers, hundreds of Ducs and thousands of Happy Eaters. Frek thought uneasily of the shuggoths. But this was different. The toons were copying themselves without eating anything. Self-replication came naturally to them. After all, they were used to deploying instances onto millions of different homes' wall skins at the same time. And, come to think of it, if the toons overran the Planck brane, who was to say it would be a bad thing?

Frek and Renata were the first two to reach the Magic Pig's arched door. Rundy's muddy wallow was to the side.

"Can you still kenny craft?" Renata asked Frek before they went in. "I'd feel better crawling into that burrow with a blaster in my hand."

It had been nearly a year since Frek had even tried kenny crafting—it just didn't work for him on Earth. But he found that, in the

Planck brane, he still had the knack. Frek went ahead and crafted heavy-duty blasters for himself, Renata, and Ida.

Ida was grimly pleased to have a gun. It only took her a second to figure out the controls, and before anyone could stop her, she'd widened Rundy's burrow to a height of three meters. She had a deft touch; she only excavated as far as the spot where the entrance burrow met the living room, leaving the Pig's quarters and furnishings fully intact.

Rundy's main room was much the same as before, with its clean piles of straw and its cupboard of yams and beets. One immediate fact they gleaned was that the Magic Pig hadn't been gone all that long, for there was a bubbling kettle of porridge on the hearth.

Frek went and tried the locked door of the Magic Pig's study. He was curious what was in there.

"Blast it open," suggested Flinka, who'd pushed her way in with them.

"Let me," said Ida, and raising her gun again. One quick needle of power punched out the lock. The door swung open.

What Frek saw in there was, strictly speaking, impossible. A green chair faced to the left, and at the same time the chair faced right. The Magic Pig was in the chair, but the chair was empty.

Frek was looking into a wholly different form of reality, a world of multidimensional time, with every alternative coexisting. A map, perhaps, of the Magic Pig's mind.

The Pig in the chair looked at Frek and made a spiteful face. But no, come to think of it, the Pig and the chair weren't there at all. The room was filled with images, like a thousand stories wanting to be told.

The Magic Pig was on all fours, bucking his back. He coughed out a soft pink bean. The little shape writhed and grew, it became a ruddy pouch with twitching tendrils, expanding like a house tree. The red flesh forked and split, branching into higher dimensions. A lowering face appeared upon the dark meat—Zed? *"Wheenk!"* laughed the Magic Pig.

"Lots happening," said Flinka, her glowing body at Frek's side. None of them dared to actually enter the study.

The Magic Pig was definitely gone—though at the same time he was sitting in that green chair in the doorway, blocking the view. Inside the study Rundy was proudly giving Cecily Pig's hand—trotter—to Sid at a fancy wedding, with all the branecasters in attendance. No, it was a funeral. All around the figures, the hallways and the mind worms of the Exaplex grew, with Zed somehow present in every part of them. The branecasters leaned over Carb, decohering him into melting pictures—

"I see suns with faces," broke in Ida, pointing toward the room's ceiling. "One of them looks like Daddy."

"Come out of there now!" called Aunt Guszti, who'd stayed outside by the wallow.

"You're just scolding because you're too fat to get in here," yelled Flinka. "Too fat and old and stiff."

"I warn you, young minnow!" said Aunt Guszti. "You get pounded very soon!"

As she said this, a hundred Hungry Eater toons pushed into the Magic Pig's quarters and started bouncing off the ceiling and walls, smashing things. The toons felt every bit as solid as normal objects.

"Back outside," cried Frek, after a couple of the hyperactive Eaters had thudded into him. He definitely didn't want to get pushed into the seething multiverse that lay beyond the study door.

They fought their way out to the wallow. Guszti was waiting there, floating close to the ground, innocently nibbling the grass. Above her the swarm of toons circled like a gathering whirlwind.

"You sent those Eaters in there because you were jealous," snapped Flinka.

"It's bad to snoop in there," said Guszti. "He might find out."

"It's like I always thought," said Flinka. "The Magic Pig's different from everyone. He's in all the possible worlds at once. That's why he's always ready for what happens next. He's been helping the branecasters lately, but soon he'll move on."

"So you know it all," said Guszti. "I'm lucky to talk with you."

"Can you weird fish stop arguing and lead us to the Exaplex?" interrupted Renata.

"Certainly," said Guszti. "I am only waiting for you to ask. Follow my niece and me. If you are finally eliminating the Exaplex, the

Hubs will be grateful indeed. The branecasters have lived too well for too long."

So the two flying fish led the way, still quarrelling a little, with Ida piggyback on Tawni, and Renata on Goob Doll Judy. Gypsy Joker padded his bony arms with a velvet cloak to make Frek's ride more comfortable. The ever-multiplying toons trailed behind them like a great scarf of birds.

Rather than flying along a straight path toward the unseen Exaplex, Guszti and Flinka zigzagged from hilltop to hilltop, as if finding their way by a chain of association. The hilltops were three or four kilometers apart from each other, and there seemed to be no end to them. They were flying very fast. Frek had the impression that, spread out as it was, the new Planck brane could be thousands of kilometers from edge to edge.

The buildings they passed resembled a wine barrel, the bust of Venus de Milo, a lion, a pool table, a bicycle, a tuba, a bed, and a curtain. It was strange to see these enormous sunlit structures beneath the starry night sky, each of them over a hundred meters tall. Tiny doors and windows pocked the buildings, the doors giving onto little landing pads from which the wingless flying Hubs launched themselves, lively as gnats. Like toons, the Hubs could tailor physics as they liked. For them, physics was a matter of Style—not Law.

But why were the buildings shaped like Earth objects? Why a stuffed lion the size of the Sphinx? Why a giant brass tuba resting on its bell? Why a skyscraping velvet curtain with its center pulled in by a tasseled tie? The Planck brane was unfathomable.

The Hubs waved and cheered, as if welcoming a rescuing army. Near an armchair-shaped building Frek saw the little family he'd seen on the tram, the girl with the parents who took turns being warts upon each other's noses. They recognized Frek and shouted encouragement as he flew past in Gypsy Joker's arms.

Onward Frek's party raced, a sky-filling flock of Skull Farmers, Goob Dolls, Professor Bumbys, and more. The toons' rate of multiplication was wholly out of control. Each of them was spinning off copies as fast as bubbles blowing off a wand, with the copies belching out copies of their own.

Frek's party cruised past a building like a lady's silver hand mirror balanced erect on its long handle. How odd it was to see a mirror that size, dizzying and unreal, especially with the hundreds of thousands of toons reflected in it. Beyond the mirror, Guszti swerved to the right and headed toward a hill topped by a hundred-meter candle, complete with a wavering flame. As they approached the candle, a tang of salt air blended with the waxy smoke. And now Frek heard the roar of waves.

Like some otherworldly lighthouse, the candle was on a promontory above the beach of a boundless sea. The ocean was limpid, sunlit, aquamarine. Above it was the starry night sky.

Hubs were darting in and out of the candle's giant flame, quite immune to the heat. As Guszti and Flinka led the troop of toons past it, a single Hub flew out to them.

It was a woman with a round head, a stylized hank of yellow hair, and a vivid green line down the middle of her face. The two halves were different hues and were mapped from different angles, one side a profile and the other seen straight on. Dora from the tram.

"Hallo, Frek," she called. As before, she had a large aura patterned with lightning bolts of bright gold.

"Pull over here for a minute," Frek told Gypsy Joker.

"Okeydoke," said the Skull Farmer giving his head an unsettling twist to look back at the trail of copies behind him. He dodged over to where Dora hung in the air.

"Hi, Dora," said Frek. "As usual I'm looking for the Exaplex."

"And losin' our place at the head o' line," muttered Gypsy Joker, fingering his dice earrings. "I want to drop my bomb. Get that first punch in. That's how we do it back in Kentucky, you wave?" The Skull Farmers had an elaborate back story.

"I know all about your mission," Dora told Frek. "We Hubs have been expecting you all along. There's such a level of interest in your case that it's quite skewed our last few renormalizations."

"Expecting me?" echoed Frek.

"Many of us have always known you'd bring down the branecasters," said Dora. She pointed out over the sparkling sea. "The Exaplex is there. The branecasters are hiding inside it."

Frek stared across the ocean. Near the horizon was—an island?

"During the last renormalization we Hubs pushed the Exaplex out of Node G," continued Dora. "Its up to you to finish the job. Huggins versus Branecasters. Saint Frek slays the mind worms. You and your army of mind-children." The ever-ramifying avalanche of toons was already flying out across the great water.

Again Frek thought of the shuggoths. "I feel gross," he said. "Like we're overpopulating your world."

"Hardly likely," said Dora with a little laugh. "The Planck brane is infinite these days. That ocean—it truly goes on forever."

"I thought the edges wrap?"

"Everything can change during renormalization. Even the shape of our space. We're due for another storm quite soon, by the way." She swept her hands around the circle of her aura. "I, for one, am well prepped."

"A storm?" said Frek uneasily.

"You'll know it's beginning when the sky breaks up," said Dora. "Don't frown like that! There's enough time for your mission. Fulfill your destiny!"

"Yes." But now Frek sighed, remembering the day he'd ridden the solar flares with Dad. Did the good times with his father outweigh the bad? Either way, the old man wasn't coming back. "Let's get going," he told Gypsy Joker.

The Skull Farmer stretched himself out flat with Frek hugged against his ribs. "Adios," the skeleton told Dora—supposedly he'd lived in New Mexico after Kentucky—and then they were off like a horizontal rocket, streaking across the warm, pale blue sea. Once they caught up with the swarm's vanguard, Gypsy Joker decelerated with a theatrical screech.

"Oh, there you are, Frek," said Renata from the arms of Goob Doll Judy. "We were starting to wonder. The Exaplex is that floating mountain of meat." The Exaplex organism hung in midair—an enormous wobbly lump with battlements on top.

"How are we going to fight them?" asked Ida, steering Tawni closer to Frek. "What's our plan?"

"There's so many of us that we can overwhelm them," said Frek, sounding more confident than he felt. "The toons will arm themselves— you know how toons do, just reach in a pocket and pull out slingshot or a blaster or a scimitar or a bingbong bomb. We'll blast the Exaplex until Zed and the mind worms are in the open. And then we finish them off. You hear that, Gypsy Joker? Pass the word so we can get started. There's gonna be a renormalization storm soon."

"What's renormalation?" asked Ida.

"Dora stirs up trouble for nothing," interrupted Aunt Guszti in a tart tone. "You have a whole hour, maybe two. I vow to lead you back. Now press your attack."

The Exaplex meat-mountain loomed up before them, big as a town. Its lumpy lower half was lit by the sun-glowing sea. On top, its soft turrets and walls were black against the starry sky. And above the castle writhed enormous ghostly tendrils like northern lights.

Nearly one billion strong and still growing, Frek's party rose high up into the air, encircling the floating island of flesh.

"Rock and roll," said Gypsy Joker, reaching for his earring.

"Spacesuits, Frek," said Renata. This bombing was going to be realer than the one in the Goob Dolls' alley. "Hurry."

Moving fast, Frek crafted four reflective spacesuits and got the humans in his party covered up. Just as the mirrored surfaces came on, Gypsy Joker threw his bomb. And tens of thousands of other Gypsy Jokers did the same.

Flassssh.

After the light came the sound. It wasn't so much something they heard, as a force that they felt. A shock wave that threw them back a few kilometers. The humans' spacesuits shielded their ears from the overpressure of the blast. And the toons were of course indestructible.

They regrouped and, whooping with blood lust, they zoomed in on the Exaplex.

What was left of it. The battlements were gone and the mountain of flesh had been chewed down to the size of Gov's puffball. The mind worms and Li'l Bulbs were exposed. They radiated out from the meat nexus like the arms of an evil sea anemone.

And now a puckered hole upon the Exaplex pushed out a glowering ogre, his feet firmly rooted in its flesh. It was Zed Alef, wreathed by the worms.

The toons dove in with machetes, flame-throwers, cannons, blasters, dark matter bazookas, Nguyen War singularity guns and, yes, wooden mallets and water balloons. For a toon, no means of attack was too far-fetched.

At first they made little progress. Zed Alef was fending them off, batting them away like mosquitoes. And the mind worms were growing back as fast as they were killed.

"Pull Zed away by himself," Frek told Soul Soldier.

The toons surged forward with a million lassos, buzz-saws, and tractor beams. Though Zed fought with abandon, the toons managed to bind him, cut him free, and pull him away from the great knot of mind worms, to isolate him from the Exaplex tissues that he controlled. The worms' motions grew random and disorganized. And Zed began to shrink.

For a second, Frek thought they'd already won. But then Zed slipped his restraints, locked into human size—and flew straight at Frek. A wild strength filled Frek; he was eager to join this final battle. Buoyed by his spacesuit, he shot forward to meet his enemy. He and Zed met with a *thump*.

Immediately the dark controller of the Exaplex wrapped his arms around Frek's chest and began to squeeze. His fingers grew tendrils that found their way through Frek's suit, into his muscles, and now into the nerves of his neck. Frek felt an unbearable torrent of information rushing into him—realtime data about every living being in every world under the branecasters' control.

Furiously Frek sky-air-combed himself, desperately he wrestled with the Exaplex's organic mind. The data flood rolled back. Yes, Frek could win. Somewhere he seemed to hear Carb cheering him on.

Frek pushed harder, driving back the tendrils of Zed's mind. Remembering the sight of Stoo's tormented face, Frek hit Zed with a blast of will. Momentarily stunned, Zed faltered.

Frek snapped his knee upward into Zed's belly; he twisted free of Zed's grip and pounded his elbow into the creature's temple. Zed's mouth popped open—and Gypsy Joker shoved in one of his earring-bombs.

Everything went white, then black. For a timeless period, Frek saw nothing. And then he seemed to be looking at—drawings, one after the other.

Ants and a humming bird. Yessica with a snake's tongue. Goob Doll Judy juggling planets. Cawmb with the cover falling off his tail. Gibby and a baby Unipusker. A rickrack tree blueprint. A map of Unipusk. Frek's profile. A Unipusker with ickspot. The Huggins's house tree. Renata with ribbons in her pigtails. A row of artigrows in the Kritter-works. A gene wasp. The Toonsmithy. Frek and Renata together.

"Come on," came a voice. A sweet voice, a kind voice. "Snap out of it. These things are real."

Frek blinked. He was—floating? Floating on his back in the Planck brane sea. Still wearing his spacesuit. Staring up at—Renata hovering over him, suspended in the arms of Goob Doll Judy, with Gypsy Joker at her side. Renata had been holding her turkle in front of Frek's face, showing him pictures.

"You and me done finished Zed," put in Gypsy Joker. "He died and just about took you with him. Your girlfriend here's been helpin' your body latch on to your soul."

"Renata," said Frek, reaching toward her. "You always help me come back."

"You can count on me," she said, taking his hand. "I like having you around."

They flew up to rejoin Ida. "You lit off a big bomb," observed Ida. "Renata said I had to stay up here and watch for those branecasters. We can't let them get away."

Meanwhile the toons' singularity guns were snuffing out the Li'l Bulbs and mind worms. With Zed gone, the evil eels weren't growing back. In a few minutes the only remnant of the mighty Exaplex branecasting nexus was a chunk of meat resembling a skinned ele-phruk.

With the mind worms gone, Frek's brain felt private, fully his own, not under attack. No espers pried at his head; he no longer needed to sky-air-comb the parasites away. Finally he could begin to relax.

Throughout the whole galaxy, the flickerballs and esper shows would now be on the blink as well. Untold numbers of talent races were awakening from slavery. All thanks to Frek and his gang. They'd killed off the Govs, they'd healed Earth with the elixir, and now they'd finally crashed the branecast. Unbelievable.

Frek had a sudden painful memory of the melting pictures tumbling from Dad's shroud. He wouldn't have made it if it hadn't been for his father. What had Dad said? "As long as you're around, I'm still alive." It was all right.

"Can you feel the difference?" he asked the others.

"Yes," said Renata, understanding exactly what he meant. "It's good. But we're not done. It'll come back unless we get rid of *them*." She pointed to the floating lump of Exaplex flesh.

Perched on the singed meat were the six branecasters and—the Magic Pig. They looked annoyed, put out, angry, but not terrified. Their gold auras were strong.

"Nothin' we throw at them makes a difference," said Soul Soldier. "They're tough as toons. Best we can do is keep them from flying away."

"Right," said Frek, with a quick glance up at the calm, starry heavens. "If only we could drain their wham before the storm hits."

"Why does wham matter?" asked Ida.

"The Planck brane has these weird storms every fifty-two days," said Frek. "The Hubs with the most wham survive a storm, the others don't. The Planck brane's like a shared dream the Hubs make up together. A storm is a fresh start. A Hub's in the new dream if enough Hubs remember him. Or her."

"I've got it!" exclaimed Renata. "Disrespect the branecasters. Make them ridiculous. Show how plain and boring they are. And then stop thinking about them. I bet the Hubs will follow along."

So as not to hide the branecasters beneath a struggling dog-pile, Renata sent only a few toons after them. It seemed likely that the far-flung Hubs would have some way of perceiving what happened here. Even without esping, distances didn't mean much in the Planck brane.

As the humans and toons laughed and cheered, the Space Monkeys tore off the struggling branecasters' spiffy clothes. Da Nha Duc pasted feathers to Chainey's bald head and bare butt. Mean Queen scrubbed off Jayney's pancake makeup and painted her nose red. Gypsy Joker darted in to bag the branecasters' gold jewelry and pry out their gold teeth. Goob Doll Judy used her lipstick to scrawl "KICK ME" onto Sid's hairy back. Fax Frog shoved a red apple into Cecily's mouth and trimmed her ears with parsley. Professor Bumby put dunce caps on Batty and Bitty and asked them Latin questions they couldn't understand.

But somehow nobody managed to lay a finger on the Magic Pig. He was always standing somewhere different than where his would-be tormentors reached.

Now Strummer played a song, with Soul Soldier singing along.

> Branecasters, taskmasters, gold graspers—
> You take and you never give.
> Slave masters, down-casters, world blasters—
> You don't let real people live.
> It's a brand new road—you're forgettable;
> And none of us think it's regrettable.
> Let the storm come down, we won't think of you.
> When the brane grows back it won't stink of you.
> Farewell, adios, you're gone, you lose;
> Nobody's watching your daily news;
> I don't remember who I'm singin' this to.
> All I see is my friends and the sky above;
> It's a new Planck brane for Hubs in love.

They sang the verse a few more times. Hubs all over the Planck brane joined in, the sky echoing with their massed voices. The branecasters tried to interrupt, but nobody listened to them. They made as if to fly away from the chunk of Exaplex meat, but the toons pushed them back. The longer the laughter and the singing continued, the fainter the branecasters' auras grew.

Though the Magic Pig was hemmed in with the others, his halo remained bright and strong. Nothing at all seemed to get to him. He always zigged whenever anyone else zagged.

Just then a kilometer-sized cube of starry sky tumbled down and fell into the ocean. What a splash! And here came a block with the moon, followed by another splash and another.

At this first touch of the renormalization, the branecasters faded away, leaving the Magic Pig on his own. The Pig seized the moment of confusion to fly off as fast as he could go. And Soul Soldier used a Nguyen War singularity gun to blast the last remaining bit of the Exaplex into glowing wisps of plasma.

Meanwhile more cubes were splashing into the sea.

"Lead us to the branelink, Guszti!" cried Frek. "Hurry!"

Guszti and Flinka sped across the ocean, closely followed by the four humans on their toons. The billion other three-dimensional toons stayed behind to take their chances. There wasn't room for them in the wall skins of Earth.

Frek and his party rocketed past the candle—its flame had been doused by waves from the falling blocks. They passed the hilltop mirror, avoiding its shattered shards of glass. It was turning to night. Not only was the moon gone, the dropping blocks were spilling blackness, as if covering the landscape with ink. Somewhere in the darkness Frek heard the slow snipping of giant scissors.

It was good that Flinka and Guszti glowed. Frek and his companions safely followed them to the hill with the giant leaf. The luminous fish hovered by the branelink tree's stem, shedding enough light to see.

To Frek's horror, the Magic Pig was busy there, furiously digging with his trotters. He'd covered up the entrance hole with a big pile of mud!

Ida ran over and kicked the Magic Pig in the butt so hard that he rolled down Pig Hill, squealing all the way. Meanwhile Renata used her blaster to burn the dirt away from the branelink entrance.

Hearing a rush of air, Frek looked up to see a cube of sky falling straight down upon them. The hill and the giant leaf rocked and shuddered under the impact, but Frek felt only a puff of wind. And then he realized their protective spacesuits had dissolved.

"I can't see!" cried Ida. "Where's the door?" The darkness was absolute.

"It's here," called Renata's voice. "The door looks like a woman."

Yes, the branelink door was a cut-out patch of twilight against the renormalization's velvet gloom—it was shaped like the outline of a plump, motherly figure in a wide-brimmed straw hat. Visible through the woman-door were the Huggins kitchen and garden. A cozy little group sat on a cloth in the yard with a crescent moon behind them. From where Frek stood, the crescent was positioned exactly at the center of woman-door's head.

They found their way through, Frek last.

As he stepped into his home world, Frek looked back for a last glimpse of the Planck brane. He saw a blackboard with symbols marked in chalk. The symbols were moving. The branelink vanished.

Out in the backyard, Linz Martinez, Mom, Geneva, and the Unipuskers were watching Da Nha Duc toons on a show-pillow. The Unipuskers were enjoying it mightily.

"Haw haw haw," creaked Hawb, leaning back his head and letting his shell mouth crack wide open. His eye stalks were bent to focus on Da Nha's furious struggle to build a larger house than his neighbor Jones.

There was a faint mist beneath the leafy trees, and a line of pink along the horizon where the sun had gone down. The crescent moon hung just above the trees, delicate and bright.

Linz Martinez was sitting beside Mom, and Geneva was petting one of Wow and Woo's puppies. She looked very relieved to see Frek return. For the first time in a long while, he realized that his big sister cared about him. He didn't look forward to telling her about Dad.

"Command Frek to close our deal now," said Hawb, turning all businesslike. He was trying to stand up, but couldn't quite get his footing. There was an empty tree-juice mug and quite a pile of peach pits by his side. He'd been eating and drinking as fast as he could.

"No more deal," said Frek, temporarily forgetting about his father. Such a wide smile crawled onto his face that he felt as if his chin could fall off. "No more esping. The mind worms and the branecasters are gone."

"Explain!" cried Cawmb, taking on his usual peremptory tone.

"Oh, Frek!" said Lora, ignoring Cawmb. "That's wonderful."

"You should have seen your son," put in Renata. "He rocked. And Ida—Ida kicked the Magic Pig's butt."

"Just like she said she would," said Frek, grinning even wider, if this were possible.

"Way to go, Frek, Ida, and Renata," said Geneva, giving them a warm smile. "You're heroes!"

"Justify the projected delays in the Unipusker production of the humanity channel," persisted Cawmb.

"No channel," said Frek, making it insultingly simple. "No producer. No flickerball. No got. Go home."

"Might as well relax for a while and watch more toons," Geneva told the Unipuskers in a soothing tone. "I'll tell you what, Hawb and Cawmb, I could get you some urlbuds to take home. If they don't work on your walls, I bet you could rig something up. You're so hightech. Buy some urlbuds and you won't be going home empty-handed. Start a new business."

"Request one thousand toon urlbuds," said Hawb almost right away. Cawmb burst out with something in Unipusker, and the two quarreled for a minute. But then the Da Nha Duc on Geneva's pillow did something else that set them both to laughing. "Make that two thousand urlbuds," said Cawmb.

"And you pay us—what?" said Geneva. She had more of a head for business than Frek.

"Propose to pay equal weight of gold?" said Hawb. "We have a supply that was intended for the branecasters."

Geneva glanced over at Mom. "Gold will do," said Lora. "We could use some gold around here. But make it ten times the weight. And throw in some diamonds. We'll get the urlbuds tomorrow morning. Now sit down, everyone. I'll bring out more tree-juice. The fizzy kind for the old folks. And Frek, I'll make you and the girls some sandwiches. You look kind of—did you find out something about Carb?"

"He's dead," said Frek. "The branecasters killed him."

"They made him into a pile of leaves that blew away," added Ida.

"Oh no," said Geneva.

It took a while to settle down from that, but even so, the warm evening went on. Even though he'd turned his back on the family, Dad would have wanted them to be happy, wanted them out in the yard, enjoying the spring night, talking, eating, and drinking. Woo, Wow, and the puppies kept sniffing everyone and begging snacks.

The Unipuskers were in a good mood. They said that of all the races they'd met in the galaxy, only the Earthlings had thought of making toons. Made expansive by the tree-juice, Cawmb said the toons meant that Earth, just as she was, had an export valuable enough to prevent other races from wanting to crush and colonize her. Humanity could join the galaxy's other races on equal terms.

Such good news called for cheers, toasts, and songs. A few neighbors came over, among them Stoo Steiner, looking a little shy.

"Stoo!" exclaimed Frek. "It's all fixed. No more espers."

"My father's sorry about the shuggoths," said Stoo.

"Sorry?" exclaimed Frek. "That's all?"

"*You* should talk," said Stoo. "It's been a bad year for some of us."

"Oh, Stoo," said Frek, softening. "Can we be friends again?"

"That's why I'm here." Stoo's smile was wonderful to see. "I've always gotten a kick out of you and your family. You're all so—I don't know. Different."

"Thanks," said Frek. "I'm starting to think maybe different is good. The toonsmiths—they like some of my ideas. And Renata's already working with them."

"Can you take me to meet them, too?" said Stoo. "By now, I must know more than anyone about watching toons."

"Sure," said Frek.

Lora brought out some more instruments and they played music till midnight, Lora on guitar, Frek on harmonica, and Linz Martinez coaxing sweet melodies from his violin.

And then Frek and Renata were alone. When Frek glanced up at the sky, he almost felt like he could see his old man up there smiling— the crazy goof. He smiled back. The lawn smelled like flowers. A mockingbird sang in the trees; the branches blinked with lightning bugs.

"It's all together," said Frek, thinking back over the long quest. "We're done."

"No, we're not," said Renata, squeezing Frek's hand. "We're just beginning."

glossary

aircoral, airpolyp. Airpolyps are gnat-sized flying kritters that build up curvy houses called aircorals. Like sea-going polyps, they create these reeflike structures by depositing tiny bits of silicon and calcium.

angelwing. An angelwing is a kritter resembling a one-meter-long dragonfly body with a single two-meter wing. People use pairs of angelwings to fly.

anyfruit. A tweaked fruit tree that yields all the traditional fruits.

anymeat. A meat product grown in loaves for food.

artigrow. A kritter resembling a large artichoke. Serves as an incubator to grow kritter embryos to term.

autopoiesis. The process by which a living (or social) system creates, organizes, and maintains itself. (A standard word, popularized by the Chilean biologists Humberto Maturana and Francisco Varela in the 1980s.)

bindmoss. A durable ground-cover resembling wiry moss.

bobblie. An enormous sentient weather pattern in the atmosphere of the gas-giant planet Jumm.

brain nodule. A dense nexus of fungal tissue found in the Govs' puff-balls. Functions like an organic computer.

brane, branelink. A brane is a universe, and a branelink is a hyperdimensional tunnel connecting two parallel branes. (Brane is a standard word, derived from "membrane," and is used by cosmologists and string-theorists.)

branecast, branecaster. The branecast is a process by which the branecasters extract the thoughts of "talent creatures" in our universe and display them to "clients." An entire race's activities become something like a reality TV show. The branecasters are a tightly knit group of six.

counselor. A police agent employed by the Govs.

cowloon. A balloonlike cow-derived kritter that yields an intoxicating fluid called moolk.

Crufters. Rebels dedicated to turning back biotechnology and restoring Earth's original ecology.

cryptoon. A toon creature that acts as an autonomous secret agent.

decoherence. A standard quantum-mechanical notion akin to the notion of a system being in a simple, collapsed state after a measurement is performed. The terminology is a bit counterintuitive, in that a "coherent" state is a mixed state of being simultaneously in many modes, and a "decoherent" state resembles a definite, classical single-mode state.

elephruk. An elephantlike kritter with a lowered back. Used as a truck.

esp, esper. To esp someone is to see into their mind.

Exaplex. A huge organic entity in the Planck brane that acts as the machinery of the branecast. Seemingly created by the Magic Pig. The Exaplex has hyperdimensional mind worms that extend out to the brains of talent race members, as well as Li'l Bulbs that send the information to clients' flickerballs. The controlling intelligence of the Exaplex is a being called Zed.

facilitator. A teacher.

flickerball. A device resembling a crystal ball, used by espers to experience the branecasts of other beings' minds.

foamskin. The foamy, leathery skin of a tweaked thistle. Used to make casts for sprains and broken bones.

gaussy. Far out, extremely fashionable, uncompromisingly chic.

geeve, geever, geevey, geevin. Geeve is an obscenity with the force of the f-word, and is used in a similar range of combining forms.

giga. A lot.

glatt. Smooth, excellent, very nice.

glawk. To hang out.

gleep, gleepy. Creep, creepy.

glozy. Cozy and nice.

glypher. A sluglike critter that posts images onto house tree wall skins. Used by schools to send messages home to parents.

godzoon. Very, extremely.

gog, goggy, gripper. Excellent, wacky, mind-boggling.

gollywog. Weird and crazy.

googly. Funny, entertaining, cheerful.

Gov. A highly intelligent kritter evolved from a certain kind of worm. Govs live in fungal structures called puffballs and act as the rulers of Y3K Earth.

Great Collapse. The catastrophic occasion in 2666 when the NuBio-Com directorate chose, firstly, to deploy a knockout virus to block reproduction, and secondly, to destroy the genetic codes of all but 256 of Earth's species.

grinskin. A person who takes psychotropic and weight-reducing medications that render the individual's personality artificially bright and flat.

grobread. An organic, living bread culture that continually renews itself.

groover. A dumbbell, a pawn, an individual whose thoughts are completely controlled by the media.

Grulloo. A humanoid mutant with only one pair of limbs which perforce function as both arms and legs. (Derived from the medieval term "gryllos," used for fantastic creatures of this type depicted in the margins of illuminated scriptures. The painters Hieronymus Bosch and Peter Bruegel often painted gryllos creatures into their scenes of hell.)

gump, gumpy. Impolite word for a handicapped person.

gundo. A large quantity, very much.

gurp, gurpy. Very unintelligent person. A dope.

Hub. An inhabitant of the parallel universe called the Planck brane. Their appearance is quite mutable, and their continued existence depends upon their level of renown (see "wham").

ickspot. A deadly disease peculiar to Unipuskers. Symptoms include gray, flaky spots.

jocktoons. Toon shows about sports.

Jumm. The large gas-giant planet orbited by the moon of Unipusk.

kac. Obscenity for excrement, with the same force as the s-word.

kenner, kenny, kenny-crafter. Kenner is invisible dark matter, found throughout our universe. Kenny-crafters have the ability to transmute kenner into visible matter, and to "vaar" it into whatever shape they want. Objects created in this fashion are kennies.

killtoon. A violent toon show.

knockout virus. An agent used to block the reproductive processes of every species on Earth. The exact formula is continually changed. NuBioCom licenses temporary antidotes so that people can from time to time have children.

kritter. A genomically tweaked plant or animal. Generally kritters are designed by the NuBioCom corporation.

loofy. Collective word for the smallish vortex rings found in the atmosphere of a star. Larger vortex rings (such as the Orpolese) feed upon loofy.

Magic Pig. A powerful being capable of seeing—and touching—Frek's past and his possible futures. The Pig's main motive is to make a profit and survive. Due to his association with the branecasters, he has a vested interest in making Frek's life more complicated and thus more entertaining. (One of my nicknames in college was the Magic Pig.)

mapine. A tweaked plant that is a cross between a maple and a pine tree, but which resembles a maple that simultaneously bears colored autumn leaves and fresh green spring foliage.

matchbud. A tweaked plant that produces stalks with phosphorus heads used as matches.

mind worm. A hyperdimensional tendril connecting an individual's brain to the Exaplex in the Planck brane. The mind worms make branecasting possible.

mod. A jellylike substance that people smear onto themselves to change their appearance. The effects, which can be dramatic, appear rapidly, but normally dissipate within a few days.

moolk. An intoxicating form of milk obtained from cowloons. (Suggested by the moloko of Anthony Burgess's *A Clockwork Orange*.)

newbio. The radically different ecology produced by genomics and biotechnology in the Y3K era.

newstoon. A toon creature that acts as a newscaster.

NuBioCom. The ruthless company that takes control of Earth's genomes during the third millennium. NuBioCom is effectively the Earth's government, with its puffball regional centers housing the rulers called Govs.

Nubbie. A citizen of Earth who takes advantage of the NuBioCom biotechnology. A well-off citizen, comparable to a Y2K yuppie.

nutfungus. A spicy nutmeg-scented fungus that grows in the cracks of dying trees.

oldbio. Earth's original untweaked ecology.

Orpoly. An archipelago of suns near the galactic core, inhabited by intelligent plasma vortex rings.

oxymold. A tweaked mold that produces oxygen even in the absence of light.

peeker. A creature related to the "uvvy." Unlike the uvvy, the peeker is very invasive, and uses its electrical fields to pry deep into a subject's brain, causing considerable damage.

phenomenological autozoom, pzoom. The technique by which a toon show adjusts its view to the wishes of one privileged viewer. That is, whatever the viewer focuses on tends to get larger. The particular instance of the show "watches" the viewer for cues using eyes in its wall skin display. (Phenomenology is the branch of philosophy that seeks to analyze the actual perceptions that people have.)

pickerhand. A kritter like a disembodied hand, used to harvest rice and other crops.

Planck brane. A parallel universe inhabited by creatures called Hubs.

please plant. A kritter plant with eyes in its flowers. It grows seeds to match whatever shapes are shown to it.

puffball. A large, torus-shaped fungus inhabited by a Gov worm. Also contains offices used by NuBioCom functionaries. Is responsible for spreading the latest knockout viruses to block reproduction.

qubit. A quantum bit. Unlike a classical bit, which must be 0 or 1, a qubit can be in a mixed, "coherent" state that is a weighted combination of two possibilities, such as twenty-five percent 0 and seventy-five percent 1.

glossary

rassen, znag, znassen. The Orpolese have bodies that are something like tornadoes of plasma bent around into rings. These vortex rings have an inherent twist, which is either clockwise or counterclockwise. The rassen twist in one direction, and the znags twist in the other. Generally the rassen are of higher status. To complicate things, it turns out that the Orpolese actually travel in pairs, with two vortex rings overlaid upon each other. In a "mixed marriage," the two rings have opposite inherent twists. The znassen pairs are a combination of a znag and a rassen. (While working on *Frek and the Elixir* in Brussels, in 2002, I often ate at an inexpensive Moroccan restaurant called Beni Znassen.)

renormalization. A standard physics word for redefining a system's numerical attributes in some new, improved way. I use it to suggest the notion of recasting the quantum reality of the Planck brane in terms of some new set of axes (eigenvectors). During a renormalization storm, the entire Planck brane gets reformulated, and the local Hubs with a low amount of wham are likely to disappear.

rockworms. Kritters that hollow out the insides of asteroids.

roseplusplus. The ultimate futuristic gene-tweaked rose plant. (The name is a play on the "doubleplusplus" of Aldous Huxley's *Brave New World*.)

rugmoss. An attractive tweaked moss that changes its colors in rhythmic patterns, with each region influenced by the colors of the neighbors. (This is a biological form of the two-dimensional cellular automaton rule called "Rug," see, for instance, www.cs.sjsu.edu/faculty/rucker/cellab.htm.)

sextoons. Pornographic toon shows.

shecked out. Freaked-out or jaded or world-weary. (Cf. SF writer Robert Sheckley.)

shuggoth. A sluglike creature that's a glued-together hodgepodge of many other kinds of creatures. (H. P. Lovecraft sometimes wrote about shuggoths, although not in precisely the same sense. My sense of shuggoth was first described in my *Saucer Wisdom*.)

Sick Hindu. The hollowed-out asteroid inhabited by the rebel Crufters. (Name taken from a graffiti tag near Mountain View, California.)

sky-air-comb. The autopoietic meditation technique that Frek uses to restore the integrity of his mind, also to block out the espers.

Skywatch Mil. A system of jellyfishlike space stations circling Earth, ostensibly to provide a protective network.

space bug. A flammable kritter used as a single-passenger rocket ship. (First described in my *Saucer Wisdom*.)

spheromak. A standard fusion-science word for a vortex ring of superheated plasma. (I learned this word in a conversation with Gregory Benford at Con Jose 2002.)

stim cell. A tweaked cell that serves to repair and improve anyone who eats it. A necessity of life for Grulloos.

suckapillar. A kritter that functions as a vacuum cleaner.

Three R's. The physical removal, recycling, and replacement of a person's brain. Used by Gov as a dramatic and irreversible treatment to bring rebels into line.

toon. A cartoon creature that acts as an autonomous agent. Toons are artificial life-forms that evolve and have a high level of intelligence.

toonsmith, Toonsmithy. Most toons are initially designed by toon-smiths working at the Toonsmithy in Stun City. Once they are re-leased, of course, toons continue to learn and to change.

turkle. A kritter resembling a turtle. Its back can be used as a drawing pad. A turkle remembers all the images drawn upon it. (The word comes from the Mr. Turkle character in Ken Kesey's *One Flew Over the Cuckoo's Nest.*)

turmite. An enhanced social insect something like an ant or a termite. Turmites can be instructed to weave fabrics or to build papery struc-tures. (The term puns on the name of computer pioneer Alan Turing. "Turmite" was originally coined by computer scientist Greg Turk to describe a certain kind of two-dimensional Turing machine which was later popularized by A. K. Dewdney in a *Scientific American* col-umn collected in his *The Tinkertoy Computer.*)

tweet. An insubstantial colorful object created from dark matter by an Orpolese. Tweets function as a visible language. They can also fly through a person's head and pick up his or her thoughts.

Unipusk. The habitable moon of the gas-giant planet Jumm.

unny. Spooky, unnatural, scary.

url, urlbud. An url is a Web site, and an urlbud is a soft little vegetal object that includes the address and access permissions that allow a Nubbie to access a given url on a wall skin.

uvvy. A universal communication device that rests upon the back of the user's neck. The uvvy interfaces directly with the user's brain by means of gentle electric currents. Uvvies were originally made of computational plastic, but in *Frek and the Elixir,* they're organic krit-ters remotely related to electric eels. (First described in my books *Saucer Wisdom* and *Realware.*)

vaar. A term used by kenny-crafters in two senses. The process of turning invisible dark matter (kenner) into a visible substance is the first type of vaaring. The second type of vaaring is the process of forming the kenner-derived matter into some specific shape or device, that is, into a kenny.

vark, vheenk. Noises made by vigs.

vig. An edible piglike creature living on Unipusk; you can slice off a piece of vig and eat it. (Inspired both by the schmoos in Al Capp's *Li'l Abner,* and by Philip K. Dick's "Beyond Lies the Wub.")

wall skin. The living wall-covering in the rooms of a house tree. Like the skin of a squid, a wall skin is rich in chromatophores, and is capable of showing any possible color. A wall skin acts as a large, flat graphical display.

watchbird. A hummingbird-sized kritter devoted to following and spying upon a suspect individual. The watchbird wears a small uvvy that allows it to function as a remote camera for some central control. (The name is from Robert Sheckley's classic story, "The Watchbird.")

webgun. A spiderlike kritter that shoots out entangling strands of silk.

wham. The amount of credibility or recognition that an individual citizen has in the Planck brane. (The notion is related both to Google page rank and to Cory Doctorow's whuffie, as described in *Down and Out in the Magic Kingdom.*)

yubba. Hi, hello. Common greeting in Y3K.

yuga. A standard Hindu word for a long period of time. Used in the Planck brane to mean the time between successive renormalization storms.

yunch, unyunch. Yunching is a string-theory–based method of changing size. Yunching makes you big, and unyunching makes you small. (The idea comes from Brian Greene's *The Elegant Universe,* in which he describes a duality between a particle's size and how tightly its elementary strings are wound. My notion of using this method for faster-than-light travel was anticipated in Harry Harrison's *Bill the Galactic Hero,* where it's called the Bloater Drive.)